Arabella Crawford spent twenty years building a multimillion-dollar worldwide business empire. Now, she's ready to enjoy life. She begins by booking passage from France to America on a fabulous ocean liner.

On board she meets Nicholas Frayne, a famous movie star with political ambitions. The moment they see each other, the passion begins.

And during six amazing days and nights, all of their senses will be aroused...all of their fantasies fulfilled by a festival of luxury, a tidal wave of love.

Also by Roberta Latow
Published by Ballantine Books:

THREE RIVERS

Tidal Wave

Roberta Latow

BALLANTINE BOOKS • NEW YORK

Grateful acknowledgment is made to the following for permission to reprint previously published material: Chatto and Windus Ltd.: Excerpt from "Ithaka" by C. P. Cavafy from his COLLECTED POEMS, edited by George Savidis, translated by Edmund Keeley and Philip Sherrard. Published in the United States by Princeton University Press. Reprinted by permission.

Library of Congress Catalog Card Number: 83-90013

ISBN 0-345-30853-0

Manufactured in the United States of America

First Edition: September 1983

After the spirit of place, there is the spirit of friends.

For
Penelope Midgley,
Donald Munson,
and
Claude Ury

Have Ithaca always on your mind.
Your arrival there is what you are destined for,
But do not in the least hurry your journey.
Better that it lasts for years,
So that when you reach the island you are old,
Rich with all you have gained on the way,
Not expecting Ithaca to give you wealth.
Ithaca gave you the splendid journey.
Without her you would not have set out.
She hasn't anything else to give you.

—Cavafy

Chapter One

"Please sign here, and here, and here."

Arabella Crawford removed the top of the red lacquered Dupont fountain pen. She stared at the shiny gold point. Her hand was steady, her emotions controlled. Her face showed nothing of her feelings to the ten men seated at the huge, round, English Regency conference table. A small voice in her head kept whispering over and over again, "History, past histories."

The room was filled with a hushed stillness and there was a distinct tension in the air. Arabella turned to the lawyer standing next to her, holding a sheaf of papers in his hand.

She said, in her firm yet soft voice, "I think this room needs fresh air."

Then, turning her attention back to the table, she took the time to look into the eyes of the gentlemen, one at a time.

Armand Ury returned to her side after opening the French windows that led out on to the balcony overlooking the Place Vendôme, white under the first snowfall of winter in Paris.

Arabella felt a fresh cold gust of wind wrap around her ankles. It snapped her back to the reality of the moment. With her left hand she held the documents down and quickly placed her signature where she was instructed.

Armand Ury removed the papers and passed them behind Arabella to Axel Horst, who was standing to her right. Armand immediately placed several more documents before her, indicating where she was to sign.

Her beautiful mouth broke into a sweet, mysterious smile as she looked around the table yet again. Quickly she lowered her head and continued to sign her name on the papers before her.

Axel Horst, her Swiss lawyer, examined Arabella's signatures, witnessing each document as authentic by adding his own signature to it. He then placed each set of papers into separate folders. The little scene was played out several more times, with Arabella never looking up again until she had signed the last paper placed before her. Then, slowly, she put the top back on her pen, raised her eyes, and looked at the men.

The expression on their faces was infinitely more relaxed. Relief and a sense of calm replaced the tension that had held them so breathlessly rigid only minutes before. Axel was placing the last of the documents in the folders when Arabella rose. The men scraped their chairs back on the white marble floor and began to rise. She held up her hand and said, "No, please, gentlemen, stay where you are."

She closed the window and returned to her seat, relaxing into her chair. She looked serene and revealed nothing of the intense feelings she held inside.

The men at the table remained silent as Axel Horst handed the folders, one at a time, to each of them in exchange for their banker's draft. In each case he meticulously checked the amount of the bank checks against the signed documents. He completed his circle of the table, placed the small stack in front of Arabella, and waited in silence.

She looked at the sum of each, then mentally calculated the total. The men around the table appeared mesmerized by her beautiful hands, her long, slender fingers with their red lacquered nails, as she went through the drafts, assembling them into a perfect, neat pile.

She handed them to Armand, saying "All seems in order. Please deposit them as I have instructed." Then, turning to the men, she said, "I think we should have a last drink together."

She pressed a button on the underside of the table and rang for the butler.

Adrian Burt-Williams was the first man to speak. "Good

heavens. Surely not a 'last' drink? I am certain the others here feel as I do and hope you will always have an interest in your former corporations and colleagues. Should we not stay in communication?"

"Adrian, gentlemen, this *is* our last drink. On an official basis, at least. I will never have any business communications with you again." There was a sudden flash of shocked whispers in the room. How odd of her to say that! How strange! How rude! Finally Ito Hiro stood up and said, "Madame Crawford, after creating such successes, surely you would want to keep abreast of our progress? It has, after all, been your life's work."

"No, dear Ito, I will not. I have thought about this long and hard. The decision was not lightly made, but after I leave this room, I will never look back. I am leaving the business world." She smiled warmly at them and then continued. "To put it simply, gentlemen, I am taking your money and running away. I am going out there into a new world—well, a new world for me anyway—and you will be part of my past."

They all looked relieved that she wasn't angry with them, and more than one man appeared sad at the prospect of seeing Arabella Crawford walk away from them forever.

Quietly the butler, Rupert, came up beside her and offered her a tall crystal, tulip-shaped glass of Dom Perignon. As she lifted it off the heavy French Baroque silver tray, she bent forward and said very softly, "After you have served the champagne, please get my coat and wait for me at the conference room door."

She stood up, the men all following suit, raised her glass, and said, "Gentlemen, no toasts please," and took a sip. Then she casually wandered among the men, smiling, shaking hands, and kissing the cheek of several who had just bought her out of the business world for the net sum of one hundred million dollars.

Then Arabella Crawford, one of the wealthiest and most successful businesswomen in the world, casually made her way to where Rupert stood, slipped into her dark, full-length sable coat, and walked away without looking back.

Arabella's riches were not inherited nor the assets of a marriage or a liaison. The enormous profits she attained on this day, in her fortieth year, reflected the culmination of her own remarkable achievements. Over a period of almost eighteen years she had managed to convert a small initial investment into an international financial empire.

From the men in her life she received wisdom, support, and encouragement, but her incredible success was truly the result of her own skill, creativity, intelligence, and determination.

Armand caught sight of her as she disappeared through the door. He followed her and stood at the top of the sweeping white marble staircase. He listened to the clicking sound of her high-heeled shoes on the marble. Her step had a bounce to it, a rhythm, more like a two-step, as if she were dancing down the stairs. He smiled, thinking that it was just like the new Arabella to dance away. He was one of the intimate few who shared those rare frivolous moments that seemed to have emerged recently in the otherwise controlled and dignified Arabella Crawford.

The night before he had asked her what she was going to do with the rest of her life. He smiled to himself now, recalling her answer. She had looked up into his eyes, broken out of his arms, and slipped out of bed. She had stood tall, naked, and voluptuous in the firelight.

Suddenly, flinging her arms out, she had said, "I'm going to trip the light fantastic all the rest of the days of my life," and she began to dance before him.

He had never seen her like that, so open, so free, so uninhibited.

Now, the dark, handsome Frenchman leaned on the heavy sculptured balustrade of the staircase and watched the swing of Arabella's sable coat, the quick flash of her ankles as she descended.

Arabella took a few steps toward the door. He called

down in a loud whisper, "*Chérie, mon amour....*" His whisper echoed through the vast entrance hall.

She swung around, her beautiful face radiant under the shadow of her wide-brimmed brown felt hat with its band of exquisite, sapphire-blue bird-of-paradise feathers. She smiled up at him as she pulled on her beige kid gloves, saying "*Au revoir.*"

Armand quickly reached in his breast pocket and pulled out a long, slim jeweler's box. In a louder voice he called down, "Catch, *ma chère. Bon voyage.*"

He heard the smack of the box as it hit her leather-gloved hand.

The sound of the men talking in the conference room behind him grew louder. Not wanting them to share in this good-bye, he quickly called down, "*Merci, je t'adore. Bon chance.*"

They turned away from each other. She said to herself, "Lovely Armand," and remembered their time together the night before.

He had said, "Let's take a long trip together, darling. We could spend a month in the Far East, then go on to relax on a private island a friend of mine owns in the South Pacific."

"That would be fun, but..."

"Then perhaps we'd go on to the States so your family could be at our wedding." He held her so they could look into each others eyes.

"I know that you love me, Arabella. I know that you want to marry. We have been so—"

She had stopped him by gently putting her hand over his lips and saying "Armand, we love each other—that will always be. Please try and understand. We've talked about this before. Like all women, for the first years of my love life I went out into the world looking to meet my Heathcliff. It wasn't easy but I found him. He was mine for a little while. For the rest of my life I've been trying to avoid looking for another. But there are an awful lot of Heathcliffs out there and you, darling, are one of them.

"I've been luckier than most women who long to be loved, protected by a man. One whom they can admire and respect. There are countless women who are frustrated, left longing and looking, and never have the good fortune to find such a man.

"All the men in my life so far have been the Heathcliffs most women want, crave. I searched for them, needed them—or at least I thought I needed them. I've loved them as I love you, for your maturity, your success, your sense of responsibility, your mind and your sexuality. But somehow, and I know you know this too, Armand, we are not *in* love. And there is a difference."

He nodded slowly, but again held her close to him. It was a bittersweet moment. Arabella went on, telling him how she planned to live out her fantasies.

"While I'm still young and attractive, I want to go out into the world and learn all over again, with my new eyes, what the world and people are like. My new financial security will release me. I can enjoy everyone and everything for exactly what it is or is not. I'm just going to live everything and see what happens."

Arabella sighed, then hurried through the front door onto the snow-covered steps. She took a deep breath of the cold fresh air and, wrapping her coat tight around her, turned to her butler, saying, "Thank you for everything, Rupert. I will see you soon when you and the other staff arrive in America."

Her driver was waiting, as arranged, and she quickly slipped into the warmth of her chocolate-colored Rolls-Royce.

The heavy snow showers that had been falling all morning, covering Paris in six inches of snow, were diminishing. The sun, a dull, blurred disc of yellow in a grayish-white sky, was suddenly shining through the clouds. Large and fluffy flakes of snow were lazily drifting down, more like bits of white candy-floss than snow.

The white blanket crunched under the weight of the Rolls

as it purred its way into the traffic toward the Place de la Concorde.

Arabella felt a smile breaking across her face. Uncontainable, it burst forth into laughter. She looked at the box in her hand and, still laughing, put it in her lap.

Full of joy, she unconsciously placed her gloved hands over her face as if to hide. It was an absurd gesture so she put them down, thinking "Why not?" threw her head back and let her laughter rip and happiness fill the car.

She said aloud, "I am rich, very rich. No matter what I do for the rest of my life, I am always going to be rich!" She clapped her hands together and applauded herself, going on, "I am free. I am rich. I am free and I never have to think about money again for the rest of my life! I will never again have to exploit my mind or my soul for security. I will never have to take another step up to the next rung in the success ladder—that dangerous ladder that promises the higher you go the greater the reward, but you never realize until you're there how far you can fall." Arabella recalled the times her decisions and subsequent actions were thought to be grandiose or ill-advised and she was forced to defend herself publicly, to reassure her colleagues and investors and privately pray that her intuition and judgment would not fail. She was known to take risks. She had managed to overcome fear and she had never failed . . . and now it was time for her to reap the rewards.

"I will never have to think about proving myself to myself, the world, or anyone ever again. What bliss!"

She put her hands in her lap and in so doing touched the jeweler's box. She thought of Armand. It had been a lovely brief romance, and she knew she would always have a dear friend in Paris. Armand, who had always been so generous in bed, in his love for her and in his gifts, had thought to bring her yet one more present.

She pressed open the catch and gasped with pleasure at the sight of the Art Deco diamond and emerald bracelet. She held it up to the light; the diamonds shot rainbows of color around her. The setting was exquisite.

She pushed down the kid glove and clasped the bracelet on her wrist, then held up her arm to admire it. She loved it. It was a delicious gift. Arabella searched through the Van Cleef & Arpels box for a card, a word, but there was nothing. How right Armand was. He understood the end and was the generous gentleman about it.

She snapped the empty box closed and placed it on the seat next to her, bent forward, and tapped her finger on the glass that divided her from the chauffeur, Oskar.

The glass slid down silently. "Yes, Madame Crawford?"

"Is everything in order? Are we on schedule?"

"Yes and no, madame. Everything is in order but we are not on schedule. We are running late. But a message came through on the car telephone from Missy. She asked that you be told not to be concerned. The ship will wait. She and all the luggage are at customs and will meet you there. Xu, the change of clothes you asked for, and the dogs are at the heliport."

Missy, her secretary, and Xu, her personal servant, were her constant and loyal companions and would accompany her on her journey from France.

Arabella leaned back again into the seat and was dazzled by the beauty of the Place de la Concorde. It was crystalline white, the wind had dropped, and the few flakes trying to fall were more like suspended polka dots. The scene could have been a glossy color postcard or a Surrealist painting of white confetti falling over a sprawling white frosted wedding cake entitled "Paris, Place de la Concorde in Winter."

The traffic dispersed, as if in slow motion, in several directions. Just a few cars were going the way of the chocolate Rolls, over the Pont de la Concorde.

Arabella's attention was caught by the river. The Seine— dark and cold. Several boats, covered in snow, were tied up to the quay.

The car was just approaching the center of the famous bridge when Arabella said, "Oskar, pull up here. I want to get out."

The chauffeur opened the door and said, "Not too long, madame."

"No, not too long, Oskar."

She walked to the rail and looked down into the water. Paris, the empress of cities, was spread out before her. She knew the name of every building, park, and bridge in view. Le Petit Palais, Le Grand Palais, and beyond them, Le Rond Point des Champs Élysées on the Right Bank. The magnificent houses overlooking the Seine on the Quai d'Orsay. Beyond them, the exquisite Hôtel des Invalides on the Left Bank.

Arabella had been captivated by Paris on her first visit and had remained enchanted. It was not only the astounding physical beauty of the city but the spirit of the people and the rich history of art and style that overwhelmed her emotionally. She also knew it was the perfect location to headquarter her worldwide business interests.

In the early years, she found the creative environment challenging and inspirational. In recent years, it offered her an opportunity to retain her anonymity and remain protected and secluded from the public eye while living a satisfying private life.

She devoted most of her time to her work, but when she ventured out, she appreciated the many luxuries Paris had to offer. She enjoyed lavish meals at Maxims, where she was a recognized patron. She loved to attend the couture designer preview showings on the rue Faubourg St. Honoré, where she was a preferred client. She adored the opera and the theater and visiting the galleries. She developed an appreciation of art treasures and acquired a modest but valuable collection.

Most of all, she loved to walk alone or sit quietly in a café. She felt her energy renewed and her spirit replenished during these special private times. Regrettably, these times for culture, frivolity, and leisure were rare as most of her hours were spent in her office on the Place Vendôme overseeing and directing her business. In recent months her suite at the Ritz functioned as a secondary office. There was no escape—until now!

She snuggled deep into her coat and watched the bow of a coal barge peep out from under the bridge. Black smoke curled from a stove-pipe chimney in the wheel house, where the barge family lived. Standing on top of the vast hills of coal all covered with snow and leaning against the cabin was a young girl with long, straight black hair hanging down from under a red wool cap. She was looking dreamily at Paris. She caught sight of Arabella and waved. Arabella waved back, smiling. The girl started trudging through the snow toward the stern of the barge, which was not yet in Arabella's sight, signaling with both arms and smiling. Arabella impulsively pulled off her hat and waved it. The teenager pulled off her cap, mimicking the woman on the bridge.

Putting a great deal of power behind it, Arabella skimmed her hat down into the breeze. For a split second the two looked at it floating in the air toward the barge. The bird-of-paradise feathers were alive again, fluttering over the Seine in Paris. Their eyes met for that split second where a lifetime of friendship is made and lost forever. They smiled and then their attention was back to the fate of the hat.

"Run!" shouted Arabella, in French. "Go get it, to the left, the left! Catch it, oh, do catch it!"

The hat and the girl moved closer together. She jumped up and almost had it. But a gust of wind took it off to the right. She scampered over the coal and snow to the edge of the barge and, running toward the stern, bent over the side and caught it. She kept walking while calling to Arabella, "It is a bird, a beautiful bird, and I caught it!" She looked so happy with her prize and, never taking her eyes off Arabella, kept waving with both arms.

Arabella laughed and clapped, shouting "*Bon chance*, good luck!" as the barge chugged away.

She turned around and, with her back against the stone balustrade, ran her fingers through her long, ash-blond hair;

the lighter streaks were as white as the snow and sparkled like the diamonds on her wrist.

Hugging her luscious sable coat around her against the cold, she said aloud, still smiling, "Well, you change your life, you change your hat!" then hurried into the warmth of the waiting car.

Oskar caught a glimpse of his employer in the rearview mirror. He and Rupert had nothing but respect and admiration for the beautiful, successful woman for whom they worked. Their position as valued servants gave them a good deal of pride in their work. They had grown accustomed to her calm, self-assured manner, the efficient and organized way she dealt with her work as well as with her personal life. The joy she had for life and the courage she showed in living it were an example to them of a type of woman they had never previously thought existed.

She was one of those women who takes on the role of the dominant party. It was evident in every phase of her life, yet she had the ability to delegate what she knew could be handled better by others. That in itself made working for her easy and rewarding. Rupert and Oskar, Missy and Xu, worked as a team, caring for Arabella. They removed all the mundane problems of life, allowing her to work and play on a grand scale successfully.

Oskar and the chocolate-colored cars were a welcome sight on the streets of Paris, London, and New York. Arabella Crawford's team was far better known than the beautiful and successful semireclusive female industrialist herself. She ventured out infrequently and managed to remain mysterious except for her business acumen—which was written about in the financial and business publications of the world.

The entire team thought of her as kind and considerate. They were amazed at her success in the hard world of business. It was Missy who constantly reminded them, "Madame Crawford needs our loyalty and protection. We must always be faithful and caring for her because she is a woman who deserves our respect and trust." The men had always felt Missy to be instinctively right.

Oskar's eyes darted to the rearview mirror again just at the moment Arabella gave a shiver of cold.

"I am afraid you got your feet wet, madame."

"Oh, Oskar, you are so right. My feet are wet and freezing, that's why I can't seem to get warm. My shoes are ruined." She kicked them off then reached for the gray fox car robe, threw it under her feet, and covered them over.

"May I suggest a little Courvoisier or Calvados, madame, to warm you up."

"Quite right, Oskar. Whatever would I do without you to keep an eye on me? It was my lucky day when the Earl of Heversham was kind enough to convince you and Rupert to come and look after me."

She reached for the crystal flask and poured a small amount into a tumbler.

"I hope you have never regretted leaving Heversham Park and his lordship for the life we have lived these past few years, Oskar."

"No, madame, I assure you, my devotion to Lord Quartermaine and my affection for Heversham Park will never end. My family has been in service to his lordship and his family for over three hundred years. We are a part of the estate, and his lordship has made it clear that there is a cottage waiting for me any time I want to return. As long as I am in service to you, I am still in service to the Earl of Heversham."

Arabella was touched, but for the first time that day her joy was not complete. The mention of her beloved Anthony Quartermaine, the Earl of Heversham, brought a lump to her throat, a reminder that all was not perfect after all. Not allowing herself the disquieting reverie, she pulled herself back to the conversation.

"Thank you, Oskar. There are going to be great changes in our lives and the way I live. Who knows, I may have a Heversham Park of my own soon."

Arabella then fell silent again as she thought about Anthony. A belted earl, a man close to the Queen of England, his home—Heversham Park—the finest estate in England, his heritage.

She owed so much to Anthony Quartermaine. Had it not been for his courage and love she would have become the obscure, devoted mistress in his life, involved in a love that could never become public because of his wife, four children, and other responsibilities. He would not allow her the humiliation of being second-best in his life, nor the loneliness and dependency on the scraps of a life with him she would have had to endure. Had it not been for Anthony forcing her out into the world to make a life for herself, what would her life have been? She often wondered. He supported her with love all these years but it was a silent love, a distant love given to her through discreet emissaries to help her through life. They met when he was forty and she was only twenty-two, and now, eighteen years later, he remained the most important person in her life.

If not for Anthony's selfless love, Arabella might not be the happy, rich, successful woman she was today. Yes, she had known great love in the intervening years, but she had not yet met the man to take his place. Her smile returned; she never allowed herself unhappiness over what was not to be.

An unidentifiable nursery tune kept going through her head. She began to hum it but could not remember the words. The Rolls pulled into the heliport while Arabella was singing softly, "Where do we go from here, boys? Where do we go from here? Where do we go from here, boys? Where do we go from here?"

Chapter Two

The S.S. *Tatanya Annanovna* was the newest, finest, and most sublime luxury liner afloat. It lay on its Cherbourg berth, its smokestacks signaling that departure was imminent. The decks were busy and bubbling with the excitement of its passengers and the activity of its crew. The twenty-thousand-ton ship was over nine hundred feet long, with eight passenger decks accommodating more than one thousand people. The cool winter sunlight reflecting from the water enhanced her magnificent silver-and-blue exterior. She was truly a dazzling sight. Flowing down the side of the magnificent ship was a cascade of colored streamers. The gangway, with its arched canvas awning of red, white, and blue stripes, had not yet been removed. The ship's officers, in full dress uniform, were standing guard on the dock.

The masses of well-wishers, visitors, television and radio reporters, and the hundred-piece band of the Scots Guards crowded the pier. A flotilla of thirty tugboats stood waiting to surround the famous ship, ready to escort her into the Channel with whistles hooting and hoses creating fountains of water in celebration of her maiden voyage across the Atlantic.

The *Tatanya Annanovna*, the jewel in the crown of the Anglo-French line, was the most widely acclaimed luxury ship in decades. Rumors were rife about the grand, exquisite ocean liner. There was an aura of mystery about her right from her very beginning.

There were many well-kept secrets about the *Tatanya*, starting with the source of the massive injection of money into her old shipping company said to have been arranged by a woman merchant banker and a White Russian prince. Rumor had it that the investment had been made in gold through a Paris bank. The ingots had been stamped with the cartouche of the murdered Tsar Nicholas. The stories grew from there. Some said the hidden treasure, the vast fortune of the Romanovs, had been found at last. Anastasia had survived, was still alive, identified, and her identification confirmed. The banks had finally been satisfied and released the money to the rightful heir. The Communists had lost the treasure and the capitalist White Russians were now buying into the most privileged, capitalistic investments to be found. There were stories of oil money and underworld connections, of secrets embedded in the ship's hull. These were only a few of the tales about the *Tatanya Annanovna*.

The ship had been having its final outfittings and decoration for two years. During that time the news media had not let up on the story, nor had the public relations department of the Anglo-French line. This ship was luxurious in the tradition of the great ships of the past—the *Normandie*, the *Grass*, the *Ilê de France*, the great *Queen Mary*, the two Elizabeths, and the tragic *Titanic*. The *Tatanya* could only be described as a glorious water palace. Her exquisite beauty, opulence, seaworthiness, and service were legendary before she was even launched. The public the world over had been satiated on everything about the *Tatanya*, from her uniquely designed ship's stabilizers to her hundreds of handcut crystal chandeliers. Her lavish staterooms were a familiar sight to readers of design and fashion magazines and curious television viewers, long before she ever made her trial run. The world waited to hear who were the fortunate travelers who were able to obtain passage on her prestigious maiden voyage across the Atlantic.

A book had been written about her by a modern-day Agatha Christie. In every important city, the night before this, her maiden voyage, the film of the book *Farewell Voyager*, starring Nicholas Frayne, opened to rave reviews. The film crew and its galaxy of stars had lived and worked on the ship. In their seven months on board they managed to add notoriety to the ship's already interesting history and background. The gossip columns reported one attempted suicide, two divorces, one sex scandal, and endless profiles of the male lead, one of Hollywood's great actors with two Academy Awards among his professional honors and a charm and kindness that eased the broken hearts he always left behind.

The world waited for the ship to sail and live up to her reputation. The passengers waited now. Some still on the open decks, wrapped in their furs and cashmere coats, leaned on the polished mahogany rails and looked down on the deserted dock, empty except for the men ready to cast off the ship. There were half a dozen customs men standing around in the cold, blowing on their hands to keep them warm. The single sentry stood guarding the gangway, making sure no one disembarked. For fifteen minutes now two helicopters had been hovering off the starboard side like great hummingbirds, ready to follow the ship, photographing her departure for the world's television viewers to see.

Curiosity hummed through the passengers. Who were they waiting for? Was it a film star? Yes, of course it was a film star. No, it was not the President of France. It was Mrs. Reagan. No, that could not be, she was in Washington, someone had seen her on television in the cabin only a few minutes before. No, it had to be a movie star. All the secrecy, all the exclusivity. To hold up such a ship it had to be something political.

A woman in a pale-gray mink coat said, "It's the CIA."

Libby Katz said to her husband, Isador, "It's the senator's wife, I'm sure of it. When I met her in Israel the day before yesterday at the B'nai B'rith Dinner she was still trying to book passage."

"Don't be silly," said Sophie Davis, Izzy's widowed sister. "They don't do this for senators and especially not for ex-senators, no matter how many terms they've had. It's no good. You wait all your life and several ancestors to be counted as old money, remain a Democrat to show you're human and caring, and what happens—the Republicans, new money, and 'flash' are in. You can't win."

Sophie's late husband's sister, Tessie Tillman, said, "Not everything is political, Sophie. I say it's a Greek millionaire; they always have connections in shipping."

It was Libby who said, "Who cares who they're waiting for? I'm warm, I'm happy, I have a deluxe outside cabin with private deck on the *Tatanya Annanovna*, which is equivalent to first class on the QE2. I'm on her maiden voyage, I'm with my husband and my friends. So who cares who they're waiting for?"

"You're right," Izzy said, putting his arm around her. "And besides, who's in a rush to get seasick?"

Two decks below, the third-class purser was looking over his flock, happy in the thought that he had the young students, the larger families, and the occasional young poet, painter, and aspiring ballet dancer. There was even a French jazz group going on their first tour of the States and a black pop singer. It was going to be an interesting and amusing crossing.

Just then the whir of helicopter blades echoed among the buildings, the empty dock, and the great ship. The passengers reacted to the sound by assembling rapidly at the railings. Suddenly, as if by magic, it was there. All eyes looked up, watching the chopper twirl down slowly to land on the dock only inches from the gangway.

The striped awning rippled in the wind as the custom officers bent their heads down and held their hats in place. The cascade of paper streamers hanging over the side of the ship began to dance around and come alive. At that moment there were three blasts of the ship's horn. The crew took their stations.

All eyes were on the helicopter whose motor had been cut and whose blades were slowing down. The dockers took their posts, ready to heave the lines on the word from the bridge. Others went to the gangway and stood ready to roll it away after the mystery passenger had embarked.

The door to the customs shed opened and out poured

old, well-worn Louis Vuitton steamer trunks, suitcases in various shapes and sizes, hat boxes large and small. The baggage men lined them up near the gangway.

The helicopter blades had nearly stopped. The door was flung open and out jumped the pilot—Arabella Crawford, dressed in a shiny silver silk jumpsuit that showed every curve of her voluptuous body.

Nicholas Frayne was standing alone on his private balcony on the bow of the *Tatanya Annanovna*. He threw his head back and roared with laughter, exclaiming aloud, "What an entrance!"

He raised the high-powered binoculars hanging around his neck to his eyes and focused on the scene below. Distracted for a moment by the sound of the ratchets as they began to grind, pulling up the huge, heavy anchor, he focused again on Arabella, as she removed her silver lamé cap and a mass of long blond hair fell around her exquisite, sensuous face.

He examined her—the high cheekbones, the perfect oval face with its long, straight, perfectly chiseled nose. His eyes lingered longest over her lips, her mouth. What a mouth! He wanted to reach out with his fingers and trace the shape of her lips, feel the softness of them. It was the sexiest mouth he had ever seen. The shape was divine. He wanted that mouth. Erotic fantasies tripped through his mind. How delicious to be in that mouth. His body reacted to the very thought.

Arabella threw her arms around herself, jumped up and down several times as if to shake off the cold. He saw a man's arm reach out and hand her a sable coat.

Nicholas Frayne spoke his thoughts out loud. "Oh no, fella, she's going to be mine. No, she can't possibly have a man with her." He was surprised at his instant desire for the woman on the dock. He watched her every movement as she wiggled into the warmth of her furs. He focused the glasses on the pair of arms reaching out to her, handing over a dog, a silver-gray whippet. She kissed the sleek, elegant animal, petted it. Then out came another, mushroom color, and another, dark beige, and yet another, the color of desert sand. She held them all on leads while they barked and danced around her ankles.

She spoke to a diminutive, pretty, black-haired young woman who advanced to greet her. She wore camel-hair trousers, an olive-green wrap-around coat, and carried a briefcase in one hand. They exchanged comments and the woman moved on quickly past the luggage, touching each piece as she counted aloud.

The man was out now, tall, six foot six inches, Oriental, with a kind, handsome face and the body of a weightlifter. Under one arm he carried a large rectangular box of black alligator trimmed in gold. Obviously the lady's jewel case.

Nicholas was relieved when the Oriental hulk took the dogs' leads and dutifully stepped back behind the woman. Nicholas watched her shake the co-pilot's hand, then turn and walk with her small entourage toward the customs men and the line of luggage. Documents were handed to the men, duly checked, and accepted. One of the men touched the large jewel case and spoke to her briefly. The man marked the cases with chalk, she was cleared, and the luggage disappeared up the ramp.

It was all so quick. Before Nicholas realized it, she had vanished up the covered gangway. Just as quickly she reappeared running onto the dock and to the helicopter. The blades were just beginning to move slowly, gathering speed, then they were cut. She hurriedly opened the door and for a minute Nicholas gasped; he thought he had lost her.

She picked something up, turned, her face was all smiles and laughing. Her gold and silver hair blowing in the wind, her sable coat flying open, she shone like a silver sun as she ran with two blue and white Chinese porcelain bird cages, one in each hand.

Nicholas's heart skipped a beat. He threw his head back again and started to laugh. Putting the binoculars to his eyes, he had just enough time to catch sight of the brilliant, exotic yellow birds before she was swallowed up again by the striped tunnel leading to the first-class boat deck. The dogs, the Oriental man, and the small dark woman followed her.

Nicholas Frayne lowered the binoculars and suddenly the dock seemed gray and lifeless. The whole scene had taken no longer than ten minutes, and for that ten minutes a light had been turned on in his life. He didn't even know her name, but he knew one thing for sure: He had seen the woman he would one day call the light of his life. He was filled with excitement, yet calm and very sure they were going to be together.

Nicholas reached into the inside pocket of his brown-and-beige tweed jacket and took out a long, slim cigar. He absentmindedly patted his beige cashmere turtleneck sweater, looking for a breast pocket, then reached into his worn blue jeans and found his old Ronson that was more like a flame thrower than a lighter. He lit the cigar, took some deep puffs, and watched the dockers move the gangway toward the customs shack. He watched the *Tatanya Annanovna* set sail but he saw nothing. He was too filled with the vision of his pursuit of this dazzling, elusive woman and his anticipation of the voyage ahead.

The West Hartford, Connecticut, contingent aboard gave a round of applause as the dockers threw the heavy lines into the water.

"Well, we're off!" said Sophie.

"I think I'll take a Dramamine," Izzy said.

"Don't be silly," Libby said. "Go get one of those Band-Aids they put on your neck. It's very modern."

"I'm so excited," said a flushed Tessie Tillman.

Dressed in full regalia—red coats, busbees, and all—the band of the Scots Guards reappeared at the end of the quay in the afternoon sunlight and struck up "Land of Hope and Glory" as the ship sidled away from the dock. Its mammoth engines drove the giant propellers and hundreds of thousands of gallons of water churned and swirled around the *Tatanya Annanovna*, driving her forward out into the port. A festive spirit provoked those passengers on the top deck to throw confetti, which rained down on the flotilla of yachts and small sailing vessels sounding their horns in unison as the huge liner sailed out of the harbor. The sailors waved farewell and the passengers on the deck waved back.

Romanticism and intrigue are synonymous with crossing the Atlantic Ocean on a luxury liner. When almost a thousand people, strangers for the most part, come together in an isolated, floating hotel for six days, anything is possible. The ship becomes the world, the ocean the universe, and what waits beyond, irrelevant. Time zones are created at will, the only reference points being the planets, the stars, and the tides. Every person on board felt the thrill of adventure, the excitement of a voyage into the unknown.

The tugboats surrounded the magnificent liner, giving it a dramatic water cannon display and a tugboat symphony of hoots, whistles, and bass foghorns.

"What a sight, what a send-off!" said Sophie.

"Oh, it's thrilling!" said Libby, and turning to her husband, she added, "Now I bet you're sorry you're such a snob about carrying a camera."

"No, not at all. I'm not a snob—I'm a realist. I'm a retired furniture manufacturer, not a photographer. Don't worry, Lib. We won't miss a thing. Not on your life. You can be sure in an hour's time we'll be able to buy any one of a hundred professional photographs of what we've just seen. They'll be up on the board next to the purser's office. In fact, I'll buy each of you ladies one!"

Libby gave her husband a playful punch on his shoulder and said, "You can never win with him. The worst thing is, I'm sure he's right!"

"No, he's not," said Tessie.

Dead silence fell over the group.

"Well, maybe half right," backed down Tessie.

More silence.

"What I mean is, you can be sure there'll be no photographs of the mystery lady who landed in that helicopter. I'm sure she's someone famous."

Half an hour had gone by since the *S.S. Tatanya An-*

nanovna had sailed and not one of the West Hartford group had said a word about Arabella Crawford's spectacular embarkation—each one all but biting her tongue not to be the first to say something. All were trying to be discreet and show indifference by their silence. But Tessie simply could hold back no longer.

Libby railed in defense of her husband. "Of course Izzy's right! We can buy the photographs from the purser. As for the helicopter landing, well, you can be sure she paid plenty—or let me say, *someone* paid plenty—for that privilege, and privacy should go with it. I certainly hope they didn't photograph the lady."

They then resumed their promenade on the boat deck, walking four abreast. Sophie bent her head forward and looked across at her sister-in-law on the end.

"How did you like that coat, Libby?"

Libby walked a little bit taller and, pulling her soft belt a little bit tighter around her vicuña coat, raised her hands to the underpart of its Russian sable lapels, fluffing up the fur. She looked past her husband, across the faces of her two friends, and sighing heavily, said icily, "Sophie, that was no coat. That was the most exquisite Russian sable I have ever seen."

They walked on.

"Wasn't she beautiful?"

"Gorgeous."

"She has some sense of style! Imagine wearing a silver silk jumpsuit with that blond and silver hair! Let's have a man's opinion. What did you think of her, Izz?"

"I thought she looked like a goddess. She shone like a silver dollar."

The look on the three women's faces intimated they might have been happier if Isador had been a little less enthusiastic about her.

"Granted," said Sophie, grudgingly. "But a woman like that? All looks and no brains. In a way, I feel sorry for her, for all the women like her. When the looks go, where are they, the poor things?"

The first one to come to Arabella's defense was Izzy.

"I don't think she's too dumb, Soph. She was smart enough to pilot that helicopter to a perfect landing. No mean feat!"

Libby added, "Girls that look like that are dumb like foxes."

"Well, I think the whole thing was marvelous and she was beautiful, spectacular. I wonder if we'll see her again."

"Or her husband."

"Husband, I doubt; sugar-daddy, maybe."

"Maybe the Oriental is her husband," said Tessie.

The three others said in dismay and unison, "Never!"

"Well, I wish her luck, whoever she is. Girls like that are a rare joy to see," said Izzy.

"Are you kidding?" said Sophie. "In this day and age, girls like that are a dime a dozen."

Izzy stretched his arms out across the women and said, "Stop!" in a serious and authoritative manner. He reached into his pocket and pulled out a quarter and a nickel, handed them to Sophie, and said, "Okay, Soph, here's thirty cents. Buy me three."

They all laughed, and Izzy said, "Come on, my beauties, let's have some champagne. Sugar-daddy's buying!"

Chapter Three

Arabella, Xu, and Missy, after putting the dogs and birds in the ship's kennels, went to Arabella's staterooms. They stood on the private balcony at the bow of the deck and watched the water display. They heard the tugboat concert as the ship and her flotilla cut their way out of the harbor. Arabella had one of the few exquisite penthouse cabins on the ship. Each had an outside deck and a private, enclosed balcony offering protection from the damp chill of the North Atlantic but commanding a view of the sea from all angles.

After briefly enjoying the view, Missy and Xu excused themselves to perform their many duties.

A permanent smile was etched across Arabella's face, a smile that came from within, involuntarily, just there. It was not unlike the feeling in her feet of wanting to dance, or in her heart, which felt as if it were singing instead of beating. Her whole mind and body were receivers for her sensations of joy, frivolity, and love. She could only remember one other time in her life when she felt such emotion. Anthony Quartermaine, the Earl of Heversham, walked back into Arabella's mind and memory. She wondered how he would react when the news reached him about her extraordinary business coup and abrupt departure from Paris.

Leaning on the glossy mahogany rail, Arabella pulled her sable up around her face against the cold wind and watched the coastline of France disappear on the horizon. The flotilla of tugboats now looked nothing more than children's toy boats as they sailed back to the shore. She could barely hear the melancholy foghorns blasting their final farewell.

It was a moment for nostalgia about places she had traveled to in the past and might never return to, or, if she did, they would certainly never be the same. Could she ever return to Paris and be at home there again? It was a moment for reflection. And for Arabella, that always meant Anthony and their long, exquisite, strange love affair. It came as a shock to Arabella to realize that those eighteen years and the love affair might indeed be just that: the past. To her life had never been the ordinary chain of events that most women expect, and to her Anthony was always the symbol of the unexpected, a twist of fate, an inexplicable part of her soul. Where would he fit now?

She turned away from the coastline and looked out to the vast ocean that lay before her. She would look to the future now, the new, the fresh, the unknown. To being free, more free than she had ever been in her entire life. Rich, rich beyond measure. Her thoughts were of houses, gardens, and romance, yes, romance above all else. A life of leisure, fun, and romance.

She wanted to sing, dance, laugh, play, make love, wild, unbridled, passionate love. She sucked in great draughts of cold wind and her heart began to pound with excitement and expectation. She threw her head back, opened her arms, and laughed out loud. An icy wind wrapped around her body; it made her feel sensitized and alive all over. She pulled her coat about her and dashed into the warmth of her drawing room, where a fire was blazing in the fireplace, adding a glow to the soft creamy tone of the room.

Missy was opening telegrams and gathering cards from the flowers. It was the first chance Arabella had to take in the drawing room of her suite and she said, "Very lovely, Missy, isn't it?" The carpets were plush, the drapes were silk, and the furnishings combined rare antiques with solid, seaworthy contemporary furniture of the highest quality. The walls were discreetly mirrored to take advantage of the ocean view. The lacquered surfaces reflected the light. She knew instantly that this was going to be a very special place.

She walked through and examined the other rooms. There was a pantry complete with Royal Doulton china, Baccarat crystal, coffeemaker, tea kettle, ice bucket. She found tid-bits and delicacies from Fauchon in Paris and Fortnum's in London; a tin of assorted biscuits on the serving counter and, in the refrigerator, a bowl of fruit, champagne, and jugs of fresh fruit juices.

She walked down the hall to one bedroom designed as a sitting room with a marble table and chairs in the center. It was charming, more like a library or a breakfast room, a place where one might even dine *à deux*.

The master bedroom was large and lovely with a king-sized bed, a canopied four-poster draped in beautiful crewel work on beige silk. Leaves and flowers, exotic birds, and a Russian royal crest of silver threads were in the center of the upholstered headboard. The furniture was sixteenth-century French Provincial, the color of dark, sweet honey. The portholes were large and overlooked more of her private deck. The room was flooded with light. The *boiserie*, obviously original, was lovely with architectural wood carvings of flowers and birds over the door.

Arabella went through to the dressing room where Xu was unpacking and putting her things away. Then into the large bathroom of cream marble with a light vein of eucalyptus green running through it. She touched the thick towels, then walked back, dropping her coat on the bed as she passed.

She called, "Xu, come here a moment."

In the drawing room again, she turned to Missy and said, "Stop fussing with all that, it can wait. I want to talk to you and Xu about this trip. Have you two seen your accommodations yet?"

"No, we haven't," said Xu.

"Well, go now and see that they're to your liking. I want you both to enjoy this crossing. You are booked in second class and must take advantage of the service and luxury available there. That means, Missy, Xu, that until we have to get ready to dock in New York, I don't want you working. I only ask you, Xu, to finish unpacking."

Missy and Xu looked at each other quizzically.

"I really mean that. It's unlikely I will need you since there is more than enough staff to take care of my needs for the next six days. I want you both to forget about me and have a grand time."

Arabella's two companions were reluctant to obey her orders but were clever enough to know that she meant it.

Missy and Xu spoke at once. "I will take care of the dogs and birds."

Arabella said, "We all will. I hate leaving them in the kennels. If each of us spends some time every day with them, they won't be lonely.

"I may invite you two to dine with me one evening or join me at the gaming tables, but that will be strictly social, and you must decline the invitation if you have something better to do. Understood?"

They both agreed. Just as Missy was about to leave and Xu return to the task of unpacking, there was a knock at the door.

It was Pete Peters, the purser they had all met at the time of their embarkation. He had come to check that Miss Crawford had everything she wanted and that she was comfortable in her suite. He passed on compliments from the captain and an invitation to dine with him and a few guests in his quarters that evening. It would not be formal, as it was the first night out.

Peters was a handsome man. Tall, dark, and slim, with a dimple in his chin and a twinkle in his eye. Arabella thought she detected a spark of something between him and Missy, a spark that made Missy no less efficient but more flirtatious than usual.

Peters had brought with him the cabin maid and steward who would attend to Arabella during her voyage. It gave her the opportunity to reassure her own servants that she would be well cared for. The maid went off with Xu to see where everything was and how Arabella liked things done. Missy left and Arabella talked to the purser, asking him to make sure that her guests, Xu and Missy, were well taken care of during the crossing.

Arabella was handed a massive package of brochures outlining everything happening aboard the *Tatanya Anna-novna*. They included a detailed plan of the ship and a passenger list. When asked by Peters if she would like to join her fellow passengers now for tea, Arabella declined, saying she would rather have a late lunch in her cabin. She was famished. It was arranged and then everyone but Xu left.

Arabella went into the dressing room where he was putting the last of the empty suitcases away. He watched his mistress standing in front of the full-length mirror. She seemed to be studying herself. He remained where he was, silent, not wanting to disturb her thoughts.

Arabella came out of her reverie and saw Xu's reflection. She smiled, turned, and said, "I think I'll have a hot bath, Xu."

"Would you like a massage first, madame?"

"No, thanks, but if you would lay out a clean chemise and robe, that silver one with the hint of peach in it, I think. I'll go and pin up my hair, then you can do the back of my neck and shoulders."

During the years she was building up her financial empire, Xu had looked after her and protected her so well. More than once he had rescued her from hate and intrusion, the unpleasant aspects of a position as powerful as hers. He had always been the perfect bodyguard. She feared nothing as long as he was at her side. Not only did Arabella want to see that Xu was cared for and happy, but she felt it essential that he be so.

She wondered what she had done to deserve such loyalty and devotion from Xu. He was the youngest son of one of the most important Chinese officials, one of those of a Chinese cadre like Lin Piao who is periodically in and out of favor. Xu was born into the new China. His father, Chao Zhao Shi, was an old man at the time of his youngest son's birth. Before the revolution he had been a man of great wealth and stature. He was an educated, forward-thinking man, and they were a family of scholars, physicians, artists.

He had thrown in with Mao and Chou En Lai, had been one of the great financiers of the long march. He had proved himself time and time again in the fight for a new China. But the Zhao Shi family always carried the stigma of the Mandarin class.

Xu was the child of a reformed household whose father once had three wives, several concubines, and innumerable children. The surviving children were scholars of one sort or another, all working for Communist China.

At the time of the cultural revolution, Xu Zhao Shi had been in his last year of medical school at Peking University and was famous throughout China as one of their favorite and finest all-around athletes. He was engaged to marry a fellow student whom he had loved since childhood.

In 1966 Xu was in Paris on an exhibition tour with a group of Chinese athletes. He and his group were watching television in their hotel when the news flash of the cultural revolution broke. He watched pictures of the mobs rampaging through the streets of Peking. He saw his father and two of his brothers denounced, driven through the streets with hands and feet bound, placards hung around their necks, being beaten; excrement and garbage were being thrown at them. A picture of a group of his fellow students from the university being denounced, stripped, beaten, and humiliated flashed across the screen. Among them was his childhood sweetheart, his first and only love. He saw her head cracked open and her life flow away on French TV.

He had met Arabella on the very same night he saw his life destroyed.

Long before the troubles erupted, Xu's father knew they were coming. In what form or how intense, he had no idea. He had tried to stem the tide of disaster, but he was ineffective. It was then he confided in Xu and only one other son—the two men in his family that he was sure stood with him politically. They agreed that if indeed there was a revolt and any of the three were abroad, they would ask for political asylum and remain abroad until they knew the fate of the family. They felt that this was the only way to help those who might be denounced or incarcerated.

Xu had walked from the television set in the lobby of that Paris hotel to his room. There he found his address book with a list of every foreigner his father trusted. Arabella Crawford was the only Paris telephone number. Her connection with Chao Zhao Shi was through a sale of grain she had made with him to the Republic of China.

Xu had called her Place Vendôme office; she happened to be working late that night. Arabella answered the telephone. He declared who he was and that he needed help at once. She told him to leave the hotel immediately and to walk north, go into the first café, and take a table. She would find him. She did and brought him directly back to her rooms at the Ritz. They turned on the television and waited for the next news flash. The boy was shattered.

At nine o'clock the next morning, Arabella took him to the American embassy, where he was given political asylum. They had been together ever since.

Xu unconsciously made several vows during the night he saw his fiancée die on that TV screen: He would never marry, or become a doctor, or commit himself politically. It had something to do with the shock of seeing man's inhumanity to man.

Ever since he and Arabella had been together, he had kept up his athletics, become a Zen Buddhist, learned four languages, become a master of all the martial arts, and kept up his studies of medicine.

He had chosen to stay with Arabella. He protected her, kept her physically fit, and more than once had a spiritual influence on her.

Arabella unzipped the jumpsuit, sat down on the chaise in her dressing room, and pulled off her silver kid ankle boots. She stretched, jumped up, and slipped out of the garment, leaving it on the chaise like a discarded skin.

At the dressing table in her bedroom, she reached out for the white jade hairpins, which were exactly in the place she wanted them to be. Xu was a treasure: Her jewel case was open, her jewelry available to her; every pot of cream, every lipstick, shadow, brush in its place. How she loved everything in its place. Everything precise, everything perfect. Being precise, clean, and ordered came easily to her, and just as easily came her spontaneity.

She sat barefoot in her white silk chemise with its insets of ecru-colored lace, arranging tendrils of hair prettily among the mass piled up on top of her head. She laughed at herself; she looked anything but the hard-nosed executive she had been these past few years.

Arabella slowly cleansed her face and saw for a fleeting moment a beauty she had never recognized before. Caught up in the frivolity, she began to play with the pots of color and makeup on her dressing table. Suddenly she had the desire to make herself more beautiful than she had ever been. And now she had the time—and the money—to do it.

Xu appeared behind her and with strong, deft fingers worked the muscles in the back of her neck, the two lobes at the base of her skull. With one huge strong hand he circled her neck, kneaded the muscles, and felt her relax. The heavy silk satin chemise slipped forward revealing her magnificent breasts—large, lusciously firm, and voluptuously round and high. She looked in the mirror and put her makeup brush down, thinking she had never looked more relaxed and beautiful as she did right there and then.

Xu worked across her shoulders and with his thumbs massaged her spine just below the neck.

"Oh." She sighed. "What ecstasy!" Closing her eyes as he worked down one arm to her very fingertips, she felt as loose and easy as a piece of string. Xu massaged down the other arm and then, with both hands, the back of her neck again.

She slowly opened her eyes and watched the handsome Xu in the mirror. His massive strong hands became gentle as he kneaded around her neck and throat and moved across her back up her shoulders.

All tension was gone. The warmth she felt within her was delicious. She looked into his face and said, "Thank you, Xu." She slipped her arms through the sleeves of her dressing gown, and the touch of the silver peach silk against her skin made her shiver, it was so sensuous.

"Would you like me to stay?" he asked.

"No, Xu. You go now and enjoy these next few days on board ship. I promise you that if I need you, I'll find you."

He thanked her and left.

Arabella went through the dressing room and caught a glimpse of herself in the full-length mirror: her perfectly made-up face crowned by the pinned-up, tousled fair hair, the magnificent heavy breasts, the tiny waist, slim hips with full, high, rounded buttocks, and flat stomach. She had long, elegant legs. Her nipples were erect and her body, still tingling, longed for more sensations. She felt lovely and was enjoying her loveliness.

Chapter Four

Arabella heard her stomach grumble, and it reminded her of her hunger. She was slipping into her dressing gown when the buzzer rang at the stateroom door.

She called out, "Come in."

She went through into the bedroom to her dressing table to take her hair down and brush it, but before she could do so the buzzer rang again.

"Oh, dear."

She replaced the brush on the table and went into the drawing room.

"Come in," she called, approaching the door, her head down as she fastened the braided frogs on her dressing gown.

The doorknob turned hesitantly, and she instinctively reached out, her hand moving with its turning. She pulled as the man pushed and the door opened. She looked up, stepped back, and was taken by surprise.

In the door, leaning against the frame, was a man in a well-tailored, rough tweed jacket and faded blue jeans. Their eyes met. Arabella took a deep breath and tried to compose herself, involuntarily blushing.

It was he who broke their gaze by reaching out with his forefinger and tenderly tracing the shape of her lips. He raised his eyes to her hair and then slowly drank in her beauty from head to toe.

Pink with embarrassment, she was simply not able to get herself under control. She was flustered and said, "I thought you were the waiter with my lunch," still standing there with her hand on the knob of the open door.

The man straightened up and the famous smile that went to the heart of millions of movie fans broke across his face.

Nervously he pushed a heavy lock of fair hair off his fore-head and said, in his slow, deep, sexy voice, "No, I am not the waiter, but I have brought your lunch."

He turned away and pulled a serving trolley into sight. It was covered with a crisp white damask cloth and laden with a silver soup tureen and other silver covered dishes.

Arabella, mesmerized by the handsome profile emanat-ing virility and power, was not yet aware of the table. She was as if burned by the passion, desire, soul, and spirit he directed at her. They matched her very own.

Their eyes met again. He saw the confused look on her face, the fragility, vulnerability; beneath that he saw desire, excitement—the ingredients that made up this glorious beauty. At that moment it was not his or her heart—but their hearts—that skipped a beat, and they were then linked together.

It was Arabella who looked away, feeling deeply em-barrassed at having been caught off guard and giving so much of herself away. She nervously put one hand to her hair, trying to arrange it better, her other hand to her face, trying to brush away her high color. Suddenly she recog-nized him as the actor Nicholas Frayne.

"You must forgive me, I am not usually so . . ." Her words trailed off and she tried again. "Well, it's not often one opens the door to a waiter and finds a movie star in his place!"

Nicholas was enjoying her embarrassment; it brought her closer to him. With the back of his hand, he touched her cheek and said, "Do you always blush?"

His voice excited her. She felt stupid and as if she could only say inane things. She said to herself, "For God's sake, stop behaving like a middle-age groupie!"

She wanted to say something clever, but came out with "I think I'm giving myself away."

"I hope so," said Nicholas Frayne. He reached up and pulled the jade pins slowly from her hair. It tumbled to her shoulders and he touched it.

"It's like silk," he said, as he bent closer to her, tilted up her chin to his face, and kissed her mouth. The warmth of her lips aroused him, and he pressed his kiss just a little harder. He drew away slowly, trying to control the passion he felt.

He stepped back and said, "I do have your lunch, madame. May I please bring it in?"

His question snapped Arabella momentarily out of the soft-focused haze she seemed to be in.

"Of course, please come in, Mr. Frayne," she said, backing into the room, allowing him to enter. He wheeled the trolley to the center of the room and then turned and walked past her out the door.

For a split second Arabella's knees went weak and she said to herself, "How extraordinary—he's gone!"

But then he was back, and in his arms he carried an enormous florist's box, tied with a wide satin ribbon. She could see huge white lilacs, long-stemmed white roses with just a hint of peach in them, creamy tulips, and several sprays of white baby orchids.

Arabella's expression changed. All confusion gone, there was pure delight. She placed her hands together as if in prayer and touched their sides to her lips. She smiled and exclaimed, "They're absolutely gorgeous!"

"You see, I have not just come as a waiter. I've come courting," he said as he walked past her into the room and placed the box on the floor next to the coffee table. Then he went out into the corridor again, returning this time with an ice bucket containing two bottles of champagne under one arm and a box of chocolates under the other. Chatting nervously, he explained, "White chocolates. Leonidas handmade white chocolates with fresh cream filling from Belgium." He placed them on the coffee table, then turned to look back at her. He asked, in the famous, husky whisper, "May I join you for lunch?"

The sound of that familiar voice brought Arabella to

attention. It helped her get her emotions under control. She closed the door, leaned against it, smiled, and said, "Oh, yes, you must!"

She went up to him and, putting out her hand, said, "I am Arabella Crawford."

He picked up her hand and touched it to his lips. "I know," he said. "And I'm Nicholas Frayne."

"I know," she said, and they both began laughing, releasing some of the incredible tension that filled the room.

"You couldn't have chosen more perfect flowers. They're absolutely gorgeous. Let me put them in a vase." Arabella opened an antique Chinese cabinet and found a perfect cut-crystal vase, which she filled with water.

"Where shall we have our lunch?" Nicholas asked.

"Why don't you take everything from the trolley and put it here on the coffee table while I arrange your lovely flowers."

Arabella picked up one branch of white lilac and held the heavenly scented tiny blossoms forming the full, pear-shaped head cupped in the palms of her hands and buried her face in them. What madness! she thought. "What delicious, romantic madness. This can't be real! I must be in a movie with Nicholas Frayne!"

The glossy movie star, the brilliant actor, the intelligent film director, Nicholas Frayne, and the clever, aggressive business tycoon, Arabella Crawford. Four hours before on dry land, would they have even spoken to each other? Only here, on a romantic voyage made for lovers, in an isolated world away from the reality of life it all seemed right, quite normal.

Nicholas stood watching her create a beautiful arrangement. When she had finished, she held out her arms, silently asking him to help her up. He took her by the hands and raised her up from the floor. They looked at the flowers in a silence that spoke volumes.

He squeezed her hands, smiled, and said, "Oh, I almost forgot." He reached for something in his breast pocket. He pulled out a white envelope and handed it to Arabella, saying "I'll open the champagne. You read your letter."

They pulled cushions off the white sofa onto the floor and sat on them. He opened the bottle while she read:

Dear Miss Crawford,

This is a letter introducing my friend Nicholas Frayne. I hope you will forgive this intrusion on your privacy. I have been blackmailed by Nicholas for this introduction. He assures me that if you appear at all offended he will retreat at once.

I can only apologize with the excuse that not even for blackmail would I have given him your name, your whereabouts, or this introduction had I not thought that you would enjoy his company.

I hope you will show me forgiveness by being my guest this evening at nine in my quarters. We will dine with a few of the other passengers.

Yours sincerely,

Wilfred Hamilton
Captain
S.S. *Tatanya Annanovna*

Arabella put down the note and smiled. "You do very unconventional things, Mr. Frayne, under the most conventional camouflage."

"And you, Arabella Crawford," he said, with a twinkle in his eyes as he handed her a glass of Dom Perignon. "I'm sure you always go on first dates in your dressing gown."

"Oh, my God!" Arabella exlaimed as she reached for the glass, looked down at her robe, and blushed, as if it were all one motion.

They began laughing once again, but they never took their eyes off each other. The embarrassment was fast becoming a shared experience rather than a reason for discomfort. Their eyes met and soft smiles appeared simultaneously on their faces.

"Oh," said Nicholas, "it's all right then for me to stay? Now that we've been formally introduced? How lucky I am!"

"And I," said Arabella.

They sat opposite each other sipping champagne from Lalique crystal goblets, sensing the buildup of emotions and anticipating the excitement that comes with the voyage of discovery when you are falling in love. Nicholas sat with his back to the portholes. The afternoon light poured out behind him. His virile good looks against the light gave him an even more heavenly aura than the movie cameras reflected.

Arabella sat there thinking how extraordinary it was that such a sexy man should make her think of pure joy, a flock of angels singing, yet, at the same time, she yearned for him to touch her, have his hands touch her breasts and his fingers feel the passion he aroused in her. His smile caressed her and that alone made her want to make love to him, feel his lips against hers, be electrified by the touch of his skin. Whatever it was he emanated across the table drew her to him like a magnet.

He said nothing, did nothing, and yet she felt herself drawn into his arms. He reached out without reaching out and she fled to him across the table without moving.

How amazing, thought Arabella. What magnetism!

True, she had seen most of his films and had more than once gone home sexually aroused by him, wanting him. How mad, insane, a fantasy come true! He was there with her in her stateroom on board the *Tatanya Annanovna* and on this day of all days, the first day of her new life.

The light behind him spilled out around and over him to the flowers and the silver covered dishes. The light picked up his straight reddish-brown hair peppered with strands of silver gray, making it look even more golden.

The cold champagne burst upon Arabella's tastebuds. She felt a ripple of silk from her sleeve roll over her arm, a wave as if from a warm tropical ocean. It was so delicious she unconsciously put her glass down and smoothed the silk over her arms with her hands. It was glorious. She felt her nipples grow erect as Nicholas Frayne made love to her passionately, sexually, with his eyes and his smile.

He put his glass down and removed his jacket, asking "May I?" She nodded. The soft cashmere against his chest aroused his fantasies of how soft and delectable she would be in his arms.

His fantasies took flight. He had her in his arms, was exploring her body, her wonderful breasts. He fondled them; they were supple and full. He could feel the nipple in his mouth, he nibbled and sucked, it grew hard, erect, and swelled as she became excited by him.

He imagined her open and ready for him as he entered her, at the same time kissing her eyes, her chin, the tip of her exquisite nose, and her mouth. He opened her with tenderness and kisses and was deep inside her. Her mouth embraced him, tantalized him.

She would reach down, feel his erection, and make love to him. She would be thrilled by him, fondle him, suck him, lick him, She would kiss him, take him in her mouth and her throat while he nuzzled his face between her legs. He would play with her and drink the sweetness from her. They would make love that way using their fingers and tongues.

The bulge in his trousers was becoming uncomfortable, and he needed to move to adjust himself. He saw a cassette deck across the room and went to pick out a tape. He thought some Chopin waltzes might be nice—lively but not too intrusive. He inserted the tape and returned to the couch.

"That's perfect! Some background music to lunch by."

He watched Arabella remove the silver cover from the soup tureen. Smoothly, almost imperceptibly, she changed position, gliding onto her knees. She sat back on her haunches and ladled out steaming lobster bisque into the soup bowl before her. She picked up the elegant china bowl by its two handles and passed it to Nicholas, saying "I hope you like lobster bisque. May I have your bowl, please."

He watched as she put the heavy silver ladle back into the tureen and slowly stirred the thick, creamy soup. His fantasies took off again.

This overwhelming attraction he had to Arabella was one that he had played out in various ways on the silver screen many times; only then it was acting, someone's play, a role. This was no play. It was real and it had never happened to him in his life before. Not even with Maggie whom he loved, his childhood sweetheart, the woman he married, the mother of his children. Not even with Sylves, the woman he had lived with for many years, a woman who had satisfied his sexual needs and social life until only a few months before.

They spooned the sensuous liquid to their lips as they looked at each other. Their tastebuds were open and the soup was sheer ambrosia. The perfect bisque—rich, creamy, and flavorful. They were silent, taking each other in as well as their soup.

Arabella remained sitting on her haunches. Nicholas poured more champagne for them and when they touched their glasses for a second time and drank, he knew that she understood how he felt, that she felt something for him. She was in control of their destiny just as much as he was.

"You are exquisite, Arabella. I want to know all about you. Where did you come from, that is, apart from out of heaven?"

"Paris."

"And before that?"

"I'm American—Washington, D.C., and the banks of the Potomac. But that was eighteen years ago."

"And in between?"

"For business reasons, I lived in London for several years, spent time in New York, Zurich, Brussels, and Milan, traveled to the Middle East, China, Japan, and Australia, and visited Caracas and Buenos Aires, as circumstances required." She refrained from mentioning Alexandria and the other more exotic places she and Anthony had shared for pleasure.

"Why are you making this crossing?"

"Because I'm changing my life and I'm..." She hesitated and then asked, "Does any of this matter?"

"No, not in the least. We have time to learn all about each other. What does matter is that I'm here in your cabin and you and I are going to make this voyage together across all that—" He waved his arm, and they both looked out through the oversized portholes off the bow to the open ocean that lay before them.

"You seem very sure. Do you always do this—jump into a woman's life and court her with flowers, chocolates, and champagne?"

"Only on ships when the atmosphere is bursting with romance, intrigue, isolation, and the unknown, and a woman like you makes an appearance."

They were silent for a minute, looking into each other's eyes. Then he said, "I want to seduce you physically, emotionally, and spiritually. Does that frighten you?"

"No," she said, with the most tantalizing smile and sparkling eyes. "Not if you do it well and can accomplish it."

He chuckled and said, "It might be a question of who is seducing whom."

She smiled and said, "Yes, it might, mightn't it?"

The soup bowls empty, they put them aside. Arabella replaced the tureen in the center of the table with a large silver dish with a balloon-shaped cover. She opened the cover using the two small handles at the top. The lid slid down to reveal a large crystal bowl filled with caviar, the best black Beluga. It was set in a circle of crushed ice and lemon halves, covered in fine cheesecloth. She uncovered another dish filled with paper-thin pancakes, and another small silver bowl filled with thick white sour cream.

"I know it's extravagant!" said Arabella. "But that's how I felt when I ordered lunch. Now I'm doubly glad I did because I have a guest. I do hope that you like Russian caviar."

"One of my weaknesses," said Nicholas. "What a wonderful lunch and a wonderful hostess."

Embarrassed, she went a little pink and said, "May I make the first blini for you the way I make them for myself?"

"Yes, please."

Arabella then assembled the classic Russian specialty that the ancient Slavs used to eat to reassure themselves in the dead of winter that the sun would one day return. First she picked up one of the hot pancakes with the tips of her fingers and smoothed it out flat on a plate. Then with a silver spoon she spread a thick layer of sour cream over it. With the crystal spoon, she scooped up a huge portion of black caviar, which she put in the center of the pancake, then she reached for one of the lemons and squeezed it over the caviar.

"I think I should tell you," Arabella said, "that I don't roll them as one should. I never like blinis that are all pancake and a touch of the black eggs, only when they are all caviar and a touch of pancake!" She handed him the plate.

Nicholas watched her make one for herself and laughed when she filled the crystal spoon with caviar from her plate and tore off a corner of the pancake. She slid the spoon into her mouth and rolled her eyes in an expression of delight as she slid the now-empty spoon out again, quickly popping in the piece of pancake and sour cream after it.

She amused him with a hand gesture as if rubbing her tummy in a circle and said, "Oh, Nicholas, this is sublime!"

He agreed with her. It was divine. She made them each another as he opened a second bottle of champagne. They indulged themselves in silence, savoring the luxurious lunch.

He stood up and, moving around to sit next to her on the sofa, filled her glass. He put the bottle down in front of them on the table after moving some of the empty dishes.

He looked at her and said, "That was a wonderful lunch. Memorable."

Kissing her on the lips lightly, tenderly, almost hesitantly, he leaned back, moved closer to her, and drew her to him. He felt her relax into his arm. She rested her head on his shoulder. The touch of her silk dressing gown and her body in his arms was enough to release the passion and tenderness he had felt when he had seen her through the binoculars during her spectacular arrival on the ship. He caressed her hair, kissed her on the cheek, and pulled her tighter to him. He tilted her face up to his and said, "I think you are divine."

Arabella responded by twisting around in his arms, lying down with her head resting in his lap. Then she reached up and pulled his head down to hers. First she kissed him ever so gently on his lips—a whisper of a kiss. Then she pointed her tongue and outlined the shape of his lips.

Nicholas thought he would melt, the fire she ignited in him was so hot. He pulled her up tight in his arms as he opened his lips. She ran her tongue inside and their lips met again in a more passionate kiss.

She slid her hand under his cashmere sweater. The feel of his skin electrified her. She gasped at her unexpected response and quickly moved her hand away.

"Nicholas, let's talk first. I want to know all about you."

"Shhh," he whispered, as he gently touched her lips. "We already know each other. What we are both feeling now is important. We have time to talk later."

They held each other, silent and thoughtful, sometimes touching, petting, caressing, other times so sexually aroused they held back, trying not to drown out all the other things they were feeling for each other with lust.

The room was growing dark. Dusk was upon them when Nicholas kissed her on the temple. He was cuddling her to him as she dozed. She had that luscious, lazy feeling, induced by too much champagne and even more emotion.

He felt her come alive again in his arms as he touched her breasts. He unfastened the silk braided frogs that held her dressing gown closed and saw her body for the first time under the scant silver-peach chemise. He covered her with nibbling kisses across her shoulders, around her neck; he rubbed his face over the silk between her breasts and down over her stomach; then he pulled her close to him and kissed her deeply as he found his way between her legs. He unbuttoned the three tiny pearl buttons across the narrow crotch of the chemise and found the moistness it had covered. He touched her, played with her mound of golden hair. She was so soft, velvety and warm.

She sighed and whispered, "Yes, oh, yes . . ." He worked the chemise up over her body, and when he saw her heavy, firm breasts with their rosy nipples standing forth, he quickly pulled the chemise over her head and dropped it on the floor. He looked at her naked in his arms and then suddenly, with overwhelming passion, he pulled her even tighter to him. The soft cashmere caressed her, and his erection stabbed her through his trousers. He held her that way with one arm around her back, the other over her bottom, which he caressed before he reached under it to feel inside her again. He released her and his passion subsided for a moment as he stroked her hair, looked into her eyes, and said softly, "I've thought of nothing but you since you landed in the helicopter. I watched you through binoculars and imagined how wonderful you would be, but I was quite wrong. You are more wonderful than I imagined. All through lunch I wanted to feel you, to know you, make love to you."

Arabella put her arms around his neck and began kissing him slowly and sweetly over his face and neck while he touched her. He then bent to kiss her neck and whispered in her ear, "Come, my darling, come!" He felt her twinge with excitement and when, with deft fingers, he went deep into her and felt her come, she sighed and said softly, in a voice laced with sex, "Oh, Nicholas, I can't hold back from you."

He said, "Shhh, shhh, it's all right," and opened her wider, pushing in as far as he could go. "Shhh," he said again. "I want you this way. If only you knew what joy it gives me to have you respond to me like this. It's only the beginning."

Eventually he removed his hand and stroked her thighs and hips. She reached down and took the hand that had made love to her, raised it to her mouth, placed the palm over her lips and kissed it. He saw the passion in her eyes as she pulled slowly away from him, but only far enough away to slip back into her dressing gown. She wrapped it loosely around her and, still stretched out on the sofa on her side, facing him, her head in his lap, she said, "I want to show you how I feel about you." She kissed him as she undid the large silver buckle, loosened his belt, and slowly unzipped his fly. He slowly moved aside and zipped up.

"I know how you feel about me, Arabella," he said. "You told me by the way you responded to me. I'm sorry I must leave now. It's not possible for me to stay. I'll explain later." He turned his face to hers and put his arms around her. He said, "We've been like two kids. I've fallen for you, and it's true we know nothing about each other." He then picked her hands up in his and kissed them, saying "Let's take this crossing and the days and nights on board to discover each other."

"I would like that," she answered.

He took her by the hand and they walked to the door. Again he said, "I'm sorry to have to leave you now." And he was gone.

After Nicholas departed, Arabella remained in a state of shock and euphoria. She couldn't help but think how wonderful it would have been if he could only have stayed a little longer. She knew they were both sexually excited when they parted, a feeling that could only increase until they were together again. She knew she had been seduced in a way that felt uniquely special yet somehow familiar. She decided a long, luxurious bath would clear her mind. She went to the tub, poured in a packet of Caswell Massey gardenia bubble bath, turned on the gold-plated faucets, and watched the water flow. She gazed at the steady stream and the rising foam as if hypnotized.

The ringing telephone jarred her back to consciousness. She lifted the receiver from its cradle on the wall near the tub. It was Anthony. The sound of his voice was both jarring and comforting. He was calling to say he had heard the news of her departure from the business world. He was thrilled and very proud of her and what she had done and wanted to wish her well. When he asked what was she going to do, she told him of her plans to build a new life, have fun and do all the things she had missed. "I'll create a garden, bake bread, make a home, dance...who knows? All I do know is that I'm going to take each day as it comes."

She shut off the taps and reached down to feel the water. The heat jolted her.

"Anthony, why are you calling me all of a sudden? This is the first time I've heard your voice in months."

He replied, "Arabella, I want to talk to you further. I have something very important to tell you but I don't have the time or privacy to talk now. I'll call you tomorrow."

"All right, Anthony," she said, somewhat confused at this mystery. "Good-bye."

"Good-bye, Arabella."

She hung up the telephone and returned to the bath. The oval marble tub was set in the middle of the room. She stepped over the side and slid into the soft, warm water scented with gardenia. Gliding forward until the liquid-satin water engulfed her up to her shoulders, she lifted the sponge and squeezed rivulets of the caressing, soothing water over her arms. She placed a padded cushion behind her neck and stretched languorously....

Chapter Five

Alexandria, my beautiful, decadent, crumbling Alexandria! My sensual, mystic, beloved Alexandria, city of passion and intrigue languishing under the baking sun, refreshed by the steady rhythm of lapping waves.

My beloved Alexandria with your exotic smells, sights and sounds that slash at one, wound one so that you may leave a scar that will never be forgotten. Exquisitely rich in your poverty, yet still proud and regal, memories of a once affluent life. Schizophrenic, sexual, erotic Alexandria with your smell of the desert mingling with the sea.

Tantalizing Alexandria, you never stop pricking the senses. Ask E. M. Forster, Cavafy, Seferis, Lawrence Durrell. Ask me and ask Anthony Quartermaine.

Arabella had not thought about her first meeting with Alexandria and Anthony for years. Her beloved Alexandria and her great love, Anthony Quartermaine.

It all came flooding back to her as if it were yesterday. Almost unconsciously she dipped the large round sponge into the bath water and pressed it against her face. She felt the water pour over her eyes, nose, lips, chin. It ran off her cheeks, down onto her neck and breasts. She dropped the sponge into the water and spoke to the ghosts sitting around her in the bathroom on the *Tatanya Annanovna*.

I have not forgotten you, she thought. My glorious Alexandria. How innocent I was when I landed on your shores! We were a party of naive foreigners, semisophisticated young ladies and gentlemen just out of Smith, Vassar, Harvard, and Yale who had notched New York, Paris, and London under our belts and thought ourselves world travelers.

Young American innocents abroad, cruising on a Greek millionaire's yacht—the father of one of our friends, who was determined to show us Egypt. A few house parties in Alexandria and a taste of the desert and he guaranteed us our lives would never be the same. Our host was right.

It's funny, thought Arabella. Even all these years later I can still remember feeling disappointed that none of the group wanted to stay and explore Alexandria further, as I did. Yet, at the same time, I had been relieved to separate from the group and discover the life of the Levant without them.

As Arabella soaked in the steamy, fragrant bath, she remembered that time in Egypt.

The port was filled with the most exotic ships, both large and small. Dhows and feluccas bobbed up and down with caiques and schooners from every part of the world. Sailors in white suits, sailors in galabeahs with great white turbans, sailors in baggy shorts and in worn denim called out to each other in languages as exotic and sweet-sounding as one could possibly imagine.

As soon as she set foot on Egyptian soil, she knew she was in a strange, exotic land. She also sensed that a new world was about to open up for her, and she trembled with excitement as the city covered her like a blanket. She felt disoriented, slightly mad, as a Westerner walking through those ancient streets for the first time, watching the mélange of people—blue-black Sudanese; olive-complexioned Greeks; dark, sultry Egyptians; white-skinned descendants of Europeans enmeshed in a living theater. They wore exotic costumes: galabeahs, caftans, tarbooshes, turbans, and ties. The women in voluminous black dresses down to the dusty streets, black shawls over their heads, not a hair showing, their soft faces with black, liquid eyes highlighted in kohl, were in strong contrast to the most beautiful Egyptian women of wealth, who wore elegant dresses.

There were exotic cafés, taverns, and open-air coffee shops where men smoked their narghiles and drank tiny cups of strong sweet black coffee, or small glasses of thick sweet mint tea, and played backgammon, and where the occasional poet might be seen writing. As contrast, there were elegant, expensive coffee shops where handsome men and women met clandestinely to gossip and flirt and a Greek banker might be seen reading his paper. In between there were street vendors by the hundred.

Delicious Alexandria, your colorful people, the heartbeat of your city, a spectacle so rich I see it all again all these years later, thought Arabella.

The luscious city by the sea, filled with crushing poverty and exquisite beauty, teemed with sensual life, seemed to ferment in the sun. The Americans walked its streets and squares and became familiar with the broken marble fountains no longer gushing water. It was a city filled with the smells of garlic and jasmine, the desert, sea, and sun, always the sun. It was so strange how even the night smelled of the sun. Arabella would watch, mesmerized, as the darkness gave way to a white-hot moon.

Suddenly her senses seemed alive as they never had before. Alexandria made Europe and America, her friends and her life up until then, seem pale and dull, sexless and very far away. As if seduced by the city itself, she gave in to it and felt herself changing, growing away from the people she had come there with and toward something else as she mingled with the Levant and Africa.

Silently, Arabella let some water out of the bath, then turned on the tap to let some more hot water into it. Tiny beads of perspiration appeared on either side of her nose, above her upper lip, on her forehead. She stretched her foot out and turned off the tap with her big toe.

Arabella reached out to the table next to the bath and picked up a terry-cloth-covered neck rest and put it behind her. Stretching out, soothed by the heat of her fragrant bath, she closed her eyes and let long-forgotten memories return.

* * *

Arabella remembered standing up in the open horse-drawn carriage and waving good-bye to her friends after promising to meet them in Cyprus four days later. It occurred to her now how rarely she thought of her beau at the time of that cruise, Sam Waterman. Sam was a brilliant young medical student from Johns Hopkins. She could still picture his long face of disappointment at their parting.

He had been a sweet lover, a sensitive young man with whom she had had a friendly romance for two years. She had never expected to stay with him even that long, but it had been easier than breaking up. And he was nice enough. She remembered the pang of real loneliness she had felt sending him away, the fear of the unknown before her and the knowledge that she would miss him in bed that night.

Their last conversation together came back to her as if it had happened only yesterday. The others had all kissed her good-bye and boarded the yacht.

Sam had kissed her and said, "Why do you want to leave the group? Why break us up? We're all on vacation together."

She had answered, "I'm not breaking us up, Sam. I've fallen in love with this fantastic, erotic city and I haven't seen enough of it. It's been a wonderful vacation but I'm tired of island hopping, of seeing everything superficially, of glimpsing Crete and waving at Sicily and barely touching the shores of Turkey. I can't do that with Alexandria. Anyway, don't look so sad. What's four days' time? We'll be together again in Cyprus and, besides, you can still stay— you don't have to leave."

"But I want to. All I see here is dirt, poverty, and weirdness. I don't have the need to stay that you do." He kissed her again and went on. "I just don't feel the same. I want to go on with the others. I'll see you in Cyprus."

That evening, dusk came to Alexandria like a big deep bruise. The sky turned pink, pale yellow then lavender, until finally a deep purple before the black of night. For

Arabella it was a moment of depression, sadness. Until dusk in Alexandria, she had never been aware of the death of a day.

She sat in a carriage driven by the big, soft-looking Egyptian in his gray galabeah and large white turban. Around her were cars of every vintage and shape, hooting and tooting the pushcarts, bicycles, dilapidated lorries, donkeys pulling flat carts loaded with fruit, vendors, and people. Masses and masses of people.

By early nighttime, Alexandria was lit up by a soft yellow from a million dim light bulbs. The Corniche looked like a chain of twinkling diamonds. The city glowed on a low voltage and high atmosphere.

The dappled gray horse with his sway back clopped along the pavements, swinging his haunches like some seductive charmer to the tinkle of his own bells hung along a harness studded with charms against the evil eye. They worked. Arabella arrived safely back at the Hotel Cecil, that wonderful, old-time hotel. The Cecil, with its pale-pink facade of soft stone punctuated by latticed balconies under skimpy dark-green awnings. It overlooked the square of drooping old palm trees, worn-out grass, and the eastern harbor. The sweet and homey Cecil with its comfortable elegance and unprepossessing entrance was a welcome sight to Arabella. She went into the dark, old-fashioned lobby, where the ceiling fans lazily circulated what little cool air there was. There were dusty and tired potted palms, gigantic spiky green-and-white striped plants called mother-in-law's tongue, and in the slightly seedy-looking, overstuffed chairs sat the hotel's well-dressed guests. There were only eighty-three rooms in the hotel, and all their occupants had at least one thing in common: the pleasure in gossip and staring, Alexandrian pastimes.

This lobby had known throughout its history many famous poets, writers, statesmen, sheikhs and kings, presidents and prime ministers. It was the second home to the English when they were in Alexandria, as well as the French,

Italians, Americans, Saudi Arabians, Lebanese, Greeks—
the list went on and on.

In the center of the main stairwell were a pair of tiny
elevators, beautiful little black wrought-iron cages that ran
up and down constantly, silently, as if running on greased
poles. The white marble stairs, covered with ruby-red Turkish carpet on each tread, snaked around the elevators with
a matching balustrade of wrought iron and a polished mahogany handrail.

The waiters, porters, and baggage boys were dressed in
small white turbans and beige galabeahs intricately em-
broidered in chocolate brown. They were the best *sufragies*
—servants—to be found in Alexandria.

It was there, in the famous old Cecil bar that had sus-
tained poets and writers, statesmen and lovers, that Arabella
saw him again. The tall, handsome, middle-aged Englishman who appeared so proper, so staid, so conventional, so
very conservative.

It was quiet in the bar—such a contrast to the symphony
of horns, bells, and people, the exotic sound of Arabic music
blaring from the shops, the exquisite sound of the call to
prayer echoing from the slim, needlelike minarets over the
rooftops of Alexandria. There, in the quiet of the bar, the
exquisite elegance and aristocratic bearing of the man caught
her eye.

A *sufragi* showed Arabella to a table and took her order
for a long, cool drink—a Pimms—that was served to her
in a silver tankard. After a few sips Arabella looked around
the room. She took it all in, the long elegant bar of dark
polished wood, a table with several well-dressed Arab businessmen, another with two elderly women, faded European
beauties. At another table sat a handsome French homo-
sexual with a much more beautiful young Arab boy.

Arabella's eyes met the Englishman's. His face was passive but his eyes were not. She could not help but think
that under that calm, cool facade was a very sexy man. She
was disappointed when he looked away, paid his bill at the
bar, and left.

Twenty minutes later she picked up her key at the desk and left an order for another Pimms to be sent up to her room. She had decided to drink it there, looking out over the city, then change and go down to dinner.

The elevator cage door opened, the operator stepped out, then a couple who walked toward the dining room. Arabella stepped in. When she turned around to face the front, the handsome Englishman had stepped in behind her. Although taken aback, now it was her turn to look passive. He smiled, turned around, and faced the front, with his broad back to her.

The elevator stopped at the fourth floor. The galabeah-clad operator opened the little door and stepped out, followed by the Englishman and then Arabella.

Arabella heard the elevator door close as she walked toward her room; then she realized she was being followed by the Englishman.

She stopped suddenly, turned around, and said, "Are you following me, sir?"

"Why, yes, I am," he answered pleasantly.

"You would not like me to call the *sufragi* over there, would you?" she said, pointing to one of the floor servants. "What do you want?"

"I want to go to my room," he said, holding up a key with a worn wooden tag on which was written the number 406.

Arabella flushed and said, "Uh oh, I think I've made a fool of myself. How embarrassing!" She held up her key, "I am four oh five." They walked to their rooms. Arabella gratefully closed the door behind her.

Her room had the look of faded elegance with its English flowered cretonne bed cover and curtains; the great white mosquito net hanging from the ceiling was draped back and tied to the bedposts. Arabella went to the window and cranked open the shutter. Another sound so familiar in Alexandria— the wooden-slatted shutters clattering up and down trying to adjust the sun and heat for comfort. She went onto the balcony and rolled back the green awning, hoping to get a little more air into her room. She stayed there, drinking in the night under a blanket of stars. She saw the outline of the Englishman standing in the dark on the balcony next to hers.

Feeling bad about how she had snapped at him before, she leaned toward him and said, "Are you as seduced by Alexandria as I am?"

He smiled and said, "Yes, I certainly am."

The breeze, what there was of it, was still hot and not refreshing. The streets below teemed with life. Arabella heard a click and turned to look at him again. A lighter flame glowed, illuminating the Englishman's face as he lit his cigarette. An arrogant face, she thought, one of breeding and polish—an aristocrat's face.

Arabella decided to be mischievous. As he was snapping his lighter closed, she said, "I think it is the sexiest city in the world. What do you think?"

He turned to face her in the dark and, putting his foot on a chair, he leaned forward and said, "Erotic, I think. The most erotic city in the world."

They looked at each other in the dark. Was it a challenge she felt between them? If not, then most certainly a tension.

Arabella said, "Are you here alone?"

He hesitated and then answered, "Yes."

There was an uncomfortable moment of silence, which Arabella broke by saying "It would be very interesting if we could discuss erotic, sexual Alexandria together over dinner. Will you invite me?"

Again she sensed his hesitation, caution, his conservative English manner.

"Oh, dear," she said, "you're hesitating and you're quite right. You don't even know me."

"But I feel I know you."

"Oh, how strange."

"Not so strange. I've been listening to you make love for the last four nights. No, we are not exactly strangers."

"That's the second time in less than thirty minutes I feel embarrassed with you," she said.

He laughed. "Don't be. I think you are delightful. Yes, I will take you to dinner. Shall we say in an hour's time in the lobby?"

Arabella sat in her bath washing her arms with the large soft sponge wondering at how brave and self-assured you can be when youth is on your side. Anthony Quartermaine was the first and last man she had ever picked up. She smiled even now remembering how wicked she felt doing it and thought how desperate she must have been to have gathered up the nerve to carry it off.

When Arabella stepped out into the lobby to meet her Englishman, every pair of eyes in the room was on her. She looked ravishing. The sun had streaked her blond hair silver white in places, her skin was a golden brown. She wore a dress that accentuated her wonderful figure and long, long legs. Her Galanos dress showed a bare back to the waist. It was so skimpy at the sides that when viewed from the back she appeared to have nothing on above the magnificent bone-color silk skirt that billowed out as she walked. She wore several antique Indian ivory braclets trimmed in silver and reddish-gold antique Phoenician rings on her fingers. High-heeled bone sandals criss-crossed over her toes and feet. She carried over one bare shoulder a small purse, a *recamier* of spiral-chased gold with small sapphires set in the gold clasp on a spiral golden chain. This had been a gift from her mother, who had received it on her twenty-first birthday.

Arabella was taken aback to see her Englishman not waiting impatiently for her but talking to two men, one looking like another stuffy Englishman and the other a dark, handsome Arab with the bearing of a sheikh or prince. He was in fact an Alexandrian Copt.

Just as were everyone else's in the room, their eyes were drawn to the beautiful Arabella. He shook hands with the two men and left them, greeting Arabella by picking up her hand and kissing it.

"You look ravishing, absolutely ravishing." He slipped his arm through hers and said, "Don't you think we should introduce ourselves?"

Embarrassed a third time, and feeling not at all like the worldly-wise seductress she was playing at, she simply smiled, held out her hand, and said, "I am Arabella Crawford."

"And I am Anthony Quartermaine."

They shook hands quite formally and started toward the dining room but Arabella, recalling her role, stopped him, saying "Oh, no, not the dining room?"

"But the food is excellent. You may choose from an international cuisine."

"Anthony, don't be so conventional! You can't have been seduced as I have been by Alexandria or you would take me out into this sensuous city and share it with me. Nope, sorry, I will *not* settle for the Cecil. Not tonight."

She looked so annoyed, so crestfallen that he could not help but laugh at her.

"All right," he said. "Just to show you that I am not too stuffy, I'll take you out to a restaurant."

They swung around and walked down the stairs, through the entrance. He helped her up into one of the open carriages lined up in front of the Cecil, and in perfect Arabic he told the driver where to drive.

A light flick of the whip on the horse's flanks, the bells began to tinkle, and they were off.

"You didn't tell me you spoke Arabic."

He smiled and answered, "No, I did not."

"Well, how is it you speak Arabic?"

"Because I am an Arabist."

"Oh," she said, not quite knowing what that meant. "Where are you taking me?"

"To a lovely old restaurant on the Corniche where they serve delicious fish fresh from the sea and the most exquisite Arabic cuisine. It's been there for donkey's years. My father dined there before me when he was a young diplomat in Cairo."

Before they knew it, they were in front of the wide-fronted restaurant, an unprepossessing place with tables and chairs set out under a rolled-back awning that faced the sea wall.

"Good heavens, Anthony. We could have walked here!"

"With you in a dress like that? My dear, I do not consider myself a coward but I am not suicidal either. That would have been sheer folly, much too dangerous."

"My God, you *are* a bit on the stuffy side, aren't you?" Maybe there was nothing beyond the stiff British composure after all, thought Arabella, feeling slightly annoyed with herself.

They were shown to a table and made a fuss over. The owner appeared and greeted Anthony. "Ah, Lord Heversham, I had heard you were in Alexandria. How happy we are to see you again, my lord."

Anthony introduced Arabella and when the man finally left them alone, after taking over the ordering of their meal, Arabella said, "You told me your name is Anthony Quartermaine?"

"It is. I am Anthony Quartermaine; the Earl of Heversham is my title."

"I refuse to be embarrassed again," she said, turning a pleasant shade of pink.

They both laughed easily together for the first time. They chatted casually about Alexandria, and he told her he had been there many times. She admitted to him that the city had touched her deeply in some way.

"I know in my heart once I leave this extraordinary sensual city, I will never be the same and I will never return. I can't go before fulfilling something, maybe my destiny. I want to be seduced by a man the way this city has taken me."

She put her hand out and as he took it in his, she had to admit to herself that she was enjoying this role and being with the proud, handsome Lord Heversham. It made her realize just how wicked the sensual, erotic atmosphere was making her. She had never, ever behaved in such a sexually aggressive manner before. It was fun shocking him, though.

She said, "Anthony, there's something else I want you to know. I've never been sexually aggressive before, but Alexandria has turned me around."

He did not play games with her. He told her the truth.

"Arabella, I am a married man. Happily married, and I am going to stay that way." He stroked her hand gently and added, "You are an exciting, beautiful woman, and free. I am not. Now do you still want to play with me?"

Arabella did not remove her hand. She looked into his eyes and spoke openly of how she felt. "I would have preferred it if you had been single. I've never been involved with a married man before. Where is your wife? Why are you here alone?"

"She is about to have a baby. She is in our house in the country in England. Fiona loves Gloucestershire where we live. She hates leaving the children. She does not share the love I have for travel in the Arab world, anyway. Her passion is babies, herbaceous borders, and making the best family life possible for me. I have other passions. Because we love each other, we indulge ourselves by setting each other free to enjoy them."

"It sounds to me more like being let out on a long leash than freedom."

"It works for both of us, you see. And now have you decided whether we are to play together?" he asked again. Anthony Quartermaine exuded charm along with the challenge and, for the first time, an interest in her. Arabella could not resist it.

Slowly she allowed a smile to come forth and finally said, "Anthony Quartermaine, the Earl of Heversham, I will play with you."

Over dinner something happened to the couple. They gave themselves up to the delicious food, the sensual atmosphere, and spoke very little. An electricity, a chemistry began gradually pulling them together.

The cheeky bravado that Arabella had accosted Anthony

with disappeared. She felt herself slipping into genuine desire to share with this man all the erotic feeling that the city inspired in her. What was so extraordinary was that he understood it. Something stronger than words—powerful feelings—rose to the surface for both of them during their meal.

They picked up their tiny cups of hot sweet Turkish coffee and walked across the road to the sea wall. Placing the cups on top of the wall, they looked across the dark Mediterranean and listened to the sea washing the shores of Alexandria. They could make out the outline of the ancient lighthouse in the distance.

He caressed her hair and said, "I know a better place than this."

They crossed back to the restaurant, where Anthony paid the bill, and climbed back into the carriage that had been waiting for them. They drove through the city, Anthony giving endless directions to the driver. He showed her an Alexandria she had not seen before. He stopped the carriage and bought her several chains of jasmine and placed them over her head, adjusting them carefully over her breasts. The scent engulfed her; she knew she would never know such a sweet scent again as long as she lived.

Then the carriage turned away from the heart of the city and back along the Corniche in the opposite direction, away from the hotel Cecil toward Montaza and the beach. They passed the little tin train that rattled the route all day long and well into the night. The traffic thinned out and then they were there. They got out and walked away from the Avenue of Royal Palms, through thick green grass and hibiscus bushes, eucalyptus trees, date palms, and scrubby pines growing out of the sand. It was a strange exotic forest of tree trunks whose life of green was way up at the top, reaching for the stars.

The pair wound their way through the trees toward a line of beach cabins silhouetted in moonlight. As if by magic, a *sufragi* appeared with a lantern. He greeted Anthony by name, took a key from him, and went ahead to light the way. He opened the beach cabin and lit a lantern inside, then opened the front doors, rolling them back to allow a view of the beach.

Arabella and Anthony entered the cabin and watched the *sufragi* place a blanket and beach chairs down near the water's edge. There were no other people around, and the magic of the place was eerie and exciting.

Anthony said, "Arabella, leave your shoes here. Ibrahim will make us coffee."

He removed his own shoes and socks and rolled his trousers up a few inches. Then he took her hand, and they walked through the cabin and the small garden in front, across the sand to the water's edge. They stood in the dark and stillness of the night on the cool, damp sand and watched the waves roll gently on to the beach.

He turned her around and said, "There she is, your Alexandria," and there she was, all lit up off in the distance.

"Oh, isn't it wonderful! I can't begin to tell you what this city does to me, Anthony. It's as if I've never felt or experienced any other place in my life. It pricks all my senses, it's so decadent, so sensual."

The *sufragi* appeared with a small table, some fruit and Alexandrian sweets, and tiny coffees. Anthony gave further instructions to the man, who bowed and disappeared.

It suddenly occurred to Arabella that the erotic feeling she felt for the city was turning into a romantic feeling for this man. They had hardly spoken since they entered Montaza; words seemed superfluous. Anthony put his hands around her neck and undid two buttons. The silk slipped slowly down off her breasts. She stood in front of him looking into his eyes and watched him admire her. He didn't touch her.

She stepped closer to him and unbuttoned his jacket, began to loosen his tie. He reached out toward her and she closed her eyes, trying to hide the passion in them from him. She waited nervously for his first touch of her breasts, but all he did was to pull the necklaces of jasmine up over her head. He dropped them in the sand. Then he put both hands around her neck and caressed it and her shoulders. She was shocked at how electric she found his touch. She was surprised when he stopped there, still not touching her breasts, now swollen, longing to be fondled. She suddenly ached with desire. He picked up her hand and kissed it tenderly. She nearly fainted with the tension he was creating. He was teasing her, priming her. She knew it and was not happy about it. She wanted him too much to be played with.

He said, "Come, let's sit down and have our coffee." He sat in the old-fashioned striped canvas and wood beach chair. She looked down at him. He looked infinitely more handsome and sexy in the moonlight.

Arabella slipped her dress up over her head and dropped it onto her beach chair. The cool air was like a silk spider's web coating her all over. Anthony looked at her lasciviously.

He said, "Arabella, you have one of the most voluptuous bodies I have ever seen. Yours is a body that needs nothing but to be honed by lust. You were made for sex, my dear."

Arabella was beginning to wonder who was out to seduce whom. He was teasing her, just as she had planned to tease him. She slid down slowly to her knees between his legs, spreading them apart as she got in close to him. She bent forward and unzipped his fly. He slipped his hands under her armpits and pulled her up as he rose out of his chair. He picked her up in his arms and, touching her lips with his ever so lightly, he laid her down on the soft blanket.

He remained on his knees bending over and said, "Now it is time for me to warn you. Something is happening to us. Don't toy with me, Arabella. There is too much at stake for the likes of you and me together."

Arabella said, "I'm not toying with you. It may have started that way, but it's already too late."

She gently pushed him down on his back and laid her naked body alongside him. She kissed him passionately and was shocked that his lips were cold to hers. There was no response from him. Dazzled by her own intense sexuality, she could not accept his indifference to her kiss. She slid

herself down his prone body until she was between his legs.
She slipped her hands inside his open fly and released him.

Yet again she was surprised—he was flaccid. She took
the head of his penis and began to suck on it, then slowly
began to feed herself on the rest of the sweet flesh. He
began to swell in her mouth. It was thrilling. He grew larger
and larger. There were times when she thought she would
choke on him, but her desire to have him feel her presence
and the joys of sex with her drove her on. Once she saw
the wild passion in his eyes from the pleasure she was giving
him, it was even more erotic. She had never seen that look
in any of the young men she had been with previously. It
made her nipples grow erect, and her desire to give herself
to him increased. She was determined to hold back her own
feelings, to rape this man with her mouth. She wanted to
force his passion into the open. When he came in her mouth,
she felt she swallowed his very essence.

After a few silent minutes he rose and took a towel from
the beach chair. She watched him dry himself off, tuck
himself away, and zip up his trousers. He dropped to his
knees and, bending over her, kissed her gently. He stretched
out on the blanket next to her and, leaning on his elbow,
said, after pushing some strands of hair away from her face,
"You enjoyed that. I'm glad."

"You might say you liked it, Anthony."

He put his arms around her and lifted her half off the
blanket into his arms. For the first time he touched her
breasts. He took the erect nipple between his thumb and
forefinger and began to pinch it, slowly increasing the pressure.

"Oh, I loved it," he said and bent to kiss her throat.

She wriggled out of his arms. He stood up and pulled
her to her feet. She reached for her dress and from behind
he slipped his arms around her naked bottom, resting his
hands on her lovely mound of damp pubic hair. Still in his
arms, she turned around slowly and said, looking up into
his eyes, "Oh, no, I will not give in as easily as you did."

He said nothing. He helped her on with her dress, did

up the buttons at the neck, and turned her around to adjust the skirt so that she looked perfectly neat. They walked back to the cabin where she took out her gold purse, repaired her face, and combed her hair. She saw him watching her. He never took his eyes from her. When she sat down and reached for her shoes, he bent down on one knee and wiped her feet with a towel then slipped her shoes on. He picked up one foot and kissed her tenderly on the ankle. Arabella had to close her eyes and try to hold back the tremor she felt going through her. Their eyes met and she was about to say, Take me, take me here, now. Make wild, passionate love to me. I want it so much. But he didn't give her the chance.

"No," he said, "don't say anything. It's time to go back to the Cecil."

He picked up both their keys at the desk. They traveled silently in the toy elevator up to their rooms. He opened the door with her key, picked her hand up and kissed it.

He said, "You are a remarkable lady, Arabella. Thank you for this evening." He pushed the door open for her. She entered and he left her.

There was nothing for her to say or do. He had reverted to the proper English gentleman. She went in and closed the door, took her dress off and hung it up. She had planned to take a bath and go to sleep but she could not. She was too tense, unsatisfied. She needed sexual relief. She wanted him.

She lay on her bed and thought about Anthony, wondering why she had been so stupid and not let him make love to her. Her body ached for him, for him to take her wildly, madly. She knew something now, alone in her room: Anthony Quartermaine would know how to make love to her as she wanted it to be. She touched her breasts, which only fired her desire for him even more. There was nothing to be done except go and give herself to him.

She went to the door that connected the two rooms. It was locked; she knew that for she had tried it when she had first taken the room. The key was in the lock. She turned it and opened the door. Behind it was another door, locked from Anthony's side. She knocked on it. Her heart began to beat faster. She knocked again just as the key was turning.

He had taken his jacket off, but that was all. He looked her naked body over, reached out and caressed her breasts. He folded her in his arms and tilted her chin up to his face. She looked at him seductively.

"Do you really want me?" he asked.

She nodded yes. He touched her breasts again, picked up her hands and kissed them, saying "I have wanted you for days. I knew that ninny of a boy could never satisfy you the way you need to be. I lay in my bed listening to you, wanting you. I wanted to be the man with you."

She put her arms up around his neck. He lifted her by the waist, crushed her to him, and then kissed her deeply and passionately. She melted in his arms. He put her down, and they walked to the edge of the bed where they sat. He picked up the telephone and made two calls, then put the receiver down and said, "Come with me." He picked his jacket up from the chair and walked her through into her room.

He said, "Get dressed quickly. The car is waiting downstairs. I'm going to take you somewhere where we can make love properly. It will be wonderful, I promise."

They drove in a plum colored Rolls-Royce through elegant streets past huge impressive mansions built and decorated by the foreigners who had lived in Alexandria. They were mini-palaces, with stature and elegance fit for princes or kings. Each of them was set behind walls with intricate wrought-iron gates, surrounded by exotic formal gardens with marble fountains splashing into basins often filled with goldfish. Giant palms, like sentinels, watched over them.

The one whose gates the Rolls passed through had a garden that was magnificent and subtly lit. The winding drive stopped before a long flight of wide pink marble stairs that led up to a grand entrance. As if by magic, the doors were opened by a pair of blue-black Sudanese *sufragis*.

As they started up the stairs, Arabella turned questioningly toward Anthony. They stopped on a step and looked at each other.

He touched his finger to her lips and said, "This is the most erotic house left in Alexandria, in Egypt, who knows—maybe in the world. Trust me and let yourself go. I promise you I understand what you want and I am going to give it to you."

She said nothing, she could not. She was falling under his spell. He took her hand and they went forward together. Inside they were greeted by the handsome man she had seen Anthony talking to in the lobby of the Cecil. They were introduced and Anthony told her, "Prince Ahmed is our host." He led them through the vast, elegant marble hall, down a few stairs to a magnificent drawing room where they were introduced to half a dozen couples. Someone was playing jazz on the piano—so incongruous in a room such as this in Alexandria.

The twenty-foot-high windows with their arched tops were draped in heavy tangerine-colored silk, tied back in great elegant swags. They were fantastic frames for the view of the beach and the sea. The chandeliers were massive and looked more like diamonds than cut crystal. Everywhere Arabella looked she was able to recognize every chair, every sculpture, every table as being of the finest quality.

The women in the room were gorgeous, dressed by the best European designers—Givenchy, Balmain, Dior, and St. Laurent. They wore magnificent jewels and they gave off a sensual scent like a strong perfume. They were women with vast sexual appetites who knew how to handle men. She recognized it at once; it was in the air in any city—here it was simply uncaged.

The men in the room were for the most part handsome, rich, sophisticated men. She looked them over, finding them sexually interesting.

Prince Ahmed, the host, came up to her, put his arm around her shoulder, and said, "You are ravishing, Arabella. I see you looking us over. You have most likely recognized

us as the devout libertines that we are. Anthony has told
me that you have been seduced by Alexandria and that he
has brought you here to seduce you as well. Please enjoy
the hospitality of my house."

A *sufragi* came by and offered her a glass of champagne.
Anthony took her by the hand and led her to a sofa. He lit
a pipe.

"It's wonderful," he said. "The best in the Middle East.
Hashish always loosens me up. What was it you called me?
Ah yes, a stuffy Englishman."

He offered her the pipe. She took a few long drags on
it and said, "I told you before in the restaurant that I will
not allow myself to be embarrassed by my behavior with
you ever again." She had never used drugs before, or even
knew of anyone who had. In America it was still considered
"very bohemian." Somehow in Alexandria, with a proper
Englishman, it seemed all right.

They sat there flirting with each other while they drank
more champagne. They spoke to a few people in the room,
and finally he whispered in her ear, "Ahmed has given us
a lovely room overlooking the sea. Let's go."

They slipped out of the room and walked arm in arm up
the grand staircase to the first floor. A *sufragi* pushed open
a huge pair of carved French walnut doors. The room was
extremely severe and yet elegant. The walls were paneled
in walnut boiserie and mirrors, the chandelier was huge and
hung rather low. It was made of rock crystal in the shape
of apples, pears, berries, and grapes, in tinted pale colors
and mixed with droplets that looked like crystal tears. The
floor was of black-and-white marble. In the center of
the room stood a massive four-poster bed of carved ivory.
The bed linen was of ivory silk satin, trimmed in antique
ivory and white lace. The huge feather pillows were covered
in the same silk satin and lace.

There were a few chairs covered in white suede and some
Louis XV tables. Four large windows opposite the entrance
to the room were draped in heavy white silk and tied back
with huge black and gold tassles.

There was a knock at the door and two handsome young men entered with small tables, champagne, glasses, bowls of fruit, plates of fresh figs and dates. Another knock at the door and two very pretty girls entered, one a black African and the other Chinese. They came in carrying a blue silk robe for Anthony and a magnificent, diaphanous black caftan with borders of gold embroidery at the cuffs and all down the front. This was for Arabella.

The girls smiled at the couple and the Chinese girl, Mai Ling, said, "For you, miss, a gift from Prince Ahmed."

Anthony began to laugh. He said, "Don't look so surprised. This is Mai Ling and this is Coco. These two men are Dimitri and Jean Paul."

Arabella had a buzz in her head and an excitement in her loins such as she had never known before. She wished they would all go away so that Anthony could take over. From the moment they had entered this house, Anthony had been stripping away layer after layer of his defenses. With every sniff of cocaine, every puff of hashish, he revealed another part of his sensual self and she knew it matched hers. She was excited.

One of the girls went to Anthony and removed his jacket, undid his tie. He took Arabella by the hand and led her down a few steps to a sunken bathroom of white marble.

"Shall we bathe before going to bed?"

"Yes," she said. "Let's."

He sat down on one of the marble chaises, pulling her down next to him, and allowed Coco to take off his shoes and socks. Mai Ling then joined in and helped undress him.

Arabella wanted to be part of the sexy scene and said, "Let me do that, Anthony."

"No," he said. "You are to do nothing. You have done everything you are going to do tonight. We're all here to wait on you."

Arabella could not believe how handsome Anthony was naked. More handsome than any Greek god. Flanked by Coco and Mai Ling, he allowed them to fondle, kiss, and lick him. Arabella was aroused beyond anything she had ever known before.

The girls approached Arabella, removed her shoes and her dress, finally her lace panties and bra, while Anthony watched. After they pinned up her hair, Anthony kissed Arabella on the cheek and took her by the hand to the sunken tub. They walked down the steps into it and bathed together. Anthony washed her himself, and she thrilled to his every touch. When she went to take the sponge to him, he stopped her by shaking his head and insisting she not do anything. When they stepped out of the tub they were wrapped in huge white bath sheets and dried off by the boys, who were now naked and impressively well made for sex. Coco let Arabella's lovely hair tumble down onto her shoulders and Mai Ling brushed it. Arabella and Anthony were then helped into the robes Prince Ahmed had sent.

Anthony took her hand and led her to the bed. Arabella whispered, "Please send them all away, Anthony."

He said, "Darling, don't be silly. They are going to perform for us. They'll be very useful."

The men and Coco undressed Mai Ling provocatively, then produced various implements for lovemaking.

Arabella was extremely sensual looking in her sheer black-and-gold robe with her shiny blond hair falling around her shoulders. As thin as a web, the robe showed off her magnificent body—every line, every curve. Anthony looked at her and said, as he disrobed, "You are so very wicked looking, so provocative."

She could bear it no longer. She opened her robe and let it slip off her shoulders and down her arms onto the floor where she stood. She walked into his open arms. They slid sensuously onto the white silk satin sheets together. Mai Ling and Jean Paul propped up the large soft down pillows behind them.

Anthony held her close, put his arm around her shoulder, and kissed her tenderly. Coco rubbed oil over Mai Ling's nipples. Then she massaged the oil on the head of Anthony's penis. Arabella stretched out her hand to touch Anthony but he stopped her, taking her hand and drawing it up to his lips. He kissed it sweetly and gently.

"No," he said softly.

Arabella could not help herself. She began to squirm with need and excitement.

He said softly, almost in a whisper, "Open your legs, Arabella." Never had she felt so sexy. Never could she have imagined such need. Anthony pushed himself up to almost sitting position and, looking down at her, still with his arm around her shoulder, he bent his head down and kissed her on her hungry lips.

"And now it begins, Arabella."

He kissed her deeply, passionately, long and slow, while Coco was still massaging his cock with the oil and Mai Ling began rubbing the oil on the insides of Arabella's thighs.

He whispered in Arabella's ear as he stroked her hair, "Have you ever been touched by a woman?"

"No."

"It's wonderful. They are all here to do the most delectable things to you. All you have to do is lie back."

She said, "I only want you," but her body was already moving to the rhythm of Mai Ling's hands.

"No, you don't. You want everything, and everything that is possible is what you will have tonight. I'll be here holding you, making love to you as well.

He watched the girls massage her breasts and between her legs. When she would explode from desire and could hold nothing back she called out to Anthony, "Please, I want you. Please, Anthony, I beg you," she moaned.

Anthony never let her out of his arms. Every inch of her tingled and silently screamed with desire. She clung to Anthony who kissed and caressed her while tongues and hands teased her. Then Coco and Mai Ling were made love to by the men. Later, after all had performed beyond her imagination and been dismissed, Anthony still had not taken her.

She dozed off in Anthony's arms and when she woke

up, she was still in his arms. He was lying there calmly smoking a cigarette.

"Very exciting, aren't they?" he asked, looking down on her.

"It was unbelievable. I don't want to think about it."

"Why not?"

"Because with it all as fantastic as it was, I still want *you* to make love to me."

He crushed out his cigarette and said, "Listen, Arabella," pulling her up tight against him in his arms. "If I do, I will allow no one else to take you as long as we stay together. Do you understand that?"

She nodded assent.

"Good. I am going to possess you as no other man ever will. You are a magnificent, exquisite, sexy lady and I want you, Arabella. I have from the first day I saw you. I am going to make love to you, wildly, passionately. Afterward, if you want to be mine, all you have to do is say, 'Yes, Anthony, I am yours.' Don't give me your answer now. Now *we* will make love."

He kissed her on the cheek and picked her up in his arms. He carried her down to the bathroom. The two women were there. They turned on the taps and the bath filled quickly as they poured sweet scented oils into the water.

In the bath, Anthony tended her. He took a large bulbous syringe filled with herbs, perfume, lemon, alum, and liquid soap from Coco and inserted it as far as he could. He held her on his lap in the deep water, pressed his lips to hers, and kissed her passionately as he squeezed the cleansing contents into her.

It was her lover Anthony who washed her body now. It was a tender, sexy Anthony who dried her, took perfumes and oils and rubbed them over her skin. It was he who helped her slip into the caftan and she who helped him slip into his robe. They then walked up to the bedroom and to the bed.

It had been remade with fresh pale-peach silk satin sheets. There were rose petals spread over the top sheet. Anthony removed her robe, then his. Arabella felt dazed. It was so strange, as if the hours before had all been a dream. She could not understand how but she felt fresh and new, ready to be made love to as if for the first time.

He gathered her in his arms and, lifting her, placed her diagonally across the bed. He removed the long silk braided cord from his robe and stretched it the length of his outspread arms.

"Lie very still, my sweet," he whispered, "and raise your arms to me." As she obeyed, with one quick motion he looped the silk cord around her wrists and firmly knotted it to the bedpost. Arabella gasped with alarm and tried to squirm free.

"Don't move," he commanded as he moved swiftly above her. The weight of his firm, muscular body pinned her motionless and she was too shocked to speak. He had been so gentle, so loving, and now she was near terror. As he rose above her, he grew erect and every muscle in his body pulsated with tension. "I want you now, Arabella," he said as he forced her legs apart and moved inside her with one quick thrust. "Don't move," he said, looking directly into her eyes. As she attempted to cry out, he pressed his lips to her mouth and forced them open with his tongue. She could not move. She could not make a sound.

To her surprise, she felt her muscles involuntarily contract as his penis throbbed inside her. He slowly withdrew and then reentered her once more. He repeated the motion, each time moving away more slowly and reentering her with more force so that the painful, pleasurable sensations pulsated throughout her body, and all the while her mouth was filled with his tongue.

Each time she quivered, he made her be still. Then his movements became faster and faster as his orgasm came explosively. She could contain herself no longer and she felt her entire body trembling in shivers of ecstasy.

During those moments, his lips remained on hers, but his kiss was much more gentle. He shifted and felt almost weightless upon her. She felt his fullness inside her and she squeezed tighter around him. He reached above her and her hands were freed.

"Now you are mine," he whispered. "You are in my power." She knew he spoke the truth for she felt consumed and had no comprehension of the feelings that overtook her. She felt satiated.

Anthony looked into her face and lightly touched her cheek. He kissed her softly on each eye. He stroked her neck and caressed her breasts with a touch as light as a feather. He moved down and rested his head on her firm belly as his hands moved below the soft mound of hair. He placed his head there and gently kissed the soreness away.

The sensations began inside her again as his lips sweetly drank in her juices. He touched her thighs as he turned her on her side and covered each round cheek with little nibble bites. He stroked her legs, he tickled the soles of her feet. He kissed each toe. She remained motionless and silent savoring every stroke, touch, kiss, and caress.

He moved forward now and, lying alongside her, he said yet again, "I possess you now—you are mine, only mine."

The last thing she remembered before dozing off was putting her arms around him, kissing him tenderly on the lips and saying "Yes, Anthony. I am yours."

It was late afternoon when Arabella woke up alone in the great white ivory bed. The room had been cleared. Over the chair near her was draped a white silk caftan. She turned and looked at the vast empty bed. Arabella felt heartsick at his absence. She covered her eyes, trying to hold back the tears of disappointment. They were brought on by the sight of a large, square envelope on the pillow where he should have been.

She pulled herself together and reached for the note. It read:

Wake up, sleepy-head, with the knowledge that I am thrilled and grateful for your gift. I love you, Arabella, for giving yourself utterly and completely to me, for taking me as you have. The car is waiting for you. It

will take you back to the Cecil and I will meet you
there in time for dinner.

Anthony

Arabella crushed the note to her breast, closed her eyes,
and sighed.

They had fallen in love.

Arabella picked up the sponge and squeezed it. She gave
a shiver; the water was ice cold. She had no idea how long
she had been lying in the bath daydreaming about the past.
She looked out of the porthole and was shocked to see that
it had grown dark.

She was not so much concerned about the daydreaming
and Anthony Quartermaine as she was surprised at the Atlantic crossing turning out to be a kind of catharsis. She
knew very well that ocean voyages sometimes did that to
people. It was connected with the isolation, the claustro-
phobia of a ship, however large, if you were far enough
out at sea on it and for long enough.

Lying there in the cold bath water, Arabella knew how
deeply in love she had been with Anthony Quartermaine;
maybe a part of her still was. She also knew that she was
fascinated by Nicholas Frayne.

Chapter Six

From a brown leather wing chair in a corner of Captain Hamilton's stateroom on board the S.S. *Tatanya Anna-novna*, Arabella had the dubious advantage of being able to watch for Nicholas's arrival from four different directions. She could catch sight of him from the balcony if he entered on that level, or alighting from the captain's private elevator that came up into the drawing room, or from the main entrance to the room, or from the door off the captain's deck.

We all know the trepidation, the torturous despair of waiting. Arabella's was no exception. He did not show up.

She had arrived at the captain's quarters at exactly nine o'clock. She looked absolutely magnificent. The petting and foreplay that Arabella and Nicholas had experienced had set Arabella's senses on fire. After Nicholas had left her, she had realized he had awakened something deep within her and she kept hearing his voice insinuating there was much more to come.

She had dressed that evening for him, for them, and for no one else. She had chosen her new taupe leather evening dress by Armani. It was sleeveless with a high, round neckline and cut straight down to the ankle with a long slit in the front, up to the thigh. It fit her like a second skin. The leather was soft and supple like the finest kid glove. She carried a taupe-and-silver knit bolero jacket over her arm. With the dress she wore a Bulgari necklace, a choker of heavy gold chain links with an ancient Roman silver coin encircled in gold and diamonds hanging from the center. Her earrings matched the coin, and on her wrist was Armand's gift, the diamond and emerald bracelet. It was a most elegant yet sensual and provocative outfit.

Her luscious gold and silver hair hung loose and soft on her shoulders with one side pulled back off her face and held in place by a golden comb.

Arabella should have realized Nicholas would not be there when the captain had called her and asked if she would do him the honor of allowing him to be her escort that evening. She remembered thinking it odd but had not dwelled on it, too happy even to think something might go wrong.

As the party continued, she enjoyed meeting some of her fellow passengers and entered happily into conversation, but she was maddeningly aware of Nicholas's absence. When she had first entered the room, it had not occurred to her that they would not be together that evening. Then, as the minutes dragged by and she became painfully aware that he was not coming, she had a great deal of trouble keeping centered, her mind focused on the conversations. She felt like a teenager—cranky and out of control.

She tried to work out in her mind what had happened, to put the pieces together and make a picture. The pieces of the afternoon were rich, vivid, and beautiful. But now her blood was boiling for other reasons.

The captain introduced her to Millicent Merton, a widow who seemed to be chasing after the ship's doctor. She smiled at Arabella and said, "Just call me Millie, sweetie."

Arabella couldn't remember the last time anyone had called her sweetie. It just made her feel all the more like a child. Millie Merton then introduced her to Mike Mackay, an oil man from Texas who had the stateroom next to hers. The captain introduced her to the Van Renders, very affluent and highly social Americans.

Millie kept droning on about how well she knew life on board ship. She had sailed on all the great transatlantic ships and as soon as she had familiarized herself with this one, she would be happy to organize their life on board. It was during Millie's monologue that it hit Arabella—he was not coming.

How well we all know those whys. That crash of disappointment, those terrifying, anguished moments of what did I do wrong? The endless going over and over every detail and word that had passed between you. It was only hours ago and there had been nothing wrong. She recalled how it had grown dark and he had turned on the lamp. The beautiful white Ming lamp. She remembered him doing up his trousers, his belt, fastening the silver buckle and looking at her with love, affection, and a great deal of passion. He had stood and helped her to her feet, then raised both her hands to his lips to kiss her fingers. Then he had straightened her dressing gown, tightened the soft sash, and used it to pull her tight against him. He had then kissed her on the mouth and said, "I love your mouth. I wanted it from the very moment I laid eyes on you."

Suddenly she thought of Anthony again. She had been surprised by his call. He was usually so careful about showing he still cared. He was a cautious man, Anthony Quartermaine, the Earl of Heversham; so was she now, when it came to her feelings about him. She remembered saying yes; she thought it the most wonderful day of her life, looked forward to the voyage, and was thrilled with her new beginnings. But where did Anthony fit? Remembering Alexandria confused her, and the memories conflicted with the present.

Arabella felt someone poking her arm none too gently.

"Oh," she said.

"You didn't hear a thing ah've said, did ya?"

Arabella flushed and said, "I'm afraid I was distracted. My mind was wandering."

"It sure was, dahling. Now lookee here, ah'll begin again, but you pay attention, ya hear? Now then, ah was askin', are you a gamblin' lady? Cause ah figure you are a gamblin' lady."

"Well, I do play the tables occasionally, Mr. Mackay. But I've never thought of myself as a gambling lady. Maybe I am."

"Ah tell ya, you are, girl. You're a gamblin' lady. Ah'm

sort of checking out and seein' who ah'm gonna have for casino pals here."

"Then I take it you are a gambling man?"

"Ah sure am, honey. Ah figure ah gotta line a few things up so ah don't get too bored. Ah'm used to flyin' everywhere and gettin' there and chargin' on with it. This is a long, hard way to get to the States, gal."

"Oh, I'm sure you'll enjoy it. I don't think you're a man who tolerates boredom for long."

"You're damn right, honey. Ah promised my wife this here holiday is gonna be a good one and I sure as hell am gonna keep ma promise. That's her, Marcia, over there."

He pointed to a gorgeous, long-legged Texan beauty dressed in wide white cashmere trousers and a handsome silk shirt with a waistcoat of leopard skin. She was deeply tanned, with blue-black hair, huge blue eyes, and the face and body of a beauty queen. She wore gigantic earrings of black coral and gold, several heavy gold chains around her neck, and an enormous pear-shaped diamond on her finger.

"Now you just confide in me who ya thinking about. Who is he that's missin'? Who did ya leave behind? Now you looka here, gal, ya not ta worry. A gal that looks like you sure don't have ta worry. He'll come arunnin' as soon as he can. You gals are all alike. You never understand a man's gotta do what he has to do in his time, not yours."

Arabella could have jumped up and kissed that big teddy-bear Texan. She knew he was right. She relaxed, smiled, and said, "Listen here, Mr. Texas. I am enough of a gambling woman to believe you're right."

He laughed and said, "Ah know ah'm right, Arabella." He called to the waiter passing by with a tray of cocktails. "Hey, boy, how about a little bourbon for me and what ya drinkin', gal?"

"Champagne."

"And champagne for this lady, son. Now, listen here, Arabella. Y'have got one gorgeous name but it's too long for us Texans, so you can call me Mr. Texas if it pleases ya and ah'll call ya Belle. No, ah'll call ya Miss Belle. How's that grab ya?"

"That'll be fine, y'all," she mimicked him, and they clicked their glasses and laughed.

Arabella had met the first of the friends she would make on the maiden voyage of the *Tatanya Annanovna*. Shortly after that meeting, the captain took her arm and the waiter announced dinner.

They walked into the captain's dining room two by two. The captain and Arabella led the party, followed by Millie and John James Van Renders. After them came Mrs. Van Renders on the arm of Mike Mackay, followed by Mrs. Mackay and the ship's doctor.

It was nine forty-five when the captain's party sat down to dine. At the same time, in the Vanya Bar in first-class, Nicholas Frayne sat holding hands with a beautiful young woman, Wendy Sears.

The Vanya Room was one of Nicholas's three favorite public rooms on board the *Tatanya Annanovna*. The library and the music room were the other two. The room was not particularly large but it was two decks high, giving it great elegance. It was the original eighteenth-century paneled room from one of the more beautiful, smaller St. Petersburg palaces. The owner, Prince Ivanich Scherbatski, dismantled the palace piece by piece and smuggled it out of Russia to the South of France one year before the revolution.

The Scherbatski Palace on Morskaya Street, in the most fashionable quarter, was considered a jewel among the houses to be seized by the Communists. Much to their disappointment and fury, when they stormed the house they found nothing but a shell. They say that Scherbatski left not a piece of parquet floor, not an ormolu doorknob in the house.

It had to be true because the Vanya Room was perfect, intact—columns with Corinthian capitals of jasper included. From the original dull silver gilt-carved ceiling hung a magnificent rock-crystal chandelier of enormous proportions that supplied all the light needed in the bar. The parquet floor was sensational, more like a Dutch marquetry tabletop than a floor. But it was the ancient paneling and its color, dark brown tinged with olive green when the light of the chandelier reflected on it, a green-tobacco color, that Nicholas liked most.

The tables and chairs were of the period. Large, comfortable chairs covered in jasper-colored velvet. The tables were round ormolu, simple, almost modern in design but of the period with inlaid tops of solid rock crystal—clear thick slabs with the occasional cloudy vein running through, making the tops of the semiprecious stone even more interesting and elegant.

On the S.S. *Tatanya Annanovna*, the first-class dining room was organized in a more civilized way than on board most ships. The tables were reserved in advance by the passengers and dinner was served any time between eight and ten in the evening. In addition to Nicholas and Wendy Sears, there were approximately twenty first-class passengers sitting in small groups around the barroom. These guests were either having their last martini before dinner or their first cognac after dinner. It was a happy atmosphere still filled with the edge of excitement of an embarkation. People were lively, good-humored, a little clumsy, not quite having their bearings or ship-life together.

Nicholas tried to give Wendy his full attention, but it was difficult. His mind wandered observing his fellow passengers, thinking about the extraordinary woman he had spent the afternoon with and the work that would finally change his life.

He suddenly found the courage to come to the point with the twenty-one-year-old girl. He took her hand between both of his, gently put it on the table, and covered it with his palms, saying "Wendy, I want you to look around this room at your fellow passengers."

Wendy did what she was told, then turned to him and said, "What has that got to do with anything, Mr. Frayne?"

"It has to do with everything. All of us on board are alike. We share a common hope. We live individually, and as a group we have the same sole purpose—to get to our destination slowly, safely, in comfort, and, if possible, having had some degree of pleasure doing it. Why don't you do the same thing?"

"What are you trying to say, Mr. Frayne?"

"All I'm trying to say is that I don't want to be any more or less important to you than anyone else on this ship. I simply want you to have a grand time."

"You're angry, aren't you? You're angry because I got Marvin to bring me on board without telling you. You're angry with me because I got him to give me a job as his secretary to work off my passage."

"No, I'm not, Wendy. You have it all wrong. I am not angry, but I am annoyed because you are still following me, because you were clever enough to worm your way into a position with my agent where you were able to see me, hoping something would happen between us.

"I am annoyed because I don't want to hurt you, but you are forcing me into a position to do just that. You are infringing on my privacy and I don't tolerate that, Wendy, not from anyone."

He felt sorry for her, but he had no patience because although the position she had placed him in was not unfamiliar, it was particularly uncomfortable because of the ship's confines.

"Mr. Frayne, don't you see, I just had to prove I'd do anything for you. I love you!"

"You're infatuated with a movie star, chasing after an image, not after me, Wendy. You don't know me. The private Nicholas Frayne is a man who would not interest you at all! I'm an ordinary person, Wendy, with an extraordinary job."

Wendy stood up. She was nervously pale, her bottom lip trembled and pouted. There were tears in her eyes, but Wendy was a trooper—an honest, intelligent girl who had made a fool of herself over an idol.

She asked, "You have someone else?"

"Yes," Nicholas replied, "I hope I do."

Wendy started to leave. Nicholas put out his hand to stop

her. He said, "Now listen, you promise me you'll join in on this voyage and make an effort to have a good time? I won't let you go, Wendy, until you do."

She nodded her head in assent and hurried out of the Vanya Bar.

Nicholas realized that his fellow passengers were trying to be discreet about the scene they had witnessed, but they had certainly taken it all in. He ordered another cold Heineken beer, pulled a cigar out of his breast pocket, clipped off the end, lit it, and suddenly felt depressed and emotionally drained. The evening was turning out far differently than he had planned. He looked at his watch and for a brief moment he thought of Arabella and of joining her at the captain's dinner, but he quickly put the idea out of his mind. He was so late; his entrance now would only be awkward for them both. She was a new and wonderful woman for him. She was extraordinary. A woman of the world, different from any woman he had ever known. It excited him, and he didn't want to take any wrong or careless steps with her.

He was thankful that she had not seen this little scene. It was one of the less attractive aspects of being a public personality, a superstar. There would be time enough for her to face that part of his life. But first he wanted her to know the private Nicholas Frayne. Once they knew each other they could go out into the world and enjoy it all! He warmed at the thought of them in the world together and his depression lifted almost as quickly as it had come.

Nicholas thought how wonderful it was going to be learning about Arabella, how she lived, what she liked and disliked, what she had done with her life so far. He wasn't sure whether he wanted to know about her past loves, but he hoped there were no complications about any present ones. He knew in his heart of hearts that they were meant for each other. Crazy? No, certainly not. There was so much to look forward to. Thinking about her, he felt a heightened sense of anticipation about the days and nights ahead. He laughed out loud just as he had when she had first landed the helicopter on the dock.

The scene with Wendy was an unfortunate necessity but it was done now, finished. He realized that wanting Arabella made him that little bit more ruthless. He needed to be, and he liked it.

He leaned back and looked around the room again. He admired it and could not wait to bring Arabella there. He took a pair of glasses from his breast pocket, put them on, and looked at the wonderful paintings. There was a series of six huge oil paintings of Armenian dancing girls that were dark, dense, in deep browns, black, crimson, and bottle green. They had been painted by long-forgotten Armenian artists in the early part of the eighteenth century. The voluptuous, succulent figures in rich costumes and exotic painted faces enchanted him. He puffed on his cigar and thought of Armenia, Georgia, Russia.

For Nicholas, shades of Russian literature came to life in the room. Chekhov, Turgenev, Dostoevski. He thought of Nabokov exiled in America and dying in Switzerland; the giants Gogol and Gorky; and he hoped Arabella had a love of Russian literature as he did.

Chapter Seven

Early the next morning, there were deck stewards everywhere setting out the reclining chairs, writing out name cards to slip into the brass metal slots on the headrests, folding soft blue, mauve, and lavender plaid mohair blankets. One steward was plumping up feathered pillows, slipping them into matching plaid cases and tying them to the top of the deck chairs with neat bows.

Isador walked down the enclosed sun deck to a pair of doors at the end through a stream of "Good morning," "Did you sleep well, sir?" "Is there something I can do for you, sir?"

He pushed the doors open against a cold, hard wind. Out on the open deck the bright sunshine hit him like a spotlight. He leaned on the shiny mahogany railings and looked down to the decks below and the three swimming pools, empty of swimmers but full of sparkling aquamarine water rippling from side to side. Waves he would rather not look at. Swirls of steam rose up from the heated pools into the cold salt air. He looked beyond the floating hotel to the inky-blue Atlantic Ocean, inhaled deep breaths of the ocean air, and found it invigorating.

He ran his fingers through his steel-gray hair and pulled a very smart check English wool cap from a pocket in his camel-hair jacket. He adjusted it on his head, thankful for its warmth and grateful to Herbert Johnson, the English gentlemen's hatter who had been filling his standing order of one every year for nearly thirty years now, ever since Isador's graduate year at Oxford.

Eager to get his bearings, Izzy was doing an early-morning tour of the ship. He was enjoying the quiet and luxury of doing it alone. He loved the bite of the salt air and, even more, the fact that he was not seasick. At last he had found a ship that did not shudder, rock, heave, and roll to the steady beat of its muffled engines. And then again, he thought, putting his hand to his neck, maybe these silly Band-Aids work! As long as he never fixed his eyes on the sway of water in a swimming pool, his bathtub, or even a glass, he knew this would be a painless crossing. He took a few more deep breaths and did a couple of half-hearted knee bends. He swung his arms a few times as if he were hitting a four-hundred-yard shot straight down the fairway of one of the most difficult greens at the West Hartford Country Club.

Too cold, he turned to go back to the warmth of the enclosure. As he did, he took notice of a lone figure in a heavy white V-neck cable-stitch sweater and white flannel trousers, standing barefoot and making extraordinary movements with his arms and legs. The tall, athletic, Oriental man glistened in the sunshine. The graceful, slow-motion movements of Tai Chi were so spiritual they had Izzy mesmerized.

He watched in silence and admiration. When Xu had completed his morning exercises, he slipped into a pair of shoes and bent down to tie them. The two men then walked toward each other.

Izzy said, "Excuse me, I hope you did not mind my watching. It was Tai Chi, wasn't it?"

"Yes, it was."

"I've only seen it once before, in a park in Peking. My wife and I were there a few years ago. There were dozens of people out doing it. Young and old. Old retired men in their seventies and eighties would go there with their songbirds in cages, hang them in the trees for an airing, and do Tai Chi. I was very moved by it all. I even bought a book, read it and understood it, but couldn't get the hang of it, you know?"

Izzy managed one of the more simple movements with

a fair amount of grace and said, "I think it's like releasing a flock of blackbirds trapped within you."

He tried another movement and smiled at Xu.

"I will come here every morning at this time and I would be pleased if you would like to join me. You are more than welcome, and if I can help you it would give me pleasure."

"That's very kind of you, Mr. er, Mr. . . ."

"Xu, spelled X-u."

Izzy put out his hand and said, "I'm Isador Katz, from West Hartford, Connecticut." They shook hands, with Xu towering over his new friend.

"It's too cold out here," Izzy said, and they left the outside deck. "Do you play golf, Mr. Xu?"

"No, no golf. But I may learn because the lady I work for says she is thinking of taking up the game."

"It's a wonderful game, you know. I've been playing since I was a young boy and for me it's still the best sport in the world."

"Would you like your chairs, gentlemen?" interrupted a steward.

"Oh, yes," said Izzy. "I'd like to have a word with you about the deck chairs. My name is Katz, Isador Katz."

"Oh, yes, Mr. Katz. We have you over here."

The two men followed the steward. Isador was quite satisfied with his chair. Then, checking the names on either side of his deck chair, he turned, reached into his pocket, took out a ten-dollar bill, and handed it to the young man, saying "Steward, you see that chair marked Mrs. Katz, and that one, Mrs. Davis, and that one, Mrs. Tillman. Those three ladies are my traveling companions. They love to gossip and be together. So take those three nametags and move them way down to the far end of this deck, away from me."

That done, he turned to Xu, who had been settled by another steward three empty chairs away. Izzy sat down and after a few minutes asked, "Mr. Xu, how about taking a chair next to me, unless, of course, you have other people to sit with?"

"Thank you," Xu answered and changed chairs.

Izzy said, "Now then, Mr. Xu, since I am going to take advantage of your knowledge of Tai Chi, how about letting me teach you how to drive a good golf ball? They have a driving range on board—I checked it out. I'm quite a good golfer and there's a pro here who could give you some lessons."

Isador was being quite modest about his golfing abilities. He was a golfer with a bookcase full of trophies and several titles that he had held for years, such as the New England Championship Golfer of the Year.

"Mr. Katz, I'd love to!"

Izzy and Xu reclined in their chairs side by side, both happy to have a new companion.

Missy was looking very pretty. Her five feet two inches were dressed in well-tailored camel-hair trousers, a white cashmere turtleneck sweater, and a camel-hair jacket. She ran her fingers through her short, wavy, jet-black hair. It fell perfectly into place around her attractive face. She smacked her cheeks lightly to bring out the color she wanted, for she never wore makeup. She grabbed her handbag, a Purdey hunting bag of natural canvas trimmed in olive green, tossed it on her shoulder, and hurried out of her cabin to the eight-o'clock breakfast sitting in the second-class dining room.

Selina Yeats, you're a lucky devil! She said to herself. How many women are there like you whose working life is as exciting, adventurous, rewarding, and luxurious as yours? Just as Daddy Sam always says, you get what you get because you are what you are, and you've been lucky enough to get the best sides of both your parents!

She smiled to herself as she thought, Mama, thanks for my vivacity and adventurous nature, and Dad, thanks for my looks and unrelenting positive attitude to life.

Missy made a mental note to call her dad. She wanted to catch him at home on their horse farm in Wiltshire where she had been born and brought up. Sam Yeats was one of the finest racehorse trainers in England and would be leaving shortly for the sales in Kentucky. She wanted to know his plans in the hope that their paths might cross. Missy was close to both her parents, but it was Dad and Spring Mile, the farm, that were her anchor. That was where she had met Arabella Crawford and the Earl of Heversham.

Just back from secretarial college in London, Missy had spent a great deal of time with her father, Miss Crawford, and the Earl of Heversham that summer while Miss Crawford was putting together a racing stable. Missy got to know the glamorous lady very well that way. Her father had suggested that Arabella take Missy off his hands and make something of her out in the world beyond Wiltshire.

Well, thought Missy, as she stepped out of the elevator, she sure did that! Her father was very proud of her and her position as Arabella's personal assistant.

Missy pushed the doors to the dining room open, thinking how lovely it was having two families—a working family of Arabella, Xu, Rupert, and Oskar, as well as a blood family of mother, father, and two wonderful brothers.

Surprisingly, the eight-o'clock breakfast sitting was booked to near capacity. The dining room bustled. It was filled with people studying the menu, the ship's paper, the activities for the day; brochures filled the tables along with the food: "Know Your Ship"; "Where to Find What You Are Looking For"; sample menus of the ship's fare available to be ordered in advance; "Whom to Call to Book Yourself into What You Want."

Missy looked around the room. They were for the most part well-dressed, wealthy, well-traveled passengers. Most of the Americans looked like they had stepped out of Saks Fifth Avenue, Marshall Fields, Neiman Marcus, or one of the expensive shops on Rodeo Drive. The women were high on Armani, Missoni, Ralph Lauren, and Jones of New York sportswear.

The American men were for the most part divine. Well tailored, tanned, courtly, and solicitous to their wives; generous, patient, and charming to the single women, young or old; highly competitive, overly knowledgeable, obsessed with statistics, and masters of generalizations. Preoccupied with success, money, culture, and winning. Some handled it with more finesse than others.

The S.S. *Tatanya Annanovna* had American tourists who were chic and well traveled, who had been everywhere and were looking for alternative ways of travel to places where they could have the same luxurious life as they did at home. From what Missy could see, they were certainly in the right place.

Missy recognized the English passengers easily from the perfect cut of the men's suits—Savile Row, Dougy Heywood—and the Scottish tweeds and cashmere pullovers, smartly worn though patched. Turnbull & Asser shirts; no cufflinks. The well-worn school tie and those dinner suits and shirts—the epitome of 1930's good taste and lack of flash.

It was especially easy to spot the English women. They always had the best complexions; naturally white, paper-thin skin with an under color and glow, giving them cosmetics from within instead of from the beauty section of the ground floor of Harrods. They were naturally beautiful from breeding and understatement. They were strong with fragile looks, a prerequisite for living with the English gentleman. What other women could ride with the hounds, follow the shoot, kill the salmon, fly fish the trout, keep their servants for a lifetime? Or load up their cars with logs for the fire, trees and shrubs for the garden, picnics for their outings, blond Labrador retrievers or Dalmatians and terriers, then chug along the motorways and London streets only to be hooted at by their husband's chauffeur as the family (for income tax purposes "company") Rolls passed them by and streaked ahead with husband sitting in the back reading *The Financial Times*, *Country Life*, *Field and Stream*?

Praise be the English woman who can turn her hand to drawing and plucking a pheasant, muck out the stable, clean a fish, cook a gourmet meal, and keep her looks and figure.

Spend endless hours on her hands and knees with her gardener and hang on to her stately home while still managing most discreetly a lover and the children at half-term. All this in the shadow of a social calendar no less busy than the Queen's.

The delicious English woman who is tough but tender, exhausted but bites the bullet for family and country. These were the women who looked best when their hairdos looked messed. Torn between dressing like the Queen, whom they loved, and the Paris fashions they admired, they still had the ability to get away with the long evening skirt in black velvet or tartan, cotton in summer, and the St. Laurent cream silk blouse. Except when they pulled out their ballgowns, which were always divine. They were as much Ascot as the horses, that being the only time their clothes and hats were allowed to surpass those of their peacock husbands, dressed in gray top hat and tails. The Ascot Man—a species of penguin the whole world prayed would never die out.

The English couples were adored and sought after by the American passengers because they spoke English instead of American. For the Americans, every Englishman was a lord and every lord as good as a duke because of his upper-class accent, his heritage, and the fact that he had not emigrated.

The previous night at dinner Missy had seen several elegant, reserved Swedes and a group of Germans who were tall and white-haired, the younger men blond and handsome. The German women fell into two categories—extremely elegant and attractive, or the opposite. They were the present-day Marlene Dietrichs, Romy Schneiders, or Marie Dresslers, and extremely pleasant and charming to everyone.

There were almost as many French as there were Americans on board, and they were the most elegant, well dressed, and attractive of all the passengers. The women were terrific looking and the French men, from sixteen to sixty, all looked like Alain Delon, sounded like Sacha Distel, charmed like Jean Gabin, and, one hoped, made love like Jean Paul Belmondo looked. They barely spoke a word of English to anyone—insisting on their own language, as they always did wherever they went.

If the Americans were the most generous travelers and the English surprisingly open and charming once they saw Dover fade into the sunset, then the French were the most demanding and difficult, forming cliques and sending back opened bottles of wine.

All in all, quite a cross-section of cultures, thought Missy. And I consider myself lucky to be here with them.

It was odd to think that none of these people would be there, that there would be no crossing on this magnificent ocean liner and, as a matter of fact, no ship, if not for her boss. Arabella Crawford had been the merchant banker who put the money together for the Anglo-French line and the S.S. *Tatanya Annanovna*, although she managed to conceal her identity during the transaction, as was her practice with many of her successful business ventures. Public recognition was not her goal and her anonymity permitted her to negotiate more freely on an international scale.

The *maître d'* showed Missy to her table. Xu was already there and he stood up to greet her. He remained standing there while the *maître d'* introduced Missy to Mrs. Davis and Mrs. Tillman. Missy chatted with Xu, ordered her breakfast, and began looking through the brochures, eager to see what events were on offer.

"Do you play any of the games or sports that are available to us on this voyage, Miss Yeats?"

"I don't know what they are, Mrs. Tillman. I must look them up."

"Don't bother. I can tell you what they are." Looking at the paper in her hand, she read: "'For your leisure and pleasure: shuffleboard, deck quoits, golf driving, putting, and tennis are located on the upper deck aft. On the forward deck is skeet shooting and a target range. Indoor games such as chess, draughts, Scrabble, dominoes, jigsaw puzzles, and a variety of card games are available from the library. There is also a running and jogging track on the deck. There are exercise classes and, of course, the health club with Nautilus equipment, a sauna, a steambath, and a regular gym, and an indoor pool.' The outside pool is only for the very brave and strong-hearted. It's freezing cold on the North Atlantic this time of year."

"Oh," said Missy. "I might just about bring myself to a game of shuffleboard, but that's about it except for a swim in the indoor pool."

"What a relief that's all there is," said Mrs. Davis. "I've looked all through these brochures and I promise you it's a joy to see they don't have those endless schedules from the moment you open your eyes to the moment you close them."

"God, Tessie, do you remember on our last cruise those endless quizzes, dance lessons, lectures—my God, the lectures! I thought I was back at school! The classes—swimming lessons, golf lessons, bridge lessons, archery lessons, shooting lessons, table-tennis and tennis lessons; arts and crafts, *all* of the arts and crafts, I might add. Teachers for flower arranging and knitting and embroidery and God knows what. Then there were the cards, the bingo, and the casino. By the time that cruise was over, I was exhausted and had to go away for a complete rest to the milk farm—sorry, these days they call it the health spa."

Missy could not help but laugh and a wide smile broke out across Xu's face. Mrs. Davis and Mrs. Tillman looked at their table companions, then looked at each other and they too broke out laughing.

"This is much better, far more humane for us poor travelers!" said Mrs. Tillman. "Mr. Xu, how will you pass your time on this crossing?"

"Oh, I will spend a great deal of time with the dogs and birds we have on board, and I will try to learn how to play golf."

"And something else, Xu," said Missy. "I have a surprise for you." Then, turning to the ladies, she said, "Xu is an archer of extraordinary ability, and I have arranged for his target to be set up on a secluded part of the signal deck. Just ring the purser's office and they'll send someone along to help you with your things and set you up."

"Thank you, Missy. I appreciate that."

"It was partly selfish, Xu. May I come and watch?"

"Of course."

"And maybe have a lesson?"

"With pleasure, Missy."

"Would you mind," said Mrs. Davis, "if we came to watch one day?"

"Not at all," Xu replied graciously. "In fact, why don't we all meet on the signal deck this afternoon at three? I will give you all instructions, or you may just observe, as you wish. Missy, why don't you invite Mr. Peters to join us?"

"And then we can all have tea together at four," said Mrs. Tillman.

"We haven't heard what else you two ladies are going to do," said Missy.

"I'm going to swim every day," said Tessie Tillman. "I'm a movie addict so I'll go to the movies every day. All of the important new films will be shown and some of my old favorites. Did you know that the famous movie star, Nicholas Frayne, is on board this very ship with us? I'll spend some time reading and fill the rest of it playing cards. I do adore playing cards."

"What do you play?" asked Missy.

"Singles and doubles in gin rummy, duplicate bridge, canasta, can can, and, if I have to, solitaire. You name it, I'll play it. I'm a card player. You see, Sophie—Mrs. Davis here—and Libby Katz, whom you've yet to meet, and I are from the age of the social card players, a time when socially there was little else to do but play cards or go to a concert of some touring symphony orchestra. That was before television and the new American addiction for sport and the sporting life."

Sophie interjected, "I think I played cards less before I became a widow and even less than that when I was a mother. But for my husband and myself, cards were always a social occasion as well as a chance to gamble on one's skill. There were times when it helped pay the bills!" They both laughed knowingly.

"Where are you all from?" Missy inquired.

"Mrs. Davis and I," Tessie began, "together with her brother Isador Katz and his wife, Libby, were all born on the same street and grew up in the same neighborhood in West Hartford, Connecticut. We never left our immediate circle of friends and neighbors. We married people we'd known all our lives, made our families at the same time, spent vacations at the same beaches, grew rich together, and have shared tragedies together. Why, Sophie and I even became widows within six months of each other." She looked around the breakfast table and continued, "Imagine being clever enough to create a small orangerie for a breakfast room! You know, I'm sure it's a close copy of the one in Versailles. I suppose it's the glass roof that allows the orange and kumquat trees to flourish. Just look at them!

"This room makes me think of my husband, Louis," Sophie said. "We were childhood sweethearts. I wore his fraternity pin in high school and we were married before he graduated college. Then we settled down in West Hartford with our friends and raised a family. It was a very cozy world, even though, at first, there was little money."

"What kind of business was your husband in, Mrs. Doria?"

"Well, my father-in-law had a furniture store in West Hartford. He sold everything from andirons to fake Louis Quinze bedroom suites. My husband, who had studied art history in college, spent his life developing the antique end of the business, buying both American and foreign pieces at bargain prices—long before they came into vogue. He turned the shop into one of the best in New England. We made two buying trips to Europe every year for twenty years. Sitting here reminds me of the last time Louis and I went to Versailles together."

"What a wonderful story!" Missy exclaimed. "But how did he ever have the foresight or the talent to determine what to buy?"

"My Louis was a man of exquisite taste; sometimes, when he looked at an old handcrafted piece of furniture, he was in a world of his own, all alone. He and my brother,

Izzy, had an understanding of craftsmanship and European art which, I admit, surpassed mine and that of most of our friends. They were marvelous together because they never put on airs or phony graces. My Louis was a special man; Izzy still is."

They were all quiet for a moment, while Sophie smiled at a memory.

"Yes, Louis would have liked this room. He had plans for his own orangerie. A place to house a swimming pool and grow lemons, oranges, and kumquats just like these. He used the original plans of Versailles' Orangerie scaled down. It was to have been in the clearing behind our house. He never lived to get more than the foundations of it laid. Ah, but that was years ago. And here we are today!" Sophie brightened once again. "Louis really would have enjoyed the *Tatanya Annanovna* with all her glamour and elegance. He would have found it in the best of taste and he would be right, as he always was."

Missy listened to all this and thought, How extraordinary and warm Americans are. You say, "How do you do," know them for three minutes, and they tell all, can't wait for you to know them.

Mrs. Davis turned to Missy. "This ship is enormous and yet there's an atmosphere among the passengers of privacy and nonpressured camaraderie. Don't you agree, Miss Yeats?"

"Yes, I do, Mrs. Davis. It's an amazing accomplishment when you consider the catering staff alone is over nine hundred. What a monumental task it is to float a hotel like this and still have it remain an elegant and intimate ship."

"As many as that?" said Tessie. "That's nothing—think of the total staff; it's mind-boggling."

"The orchestra is twenty-two pieces and look at this," said Xu, passing across one of the pamphlets he was looking at.

"How extraordinary! Just listen to this," Missy read.

"'The S.S. *Tatanya Annanovna* must be capable of meeting the demands of an international clientele. The basic catering requirements detailed below for a normal transatlantic run include such varied items as twenty-five thousand pounds of beef, twenty-two thousand pounds of fresh fruit, one hundred fifty pounds of caviar, six hundred jars of baby food, fifty pounds of dog biscuits. She carries forty-one brands of whiskey and forty-three brands of cigarettes.'"

"It's staggering!" Mrs. Davis said.

"Shall I go on?" asked Missy.

"How much coffee?" one of them asked.

Missy looked down the list. "'Two thousand pounds of coffee, five thousand pounds of sugar.' My liver will do a turnover and go green and so will yours," she went on, "when you hear this. 'Three thousand five hundred pounds of butter, three thousand quarts of cream.'"

"Oh, my God!" said Mrs. Davis. "My cholesterol!"

"Well, there's plenty of what I like," said Missy. "There are fifteen hundred pounds of lobster."

The four tablemates were now hooked on statistics.

"If there are twenty-five thousand pounds of beef," said Xu, "how much meat is there altogether?"

"Just a minute," said Missy, running her fingernail down a long column of numbers, adding them up in her head as she went along. She looked up and said, "Fifty-three thousand five hundred pounds of meat, turkey, duck, and chicken."

"That's disgusting! It's enough to turn me into a vegetarian," said Mrs. Davis, chuckling.

"If I can remember these statistics at mealtimes, it might make me eat frugally," said Mrs. Tillman. "Forget the food, it's giving me indigestion just hearing about it. What else is listed there?"

"Sheets alone," said Missy. "Ready for this? Twenty-three thousand, two hundred—and they do laundry on board every day!"

Xu stood up and said, "Excuse me, ladies. I am going up to the kennels."

Missy said, "I'll go with you."

Tessie said, "You have a good day. We'll see you at three."

Chapter Eight

While the others were having breakfast and planning their activities, Arabella was lying on her side, wandering in and out of easy stages of sleep. Nicholas was lying tight up against her, one arm draped over her hip, his hand cupping her mound, his long, beautiful fingers entwined in her silky blond public hair, the tips of his fingers nestling between her legs.

She lay there, her eyes closed, luxuriating in the warmth of his body, the touch of his skin, the beat of his heart against her back. She was seduced by him yet again. She felt the pale, soft warmth of his light, even breathing on the back of her neck as he slept. His long, beautiful, thick penis, partially erect, rested between the cheeks of her buttocks, his knees were tucked up under the back of hers, his shins touched her calves, and her feet rested on top of his. His thighs were tucked up under the back of hers. His other arm was draped over the pillow and arched over the top of her head; her golden hair was spread over it and her hand lay in his, held firmly in a tight grip, even as he slept.

In her half-sleeping, half-waking state she was aroused, electrified by their closeness. Not wanting to disturb these exquisite moments, she dared not even open her eyes. Arabella lay there, content to relive the night before while he slept on. She conjured up pictures of every step she had taken after her return from the captain's dinner.

Arabella thought she felt a change of pressure on her hand, as if Nicholas had squeezed it in his sleep. She listened for a change in his breathing, any movement. There was none; he remained in the world of dreams.

Only while reliving what had happened after she had

slipped into Nicholas's bed did Arabella realize they had barely spoken a word to each other. Yet through the hours of lovemaking they had discovered parts of themselves and each other that no one else in their lives ever had.

Now, as she relived the very first kiss after he had woken to find her in bed with him, it brought butterflies to her stomach, fire to her loins, and an aching desire to be loved.

His first kisses were gentle and when he felt Arabella give way through them, the kisses became more passionate. Wherever he touched her with his hands she felt as if her flesh was melting, the marrow of her bones liquefying. He put his hands on her breasts, stroking them upward toward the nipples. He took her erect nipples between his thumb and forefinger, twirled them and stretched them. She reached down, found his cock fully erect and throbbing.

His arms wrapped around her and he lowered his mouth to her nipples, sucking and licking long and hard. He stopped only long enough to put his mouth to her lips, kissing her deeply. In one slow continuous motion he rolled her on top of him. He spread her legs apart and felt her sweet warm wetness as he went between them with his thick penis, fast and hard. He filled her completely, and his swollen balls lay pressed against her. He pulled her to his chest tightly and they kissed, filling their mouths full with each other's tongues.

Once inside, he allowed his cock to rest there, throbbing against her soft wetness while he kissed, sucked, and fondled her. She reached over his flat buttocks and found his balls damp with her wetness. She fondled and played with them, massaging them gently.

Arabella was aroused as never before when he began to press into her with deep slow strokes. He kissed her tenderly, aware of just how much she had come. He licked her ear and whispered to her, "You are so wet, so tight, so wonderful. I want to keep you like this always."

Their beautiful, fierce lovemaking seemed endless and made their heads and senses swim. Arabella was giving and demanding, yet soft and passionate, and Nicholas was just as giving and demanding, just as soft and passionate. They were equally matched. He devoured her femaleness; she could not get enough of his maleness. Only when they were dizzy with exhaustion and satiated from their orgasms did their passion subside and they fall asleep entwined.

They had dozed off in the position they were lying in now. As Arabella was listening to his heartbeat against her back, she wanted him all over again. She felt a kiss on the back of her neck and in one easy turn he had her on top of him, encircled in his arms.

He kissed her and said, "Good morning."

She kissed him back and answered, "Good morning."

He put his hands around her waist and lifted her high above him and pulled her down slowly over his morning erection. Just as had happened half a dozen times the night before, they surrendered to each other body and soul. This time their very bones seemed to melt and they dissolved together in a crashing roll of orgasm. As the wall of waves broke from somewhere deep within them he called out, "Arabella, I love you!"

She whispered, "I love you too, Nicholas." They were both startled by the intensity of their passion and the depth of their feelings. Their declarations of love seemed premature, as they were virtually strangers to one another. As if by mutual agreement, neither spoke and they parted in silence.

On the way back to her cabin, Arabella smiled and said hello to various people, from a stiff, sour-faced stewardess, to a young, somewhat harried cabin boy, to the ship's doctor, to Marcia McKay. Arabella used the same tone with each—all too happy to greet them, or anyone for that matter. So filled with the joys of life, she smiled and greeted all who passed by.

Henry, her steward, saw her approaching the cabin and rushed forward to open her stateroom door. Her heart was singing. When she heard Henry click the door closed behind her and she knew she was alone, she broke into a two-step and danced over to the flowers Nicholas brought the previous day. Sinking to her knees on the carpet, she buried her face fully into the bouquet and inhaled its perfume. She moved her head from side to side among the blossoms and scooped up the few petals which had fallen onto the table and put them in her coat pocket.

She had come back to the cabin to change clothes and make her face up before going with Nicholas for a stroll around the decks and a visit to the kennels before lunch. She suddenly thought of Anthony, but quickly erased the image from her consciousness. She wanted no trace of conflict or reflection of reality to mar these precious moments.

There was a knock at the door. She opened it to a delivery boy in a smart gray uniform covered in round silver buttons; he presented Arabella with a parcel wrapped in shiny gray paper and a pretty white silk bow. She rushed to the dressing table, sat down and opened it, thinking it was a gift from Nicholas. She was overwhelmed when she saw the lush gray velvet necklace box with the neat lettering, VAN CLEEF & ARPELS. She pressed the catch open and was dazzled by a magnificent dark-blue sapphire as large as her thumb. Square cut and very deep, it was set in an octagonal double row of diamonds and strung on a chain of octagonal platinum links an inch wide set in magnificent blue-white diamonds.

Arabella knew without question that something was wrong. Nicholas would never give her such a gift. His would have some sort of emotional content. She was sure of that. She quickly opened the small white envelope tucked inside the satin lining of the lid. It read, "Arabella, my love, remember Alexandria. Anthony."

She sat staring at the magnificent necklace, quite speechless, unable to cope with the coincidence of her vivid memories yesterday in the bath and Anthony's own remembrance. How extraordinary that they were both thinking of the beginning of their affair almost at the same time!

She noted, of course, that the card was not in his handwriting. He had probably dictated the message over the telephone. What did it all mean? Why was he beginning it all again?

As she was mulling it all over, the telephone on her dressing table rang. She picked up the receiver distractedly.

"Hello."

"Do you like it?" It was Anthony.

"Well, of course I like it, Anthony. It's magnificent. What are you doing, Anthony? Why the necklace?"

"It's a bribe."

"Why do you think you have to bribe me? You never have before."

"That's true. But I sense that I'm losing you. I couldn't bear that. Do you remember Alexandria?"

"Of course I do, dear, just like I remember the house you bought me in Wiltshire to keep me close to you, just as I remember all the years of happiness we had together." Arabella was very aware that he was still able to excite her with his intimations of their past, his voice, his arrogance.

She went on. "Just like the other gifts you've given me and the love. How can I forget the world you showed me that I might never have known or seen without you? Do you think I could ever forget those wonderful years? But surely you aren't sending me this magnificent necklace because of the past?"

"No, I told you, my lovely Arabella, it's a bribe. I've something to tell you that I should have before. Arabella, Fiona is dead. My wife died nearly three months ago."

There was a long silence between them and then Arabella said, "Why didn't you tell me before now?"

"I couldn't tell you sooner. It was so sudden. It was an accident. I was devastated and I just could not talk to anyone or see anyone. I needed time to sort out my feelings, to recover from the pain. I wanted to call you, to see you, but I wasn't strong enough. The necklace is a bribe so I don't have to talk about my not telling you. I know it may have been a mistake not to have told you sooner and I know I can't expect you to understand. But I'm telling you now. I am free, Arabella. There is a new and wonderful Alexandria coming up for us again. A new beginning.

"Please don't say anything now. Think about what this means and I'll call you tomorrow. We'll talk then when you've had time to absorb and digest all this. Just wear your lovely new necklace this evening and remember how very long we've loved each other and how well."

Arabella closed the lid of the box as she hung up the telephone. The news of Fiona's death shocked her, but at the same time, the new sense that she was truly free from Anthony—who behaved as if he still possessed her—made her more able to appreciate Nicholas and his loving courtship of her.

She put the thoughts of Anthony out of her mind and concentrated on remembering the events of the previous night.

She saw herself using her stateroom key. As she had turned it in the lock, she had pressed her forehead against the polished walnut door, weary from trying to rid herself all evening from that dreaded feeling, fear of loss. Despite the fact that they had made no specific arrangements, she had been certain he would appear at the party.

She pushed the door open and, stepping into the darkened room, closed it and leaned against it. Eventually she stretched her arm out and switched on the lights. She tried being rational, explaining to herself that she had been seduced by a famous movie idol. She blamed herself for falling for his style, his sexiness, his being a movie star. But the rationalizations would not work. It was something more.

Arabella was reacting to the man, Nicholas Frayne. The handsome, intelligent man who had come courting her. That was what she had been drawn to; it had nothing to do with his image.

There it was again, that tear at the heart. Where was he? Had he used her up so quickly? For her it had been a beginning. Was it vanity alone that made her believe it had been the same for him?

In her anxiety, she had swung around and looked on the floor by the door, hoping he had slipped a note under it. The carpet remained bare and obstinate. It held no message for her.

Disgusted with herself, she had walked toward her bedroom. Visions of his lips, his ears, the taste of him bewitched her, made her ardent, passionate for him.

She stood before her dressing table, reached around to her back, and unzipped her evening dress. It fell around her feet. She crossed her arms and ran her hands over her naked shoulders, arms, and breasts, sighing with relief at the caress, even if it was only from her own hands. She wanted him so much; no one else, just him. How could she have been so mistaken? She had been so sure they were to be together. No call, no word, not even a note. There was nothing. Best to forget it. Just another one of those affairs that happens and dies because no one nurtures it, she thought.

She walked across the room naked, in the dark, to her bed, remembering scenes of their erotic afternoon. She thought she was left with no choice but to slip between the crisp linen sheets and touch herself, pretending it was him. She switched the lamp on next to her bed and lifted the peach satin eiderdown. Just as she was about to crawl between the sheets, she saw a large brown envelope lying on the pillow; her name was written boldly across it in dark-blue ink.

Her reflex action was to put her hands to her face and cover her lips with her fingers. She knew at once it was from him. It had to be Nicholas Frayne's handwriting. It was a handsome, sensitive, sure, and sensuous script. She grabbed the envelope, pressed it to her bosom, and slipped into the bed. She closed her eyes, trembling with joy and relief. She relaxed against the pillows and opened her eyes. Inside the envelope she found a key and a small leather-bound book, worn with age, and a note written on ship's stationery.

Arabella, this book is a rare and wonderful love story—

a first edition I found by chance and sensed I had to have. Now I know why. I love you, Arabella Crawford. I want you. Come to me. If, for whatever reason, you cannot, then keep the book and you will understand my loss.

Nicholas

The book was *Abelard and Heloise*, the story of a powerful passion and enduring love between a man and a woman from vastly different worlds.

Arabella read the note a second time, then lay it gently on the bed next to her. Consumed with emotion, ecstatic and excited, she slid down the bed until she was lying down with her head resting on the pillows. She pulled the soft eiderdown up over her shoulders and slipped her arms under it into the warmth of the bed. Arabella had always liked the sensuous feeling of lying on crisp, cool linen sheets and being cocooned in satin and the warmth generated by the eiderdown and body heat.

Her thoughts were of Nicholas and his declaration of love, of the romantic Nicholas who wanted their love to be as extraordinary in its own way as was Abelard and Heloise's. She though of the Nicholas she was sure was capable of making the most erotic love with total passion, body and soul. Her thoughts set her ablaze. She stroked her breasts. The soft, supple skin of her firm, full, rounded breasts filled her hands and she thrilled to the sensation of caressing and being caressed. With the flat of her palm she stroked her voluptuous nipples in a circular movement, round and round, tantalizing and teasing them until they were long, hard, and erect. She pinched the sensitive nipples, pulled them, and the sensation she felt made her think of Nicholas's exquisite sucking of them earlier.

Her passions aroused by her own hands and thoughts of Nicholas made her wish he was there filling and titillating her, tormenting her with pleasure. Arabella had yet to have all of him inside her. She longed for him now, full and hard, filling her completely. Her hands moved down her body slowly, as she imagined his would, and finally her hand slipped between her legs to the warmth and moisture there. She opened herself with deft fingers, closed her eyes, and massaged herself until she became almost unbearably sensitive, all the while thinking of Nicholas playing on her body. With her free hand she reached for her breast as her body began to tense up, her back arch. She came in crashing waves calling out softly, passionately, during her climax, "Nicholas, Nicholas!"

Her body relaxed and went limp; her heart was pounding. Arabella had only one desire—to come and come and come again with Nicholas. Her body stiffened once more and she came yet again with a crescendo of orgasm.

She looked now at the small, worn, Celidon green Moroccan leather book with faded gold lettering and trim of faded gold feathers etched around the cover and binding. *Abelard and Heloise*. The aroma of beautiful antique books filled her nostrils. She held the novel to her nose and inhaled deeply, holding on tight, so tight her knuckles went white.

For eight hundred years romantics and idealists have been emotionally branded by the story of Abelard and Heloise. The story came back to Arabella as she lay with her own lover's gift, this book, lying next to her on the pillow.

Abelard, the most famous scholar in twelfth-century France, a man in his late thirties, fastidious and chaste, and Heloise, a girl of seventeen, virtuous, convent-bred. Two innocents pure of flesh, heart, and soul. He the tutor and she the pupil are brought together, and they fall desperately in love.

Arabella remembered that some of the most excruciatingly beautiful words and sentiments ever spoken between two people were those between the lovers while they lived in bliss together in Brittany. Arabella clutched the book to her bosom, remembering how moved she had been when she had first read the story and, later, when she had seen the London production of Ronald Miller's play at Wyndham's Theatre.

Could Nicholas love her? Could they be lovers with the same power and passion as Abelard and Heloise? Could they pay the price of such a love? More to the point, *would* they pay the price for such a love?

She opened the book. In faded lavender ink someone had written on the flyleaf: "Catherine, my love, once is forever. Jean Louis. Avignon, April 8, 1781."

She had placed the book back in the envelope after reading a few pages. She was touched by the gift and felt an urgent need to go to Nicholas immediately. All of her senses were aroused. The wide, white flannel trousers and heavy cream silk blouse with balloon sleeves made her even more aware of her body. She slipped into a pair of Manolo Blahnik white pigskin shoes and looked in the mirror briefly, just time enough to repair her makeup and run a brush through her hair. The Bulgari necklace and earrings, ancient silver Roman coins framed in diamonds and gold, looked just as well with her change of clothes as they had with her evening dress. Even her diamond and emerald bracelet looked right.

She picked up the key and left her cabin. The aft section of the signal deck was open to the cold wind, which she needed to get herself under some control before going to Nicholas. The black sky and endless sparkling stars in space, the dark, seemingly bottomless ocean below brought things back into proportion. Arabella was composed now, ready for her next step.

She found his cabin, used the key and, as quietly as possible, slowly opened the door, her heart pounding for the moment of their meeting.

His stateroom was handsome, softly lit by candlelight, and the walls of antique cherry paneling added a feeling of warmth and welcome. On one wall hung a large, romantic Aubusson tapestry of a hunt in a wood, showing a man and a woman on white stallions, shimmering against myriad shades of green and beige. But there was no Nicholas to welcome her.

Arabella wandered through the other lit rooms until she found the master bedroom, its door open. The light from the lamps cast shadows on the paneled walls of antique Florentine leather painted with scrolls, flowers, and birds. The colors, dulled by time but still beautiful, were highlighted by gold leaf work as only the Florentines could do.

The large four-poster bed was heavily carved, reaching nearly to the ceiling, but had no canopy. The large lamps on either side of the bed gave off a soft light and a warmth to the majestic room. Arabella felt as if she had come home.

Nicholas was lying in the middle of the bed, partially covered by a quilt, with some papers lying face down on his chest, his glasses halfway down his nose. There was no welcome.

He was sound asleep. Arabella stood there at the foot of the bed watching him for a long time. She drank in his handsomeness, his male beauty; he was a joy to look at. There was a goodness in the beauty that came forth even as he slept. She was able to recognize a kindness and strength she had missed that afternoon.

Arabella removed her coat and shoes, walked through the rooms, and turned off all the lights. She returned to the bedroom and very carefully removed the documents and then the glasses, put them on the bedside table, and turned off the lamps. Quietly she removed her clothes and very slowly, gently, and silently, slipped under the covers into the bed. Then she slid as close to him as she dared, not wanting to wake him. Still tense, holding her breath, excited yet timid, and careful, she turned onto her side and leaned on her elbow, facing him.

The curtains in front of the glass door that opened onto his private deck were open. Arabella lay there looking at Nicholas Frayne and the stars twinkling over the Atlantic Ocean.

As the night turned from black to navy blue and was on the verge of dawn, his breathing changed and he opened his eyes. Feeling her presence, he rolled over onto his side and faced her. Their eyes met in the newborn light. He looked at her and said, "It's a new day." She looked back at him and smiled. He took her in his arms, found her lips, and kissed them. And then, throughout the early hours of the dawn and beyond sunrise, they made love to each other.

Arabella was ready when Nicholas knocked at her state-room door. She was dressed in a navy-blue and white checked silk dress with a high neck and soft Ascot of the same material. It had a pleated skirt that flared from below the hips, over which she wore a navy-blue cashmere jacket that ended where the pleats began. The jacket had wide shoulders and long, narrow lapels. The sleeves came to just below the elbow so that the long, full sleeves of the dress ballooned out before buttoning tightly on the wrist.

She wore large Cabuchon ruby earrings mounted in heavy gold and, on her Chloe jacket lapel, a Georgian dia-mond and ruby firefly that shimmered and trembled on a small spring as she walked.

She had swept her hair up under a charming white felt hat with a narrow brim and a band of red, white, and blue grosgrain ribbon. She wore the hat tilted slightly to one side. It was a hat reminiscent of those worn by ladies on transatlantic cruises in the 1930's. Her long, shapely legs were encased in bone-color stockings and her feet shod in matching calfskin Ferragamo shoes, with a medium heel, suitable for walking.

She opened the door. He stood there, silent and hand-some. She said, "Hello, Nicholas Frayne."

Nicholas remained silent for a few seconds after she had greeted him, then said, "Hello, Arabella. You look so pretty."

He picked up her two hands in his and said, "Let me look at you. You are a feast!" He squeezed her hands and went on. "I don't dare kiss you—I don't trust myself!"

She laughed and, removing her hands from his, used the back of one to gently rub his cheek. It was a gesture filled with affection.

She twirled around, her skirt rising with the motion and falling back against her legs. She thought to herself, I like my new look. Before she left Paris she had gone on a massive shopping spree, the first of many self-indulgences she intended. It was all part of her new life. She used to be the navy-blue pinstripe suit type, tasteful but businesslike. But now she was happy about no longer needing to create a certain powerful impression. She could appear exotic, sophisticated, or frivolous. It was no longer necessary to disguise her moods or camouflage her voluptuous body.

He put his arm around her shoulders and they walked into her stateroom together. "Do you think I'm beautiful, Nicholas?" she asked.

"What a strange thing to ask, Arabella!"

"You are beautiful," Nicholas said, kissing the tip of her nose. "I want everyone to see you. I want to show you off to the world!"

Teasingly, Arabella said, "First I want you to meet my very special traveling companions, my loyal friends who've agreed to join me on this voyage."

"I assumed you were traveling alone," said Nicholas, "but I can see how little I really know about you."

The kennels were two decks above their suites in a section next to the ship's enormous smokestack. The kennel boys opened the cage doors and the sleek, beautiful whippets—Cecile, Cyrile, Cedric, and Carmen—pranced, leaped, and ran out. They played ball with them and Arabella showed Nicholas what excellent retrievers they were. She was astonished that in five minutes he was able to teach Carmen and Cedric how to jump through a loop made with his arms. They hid biscuits and watched the dogs sniff them out. They put all four on leads and walked them up and down the deck twenty times. Finally they all bounded into the kennel steward's cabin to warm up and greet Sylvia and Sarah, the two yellow canaries who were singing away while the dogs barked and yelped.

Nicholas caught her attention by putting his arm around her shoulders and shouting in her ear, "Arabella, you don't have more of these stashed away in houses anywhere, do you?"

"No, no more dogs or birds, and no houses or flats. No, my whole family is right here, except for Xu and Missy." Arabella thought she noticed a moment of insecurity in Nicholas at the mention of Xu. She was quick to put her hand on his sleeve and say, "Xu is my manservant. He's been with me for many, many years."

"Ah," he said, "the Oriental man I saw you board with."

"And the girl, Missy, has been my secretary for the past twelve years. They're family to me and they are very special. I'm anxious for you to get to know them both during this trip. I also have a real blood family—my mother and brother—whom I hope to see very soon. Tell me about your family, Nicholas."

Arabella waited, but instead he changed the subject by saying "This is mad! Why are we shouting above this din? Come on, let's go to lunch."

Cotille Jefferson was in her cabin, third class, Deck A. Her cabinmate had chosen first sitting for her meals. Cotille had taken second. She was taking advantage of the lady's absence to learn some lyrics, try out her voice, and do a little coke.

There was no question about it—she didn't have a voice strong enough to match her ambition. Everyone else knew it and now even she accepted it. Well, she had tried her best but the voice was simply not there. It never had been.

For the first time in seven years she had been in Paris for the collections and was far more successful than she had anticipated. She still had what it took down the runway. Cotille had been a top—*the* top—black model, the best there had ever been. She was traveling back to New York on board the S.S. *Tatanya Annanovna* on a job with a photographer for *Vogue* magazine. She should be happy to get such a good assignment and forget about her fifth-rate career as a pop star. Cotille was cursed with the good looks most girls would kill for, and yet she had a self-destructive, painful need to be good at something she knew was out of her reach.

She was black—black and beautiful, sleek as a panther with the face of an Abyssinian princess. She had modeled her way out of poverty and onto the glossy pages of every top magazine in the world. She had done the runways of the best couture houses. But all that did nothing, she would say, for her soul.

Now deeply in debt and disgusted with herself, she was trying to prove there was more to her than a black clothes-horse for high fashion and a high-priced piece of beautiful black flesh to be displayed and used by the rag traders.

Cotille tried the lyrics again. She thought her voice sounded better and began to fool herself until it cracked. At the disco in third class the night before the master of ceremonies had asked her to give them a song. Passenger participation, he had said. The audience liked her so much he asked her to learn some of the band's lyrics and maybe sing with them one night. What a joke, she thought. All because he wants a piece of black ass. He had made that very clear. Jesus, life really is a bowl of shit, she thought, and pulled out a small bottle of coke and a tiny silver spoon. A little toot and it'll all hurt a lot less.

She was stopped almost before she got going by a knock on her cabin door. She quickly put the things in the drawer, checked herself in the mirror to make sure her black nose wasn't edged with white powder, and pulled the leather belt around her waist tighter. Cotille opened the door, thinking it was her cabinmate.

"Oh, for Christ's sake!" She was astonished. "Marvin Kandy, what the hell are you doing here? How did you find me?"

"It was simple—I read the ship's passenger list."

"Listen, Marvin, the last thing I need is an old lover."

She turned her back on him and walked into the cabin, went to the drawer, and took out the things she had so hurriedly put away. Marvin followed her. When he saw what she was preparing, he said, "I see you haven't changed, Cotille. Still busy screwing up your life."

"Listen, Marvin," she hissed, "get out of here. Who the

hell do you think you are walking in here like this, judging my life? You walked out five years ago, Marvin; five years ago and how many wives and kids later?"

"One wife, four children," he said. "Now, are you coming to lunch with me or not?"

Still angry, she sat down in a chair and said, "Still the same old caring Marvin Kandy trying to save me."

"Is that so bad?"

"No, not so bad, just dumb."

"What would you prefer?"

Cotille melted at the sight of Marvin-the-do-gooder. A rare bird. "Never mind. How about that lunch?"

Marvin sat down on the bed and pulled Cotille down next to him. He said as he stroked her cheek and neck, "I wish you weren't such a crazy lady."

Cotille replied, "And I wish you weren't such a nice guy."

Chapter Nine

The travelers on board the S.S. *Tatanya Annanovna* were settling quickly into the pleasant monotony of having nothing to do and nothing to worry about. Life on board ship had begun to arrange itself, giving the passengers the luxury of enjoying a life on a grand scale.

On the boat deck, passengers were wrapped up snugly in down comforters, relaxing in lounge chairs, some sipping steaming mugs of bouillon. Protected from the wind by a Plexiglas shield, they were able to enjoy the bright winter sunlight usually only encountered by skiers at the very tops of mountains.

The main deck featured the all-season health club—allowing everyone a chance to exercise in the gym or swim in heated indoor pools. For the heartiest souls, there were two outdoor pools, filled with seawater and heated to 80°F, for a quick dip followed by an invigorating dash into the sauna.

Inside there was a continuous round of fashion shows, films, and lectures available to anyone who wanted to attend. Of course, the bars and casinos were open twenty-four hours a day. A variety of restaurants offered to satisfy guests' culinary cravings at any hour—in addition to the six regularly scheduled repasts.

Services available included a doctor, hairdresser, masseuse, babysitter, secretary, shoe repairer, dry cleaner, launderer, manicurist and seamstress. One could have a facial, a leg waxing, a pedicure, or a palm reading. Everything anyone could want in the way of personal pleasure was available on the *Annanovna*.

Arabella and Nicholas approached the Trocadero, one of the three first-class dining rooms on board. Arabella put her hand out and stopped Nicholas from pushing open the etched, frosted-glass door. She said, "I've never experienced anything like this. It's as if I'm on the first vacation of my life."

He bent forward and quickly kissed her on the cheek, saying "Well, aren't you?"

She hesitated a moment, then said, "Well, maybe I am, Nicholas. I've had access to a great many wonderful things in my life, but I've never stopped to enjoy them before. It's a very reckless feeling I've got!"

Nicholas pushed the door open into a light, bright Art Deco world of honey-color polished wood, silver and pink mirrored columns, period sculpture, and paintings, decorative designs, and architecture. The dining room was large enough to hold the 220 first-class passengers in one sitting with vast spaces between the tables and palm trees to ensure privacy.

"My dear, it's the *Orient Express* goes to Casablanca!"

"Oh, it's charming!" said Arabella. "Absolutely charming."

Cole Porter music was playing as the *maître d'* greeted them and led them to their table. They were stopped several times—once by Mike Mackay, who stood up as they were about to pass his table.

"Howdy there, Miss Belle."

She said hello and introduced him to Nicholas, then Mike introduced them to the other people at his table. The Van Renders, a few tables away, nodded, and Mr. Van Renders rose out of his chair as they walked by. It was Nicholas who stopped at the table just before theirs and introduced her to Jacques and Bibi Roget, who in turn introduced them to the other three French couples at the table.

At last they were seated and a chilled bottle of Dom Perignon was opened immediately. Arabella looked out of the oversized porthole across the endless stretch of water and the vast, cold blue sky. She turned back to Nicholas, bent her head forward, and inhaled the luscious sweet scent of the yellow and pink freesias in an Art Deco bowl in the center of the table.

Two enormous menus were handed to them, and they began to study the list of culinary delights. Arabella, hidden by the menu, lowered it in order to tell Nicholas what she had decided on for lunch, but the words did not come. She was suddenly startled into silence yet again by the handsome man sitting opposite her.

His longish taffy-color hair had fallen to one side over his forehead. The glasses he wore as he studied the menu only enhanced his features. He was dressed in an Oxford gray flannel suit and a blue-and-white striped button-down shirt, with a handsome red-and-white checked silk tie. No wonder the world adored him, she thought. He was the epitome of the perfect, handsome, all-American man. He was a successful, powerful man of beauty and depth, living in the middle of a make-believe world, yet he managed to remain a man unto himself. In the way he had spoken to people on deck, in the dining room, in the way he had played with the dogs in the kennels, in the way he was with her, she could sense that he was a real person, kind and genuine.

As he looked up from his menu and smiled at her, she was jolted out of her reverie.

"I didn't mean to stare."

"Oh, were you staring?"

"Actually, I couldn't help myself. I'm so happy to be here with you. It feels so comfortable I'm amazed."

"I am glad you feel that way, because, frankly, I feel as if we've known each other a long, long time."

He reached across the table and lifted the white linen napkin etched in an Art Deco design of ecru lace, folded in the shape of a star. It revealed a small package. There were gold letters across the tan velvet box spelling out the word Joy. Arabella picked the box up in her hands, lifted the cover, and took the elegant sealed crystal bottle and held it to her nose, getting only a light whiff of the exquisite perfume. She placed the bottle back in its box, took the napkin from Nicholas, draped it across her lap, saying "How divine! What a sweet thing to do, Nicholas. Thank you."

"I told you I was courting you. Let's see: flowers, chocolates, and now perfume. Do you think I'm being too old-fashioned, too obvious?"

"No woman thinks a man she likes is too obvious," she answered, and the two of them laughed.

He said, "Let's be serious. We have some very high-level corporate decisions to make! What have you chosen for lunch?"

"Oh, I think I'll let you make a unilateral decision."

Nicholas called the waiter hovering close by and gave him their order. The wine steward appeared almost immediately. Nicholas chose a vintage Puligny-Montrachet from the Moillard vineyard and a vintage Château Palmer, a third-growth Margaux.

The order given, their glasses refilled, they relaxed and talked about the dining room and its charm. Arabella looked around at the people and said, "Nicholas, isn't it fascinating? I would love to know what made each of these people make this crossing. As a matter of fact, I'd like to know why you decided to. Why are you here all alone?"

"I'm not here alone."

Arabella felt the blood drain from her face. She recalled his silence earlier when she inquired about his family. Then she saw a mischievous twinkle in his eye.

"I'm crossing with my agent, who is my business manager and best friend, and two secretaries. One who handles my affairs exclusively and a young woman who is a temporary assistant to her for this voyage only."

"Do you always travel with your agent?"

"No, this is a special occasion."

Arabella found him hardly forthcoming but she persevered, wanting to know about his life and why he had chosen to travel by luxury ocean liner with a business associate. More to the point, where was the woman in his life? She could not believe a man like him was not married or involved. He appeared to be waiting for her to ask more questions.

"Nicholas, where is the—"

He interrupted her with "Ah, the asparagus—they look perfect."

The waiters served them; she had lost her moment. The hollandaise was excellent, the asparagus cooked to perfection.

Arabella picked the tail of one up between her fingers, dipped it in the sauce, then dangled it over her mouth before slipping it between her lips. The crunchy texture of the vegetable, coated by the rich, piquant lemony sauce, was a delight.

The Montrachet was one of her favorite wines. It was chilled and just right. Nicholas ate his asparagus, never taking his eyes off her mouth while she devoured the long thick green stalks. When she had swallowed the last one, he refilled her glass and said, "Arabella Crawford, I have never seen anyone eat asparagus in a more obscene manner. You have the greatest mouth and I have the greatest erection."

"I think I'm embarrassed," she said, with a seductive smile.

"How can the most extraordinary, interesting, beautiful, sexy woman aboard this ship be embarrassed by a compliment like that?"

"You're flattering me!"

"But I've watched other people today looking at you with admiration, with desire."

"And you are exaggerating. *I* am not the matinee idol, adored by millions, you silly thing. Are you sure you're not projecting your own image on me? I think they were looking at you."

"Arabella, we've met on the tail end of a comet. My days as an actor are over. I'm about to take on a new and different role in life. One I have wanted for a very long time. I've worked for years preparing myself for it."

She was about to ask him what he meant, but he held

up his hands and stopped her before she had a chance to utter a word.

"Not now. I'll tell you more about that later. But what about you, Arabella? I saw a dazzling performance when you landed in that helicopter on the dock at Cherbourg, but I know nothing about you. My instinct, however, tells me, you are one of the special people in this world."

They were quiet for a moment, both thinking of how to verbalize what they were feeling.

Nicholas reached across the table for Arabella's hands. "I want you to know I've never given myself to any woman as I did to you, and no woman has ever surrendered to me as you have."

"You made it easy for me. Until I was in your arms I never understood what it was to surrender to a man. You have taught me surrender is no defeat for a woman."

It was at that moment that two waiters arrived with the second course. The silver serving dishes were presented for inspection.

For Arabella it was *La Degustation d'Huitres Chaudes*— a selection of oysters poached and covered in a sauce blended from four different sauces: champagne, *l'Francy*, lobster, and green peppercorns with saffron. For Nicholas there were a dozen of the best Belons, his favorite oysters, on the half shell.

The waiters served them, then left. Arabella and Nicholas clinked their glasses together again and drank.

Nicholas said in a husky voice, "It's as if we've been waiting for each other all our lives."

They both laughed, toasted each other again, and ate their superb second course. They laughed a great deal during this, their first lunch together in the dining room. He told amusing anecdotes about his fellow actors and himself, about how disguise was unnecessary when he walked through the streets. Few people ever bothered him in public because he behaved just like any other man on the street. He told her about the wonderful experience it was to direct a film, about Hollywood in general and California as a whole.

Before the main course, they had the sublime treat of a large truffle baked in a pastry shell, which was followed by *Tournedos St. Claire*—steak charred on the outside and very rare in the middle with a light wine, mushroom, and shallot sauce—with *haricot verts* and a salad of Belgian endive.

Arabella was becoming confused by Nicholas's reluctance to reveal more than the superficial details of his life. But she was aware that she was holding back too. She'd become so accustomed to being secretive and silent about personal matters that she hardly knew where to begin. She decided to try to talk about herself and, perhaps, Nicholas would feel more open and share his history with her.

While they ate, he asked her where she had been all her life. She answered that she had been around the world many times. Arabella told him that she had usually been in boardrooms, at the bottom of a mine, or in a hotel room working on company takeovers. In her travels, though, she had glimpsed the magic of Africa, the sweetness of the South Pacific islanders, the excitement and vitality of Hong Kong, the magic of the desert.

She spoke about the loneliness of a woman on top in the world of finance, the isolation from people's honest reactions, brought on by one's position of power. All the accompanying perks—the private jets, the helicopters, yachts, cavalcades of Rolls-Royces, the servants, clothes and jewels—were, in truth, cold comfort on birthdays and holidays. And then there was that endless stream of meals one had alone in hotel suites rather than face a room of people watching a woman dine alone late at night. How everything from traveling to making love is laid out before you, made easy, convenient.

She told him of the sense of desperation one feels looking back at a car full of flunkies, men interested in who you are, what you will do, how your decisions will benefit or chop up their lives, while they smile and watch you play the tourist for ten minutes at the Acropolis, Sakkarah, or walking among the giant gods of stone on Easter Island,

and about those rare moments of peace, pure beauty, and spirituality at these same places.

Not twenty-four hours before, that had still been her world. Now, here with Nicholas on the ocean, it seemed a million years ago. For a split second while thinking about it she suddenly felt dislocated, as if she had double vision. She shook her head and it all came together again.

She was laughing at something he had said but she was laughing as well with an inner joy about herself.

"I would truly love to take you in my arms right now," said Nicholas, "because I find you absolutely delectable. But for the moment, it would be better for us to be discreet."

Discretion was something Arabella knew all about. She had, after all, practiced it constantly both in her business and personal life for the last eighteen years. Understanding it, however, did not prevent her from blurting out the question that had been twisting around in her mind.

"Is there a Mrs. Nicholas Frayne?"

She could see by the expression on his face that he was surprised by her question.

"No," he said. "There *was* a Mrs. Nicholas Frayne. We had an amicable divorce nine years ago. Is there a Mr. Crawford?"

"There is a Dr. Crawford, but he's my brother. I've never been married."

"That's so hard to believe. It amazes me that no man has been clever enough to make you his wife.

"What are *you* doing on this ship? Why have *you* chosen to take this maiden voyage? Where are you going and what have you left behind? What's waiting for you on the dock in New York, or, should I ask, *who* is waiting at the foot of the gangway on the other end of this voyage?"

Nicholas's questions were interrupted by the appearance of a curly-haired man who stopped at their table. At the same time two waiters appeared with a platter of assorted cheeses, breads, biscuits, butter and fruits of all kinds.

The curly-haired man said, "The cheese looks terrific. Smell that Camembert and just look at that *chèvre*, Nicholas!

I can also recommend the Stilton. By the way, how was lunch?"

Nicholas stood up laughing and said, as he went to shake his friend's hand, "Hello, Marvin. Been watching Julia Child again, eh?" He patted him affectionately on the shoulder and said, "Marvin Kandy, I'd like you to meet Arabella Crawford."

"How do you do, Miss Crawford?" he said, shaking her hand.

"Hello," Arabella said.

"Won't you sit down with us for cheese and coffee?" Nicholas asked graciously.

"No, please sit down, Nick. I'm going over to my table and have some lunch. I am famished. I really don't want to intrude on you."

"I don't think we should let you eat alone, do you, Arabella?"

"No, certainly not. Please join us."

Marvin was given a chair immediately, and a place was set for him. He looked at the menu briefly, made a quick choice, and placed his order with the *maître d'* who had been hovering by his shoulder.

Nicholas was telling Arabella, "Marvin is my agent. We started out in Hollywood together, didn't we, Marv?"

"Yes, we did," he answered.

"The only difference was when we started out, Marv started at the top and I began at the bottom. His father was vice president of Cougar Films. His grandfather owned the largest block of voting shares in the two greatest studios when Hollywood was in its heyday. His mother was a chorus girl in the line for Busby Berkeley, and his brother is an actor."

"You forgot to mention that my Aunt Sarah has been an extra at Cougar Studios for forty-six years," added Marvin.

The two men laughed.

"I think I should explain," said Nicholas. "Sarah Pinsky, otherwise known in the family as the 'extra,' is Marv's father's eldest sister. She's the richest one in the family, owning enormous blocks of stock in several movie companies. She's never been on the board of directors, has no decision-making power in the companies, yet she's more Hollywood than Hollywood. She knows and loves the movie business more than all of them put together.

"Having been born rich and in the business, she was determined to start from the bottom and make her way up to the top as an actress without the influence of her family. She fell for the old Hollywood image of the face in the crowd or the girl on the Schwab's drugstore stool being discovered and made into a star."

Marvin continued the story. "Sarah has not one fraction of ability as an actress, and I am not being unkind. It's a fact. Over forty years ago she registered as an extra with our father's studio and she's been driven there in a chauffeured car at least twice a week, checking in for work, ever since. Sarah Pinsky is a legend in the business. I'm sure you've seen her time and time again in crowd scenes, costume dramas, walk-on parts. She's the only extra important enough to be thrown off sets for interference in production."

"Who knows? Hollywood is so crazy, she may very well have her day yet," added Nicholas.

"You're the real, original Hollywood baby then, Mr. Kandy?"

"I certainly am. Don't call me Mr. Kandy, please. Nicholas calls me Marv. My wife calls me Marvin, although she hates the name. My friends call me Sweets, and the guys in the business call me Kandy. I answer to all of them."

"What would you like me to call you?"

Marvin turned and looked at Nicholas, then he turned back and looked at Arabella and said, "I think you had better call me Marv.

"I just came up in the elevator from A Deck," he continued. "Two women got in on the promenade deck. They were upset because one of the women had left her glasses in this dining room. The other one told her that she wouldn't have forgotten them if she hadn't been so busy watching that couple at lunch. And then they tittered on about how *he* looked like Jay Gatsby, and *she* could have been the heroine of *Tender Is the Night. They* could have been Zelda and Scott Fitzgerald. Anyhow, I had a hunch I'd find my Nick here, but I'm delighted to meet you, Arabella."

"My pleasure," she said, smiling.

Marvin told Nicholas that he'd found out Cotille was on board and had asked her to lunch. She was unable to do so but agreed to meet him later. Arabella was amused by the banter between Marvin and Nicholas. Their friendship was obviously deep, their affection for each other touching. She liked Marvin and everything about him. Arabella Crawford had risen to the top of the financial and business worlds by intuition and by judging people correctly. She saw Marvin as honest, honorable, quick-witted, intelligent; a good, kind, caring human being. There was a sexiness about him as well.

The two men kept Arabella amused with jokes and anecdotes until she pleaded with them to stop. They had convinced her that Los Angeles was now a must on her list of places to visit. Their descriptions of the high times and low life that existed simultaneously in "the business" offered a fascinating inside glimpse into a world which thrived on portraying mindless perfection. Every once in a while, it seemed that quality accidentally crept onto the scene and when it did, anything could happen. They spoke about Ingrid Bergman, Jane Fonda, and Nicholas Frayne. Suddenly Nicholas realized it was getting late. He apologized to Marv for leaving him to finish his meal alone but said that he needed to walk, get some fresh air, and have a few telexes sent before noon time in New York.

Marv said, "Please do go ahead, but there are just a few things I'd like to talk over with you. It'll only take a minute." He looked at his watch then went on. "I've got to telex our broker by four o'clock, our time.

"Do you mind, Arabella, some boring money talk? I know how women hate to hear men talking business."

Nicholas grinned at her and, turning full toward her so Marvin could not see, gave her a big stage wink.

Arabella tried to stifle her laugh and nodded yes, like a docile little girl, saying "Please don't worry about me. I'll just powder my nose."

She reached into the bone color Hermès alligator handbag hanging from a heavy gold-linked chain hooked over the arm of her chair. She pulled out a Fabergé powder box of gold inlaid with stripes of rose-cut diamonds. The clasp was a circle of Cabuchon sapphires with a large oval diamond in the center.

Marvin continued, "Nick, I've had a telex advising us to sell our stock in Abcore, Telecone, Diamine, and Execair and put it all into Hero Ashimo and Great Britannia. The word out is that there has been an enormous merger, that Hero Ashimo and Great Britannia are the new parent companies and their stock will double its present value within a year."

Arabella was, in fact, still powdering her nose as she said, "Eighteen months; sixteen at the earliest. Sell all the Abcore and Telecone. Hold all you have of Diamine. Sell half your Execair."

Marvin looked at Nick and then they both looked at Arabella. She still had her compact held up in front of her eyes, the powder puff at work on her nose. She closed her eyes for a second, opened them, and put the puff back on its jewel-encrusted box.

Nicholas leaned back in his chair, and folded his arms across his chest, never taking his eyes off Arabella. This was a woman to reckon with. This woman was his equal. It thrilled him and frightened him all at once.

With his eyes still riveted to hers, he said, "Marv, how does that sound to you?"

Marv looked first at Arabella, hardly believing what he had heard, then he looked at Nicholas. "It's a smart move," he said. "But I don't know. I'd have to make some phone calls."

"Never mind the phone calls. Do what Arabella says."

"Wait a minute, Nick. Do you know how much money we're talking about?"

"No, but just do what Arabella says."

"We're talking about three quarters of a million dollars." Marv turned to Arabella. "How do you know that's the way to handle the stocks, Arabella?"

Biting her lip, she broke her gaze away from Nicholas's eyes and said, in a sure, calm, cool business voice, "Selling the Abcore and the Telecone is a perfect move. In four days Diamine will announce the discovery of an enormous diamond strike in one of their mines. Their stock is undervalued now and no further stock will be issued. The stones mined from that strike are under analysis right now. The preliminary reports are that they are perfect—blue-whites, extremely large, all over thirty carats each.

"Execair has a small stock issue. It's about to receive a massive injection of capital backed up by the announcement of a new jet contract from the United States Government, irrevocable for five years."

Arabella picked up her handbag and put the compact away. Marvin was speechless. Nicholas was awestruck. Neither of them knew quite what to say to her.

Marvin turned to Nicholas and said, in a subdued voice his friend had never heard before, "Nick, you say go, I say we go."

"Well, that's it then, Marv," said Nicholas. He stood up, walked around to Arabella's chair, and took her by the hand.

She stood up, slightly embarassed, and said, "It was a lovely lunch. Your stories about L.A. are wonderful. It was nice to meet you, Marv."

Marv stood up, picked up her hand and kissed it. He said, "You are quite a lady, Arabella Crawford. I wish I had found you first."

Nicholas and Arabella walked from the dining room and he said, "You never did answer how you knew to make those moves with the stocks."

"No, I never did, did I."

They walked a bit farther in silence and then Arabella said, "Oh, I hope that wasn't a blunder, advising you about stocks. You see, I'm still in transition from being a woman in power to a woman at play. In the 'old world' it would have been just as natural for me to order those moves. You see, it was, after all, my work. I blurted out the right moves for Marvin to make because it's a habit of taking over and directing, built up over many years. I suppose it was natural. You don't shake off a habit overnight. I'm no longer interested in stocks, bonds, and conglomerates. It was an automatic reflex of having to make a quick decision, do the right thing at the right moment, of having to win, having to succeed. It's hard to believe that the 'having to' for me is over, but that's why I acted that way. How I knew the information about those specific stocks is another matter. Nicholas, when the right time comes, I'll tell you more about it, okay?"

"Of course it's okay, Arabella. Listen, you don't have to tell me anything. We have a lifetime to talk to each other."

He slipped his arm through hers, held her hand, and squeezed it as they walked on.

It's too soon to tell him, she thought. I knew what to do because those were my companies, which I sold yesterday. I wonder how he'll react when he finds out I've just pulled off the largest sell-off any businesswoman has ever made and that, as of yesterday, I'm one of the richest women in the world? How am I going to feel about shedding the old skin and getting into a new one? I wonder if a fantasy can ever be lived out and be as satisfying as the dream!

Arabella's mind wandered as they walked arm in arm through the shopping arcade on the promenade deck while they waited for a steward to bring a coat from Arabella's stateroom. They were doing what Arabella called "serious window shopping," barely saying a word to each other, looking at the extravagant array of clothing and jewels, crystal and china. Suddenly she wondered whether Nicholas was spoiled, a handsome but spoiled film star who expected her to fall at his feet, body and soul, babbling about her life story. Perhaps he was too egotistical to care or too proud to ask questions; he would learn what he wanted by not asking but creating a silence between them.

They were looking in a window at exquisite handmade lingerie, but all she was seeing was his reflection in the glass. There was no getting away from it. She was madly attracted to him. The man had sexual charisma and beauty—a lethal combination for a woman. Was it any wonder that women spoiled and adored him?

He turned from the window to face her and said, "When next you come to me in the night you need not bother with any of these enticing bits and pieces. Come to me naked, natural under your coat."

"Oh," she said—a very haughty "oh"—"you seem very sure that I'm going to come to you in the night. Do all your women?"

"Yes, mostly. I don't usually have to chase after the women I'm interested in."

"Oh, are you chasing after me?"

"Courting, that's what I'm doing with you—courting you. I told you that." He smiled down at her.

"Why do I get the feeling that you're laughing at me, Nicholas?"

"Because I am. You're angry with yourself because you gave away something about yourself that you would rather not have."

Arabella started to defend herself, but Nicholas kept going. "Now, simmer down. I won't ask you anything. You and I will tell each other whatever we like when and if we want to, voluntarily. Nothing has changed. I've known from the very first moment I set eyes on you that you are an extraordinary woman. Beautiful and full of life." He bent close to her ear and whispered, "And very, very sexy. Don't be anxious and try to look for a wedge to put between us. Relax, give us a chance!"

Thoughts were racing through her mind. Was this some old movie he was replaying? Was it true emotion? Was he more ready for this than she was? Why did she feel so out of control?

"Arabella, right now we're exploring each other through lust, passion, and sensuality. We are finding love, I know it. I'm not so sure you do. In bed I recognized in us a touch of the animal—a hint of the bestial—as well as the human and more spiritual. All the things inherent in every man and woman. If we can give ourselves to each other like that, the talking will come in time. Right now, does it matter what we do or don't tell each other?"

Arabella was so relieved at his frankness she hardly realized that he had seduced her yet again. This time, merely with words, he had managed to arouse her sexually. A flash of desire to break through into the very heart, the core of Nicholas Frayne, tore through her.

She smiled at him. It was a sensual, seductive smile and he squeezed her arm, letting her know that he was grateful that they were together. Arabella regained her self-control and said, "I've never been courted quite like this before, Nicholas. You're full of surprises. What comes next?"

"Ah, I believe a not-too-serious piece of jewelry comes next, a simple token of my admiration. Let's see what Cartier has to offer."

They walked across the arcade to the window, passing Monsieur Gerard and Boucheron. He said, "Don't even bother to look. This is courtship and in the early stages. Those windows are very serious business, not to mention money."

She laughed, and at that moment the steward arrived with her sable coat.

"What luck!" Nicholas said. "Saved by the coat! Too bad, you lose and we go up for our stroll in the fresh air."

He teased her as he helped her on with the coat by saying "How sad for you. I was quite prepared to buy you anything you liked if we had the time, but you know how busy life can get on a cruise!" He propelled her by the elbow, down the glittering shopping arcade.

"This is unbelievable," he said. "It is a mini-version of the Avenue Montaigne, Rodeo Drive, Bond Street, Fifth Avenue, and the Via Veneto all rolled into one."

The small boutiques were indeed all there—Van Cleef & Arpels, Cartier, Boucheron, Bulgari, Gucci, St. Laurent,

Chloe, Dior, Givenchy, Halston, Armani, Mary McFadden, Calvin Klein, Ralph Lauren, Elizabeth Arden with its red door, Germaine Monteil—all directly opposite the ship's cinema.

Like everything else on the *Tatanya Annanovna*, the shopping arcade and the indoor balcony in front of the theater had a unique charm and atmosphere. It was busy with some passengers having cocktails before going in to see a film. Others were shopping, window gazing. Arabella and Nicholas blended in, just another component of the atmosphere. Though involved with themselves, they were fascinated by their fellow travelers who assembled in this part of the ship from all three classes. It was here they would see and mingle with a real cross section of the ship's passengers.

Nicholas said, "The atmosphere reminds me of strolling up Fifth Avenue on Easter Sunday, only without the hats. Everyone looking at everyone else, pleasant to everyone else. Strangers meeting and greeting who would never do so elsewhere."

He bent his head to hers and spoke in a low voice so that the passing parade would not hear him. "It feels as if I'm Fred Astaire and you're Ann Miller. You should have your four sleek, elegant dogs on golden leashes, and this is Fifth Avenue where we're out for a stroll after church. The music swells and I begin to sing, 'In your Easter bonnet, with all the frills upon it, et cetera, et cetera. The most beautiful girl in the Easter Parade.' Cut, it's a wrap."

Arabella could not help laughing and neither could he. She wanted to throw her arms around him for being so adorable, for having a smile that embraced the onlooker, created dimples, and appeared to be hooked up to the twinkle in his eyes.

Still laughing at his little sing-song, she said, "Nicholas Frayne, you sure must have been in front of the door when God went by passing out favors! You're only just barely saved by your nose!"

"My nose?"

"Yes, your nose. Just when I think you must be the most handsome, perfect movie star in the world, your, shall I say 'substantial' masculine nose, a bit askew there to the left, looks like an intelligent nose and it reminds me that you are a man with a purpose, not just a pretty face."

"Well, I should hope I'm not," he retorted, feigning hurt—or *was* it feigning? she wondered.

They reached the pair of doors to the outside. He pushed and they were pulled open by two stewards dressed in white yachtsman caps, with black patent-leather visors and the insignia of the *Tatanya Annanovna* emblazoned on the front. They were dressed in thick knitted white wool turtleneck sweaters and dark-brown wool trousers with turned-up cuffs, razor-sharp pleats; white shoes finished off the outfit. Their clothes were reminiscent of what the well-dressed steward on board the tsar's yacht might have worn.

One of the men tipped his cap and announced the temperature, then offered Arabella a heavy beige silk scarf piped in brown and royal blue, saying "Excuse me, madame, may I hold your hat and offer you a scarf? The wind has turned sharp."

The other steward offered Nicholas a cap. Arabella left her hat but they declined the replacement, saying thank you but they were out there for the nip in the air. However, they did have a pair of deck chairs set up.

They walked around the deck, the wind playing havoc with Arabella's hair. The gold and silver strands flew up and danced to the wind's tune. She loved the sensuous feeling.

They were passed by a pair of joggers in blue tracksuits. Arabella and Nicholas looked at each other, said nothing, but picked up the undeclared challenge, the pace and beat, and jogged behind the couple for twenty yards. Arabella was the first to give up. Winded, she leaned against the wooden rail and stared down into the heavy dark-blue waves as the ship cut through them. Nicholas felt her absence and jogged back to her. Standing beside her at the polished rail, he kept the beat and pace up while staying on the spot, tousled her hair, and teased, "Not your scene, jogging?"

"No, not my scene."

He stopped, reached out, and touched the tip of her nose with his finger. "I can't wait to find out what else you can't do." He went on. "Come on, let's go and sit down in what's left of the sun."

There were about twenty people lying on their deck chairs forming an arc against the wall. Arabella and Nicholas were tucked up among the other passengers. They looked at each other, then up at the sun. They closed their eyes, luxuriating in its warmth. After a few minutes, Arabella sighed heavily. The kind of sigh that comes with pleasure, deep, relaxed pleasure. She said softly, "Nicholas?"

He answered, "Mmmm?"

"I want to tell you something."

"Mmmm?"

"I've missed a great deal in life. A great many simple things. Things that many people take for granted. Like sitting in the winter sun with nothing on my mind. Like jogging. Like long, luxurious vacations. Like taking a boat instead of a plane. Like being close to nature, people, beauty. Now I'm going to learn the names of flowers; know one bird from another; watch the stars and learn their patterns in the sky. I'm going to spend endless hours swimming with the fish, cultivating a garden, learning to bake bread, enjoying poetry, maybe even playing the piano or watching a ball game—oh yes, burn up time playing games."

"Didn't you do any of those things when you were growing up?"

"Oh, I don't want you to think I had a deprived childhood or bad parents. Quite the contrary, I've been lucky enough to have had extraordinary parents and a wonderful relationship with both of them."

"Your mother must be wonderful, extraordinary, and beautiful. I can't imagine her being anything else," said Nicholas, reaching between the two deck chairs and taking Arabella's hand.

"Yes, she is. Her name is Raine."

They turned away from the setting sun. Arabella, feeling relaxed and lazy, looked at the handsome Nicholas and thought how very much Raine would like him. She wondered what her father, W.R., would have thought about him.

She said, "I was blessed, I think, to have had a very intelligent father and a mother, just as you guessed, beautiful, intelligent, and courageous. In fact, both of them were."

Arabella thought about her parents for a moment. It had been years since she had wanted to tell anyone about her background or since anyone had asked. In the business world, no one cared where you'd been. They only wanted to know where you were going.

"I'd like to tell you their story," she said.

"I'd like to hear it," said Nicholas.

Chapter Ten

Arabella began.

"My father, William Rothberg Crawford, known to everyone as W.R. Crawford, was fifty-nine years old when I was born. He was a political columnist in Washington, and his best friend was the President of the United States—"

Nicholas interrupted. "W.R. Crawford—America's finest political journalist of the thirties and forties? Franklin Roosevelt's lifelong friend? Arabella, it's unbelievable!"

Arabella nodded and said, "Let me tell you about him.

"W.R. was born in 1882, the same year as his best friend, Franklin Delano Roosevelt. At that time America was an entirely white, Anglo-Saxon Protestant nation with a huge melting pot of minorities, called, usually disdainfully, the 'ethnics.' This group included the Irish, Italians, Jews, Catholics in general, Spanish-speaking peoples, Orientals, and millions of blacks in the South. But until 1935, America was a WASP country in all significant respects. A country of WASP history, culture, economy, with only a small percentage of the economy controlled by Jewish Americans.

"W.R.'s family was part of that small percentage. He was a third-generation American Jew who took on the WASP protective coloration because of his family's material wealth and success. The Rothbergs had always been included in the one percent that went to Groton, the ten percent allowed at Harvard. They were the almost-WASPs.

"It was at W.R.'s father's suggestion that he changed his surname from Rothberg to Crawford. The intelligent shrewd Daniel Rothberg understood that in the WASP world they lived in there was little room for a political journalist called Rothberg.

"He chose Crawford for his son, saying, 'If you are a Jew, Willie, you are a Jew. If you are a political columnist and a Jew, you had better have a WASP name—not to hide who or what you are but to ease the pain the public will feel having to accept your work.'

"That was quite a piece of advice to come from D.R. Crawford was the maiden name of his wife, William's mother, my grandmother: a magnificent Protestant beauty who embraced the Jewish faith before she and Daniel were married. She was long dead by the time W.R. took her name, and he was proud to have it, knowing full well how happy it would have made her.

"The Rothberg family had the wealth of the Warburgs or the Goulds, but unlike those Jewish millionaires, the Rothbergs had made their fortune through commerce, not banking.

"They were Jewish settlers who saw the potential in what America needed, went in and satisfied the market, investing their hard-earned profits in railroads, timber, coal and oil.

"They had their forty-room summerhouses in the Berkshires—Massachusetts—next to the WASP robber barons of the time. There was the town house on Fifth Avenue near the Vanderbilts and estates in Virginia and stables in Kentucky.

"Going back three generations, they had participated in their country, were part of the American dream and history they so fervently loved and supported, believing wholly in its future, democracy, and especially the Democratic Party.

"My father and F.D.R. first met as youngsters at Groton in Connecticut, then the finest prep school in the country. My father spent many weekends at Hyde Park, a place he truly loved, with its breathtaking views of the Hudson Valley, the gardens and stables.

"Their friendship was sealed forever when they became close at Harvard. Franklin became editor of the prestigious school paper, the *Harvard Crimson*, and wrote about what he knew best—social amenities, football scores, and school spirit. He brought his friend Bill on board to be 'the *real* reporter.' And W.R. Crawford loved it. They had a healthy respect and admiration for each other. Those years were the foundation for the deep friendship and loyalty that remained with them all their lives.

"After graduating, W.R. broke away from the two opportunities ready and waiting for him in business or law. He felt that there were enough competent people to handle the family's financial empire and that there were enough lawyers, judges, and professors from the Rothberg clan at leading universities.

"Bitten by the taste for journalism, with a love for his country like his father and grandfather before him and his best friend, F.D.R., intrigued by political events, the thought of spreading the word to the people through writing captivated him.

"Roosevelt and my father often laughed together because they were both called a traitor to their class. Despite his twelve ancestors who came over on the *Mayflower*, Roosevelt was sometimes a thorn in the side of his very own WASP society. He claimed the government was responsible for every American's financial security and went on to change his country, giving tens of millions their rightful share.

"As for W.R., his own people labeled him a turncoat, more WASP than Jew, and a snob for mingling with the men of political clout like Roosevelt. He became a famous and familiar figure in the background of American politics and international affairs. He was said to have had more political understanding than most, and his syndicated column was respected and read by millions.

"Anyhow, on one of his fact-finding missions to Singapore, this handsome, well-known bachelor met and fell in love with a twenty-five-year-old English beauty named Raine Russell. She was the daughter of the retired Surgeon-General in the Far East for His Majesty King George VI, Lord Richard Charles Winkfield Russell. My maternal grandfather was one of those Englishmen who earned his title by becoming an important figure in one of His Majesty's Far East outposts. Although I'm told he was a fine doctor and scientist, I know for sure that he was handsome, charming, and dedicated—with Raine's mother, Lady Caroline—to the machinations and proceedings of the upper echelon of English society in the Far East.

"Lord Richard and Lady Caroline were the Beautiful People of the twenties and thirties. Their only child, Raine, my mother, was brought up in a home along the lines of those migratory British stationed in the Far East. The constant voyage back and forth to England regularly made the P&O Steamship Company as much a part of their lives as England and Singapore.

"However, until adolescence, Raine was spared the P&O trips and remained in Singapore with her father and an endless stream of Chinese and Malaysian servants, nannies, and Lord Richard's Eurasian mistresses who magically disappeared on Lady Caroline's return from home leave.

"It was a childhood of contradictions, of formal English gardens and lush jungle, ponies and tigers, restriction and freedom, until Raine was shipped off to boarding school in England. She only just tolerated her time in those schools in Gloucestershire and Oxfordshire, but she adored the times she had with her mother.

"Beautiful, blond, and lithe, Caroline, so elegant and amusing, pampered her daughter with beautiful clothes, all too brief holidays in Paris, Nice, and Monte Carlo. She shared her many friends—male and female—with her daughter, several becoming foster uncles and aunts. Raine was brought up loved and adored by her parents. She always had the best of both worlds laid out in front of her—the Far East and the civilized, elegant West.

"When Raine's parents were together, they were a powerful presence in the English society of Singapore, and in time all Singapore knew that if they wanted to cut through bureaucracy to accomplish something, their best hope was Lord Richard Russell. Respected by Eastern potentates and English authorities alike, there was little denied the dashing doctor and his vivacious wife.

"So you can imagine it came as a great blow to all

Singapore as well as Lord Richard and Raine when Caroline died of a heart attack at the Ritz in Paris. Richard never married again—not his English society ladies nor his exotic mistresses. After his retirement, he remained in Singapore working on tropical diseases. He became one of the most prominent men in that area of medical research. He established hospitals and services, research centers for tropical diseases and medicines. Once she had qualified as a doctor herself, Raine returned to Singapore to work with him.

"The life and manners in Malaya in 1941 for Raine and all other well-placed British was not all work. Far from it. It was an elegant, happy social affair with the dance floor at Raffles filled with beautiful people. It was a life of good manners, many servants, handsome lovers, gin slings, rattan furniture, and home leave.

"Raine Russell was one of Singapore's darlings. Her beauty and elegance was talked about constantly. W.R. and Raine's was a simple story at the beginning. They met and fell in love. Raine filled his heart as no other woman ever had. He was fifty-eight years old and she was twenty-five. He had much more to offer than the other men in Raine's life. With his big, handsome good looks, his powerful connections, his maturity, and intelligence, he had no difficult task in sweeping her admirers away. They married less than a month after they met, at the White House, with only her father, Eleanor, Franklin, and W.R.'s publisher as witnesses.

"Those were tough and busy days for the President and for America, trying to stay out of the Second World War. W.R. and Raine understood how important it was for them to stay close to Roosevelt during those difficult times and so they honeymooned at the Crawford House on the banks of the Potomac, not far from him.

"Six weeks after their wedding, Raine discovered she was pregnant. The couple then separated, as Raine had to go back to Singapore to tie up her affairs and train colleagues to take over her work and housekeepers and assistants to keep her father's life ticking smoothly.

"They met several times over the next few months, when

W.R. paid quick visits to see her. He was much relieved when Raine arrived home for good to have her baby.

"Those days before my birth were probably the happiest of their lives. Raine went into labor, and, like everything else in Raine's life so far, my birth was easy. W.R. insisted on being there and, having watched the miracle of birth, was even more in love with his young, beautiful wife than ever. Only one thing marred their joy: I was born on December 7, while the bombs from the Japanese imperial forces were falling on Pearl Harbor. On December 8 the Japanese Imperial Army began their invasion of the northeastern coast of the Malay Peninsula. Twenty-four hours later the first bombs fell on Singapore.

"It was a double tragedy for my parents—both their countries were at war. Both countries were unprepared. Both of them were desperately needed by their countries. Their personal joy was immediately put aside.

"For W.R., it was a desperate, depressing time because he had a hollow victory. He had, for four months, been advising Franklin of facts that should not have been ignored. He had advised him and his cabinet of moves that should have been made and had not been.

"For Raine, there was no way out. She insisted on returning to Singapore to help her father move the research hospital up into the hills where it would be safe. She felt duty-bound to save a lifetime of his work.

"Assured by the highest British military personnel and reinforced by conversations between Churchill and Roosevelt that Singapore was impregnable, my parents parted once again. My mother promised to return to her infant and husband in a month's time. I was only three months old when Raine flew out to Singapore. I was nearly four years old when my mother was released from a Japanese prisoner-of-war camp on the island of Sumatra."

Arabella paused and shifted in her chair. Nicholas remained silent, totally absorbed in Arabella's story, not wanting to interrupt or distract her.

"W.R. had been a man of many love affairs and mistresses

and had waited a lifetime to fall deeply in love. He was determined that no Japanese or missing wife was going to destroy that love. He was singularly bullheaded, patient, realistic, bold, and decisive. Having been given the gift of a beautiful daughter in the waning years of his life, there was no way that he would allow her to be separated from him.

"You see, he couldn't bear the house on the Potomac without Raine, and since he had to be in Washington, he moved my Malaysian nurse, Yap, his chauffeur, and the both of us into a six-room suite on the top floor of the Mayflower Hotel in Washington. W.R. was determined to spend every possible moment as both mother and father to me until Raine returned home. Never once did he think she would not, in spite of the fact that the last word he had from her for three and a half years was a cable sent on February 10, 1942. The cable said:

Invaders five miles from Singapore stop Evacuation fleet of forty-four ships in harbor stop Will be on one of them stop Letter arriving diplomatic pouch soon stop Pray will be together again stop Love you my darlings   Raine.

"A week later a letter arrived through the diplomatic bag of the Australian Embassy." Arabella could visualize it scribbled in a soft lead pencil on scraps of different papers. She could quote it from memory. It read:

"My Darlings,

"It is February 12, 1942. I could never imagine such hell. Still do not understand it. We are so unprepared. Father refuses to leave, is settled upcountry in a make-shift hospital.

"As soon as I finish this letter, I will make for the docks. All of the city seems to be shrinking behind me, pushing us into the harbor. There is no going back; our men are blowing up the city behind us. Until yesterday the government was still assuring us the tide would turn, that Singapore would not fall. Oh, my darling, I believed them in spite of the city swollen with refugees, the relentless bombing, and the arrival of the retreating servicemen, wounded and dying.

"Spoiled child that I am, I closed my eyes to this schizophrenic city and believed it was all going to work out somehow because I bought silk stockings yesterday, lunched at the swim club, and watched a bombardment off in the distance. Because there were dances to attend every night and even some at teatime. Because I worked fourteen hours a day at the hospital yet still dined on sumptuous food at elegant private dinner parties and because it is not done, to run away.

"My beautiful Singapore is finished. We are without gas or electricity in most parts of the city. The city is covered with a cloud of smoke, and the stench from decaying bodies and burning buildings is mixed with the strange perfume of millions of dollars collected from the banks being burned in the streets.

"The mass of women and children moving toward the docks is half drunk with the fumes of gin and whiskey filling the fetid air. Thousands and thousands of bottles were smashed against buildings, pounded against pavements, in the hope of keeping the Japanese from drunken rape and murderous orgies.

"This is an evacuation ordered by the authorities, but too late. Not too late to save us, the women and children, but too late to save my dying city and so many good and brave men who will now be left behind.

"I must go. There is room for all of us. I will be safe. I must be safe to come back to you and Arabella. I will try for the ship *Vynner Brooke*, but that means nothing. The chaos is unbelievable and I will board wherever the launch takes me. I love you. Forgive me for leaving. I will come home as soon as I can. I kiss you,

Raine.

"By the time the letter arrived, W.R. knew the evacuation fleet had limped out of Singapore harbor on February 13, 1942, in the early hours of the morning, ships bursting with women and children. Only a fraction survived sinking or capture. My father was devastated by the news, and never forgave Churchill or the English for the tragedy of Singapore.

"I hope this isn't all boring you, Nicholas? I seem to be droning on with my life story."

"Boring me? Absolutely not. I'm fascinated. Go on. I don't want you to leave anything out."

"My first five years were filled with love and affection from my devoted father, care and loving from my nanny, being watched over and coddled by the chauffeur, and loved and cherished by some of the most powerful men in the world. I was their little stray, W.R.'s little burden. Men like Harry Hopkins took time to bring me candy. Franklin doted on me. Eleanor, my godmother, made an effort at birthday parties and rides in the country. I wailed and cried at the sight of Winston Churchill, who tried bribing me with a painting set. I played with the buttons of General George C. Marshall's jacket, learned to add and subtract with Bernard Baruch, who always gave me a dime when he saw me, instructing me to 'Buy a lollipop with two cents, Arabella, and put the rest in the bank. Think that way and you will always be a rich woman.'

"What little girl could ever forget all the times she was allowed to cuddle the most famous dog in the world, Fala, in her arms, to sit on F.D.R.'s knee? He had a weakness for his best friend's little girl and I loved him the most after Daddy. I was the little girl who asked General MacArthur to please bring her mummy home.

"My father's friends, all the famous public men and their

neglected wives who gave me so much love and affection when I needed it, will always have a place in my heart. They were, after all, my beginnings.

"I remember I was only three years old when the first great loss came that I understood. It was the death of my beloved F.D.R. The first sorrow I had ever seen was that of my father for his best friend, his president. I recall being dressed in a yellow hat and coat, black patent-leather shoes, and white stockings. I rode on the train bearing the body of my adored Mr. President from Washington to Hyde Park. I watched the thousands of people lining the tracks as the black-draped funeral procession rolled on its way. I walked, holding my father's hand, to F.D.R.'s last resting place in the Rose Garden. It was the saddest day of my life, but I did not shed one tear because my daddy had said Mr. Pres was going away and would not come back, but he would send my mummy home soon to replace him.

"I also remember that on August 14, 1945, the Japanese agreed to an unconditional surrender and the formal ceremony took place on September 2, 1945.

"During the last days of August my mother was found in the worst of all the Japanese war camps for women, Loebok Linggau, on the island of Sumatra.

"I heard that Raine was lying on a stretcher, looking out of the aircraft's window as they flew low over Singapore. She wept uncontrollably when she saw the vast Allied armada in the sun on the sparkling water. She felt the first strength and security she had known since she faced the evacuation fleet in Singapore in 1942.

"Five days later I spoke to my mother for the first time.

"Raine was dying of starvation and suffering from a particularly ferocious type of malaria. She was carried into the hospital in Singapore a skeleton of sixty-one pounds covered with scabies. She remained there, W.R. at her side, until she was well enough to be flown to the United States.

"During the two years Raine was in the hospital, she eased herself into my life through telephone calls, letters, and tape recordings. When we finally met, the care, love, and preparation had been well worthwhile. The reunion was far less traumatic for all concerned.

"Her health restored, her beauty revived, Raine was at last with me in time to celebrate my sixth birthday.

"F.D.R. was gone, the war over. W.R. retired to a life of making us happy, writing political essays, and remaining close to his old friends in the government.

"We lived at the Mayflower in the middle of Washington, close to the White House. It was a first-class transient hotel. A great, old-fashioned place, a Democratic stronghold for visiting VIPs of the party from all over the States. Several senators and congressman kept rooms there. The hotel maintained a certain conservative glamour in remembrance of Roosevelt inaugural parties held there—and later the Kennedys' comings and goings—and took pride in serving the powerful Republican visitors who were occasionally invited to the walnut-paneled dining room.

"It was the 'Who's Who in the Government' hotel and instilled an atmosphere of solid party and family unity, government solidarity. I was brought up there; the only baby ever reared there! The Mayflower and all its staff and elegant public rooms were my home.

"There was, however, the rare visit to the house on the Potomac. I longed to live there, play in the gardens, walk along the river with my playmates. It grew to be a symbol of something I yearned for, missed with all my little heart. I dreamed of living in a house with my mummy and daddy, just like my school chums did, having a swing in the yard, girlfriends to stay the night. I wanted to be just like all the other children I knew. But I wasn't.

"My parents held nothing back from me. When I questioned them about why we were living at the Mayflower and the differences between my life and my friends', they always answered me. They openly explained how Raine had been away, stranded with strangers, not nice strangers, and how she had been ill for a long time. How Raine had lost her father forever like I had lost F.D.R. They told it all as honestly and simply as one could to a six-year-old without the horror or gruesome details of Raine's incarceration. They promised that one day, when Raine was tired of the hotel and wanted to take on more responsibility, we would all move back to the Crawford house.

"Living at the Mayflower was one of Raine's eccentricities. She was unable to live in the house on the Potomac. She felt fearful of leaving all the strangers who lived together in the hotel. She had been too long and gone through too much in the camp with strangers and felt that to leave the hotel was to abandon them once again as she had done when they were released from the camp in 1945.

"As I grew older, I was able to accept the fact that occasionally my mother did peculiar things. While dining in restaurants, it wasn't unusual for Raine to sneak a potato, a few green beans, a chunk of bread from her plate and slip them into her handbag in full view of everyone at the table, without ever realizing what she had done. This was a throwback from days of starvation in the Japanese prison camp.

"On rare occasions she could be seen trying to coax people sitting alone on the fringes of the lobby in the Mayflower to move into the center of the room. Once she had accomplished her task, she would say something like 'It's safer here; we are safer in a group,' and then go about her business.

"The one thing that disturbed her family most, filled us with heartbreaking pity for her, was when we were out walking in the streets or in the countryside. Something would click inside her head and she could not stop; she felt compelled to keep walking. It was virtually impossible to stop her and the farther she walked, the more depressed and panicky she became. In time we learned how to control that awful throwback to the forced marches she had endured on Sumatra, which she had survived when more than half died en route.

"Because our family was so strong, it was easy for the three of us to sit down and work out any problems that entered our lives. That was how we all learned to understand and accept Raine's sometimes erratic, strange behavior.

"We lived at the Mayflower Hotel for years, expanding the rooms to fit the family's needs. I was ten years old when, to many people's astonishment, my baby brother, Robert Franklin, was born.

"My mother's fear of being isolated from the group as she had been during her many months of solitary confinement, along with most of the other fears, finally subsided after Robert was born, and we moved home at last when he was one year old.

"The house on the Potomac was a magnificent white clapboard colonial affair, large and rambling, set on six acres of lovely old gardens with luscious green grass banks undulating down to the river's edge. My parents filled it with guests, glamorous dinner parties, laughter, fascinating and interesting people who all understood and made light of Raine's sudden disappearances in the midst of a party, from the dinner table, or even during the middle of a tennis match.

"Strangely enough, she forgave the Japanese, but insisted on appearing as a witness at the Japanese War Crimes Trials in Tokyo. Not for what horrors and degradations, torture and inhumane acts they had inflicted on the unfortunate, innocent women and children; there were hundreds of others to give evidence about that. Nor was it as a witness to the merciless death by disease and starvation of a third of all the women prisoners who were buried in shallow unmarked graves. The jungle rapidly grew over the graves so that they were lost forever.

"My mother went to Tokyo to tell how they had bombed the evacuation fleet; how the survivors had struggled through the burning sea in whatever they could find to float on; how after the ordeal of surviving that, they had landed on a deserted beach to eventually give themselves up to the enemy. How the soldiers had separated the Australian nurses from the group and marched them to the water's edge. In the hot sun, the brave women had stood on the white, white sand, with a clear bright-blue sky above. They had been marched backward in silence, except for the sound of the waves breaking against their legs and the occasional shouted order from the Japanese officers. They had been machine-gunned down from a clump of jungle where their murderers were hidden and left rolling in and out of the waves with the tide. Their blood had turned the water deep pink.

"She was marvelous, and we were very proud of her courage. But during the years that followed, definitely by the time I went to college, we all began to realize Raine was spending more and more time cultivating her garden. I suppose you'd say it became an obsession. It was a 'safe' thing to do, but it wasn't normal. Yet, it was so beautiful! It boasted the most luxuriant, exquisite herbaceous bor-ders—a wild English garden filled with everything from hollyhocks to lilies, poppies to little English primroses. There was a rhododendron garden, a water-lily garden with ponds, a 'jungle' garden with orchards. Raine lost herself in them and the pavilion W.R. had built for her in one of the more secluded tropical gardens.

"W.R. was an old man by then, though still handsome and active. Robert was a lovely brother and a wonderful son, extraordinarily close to Raine. I was more like my father with my mother's looks. I passed through the awk-ward stage between girlhood and womanhood swiftly. I was said to be beautiful, with a rich, passionate sort of beauty that swelled the hearts of women and aroused the hearts of men. I was rather highly sexed, like my father, free and uncomplicated about it. I had my first lover when I was sixteen—a naval attaché of thirty, my father's friend's son. He was a handsome, kind young man who watched me and wanted me for two years. When he finally took me, he was gentle, sweet, loving, and kind. A perfect introduction to sex. I felt quite comfortable and passionate in my love-making but was actually not promiscuous.

"I had a flair for money and mathematics. I was quick, understanding the bottom line of things, the core, the so-lution, at once. I was encouraged by my family and teachers to challenge myself with remedying failing projects, small businesses and investments of my friends, turning them around into successful enterprises for them. By the time I was twenty-one, I felt I had nowhere to go but up!

"I came into a small trust fund from W.R., who by that time had begun to turn his affairs over to his attorneys and his children, making it clear that everything was to be kept in trust for Raine, that we children were to see that she never lacked for anything after he was gone.

"It was a wise and clever W.R. who sent his children into the world when we were twenty-one with a firm foundation to build on. He wanted us to be independent and live our lives without feeling responsible for Raine and himself. Raine's eccentricities had multiplied with the years.

"It was a sunny Sunday in June, teatime in the rose garden that rambled down to the water's edge. The air was heavy with the scent from two acres of forty-one different varieties of rose—full blown, rich in their colors, beautiful in their shapes, endearing in their romanticism.

"We always called this Raine's week of the roses. Robert and I always returned home for that week. There were lunches and tea parties on the lawn. Guests drifted in and out. There was even a formal summer Ball of the Roses, when a dance floor was laid on the grass and lanterns were strung across the lawns. The rosebeds were lit from below as well as from above.

"Raine was dressed in a white sheer cotton dress, tight at the waist with a full, soft skirt that rippled in the warm breeze. It was a gift from me, one of the St. Laurent collection of romantic summer dresses. She wore a large, once-elegant straw hat that was tied under her chin with a cord of blue silk. Robert and I were walking on either side of her close to the bank of the river, in worn blue jeans and white shirts. All three of us were barefoot.

"I said, 'When I come home next time I must bring you a new hat. I saw some lovely ones in Paris. I should have thought about it.'

"'Oh, don't do that dear,' said Raine. 'Your father loves this one. He says it makes me look like a faded Vivien

Leigh in an updated version of *Gone with the Wind* when I wear it in the rose garden.'

"Just then we heard W.R. call. We turned and saw him sitting in the Chinese pavilion in the middle of the rose garden. The silver tea service sparkled in the light. He waved and we waved back. Then he called us to join him for tea.

"We wandered slowly back toward him through the rose beds. Suddenly Raine called out 'Oh, no, W.R.!' touched her hand to her head, and slumped against Robert. In seconds she had herself under control and, with tears streaming down her face, she said, 'Hurry! Your father is dying!' Robert rushed to Father's side. Raine and I followed as quickly as we could. W.R. was dead.

"Robert and I were fearful about how our mother would take his death. We need not have been. She was remarkable. She sat us down and said, 'Your father and I never intended you to be distressed at my being left alone now that he is gone. I have always felt since I survived the detention camps that I have been living on borrowed time. I have had more, more than I ever dreamed I would have in my life. Every day your father and I were together was a bonus. Every moment of shared love with him was like a miracle. That was the lesson I learned from being a prisoner in Loebok Linggau. Only your father's body has gone. He will be with me always. Nothing will change for me. I will live my life out here with him by my side the best way I can.'

"After father's death, my brother and I often talked about our parent's love affair, wondering if we ourselves would ever be lucky enough to have such an experience. We were young then, but we recognized that theirs was a very special relationship.

"It was Robert who said that he supposed that if we didn't, then the love affair we had as a family was at least a fair compensation. I had to agree with him.

"W.R. had been dying of cancer for six months. He did not tell Raine or us because he felt that he could not bear to inflict one more agonizing death on his adored wife's life. He swallowed one lethal tablet at teatime on that Sunday afternoon in the garden because he knew the secret could not be kept from her much longer. The roses were blooming, the family was happy and together. It seemed the right time to leave us. That was what he wrote in his letter.

"Robert and I feel that our father died as we had always known him—a courageous, responsible, honorable gentleman, deeply in love with his wife and children.

"Well," said Arabella, "now you know from what stock I come! I've told you more about myself then I've ever told anyone. I didn't intend to go on at such length. I've held it all inside for so long."

Nicholas replied, "I knew you were extraordinary but I could never guess that you were part of the two men I most admire—your father and F.D.R. I'm speechless!"

They smiled at each other, then closed their eyes and relaxed in the dying rays of the sun.

Later Nicholas touched Arabella lightly on the shoulder. "The sun's setting now," he said, as he helped her out of her chair.

They walked away from their fellow passengers to the rail and looked down into the waves. Nicholas turned his back to the ocean, leaned against the rail, and looked at Arabella.

"I love the sound of the ocean," he said, "the way it calls out as it laps against the ship and sings a watery refrain while being sliced through by the prow of the ship. I have a wonderful schooner. She is worse than a mistress, demanding to be cared for and loved, used all the time. I do love her and I think you would like her too. She's called *Marigold*."

Arabella imagined a sleek, elegant schooner in full sail against the wind, Nicholas at the helm. She had a jolt as she realized she had included herself in the picture, standing next to him, an indication of how much she wanted to be with him.

They moved toward the door to the bar on the observation

deck. Sensing that Nicholas seemed preoccupied, Arabella smiled at him and said, "Nicholas, if you have things to do, don't worry about me. I'm quite happy."

She saw the look of surprise come into his face and, to her slight annoyance, a touch of relief close behind.

"It's been a lovely day from the moment I woke up and found you next to me," he said, in what seemed an almost too-smooth manner, as if the spell of the moment had been broken.

Suddenly Arabella suffered that dreadful sinking feeling most women experience at some time in their lives when the man they want seems inexplicably distant. There is that terrifying split second when you feel him drift away, making you want to call out and say, "Don't leave me." Then all the traditional female conditioning compounds the agony by requiring silence, because, in most cases, if you let a man know you are suffering from fear of loss, you are sure to lose him. Funny, thought Arabella, it's never like that when the circumstances are reversed. It's still unfair and lopsided, the man-and-woman game of love. She pulled herself out of that lurching, downward emotional spiral and smiled to herself, thinking how fortunate she was having learned how to think of herself as an equal with men—in business and in love. All thanks to Anthony Quartermaine.

Nicholas said, "I'll call you soon."

"Yes, soon," she repeated, all the while thinking, Why do they do it? How many women get hung up, are made to wait by the telephone because some man has left them dangling with that "I'll call you soon"? Have they any idea how cruel it is and, if they did, would they stop? Arabella doubted it.

Nicholas could tell by the tone of her voice that Arabella was annoyed with him. Yet it was that same something, proud and sure, that attracted him to her, in addition to her beauty and sexuality. He felt a twinge in his loins thinking of the night before when he had broken through that pride, beauty, and confidence.

For a moment he had the notion to change his mind, his

plans, bend forward and whisper, "Come on downstairs. I have a tremendous yen to make love to you." He wanted to reach out and touch her, but instead he gave her the charming Nicholas Frayne smile and said, "I'm sorry about dinner tonight, but I have plans I can't change. I'm having a working supper with Marvin. I'll tell you more about it tomorrow."

"Tomorrow?"

"Yes. How about some skeet-shooting tomorrow before lunch? Will you join me?"

"Yes, I'd like to."

She turned back to the ocean. He moved closer to her and said softly, "I won't kiss you good-bye—it seems so public here. Don't you sense all the eyes in the bar are fixed on us?" Automatically they inched away from one another, remembering that they were, indeed, not alone.

"Yes, I think you're right." Arabella looked at the windows of the Observatory Bar. There was a glow from within that increased as the night grew darker around them.

"If you want to come to me later, Arabella, you have my key." He brushed her cheek quickly with his fingertips and was gone.

She listened to his footsteps as he walked away, astonished that he assumed she would go to him a second time. She had actually forgotten to return the key to him, but now she made up her mind that she would not use it. If he wanted her, he would have to come after her, make the moves.

To resist any temptation, Arabella pulled her hand out of her pocket, stretched her arm straight out over the ship's rail, opened her fist and, smiling to herself smugly, said, "I *had* your key," as it dropped into the ocean far below.

There was just a twinge of regret and then she remembered one of W.R.'s most famous lines: "Empty gestures are full of vanity, selfishness, and ego."

She began to laugh at herself, an ability that she considered one of her greatest assets. Pulling the lapels of luscious fur up around her neck, she hurried inside.

Chapter Eleven

Nicholas Frayne stood in the doorway between the sitting room and dining room of Marvin Kandy's suite. He listened to the tap-tap-tapping of rapid typing and watched the two secretaries, Wendy Sears and Margaret Nettleworth, their fingers flying, working over the revised press release and personal letters.

The intricately carved antique dining table was piled high with neat stacks of Nicholas Frayne's letterhead, boxes of envelopes, and printed invitations. Several posters were rolled up and secured by rubber bands. One large poster was stretched out flat and held down at four corners by a box of paper clips, a Scotch tape dispenser, a bottle of Perrier, and a dictionary.

Marvin finished reading the typed sheet of paper in his hand. Smiling, he looked up at Nicholas and walked past the two women working at the table. He patted each of them lightly on the shoulder, saying "Terrific. Just perfect. These are the last pages to be typed, aren't they?"

"Yes," said Mrs. Nettleworth.

Marvin had a broad smile across his face, the sort of smile that comes with deep satisfaction for a job well done, a certain knowledge that you are right, on a winning ticket. He put a hand on Nicholas's shoulder, looked up, and said, "I figure about fifteen minutes. That's all, Nick, just fifteen minutes to proofread the last page."

"Right," Nicholas said and looked over Marvin's shoulder at Mrs. Nettleworth. "Margaret, you must be exhausted. You and Wendy have both been wonderful."

The two women looked up from their typewriters. These

few appreciative words and the famous Nicholas Frayne smile were like a shot of adrenaline for them.

Mrs. Nettleworth said, "Not exhausted, Mr. Frayne, just a bit overworked, but well worth it. I've often worked this hard before, but never have I been 'forced' to take a cruise to do it!"

They all laughed at that and then she continued. "The press announcement is marked for 'immediate release,' so the telex ought to be sent before the New York newspapers close."

Mrs. Nettleworth picked up a folder and said, "This is the personal statement explaining why you are leaving films and going into politics and the evolution of that decision. It's edited now. Would you like to look through it?"

"Yes, I think that's a good idea." Nicholas sat in a large wing chair, put his glasses on, and read the statement he'd begun drafting in his mind years ago. He let his hands fall into his lap as he considered for the thousandth time how different life would be—and now it was all going to happen in a very short time. And what would Arabella think! One day she'd been courted by a movie star, the next day a gubernatorial candidate. One day he was an unattached bachelor, the next day . . .

Marvin interrupted his thoughts. "What do you say, Nick—let's the four of us have our dinner here in my dining room to finalize all the details before the news media hits us."

"That's fine, Marv, fine."

Marvin ordered a delicious meal for them. The two women continued their work and the two men left for a quick drink together in the Vanya Bar.

As they were walking down the long corridor, Marvin, burning with enthusiasm and eagerness to begin what was a new life for him as well, said, "Nick, it's a terrific press release, and in less than an hour's time we'll have telexed our news around the world. We begin a new era together, and I feel great about it!"

"So do I. It has been a long time coming, Marv, and I'm very glad you are with me."

"There are many, many people with you. Although I hate losing you as an actor and director, I sure as hell am going to like working for you as Governor."

"Thanks, Marv. It helps a great deal to know you're always there."

"You know, that Wendy's been just great. And of course Mrs. Nettleworth keeps us all going. They've both been real troopers. As a matter of fact, let's go down to that floating Rodeo Drive and see if we can't find a surprise for them. I wouldn't mind buying them each an expensive bottle of perfume or something. Just a little gesture to show how much we appreciate their work."

"I should have thought of that. Of course let's go."

The perfumery was still open. The two men stood among the crystal bottles and jars, boxes of soaps, dusting powder, and exquisite perfumes, while the salesgirl wrapped up Marvin's selections.

He said to Nicholas, "I wish you weren't so set against that poster—the one you rejected with the emphatic no. That poster could get you a million votes."

"I won't have it, Marv, and that's final. It's too Hollywood, too movie-starish. Granted, it says it all, but it's too flip an image. It's too slick. It has too much of a playboy look to it, an image I never really had as an actor and I certainly don't want now!"

"You're wrong, Nick. You're oversensitive about winning politically on your good looks. No one is hanging a label of playboy on you. The serious part of your character is well established. The whole world knows you've spent a lifetime committing yourself to things that could easily have ruined your career—like your antiwar protests, your conservation efforts, your support of ERA and gay rights. You may be a handsome profile on a poster, but the public will relate to the Nicholas Frayne they know—the actor *and* the supporter of ideals and ideas.

"The public thinks of you as a socially significant actor,

like Brando, Redford, Fonda. No, I'll tell you—you're wrong, Nick. The more handsome the poster, the more they'll see the man behind it. Don't be a schmuck, Nick. Look at the Kennedys. They understood that it was no sin to be a good-looking politician."

"Oh, I don't know, Marv. You may be right. But I just feel this is no time to be the least flippant about my intentions."

"Well, I think you're overreacting. You've always been taken seriously, in everything you've ever done. Why should they see you any differently now? Look, you'll feel much better after the first press conference on the dock in New York and we've heard what the papers have to say. Forget about the posters for now. We can hold off until then."

"Good idea. Let me think about it."

Nicholas picked up a bottle of Armani perfume, unscrewed the top, and took a whiff. He listened as Marvin went on. "I just have to say, Nick, you've got to get over this thing you've got about photography in general. This poster can wait, but not forever! And really, it's such a great shot!—standing with one foot up on the rail, bending forward and throwing your hat into the ring."

The essence of Armani flooded Nicholas's senses and he momentarily forgot about the press release, the poster, and the campaign to put him in the Governor's mansion in his home state, Rhode Island. The fruity, floral aroma of jasmine, Bulgarian roses, cassis, basil, coriander, and musk reminded him of Arabella. She was indeed like flowers and fruit, spices and sexual secretions all blended together. Natural yet exotic, a vision coming from the earth and ripened by the sun and the moon.

He passed the tester under his nose again, then held it under Marvin's nose and said, "How about this for a fragrance? Mmmm. I wonder how Arabella would like to bathe in this."

"Well, why don't you find out? It's a terrific idea!"

Nicholas purchased two giant-sized bottles. He had one

sent to Arabella's stateroom and the other to his, a note attached to each.

Then the two men left for a drink at the bar. From there they went to the communications office to deliver the press release tucked away in Marvin's breast pocket. The communications office on board the *Tatanya Annanovna* was an average-sized room with several telephones, telex machines, and telegraph operators. The center contained the most sophisticated equipment available, enabling the ship to communicate instantly, twenty-four hours a day, with any place in the world without delay. Linked to satellites and computers, it offered better telephone, telex, and cable facilities than the average small city in Europe. Gone were the days of having to link by ship-to-shore radio in order to receive or make a call.

Nicholas and Marvin were standing in the communications room with the purser and the communications officer. An assistant was telexing the press release to Reuters news service and several specific top reporters on newspapers across the States. Nicholas wondered why in God's name he hadn't taken the time when they were up on deck that afternoon to tell Arabella of this enormous change in his life.

Why wasn't she there next to him when he telexed his news to the world? That afternoon their relationship had seemed all too new to him and holding back seemed natural. Was he mad? Here he was, only hours later, and her not being there felt *unnatural*. Well, it wouldn't happen again, he thought. We'll have a lifetime together and there'll be just as many important moments like this for us to share.

Marvin Kandy was not considered to be one of Hollywood's top three agents for nothing. His devotion to his clients and interest in their welfare combined with an innate ability to do the right thing at the right moment was common knowledge. As the message began feeding itself irretrievably around the world, a waiter arrived with champagne glasses and a jeroboam of Dom Perignon 1967.

The communications officer began reading aloud from the printout:

"'This evening, on board the S.S. *Tatanya Annanovna*, somewhere at sea, Mr. Nicholas Frayne announced his candidacy for the Governorship of the State of Rhode Island, his home state. After considering at great length the choice between his work as an actor and director, bringing entertainment to a vast public and a political career, he has made the decision to run. Mr. Frayne is retiring from the acting profession in the hope of representing the people of his state in their rights for good government. It is with heartfelt thanks to the public around the world who have supported him as an actor and director that he leaves them. Mr. Frayne hopes that the people of his state will support him, not as an actor now, but as a representative of their wishes so that he may fight for a better life, a better homeland, and a better world....'"

The small group broke into spontaneous applause. The communications officer continued, breaking off only briefly to say, "Congratulations and good luck, sir."

As usual, with precision timing, Marvin let the cork on the champagne fly.

The party in the purser's office became excited when the communications officer completed his telex and the machine immediately began tapping out a message from Reuters:

REFERENCE YOUR TELEX SIGNED NICHOLAS FRAYNE. PLEASE CONFIRM: IS MR. NICHOLAS FRAYNE ABOARD? WILL HE GIVE A PERSONAL STATEMENT OR INTERVIEW OVER THE TELEX?

"Here we go," said Marvin, as he drained his glass and held it up to be refilled. Then he began dictating the reply to the communications officer:

"'Nicholas Frayne on board. Marvin Kandy, his former agent, will act as campaign manager for the moment. All questions or interviews will be handled

by him until the ship docks in New York. Mr. Kandy
is available to the press through this telex wkib 39876
on board the S.S. *Tatanya Annanovna*.

"'Mr. Frayne will hold a press conference upon
his arrival in New York in three days. Any further
telex replies required will be handled by Mr. Marvin
Kandy or Mrs. Margaret Nettleworth, his personal
secretary. Thank you. Marvin Kandy.'"

The ship's purser and his assistant were obviously thrilled
to be present at such an event and asked if they might post
a copy of the press release on the purser's announcement
board. It was Marvin who tapped on the desk for attention and emotionally gave the toast that no one else dared
to.

He said, "I should like to propose a toast to a good friend
and brilliant mind, a caring human being, Mr. Nicholas
Frayne, the next Governor of the State of Rhode Island,
and a future President of the United States."

There was a split second of silence, almost reverent,
broken by "Hear, hear," from the assembled company.

"Well, it's all out now," said a very happy, smiling
Nicholas.

The four campaign comrades reunited in the dining room
of Marvin's Yalta suite and had a delicious dinner of pâté,
saddle of lamb with tiny peas and potatoes, and a Grand
Marnier mousse served to them while they talked politics
and planned the next moves to be made. During the meal,
Marvin slipped a sealed envelope to Nicholas. "Take this
with you to read later," he said. "I know you'll find it
significant."

At a little past midnight Mrs. Nettleworth excused herself, took her package of perfume—Balenciaga's Le Dix—
kissed Nicholas and Marvin on the cheek, thanked Wendy
Sears for being so conscientious and good in her work, and
left.

Nicholas thought Arabella must surely be waiting for
him, wondering where he was.

When he entered the room, the curtains had been drawn and a light had been turned on. The huge package from the perfumery was sitting unwrapped on the coffee table. He called for Arabella; no answer. He went into his bedroom. The bed had been turned down but she was not in it and, it seemed, had not been. He was suddenly distressed and overcome with feelings of anxiety. What if she would see the announcement before he had an opportunity to speak with her? Would she feel betrayed? He knew he had to see her now.

He picked up the telephone and called her cabin. The telephone rang and rang. He hung up and went to the small pantry and poured himself a cup of coffee, walked back to the drawing room and sat down, wondering where she might be, why she had not come. He untied the parcel meant for her, broke the seal on the Armani, and passed the stopper under his nose. The mixed aromas of the coffee and perfume aroused his senses and his thoughts turned sexual.

Nicholas finished his coffee and went searching for Arabella. Not finding her in the ship's public rooms, he began looking outside on the various decks—even going to the spot where he had left her that afternoon. She wasn't there either. He hoped she was not with another man.

It was past two in the morning as he continued looking for her on the lighted decks. There was an eerie vastness, an unending emptiness as the ship seemed to meld with the night. The Vanya Bar was nearly deserted, the library silent. The only signs of life were the few sailors going about their duites like sleepwalkers on a ghost ship, the muffled sounds of people finishing off their evenings in their rooms, or the occasional couple strolling arm in arm through the long, softly lit corridors to a cabin. From behind a glass door on deck Nicholas watched a ship's officer slip his hands beneath the fur coat of a beautiful young woman. There was something sensual, isolated, and raunchy about the deserted ship that made Nicholas feel not only sexy but a particular combination of romantic and depraved.

He thought it might have something to do with atmospheric contrasts—the rough, stormy weather building up outside while he was cocooned in the warmth, safety, and luxury of the quiet ship. Most of the passengers were secluded in their cabins now. Nicholas liked the pounding of the waves against the ship as it thrust forward, the sound of the wind slapping against the portholes. The soft overhead lighting down the long, empty passageways was exciting to him, knowing that the ship teemed with life behind closed doors.

Couples coupling in seclusion were isolated from the outside world and cushioned in comfort against the mighty caprices of nature and the elements. Yet there was danger too because of the fragility of the comfort and security as they were floating on the seemingly bottomless ocean, totally dependent on the whims of the winds and the tides.

Nicholas's imagination played games with him of wild, thrilling sex acted out between partners, odd sexual combinations, lust and some pain. Aggression, submission, exquisite desires and release and with it all, always lots of love and affection.

Where was she? Where could she be? Why had she not come to him?

In the card room he found several poker-playing men in dinner jackets, dress shirts undone and black silk ties dangling like ribbons round their necks while they chomped on expensive Corona cigars. A sleepy-eyed barman and two stewards stood silent and tired against one of the oak-paneled walls.

The other bars were closed. He even tried second class, on the lower deck, but she was nowhere to be found. He was on his way down to third class when suddenly it struck him—of course, the casino! She had to be in the casino.

He turned and, rushing through the corridor, he bumped into Cotille, who was looking for Marvin's cabin.

She said, "It's all right, Nicholas. I called and asked him if I could come to him. But I'm lost."

Nicholas put her in the right direction and thought to himself, poor Cotille, she certainly is lost. I hope Marvin can set her straight. He watched her scurry down the hall and he remembered what a perfect beauty she once was. Then he hurried to the casino.

He saw Arabella the very first moment he entered. She was sitting at the roulette table. The light from the silk-covered shade hanging over the center of the table fell over her like a soft, amber spotlight. Mike Mackay, the Texan, was sitting on her left. A handsome gigolo, Weston War-field, was on her right with Missy, Arabella's secretary, next to him. Xu stood squarely behind Arabella's chair.

Nicholas recognized a French couple he knew playing opposite her. The rest of the table was occupied by several Arab sheikhs, and a few well-dressed beauties standing behind them. There was a woman, an octogenarian, dressed in black lace with a diamond choker and ropes of pearls. Her fine white hair was swept high on her head framing what was left of a once-beautiful face, now ravaged by time. In her bony, wrinkled, liver-spotted hand, she held a long, slender cigarette holder; her diamonds sparkled.

The croupier called, *"Vingt-cinq, rouge,"* and raked in the chips, paying out thousand-dollar chips to the elegant elderly woman and one of the Arab sheikhs. The second croupier, who was sitting on a high chair overseeing the table, climbed down and called, "Place your bets, please, ladies and gentlemen, place your bets." Then he changed place with the working croupier.

The casino on the *Tatanya Annanovna* was reminiscent of the casino at Monte Carlo on a smaller scale, but it was no less luxurious. Ships in international waters are allowed gambling, and on this ship there were no slot machines— only baccarat, roulette, and similar high-stakes, high-risk games. At this time of the night all the small bettors had departed, along with the losers and those who feared losing. The tension was high as fortunes were gained or lost by the real high rollers.

Nicholas slipped into the casino without being noticed and stood in the shadows, drinking her in. She looked delectable, ravishing. He wanted to eat her up, mouthful by mouthful, swallow her whole.

He had to smile. There was something about Arabella that always made him want to smile—the type of smile that rises right from the toes and goes all through the body and leaves you infused with joy. That was the way he had felt when he first saw her step out of the helicopter, when they made love, and now, when she had forced him to come after her, to the casino, it was the same thing. Was it because she had the world by the tail and shook it the way she wanted to and didn't know it? Or was it that she had the world by its tail and knew it? He wondered. He reached in his breast pocket and took out one of his cigars, clipped the end off, and lighted it while standing in the shadows of the room. He admitted to himself that he was more than infatuated. Perhaps he was in love with Arabella Crawford.

Arabella had just picked up one of her ten-thousand-dollar chips from the stack in front of her when she saw the flash of a flame in the shadows across the room. His face was lighted as he puffed and turned the cigar slowly, lighting it evenly. Her heart skipped a beat. He had come for her, after all.

The croupier called out, "Ladies and gentlemen, place your bets, please. Place your bets."

Mike Mackay put eighty-seven thousand dollars on the red six. He turned to Arabella and said, "Ah knew you were a gambler, Belle. Come on, let's see what stuff you're made of now! Ya not gonna hold back now, gal, are ya?"

"Ah sure am," mimicked Arabella.

"Ah'm on to you, gal. I been watchin' your play. You always hold back a portion of your winnings and your original stake. But you're a heavy winner; tonight, go with your luck gal. Let's see you gamble."

Other bets were placed—some heavy, very heavy, some not so dramatic, and some meager but still acceptable.

Arabella listened to Mike while discreetly watching Nicholas walk slowly around the shadowy room toward the roulette table. Until his arrival she had been enjoying the gambling. But the fun of the table slipped away because now she could only think of him and how much she wanted him.

The action at the table was quick, electric, and exciting. Arabella was still in it but part of her wasn't. She looked across the room and saw him talking to a man and woman. He was laughing. Then he turned and their eyes met. She felt herself inadvertently stop breathing. The way he looked at her made her feel aroused, so feminine, and longing to feel him inside her. She contracted her vaginal muscles, drew in her breath, and thought about what coming had felt like with him that morning. He broke their gaze to say good-bye to the couple and then continued walking toward her.

Arabella made up her mind she was for the red six, the same as Mike Mackay. It had not come up and should have long before now. It was time. Mike had made a good choice; she was sure it was the red six to win.

Arabella pulled out twenty-five thousand dollars' worth of chips, her original stake for the evening, and put it to one side. She took off all but ten percent of her winnings and added that to it, having never forgotten her gambling skill that had helped make her a millionaire. Then she placed the remaining forty thousand dollars' worth of chips on the red six.

Arabella heard Mike Mackay say, "Now you're talking, gal. I tell you that number is ours for sure. This is no time to hold back. I wish Marcia could be here to see this. She'll be sorry she retired early when she hears about this action."

She felt a firm hand on her shoulder and for a split second closed her eyes, ecstatic from his mere touch. He squeezed lightly; she felt her nipples grow erect and she blushed but did not turn around. He bent down and whispered in her ear, "You've won. He's right. This is no time to hold back."

She turned around and looked into his face. He smiled at her and said, "Let's go all the way. Throw caution to the wind. I promise you, you'll never be sorry. We cannot lose."

Was he implying more or making a promise? Was he being obscure, or did he detect her slight hesitation or moment of vulnerability? She waivered briefly but then turned her attention from him back to the game.

"Hi there, Nicholas!" said Mike, putting out his hand. The two men shook hands. "How about a bet, boy? Last chance for tonight."

"No, Mike. I'm going to leave this to Arabella."

Arabella turned back to the table. She watched as the croupier bent forward, ready to spin the wheel. Very quickly she put all the rest of her chips on the red six, then turned and smiled broadly at Mike and Nicholas. Looking lovingly into Nicholas's eyes, she said, "This is the first time I've ever gambled everything on one number."

She stood up and watched as the wheel continued to spin. Nicholas, standing behind her, attempted to put his hands on her waist but could not quite make it because Xu was solidly in the way. Arabella turned to her handsome Chinese bodyguard and said, "Xu, this is Mr. Nicholas Frayne. It's all right. He is a friend."

Nicholas said, "How do you do, Xu?"

"Mr. Frayne," Xu replied and dutifully stepped back to one side.

Nicholas moved up behind Arabella, both hands on her waist now, and pulled her back against him, pressing her body against his erection. He couldn't keep his hands off her. Her looks were delectable, the moment so exciting. He wished the room were darker and he had the courage to discreetly lift her dress and take her right there where they were standing. He imagined his throbbing erect cock moving in and out of her sweet warmth and wetness as she came, while they continued to watch the wheel spin and the little white ball bounce along.

Everyone seemed to stop breathing. The room was silent with anticipation. There was more money at stake on this one game than many people would see in a lifetime.

The wheel slowed down. Mike Mackay stood up and the ball popped right into fate's slot—the red six. Mike banged his hand on the table, grabbed hold of Arabella, and gave her a hug.

Arabella looked over the big Texan's shoulder and smiled at Nicholas, saying softly "It's thrilling taking the high jump with you. Just look at all those lovely chips!"

Nicholas kissed two of his fingers and pressed them to her lips. "Fantastic, Arabella. You're the big winner. How much, do you reckon?"

"Oh, somewhere about two hundred thousand dollars," she said, smiling, feeling very proud of herself.

"Ah told you, gal, you're a gambler!" said Mike. "Nicholas—or can I call you Nick?"

"Yes, fine, Mike."

"Nick, she's fantastic! What did ah tell Marcia? Ah told Marcia she was a clever girl, a gamblin' woman. Remember gal, except for makin' whoopee there's nothin' better than winnin'. I only won half of what she did—about one hundred thousand—and ah'm real happy 'bout that."

Nicholas put his arm around Arabella's waist and pulled her toward him. He smiled at her and said, "Happy? You do like winning, don't you?"

"Who doesn't?" she said. "Yes, I'm happy."

Weston Warfield did not look happy. But Mike Mackay ordered champagne for everyone.

The losers were not really unhappy. They had the essential quality so necessary in a gambler—they knew how to be good losers. And they all believed they would be winners tomorrow night. Bottles were opened, champagne poured, toasts were made. It never really became a party; it disintegrated before it even began. The excitement of the spinning wheel was gone, the gamblers were tired, the evening was over.

Nicholas stood at the end of the bar, talking to Xu and Missy. Arabella had been swept away from him by Weston Warfield to a table where Mike Mackay was sitting with a French couple, drinking Dom Perignon.

Nicholas recognized the none too subtle play Warfield was making for Arabella and was amused as he thought, Poor bastard, he hasn't got a chance.

Pete Peters, the purser, joined the three of them at the

bar. He was clearly flirting with Missy, who didn't seem to mind a bit. Nicholas also knew this was no hour for mere socializing. This was the time for love and sex. He considered going directly to Arabella and whisking her away from the lusting Warfield, but that was not his style. He also did not want to force Arabella to expose any of her private life in front of that dolt. Was he feeling a tad jealous? Causing embarrassment was not the Frayne way of doing things. Instead he called a waiter over, and asked for a pencil and paper to write a note. The message read, "My room or yours?"

He watched the waiter whisper something in Arabella's ear, then pass her the note. The waiter returned to Nicholas and discreetly handed him the folded piece of paper. Inside was a key. She had scribbled "Mine." He looked across the room at her as he slipped the key into his pocket and began to smile. Their eyes met and she smiled back at him, then quickly looked away to the people at her table.

A few minutes later Nicholas said good night to Xu, Missy and Pete. He walked over to the table where Arabella was sitting and said good night to everyone. As he was thanking Mike Mackay, the big Texan stood up and put his arm around Nicholas. They spoke for a few minutes while walking through the casino, then shook hands, and Nicholas was gone.

Nicholas took the key from his pocket and let himself into Arabella's suite. The lamps were on, and although the room was not in disarray it had the appearance of activity going on. He walked through the room to the sofa and noticed that the coffee table on which they had lunched the day before was now stacked high with books. The flowers he had sent were there and still filling the room with their sweet scent. He noticed that the large bottle of Armani had not been opened. It had been placed squarely in the center of the console near one of the sofas.

He touched it as he went by, then slipped out of his shoes, placing them neatly against the wall, out of the way, then removed his jacket and his tie and draped them over a chair. He undid the top buttons of his shirt and sat down on the sofa, next to a stack of portfolios and more books. He put his glasses on and began looking through them.

There were books on travel, maps, books on typography, photographs of a ranch, magnificent estates in France and America. Books on architecture and several folders marked "Real Estate." He picked them up—California, Florida, Rhode Island, Massachusetts, Nevada, Barbados, Fiji. He put them down again and looked at another stack of books: *The Joy of Cooking*; *The Settlement Cookbook*; Elizabeth David; *Real Bread*; *Mastering the Art of French Cooking*; *The Constance Spry Cookbook*; *Cuisine Minceur* and *Cuisine Gourmande* by Michel Guerard.

He picked up some papers in a folder marked "Special Recipes From Friends" and looked through. Absentmindedly he held them in one hand, reading with fascination while with the other hand he peeled off his socks, leaving them on the floor. He pulled one knee up to his chin and rested his bare foot on the sofa and continued reading.

There were hand-written recipes from some of the greatest French chefs—Paul Bocuse, Jean and Pierre Troisgros, Madame Point (with a personal letter attached), Alain Chapel, with a photograph of him and Arabella together in his kitchen. There was a color photograph of the most perfect-looking soufflé. On a large yellow pad, he saw her writing for the first time. He knew at once that it had to be hers. He read: "How to: bake bread; the perfect soufflé; the perfect omelette; duck in sauce of oranges and peaches; *creme brulée*." The list went on and on.

She had done it again, and she was not even there. She had made him smile. He tried to put the the pieces together, assemble a story that would fit the magnificent, beautiful woman he had fallen in love with.

He glanced at his jacket slung over a chair and saw the white envelope peeping out of the inside pocket. He could have easily found out something. All he had to do was open the envelope Marv had given him earlier that evening— answers to some inquiries Marv had made as to how Arabella Crawford could have such inside information on the stocks he had been interested in. The answers had come through on the telex machine and Marv had said, "Okay, Nick. Do you want to hear it from me or from her?"

He had answered, "From her," and Marv had sealed the envelope and handed it to him, saying, "I won't spoil it for you, then. All I will say is that she is an original," and he slapped Nicholas on the back.

No, he thought. I'll wait, but I'll know more about Arabella before this day is out.

He went back to his investigations and thought, So she's a cook, plays with ten-thousand-dollar chips, and only gambles ten percent of her winnings? A cook? A gambler? How many chefs fly helicopters, are rich enough to be blasé about a $200,000 win, and are as beautiful and well built as a goddess? She did it again, only now he began to laugh out loud about Arabella Crawford.

He chose another pile of books on the table. Shakespeare and Yeats. Ah, he thought, things are looking up. T.S. Eliot, Marcel Proust, and Cavafy were mixed up with *The Gardener's World*, *The Great Gardens of England*, Shelley, Graham Greene, Camus, and *How to Breed Carp*. How to breed carp?

On the far side of the room piled up on the seat of a large club chair was yet another stack of books. He picked them up and sat down in the easy chair. Bending forward, he placed them on the carpet and went through them. *Are You a Poker Player?* She sure is, he said to himself. Then there were several books on bridge for beginners, a paperback entitled *How to Be Significantly Social—Play Card Games. The Basics of Gin Rummy.* Well, he thought, she's no card sharp and obviously doesn't know how to play games—card games anyway....

On a table next to the chair was a large lamp with a white silk shade. He switched it on and admired a handsome blue-and-white bowl of the Han Dynasty. Next to it there was a small pedestal dish of the white chocolates he had given her the day before. He put one of the Belgian delicacies into his mouth. It was wonderful. More books in a small pile faced him. He read down the list of the spines: Iris Murdoch, Bruce Chatwin's *In Patagonia*, Patrick White's *Fringe of Leaves*, a book of Jorge Luis Borges. What a bizarre combination it all was!

The key he had left in the lock of Arabella's door turned. He glanced at his watch. He had been waiting for her just over forty minutes and thought she had not exactly rushed. The door swung open and he heard her say as she backed into the room, "Thank you very much, Weston. Good night."

The door was nearly closed when it was pushed open again. He heard her say, "No, Weston, certainly not. Good night."

She quickly closed the door and double-locked it. She swung around, and they both said hello at the same time as she went toward him. She dropped her silver handbag down on chair.

"No," she said. "Please don't get up. You look comfortable in my library."

Nicholas said, "That's a very strange library you're traveling with."

"Oh, do you think so? Well, you might as well know that that library there is only a fraction of the things I don't know about and want to learn. You have no idea how ignorant I am. I did tell you this afternoon that I've missed a great deal in life."

"Oh," he said, "then you don't want to go into the real estate business or open a restaurant or plant a garden? Those were the things I was guessing while I waited for you."

She began to laugh and said, "Why don't you just ask me anything you want to know? Go on, ask me."

She slipped off a black maribou jacket, which had puffed sleeves and fitted tightly into the waist. Her Mary McFadden dress of silver-pleated lamé was made from a material similar to one of her antique Fortuny dresses. It had a high collar of ruffles around the neck, the long, full sleeves were gathered at the wrist by an inch of elasticized smocking, finishing the sleeve in a four-inch ruffle. The bodice clung to her and the pleats partially opened from the fullness of her breasts. From the waist the long skirt fell in three tiers to her ankles.

He watched the tips of her silver kid shoes flash as she hurried to him, making the sound of a million tiny silver bells tinkling. He loved her in silver; there was something about it that set off her eyes and her silver and blond hair. She had swept a piece of her long, silky hair off her face and pinned it in a flat, smooth spiral on top of her head with a fan-shaped diamond comb.

He said, "Well, there is something I want to tell *you*! I saw the way you made short shrift of Weston. I want you to know you will have much more difficulty in getting rid of me."

"Oh, you think so?" she said.

"I know so."

He held both his hands out to her from the chair where he sat.

She walked up to him and put her hands in his. The light from the Han lamp made her sparkle. He slowly pulled her into his lap.

"You're like a shimmering star," he said, as he put his arms around her and held her close to him. He tilted her chin up and lowered her face to his. They kissed, a soft warm kiss, and Nicholas put his hand on the softness of her breast. He ran his hand over her bodice to her waist, then he kissed her again. It was a long, deep kiss that put an eagerness in his loins. She put her tongue between his lips, licked and nibbled, hungry for him. Lying back on his arm, she said, "Nicholas Frayne, you taste like the finest chocolate in the world."

"So can you," he said. Reaching out and picking one up, he fed it to her. He watched her nibble the delicacy until it was gone.

She said, "Oh, it's divine."

He kissed her deeply, tasting the fresh sweetness of her warm, chocolate-coated mouth. He reached behind her while they were kissing and unhooked her dress. She bent forward, eager to help him, and he slid the zipper down as far as her waist. She raised herself up off his lap just high enough for him to continue down her back.

She rolled over on her side facing him, and he caressed her naked back, hips, her succulent buttocks, while he kissed her. Slowly and gently he pulled her dress forward off her shoulders, down off her breasts and, while kissing her, he raised her just enough to remove the gown completely.

She lay across his lap. Her large firm yet soft breasts and erect nipple were like luscious ripe fruit in his hands. He fondled them, first one, then the other. His mouth sucked and licked her flesh, more wonderful than any tropical fruit, real or imaginary.

"My Lord, you're glorious! Have you any idea how much I want you? Can't you tell how much I want to devour you, love you?"

She reached up and slid her arms around his neck, smiled, and said, "Yes—enough to come after me."

She slowly slid her fingers through his red-blond hair and held it tight, pulling his head down to her lips. She said, "I would have been disappointed if you hadn't found me."

"How disappointed would you really have been?"

"Can't you tell by the way I'm lying here in your arms, open, vulnerable, melting with every lick, every kiss?"

Bone-color stockings with elastic tops held high up on her thighs and a pair of silver kid shoes were all she had on now. She kicked off her shoes and drew her knees up, raising herself to a seated position. The light from the table lamp cast a shadow over her belly. She looked magnificently wanton, reckless, and beautiful—a man's delight. Nicholas gently pushed her knees apart so the light fell across the inside of her thighs. He explored her under the warm light, first with his eyes, then with his hands. Then he buried his face in the soft, flat belly and moved it from side to side, giving her sexy wet kisses. He reached up and hugged her in his arms, cuddling and petting her, stroking and fondling her everywhere. He slipped his hand under the top of her stocking and caressed all round her thigh, then moved his hand away and smoothed the stocking higher. He ran his hand all over her lovely long legs, feasting his eyes on every inch of her in the lamplight.

"You are a strong aphrodisiac. The more I taste you, the more passionate I become."

He put his hands on her waist and pulled her up onto his lap. Taking one of her legs, he placed it high up on his shoulder, exposing her to the lamplight. With his hand he gently opened the lips and ran his fingers deftly up and down. The deep pink flesh parted, revealing a paler, moist pink opening. He stroked her gently, reveling in her sensitivity to his touch, in how much pleasure she derived from the stroke of his fingers.

"Oh, yes," she said in a sexy voice. "Oh, yes."

He felt her rise to his caresses and so he pressed two fingers into her. As he stroked her and fondled her, his desire to push deeper became urgent. He saw her face flush a soft pink color and felt her pelvis move round and round, slowly, the contractions of her muscles sucking his fingers higher inside her.

"I love you for this," he said, kissing her lips, the tip of her nose, her nipples. "I love you for not holding back from me. Promise me you'll never hold back from me."

"You know I won't," she said, stroking his cheek, "but you must promise the same."

"I will, Arabella, I will!"

He kissed her belly, put his mouth to her breasts. He cherished every second of playing with her body like a favorite toy.

"I want us to do everything together," he whispered muskily. He bent his head and while tenderly but powerfully sucking on her nipples he brought his teeth together and bit her. She called out softly, and he kissed and licked the pain away. She kissed him, a kiss filled with passion.

He said, "I like the idea of sweet loving sex mixed with a touch of the animal, completely free of inhibition. Knowing that you do too makes our lovemaking all the more exciting."

He felt her body tense as she moved more quickly, his fingers still inside her, his thumb fondling her gently. Her eyes opened wide and she let out a small gasp as she came. He spread her knees apart, kissing the inside of her thighs and moving toward her belly.

"Oh, you're so wonderful!" he said. He put his lips to her and kissed, his tongue lapping as deep as he could reach.

Arabella had never known such tender loving, such sensitive caressing. She wanted to split herself open for him. She wished he could see into the depth of her; she wished he could see everything he caressed with his tongue and kissed with his fingers. That was how much she enjoyed giving herself to him.

They moved to the floor and lay together on the soft carpet. He planted kisses, passionate kisses, all over her, from her neck down her back and over her bottom. He bit her on one cheek of her behind but before she could call out, he rolled her over in his arms and kissed her deep on the mouth. She reached down and held him in her hand, stroking with a firm grip. His hardness throbbed.

She was soft and warm, and he nuzzled her wherever he found a curve to tuck himself into. She shivered under his touch and his kisses. Wherever he planted those kisses, she seemed to bloom. Her face, neck, and chest flushed pale pink as in orgasm. She welcomed everything he did to her.

Nicholas was nearly overcome with desire for the sensuous Arabella. They were silent and he cradled her naked in his arms, both reveling in her contentment, not wanting him to spend himself yet.

After a few minutes he fed her a chocolate, saying "When girls make love so much they need a little treat to maintain their energy."

"And when boys use their mouths so much, they need a little champagne to refresh themselves," she said, as she got up and went toward the kitchen.

"Lovely. Why don't I go run us a nice hot bath? I bought

you a bottle of this wonderful perfume. The minute I took a whiff I wanted to give you a bath in it."

"How scrumptious! What an exotic thing to do! I'd love it. You're always surprising me, Nicholas," she called from the other room.

"Why are you surprised by my wish to bathe you in exotic scent? Just the idea makes me want you with wild, passionate lust."

"Because when I look at you I think of the screen Nicholas Frayne I knew two days ago, the one with the Midwest blond good looks. The original sunshine boy who might take a lady out into a field of corn, turn her over on the plowed earth, and give her a peck on the cheek. It's what's beneath that all-American boy look of yours that's the surprise. You are a surprise, Nicholas Frayne, but one I find thrilling."

"And you, Arabella, are a revelation." He had come up behind her in the kitchen as she was placing the champagne and glasses on a silver tray. He reached around and held her breasts. His view of her round, firm buttocks and the back of her long, elegant legs in their sexy stockings high up on her thighs inflamed him. His erection throbbed. He enjoyed the rigid desire he had for her and wanted to plunge into her hard and for a long time until she begged him to stop.

Arabella swung around and faced him at that very moment. Their eyes met and she understood. She leaned forward and kissed him on the lips. She felt them tremble with passion as he cupped her breasts in his palms.

She said, "I will say no to nothing, Nicholas."

The water was pouring into the marble bath and the steam swirled up. They placed the champagne tray and the perfume on a small laquered table beside the bath. She peeled his clothes off and was pleased to see that his erection had not subsided. He held the long, throbbing, thick phallus in his hand and stroked it.

Arabella, her hair wrapped up in a turban, watched him

as he opened the bottle and splashed a generous amount of the heady fragrance under the running faucet. She put her hands lightly on his waist and stroked him down over his hips as she slowly slid against him onto her knees. She gathered him up in her hands, bent her head toward him, and kissed him sweetly. She gently pulled his erect cock toward her lips and took him into her mouth.

Nicholas held his breath, not wanting to give in to the tender sweetness of her sucking. She slowly eased off, kissed the tip, and raised herself off her knees. She put her arms around him and said, "Just a kiss, to let you know how much I long to have you inside me. I adore making love to you too is what I'm trying to say."

"You're going to smell like one of the girls." She laughed.

"I'm not getting in. It's for you."

"No." She smiled. "*We* are getting in. We are going to have a bath together. You can get rid of the scent in the morning with some men's soap." The two laughed and, holding hands, stepped up and into their perfumed pool. Arabella bent down and turned off the taps.

He put his hands on her waist, turned her around so her back was to him, and lowered them both into the bath. He spread his legs wide apart and she sat between them, leaning against his chest in the hot, perfumed water. She handed him a sponge and while he washed her back with one hand, he caressed her wet breasts with the other. He kissed the back of her neck and, inhaling the heavy, sexy odor, he said, "There are things I want to tell you."

Nicholas stroked her lovingly and said, "Because I too am changing my life, ending one career and beginning another. Because by now all the world knows that Nicholas Frayne, the actor, has retired, and that Nicholas Frayne, the man, is venturing into politics by accepting the nomination for the governorship of his home state, Rhode Island. Also, Marvin and I thought it far more advantageous for me if I was not too accessible to the press until they had had a chance to digest this change.

"I made the announcement last night by having a press release telexed to the world's news services. Marv and Mrs. Nettleworth, my secretary, are answering all the telex inquiries, and I'll give my first interview at a press conference on the pier when we dock in New York."

Nicholas was concerned that Arabella might not be happy with the change he was making in his life.

She closed her eyes and said, "And?"

"And what?"

"And what else, Nicholas?" Then she opened her eyes and looked deeply into his.

They both said at the very same time, "And I want to be President of the United States."

They smiled at each other. They were serious smiles. The silence hung between them like a curtain.

Nicholas pulled it back when he said, "Arabella, please, say something."

She smiled sweetly, almost compassionately, then touched his cheek with the back of her hand and finally spoke. "Well, Nicholas, and I thought I had a surprise for you! That's a pretty awesome ambition. It's rather taken me aback. Stunned me more than surprised me."

"Does it make a difference to how we feel about each other?"

"No, to the contrary, it makes my falling in love with you more extraordinary."

He stroked her hair, kissed her cheek, and said, "You know, that's the first time you've admitted being in love with me."

"Nicholas, it occurs to me that ours is a matter of destiny."

She leaned back in his arms and went on. "I give up power, leadership, control for something less demanding, something I've missed all my life. Being just a normal lady in the real world, living a self-indulgent life and having fun. And what happens? The first man who walks into my life turns out to be a man who has taken the lighter side of life and worked it out seriously and successfully, not only amusing himself but bringing entertainment to most of the rest of the world in the process.

"We are two people who when we met could go no further in the roles we were playing. We knew we had climbed to the very top; we knew our limitations and what's more, what we wanted to do for the rest of our lives.

Nicholas buried his face in the crook of Arabella's neck and kissed her. "It's all too amazing your being W.R. Crawford's daughter! You know, I've read nearly everything he ever wrote. I've studied and supported the idea and ideals of the New Deal men and what they accomplished for the United States. I can hardly believe that the woman I'm falling in love with was born into and has always been a part of that world.

"I can barely believe my luck! One of my campaign slogans is going to be: 'The Democratic Spokesman for the Republican Party—Nicholas Frayne.'"

Arabella pulled away from him and turned around. She looked at him aghast.

"Oh, my God, you're a Republican!" she gasped.

Their bodies were wet and shining like silk satin. The odor of their own body scents was mixed with the perfume of the bath water. They had come to know so much about each other—about their lives and their desires—there was only one way to complete the intimacy.

He took her in the water first from behind, putting her on her knees and bending her over. Her breasts dangled in the water that covered her up to her shoulders and back. He raised himself to his knees and spread her apart, then he rammed into her. Both equally dazzled by their lust, he took her roughly and filled every orifice. She gave herself even more completely, it seemed, than she had the night before and was rewarded again, as huge crashing waves of her orgasm mixed with his seed and were spilled into the bath water.

Chapter Twelve

He helped her from the bathtub, wrapped her in a bath sheet, dried off her hair and then her skin, dabbing it tenderly with the towel. He folded her in his arms and said, "You are all the flowers and fruits of the world, all the spices of life."

She stepped back and began to dry his moist skin briskly with the towel, drying his back, his chest and arms. She dried his thighs, legs, and feet. He stood motionless, savoring the attention. As she dried his skin, she lightly kissed each limb, each muscle, each crevice and, finally, placed one light kiss on the tip of his penis. He shuddered as the sensitive nerve endings sent a shiver through his body. They quickly embraced, surrounded by the exotic fragrance of the bath water and their own body scents. Arabella reached for the white crêpe de chine caftan, and Nicholas casually draped a dry towel around his waist.

He handed her a glass of the exquisite Dom Perignon from the cooler on the tray and touched his glass to hers. Together they walked hand in hand toward the bedroom. Arabella reclined on the chaise while Nicholas stretched out on the bed. He moved the bucket of champagne onto the bed, bracing it with pillows so that it stood upright. He put his champagne glass on the tray and tucked pillows behind him. They were facing each other. Arabella lowered her eyes and broke into a broad smile. She moved from the chaise and joined Nicholas on the bed, propping herself on the pillows beside him.

After some time Arabella asked, "Nicholas, what will happen to us if you find I'm a very different Arabella from the woman you know?"

179

"I would stroke your hair like this"—he bent down and kissed her on the forehead—"and I would kiss you like that, and then I would tell you that we are what we are in subtle variations and we have become what we were meant to be with some significant changes, if we were wise enough to make them. I'd hope that you'd agree with that and remember it, because I too am here on this maiden voyage for a similar reason.

"I'm retiring from one life and entering another. It sounds somewhat like your story and makes our meeting even more extraordinary."

"Nicholas?"

"Mmmm?"

"If we were in New York now, not in this wonderful floating island, and we were walking up an avenue and passed a newsstand, it's just very possible that you might see on the front page of the *Wall Street Journal* a leading article about me. Or you might see me on the front page of *The New York Times*. Some smart journalist might have written a caption under the photograph: 'Who is this woman?' or, 'The Garbo of the business world.'"

Nicholas bent down and kissed the top of her head, then her cheek. He stroked her breasts under her crêpe de chine dressing gown and said, "And what might the article say?"

"Oh, it might say something like, 'Arabella Eleanor Crawford, American, business address 19 place Vendôme, Paris. Until a few days ago, Crawford was the major stockholder and managing director of thirty-seven companies including Abcore, Execair and Telecone.'

"I sold all my holdings in a secretly planned, unannounced sale three days ago in my Paris office to thirteen corporations, for one hundred million dollars. The companies sold are all sound and heavy profit makers, mini-blue chip."

Arabella thought she felt Nicholas's body tense up, but she gamely continued with her imaginary article.

"'The terms for the sale were tough and tight. No chance of asset-strippers getting hold of her companies. She set the sale up with such rigid terms there is no way those companies can go but up. The sale took thirty days exactly from offer to final signatures. Every one of the buyers was on edge until the last minute for fear she would back down.'"

Nicholas laughed and asked, "How did it all happen? How did you do it?"

"Well, Nicholas darling, it didn't just happen. It's been a long, hard struggle—eighteen years. Eighteen years of everything else in my life coming second to my work. No husband, no home, no children, all relationships shared with my work. The occasional vacation, living sparsely. I sacrificed a great deal, but I gained a great deal too. It was exciting and thrilling. It stretched my mind, allowed me to use my power constructively through my companies.

"One does not make that kind of success being a goody two shoes. I was hard, tough when I had to be. I did my sneaky deals when I had to, made some bad enemies of some bad men. A woman in big business must work against some heavy prejudices.

"I've made an immense financial success. There have been a few added bonuses. The money and power I generated did, in some cases, add to the quality of life and, in a few instances, did a little something for mankind. It even destroyed a few miserable, cheating Fascists.

"I made my mistakes but was lucky. They were few and far between. It was a wonderful experience. They were thrilling years for someone who never planned to conquer big business. But once I was in it, there was nothing to do but get to the top."

"Arabella, those are massive amounts of money you were involved with, and you worked at it for eighteen years. Where did you get your training, your background, your ability to succeed on such an enormous scale?"

"I suppose partly from being brought up and influenced by the politicians that were part of my life from early childhood. Another factor is that I have an uncanny ability with figures and mathematics. Another is that I was taught strategy by my father and his associates. I grew up surrounded by men who knew how to go forward quickly and get a job done. They had courage, were leaders. It was my background. All their qualities were so much a part of me it was natural to use them when the time came."

"My dearest Arabella, why did you *want* to be one of the richest women in the world? What made you want the power that goes along with that? Why weren't you satisfied with one company, two? Why weren't you satisfied with ten million dollars, instead of one hundred?"

"Nicholas, I didn't want to be one of the richest women in the world. That wasn't my aim in life. I *am* one of them only as a result of certain circumstances. Why I wanted the power that goes along with such a position is a more interesting question.

"You see, until I was twenty-one, money was something I didn't deal with. It was a subject that was never discussed in our house. I knew that we were rich, privileged, had always had money. There was nothing ever denied us that money could buy. My grandfather and his father before him were very rich men. My father was wealthy enough to be extremely generous to his country as well as his family. We were very comfortable—not ostentatious—but comfortable, and I seemed, simply, to have an understanding of money the way Father did. It was only in his later years that he spoke to my brother and I about wealth. He taught us to understand that money and power went together, and that if one wanted to do extraordinary things in one's life for oneself or for the public, money and power made it a great deal easier.

"He taught us that monetary wealth meant freedom. He was quick to point out that my brother and I, just like him, were fortunate to have been born with these things, that they were part of our lives. Probably the one thing he tried to instill in us more than anything else was that accomplishments could be made much easier if one stayed in the background, hidden, reclusive, and had power. I learned to know that meant one had to have money.

"I don't believe that I could have done what I have all

these years had I not listened to his advice and lived very simply, stayed out of the limelight.

"My father was a clever man who managed a very public life because of his work. But his private life, the family and what he did with his money was always played down. In a way, I copied him. I learned my lessons well and accomplished what I had to in the business world in a great part thanks to him.

"You ask why wasn't I satisfied with one company, even two. Why did I go on building up and creating the empire that I did? I suppose when you spend eighteen years and work on approximately thirty companies the main reason is that you enjoy it and do it well. It was always exciting, thrilling, to take a failing corporation, turn it around, and make it flourish. It was an act of constructive creation. Then it snowballed, success breeding success.

"I went for the high jump in the money world when I came of age, twenty-one, and came into my trust fund with a cash gift of ten thousand dollars. My brother, Robert, was only eleven then. It was not until then that I realized what having money or not, having power or not, meant. I was shocked when I realized that the trust funds set up for my mother, brother, and I, plus a few hundred thousand well-invested dollars, were all that was left of a vast family fortune. It had been founded by my great-great-grandfather and my great-grandfather. The succeeding men of the family had only managed to run the fortune down. There was enough to see my mother and father out in the style to which they had always been accustomed. The trust fund for my brother and I was sufficient to keep the wolf from the door, but it was hardly the lifestyle of our family.

"That's why I spent the eighteen years making money. I wanted to live as I always had, as all the Crawfords have for a very long time. I wanted the freedom that money and power brings.

"Well, the Crawfords have their money again. One hundred million dollars is mine. My mother has her share, and my brother has his. That's just about that."

"That's an amazing story. A real American dream come true. But you only told me *why* you did it. Now I've got to know *how*!"

"How? I think you're going to think it was beginner's luck—and to some extent, it was. I invested my ten-thousand-dollar birthday present in three commodities after checking out the geopolitical situation at the time. Then I did a quick but thorough study of the agricultural successes and failures of the larger producing countries and their purchasing powers.

"Without realizing it, I began practicing what I had learned from my father's friends and the environment I had been brought up in. Behavior patterns and movements that had lain dormant for so many years came to the fore. I used what I had. There were a few ground rules I made for myself and abided by. I never invested in anything I didn't understand thoroughly. I investigated meticulously, knew my subjects well. I worked on the adage that 'it takes money to make money,' and I had the moral support of my family and a friend.

"As I told you this afternoon, we're a very close-knit family, closer than most. There is a ten-year difference between my brother and I, but that makes no difference. I watched him grow up and learned to have a special feeling for my little brother. He was the youngest student ever to be enrolled at Harvard Medical School, and by the time he was twenty-one it was evident he would be a remarkable doctor, just like my grandfather, Raine's father.

"Robert admired me, what I was doing, and wanted to participate in building up the family fortune. He didn't have my business acumen so he used his profession. Before his graduation he had discovered two antibiotic formulas that I sold for him to a pharmaceutical corporation. He turned that money over to me along with his ten-thousand-dollar coming-of-age gift. All he said was, 'Use it, Arabella, any way you like.'

"After Robert's earnings topped the two-million-dollar mark, we agreed that a portion of all future profits from his investments should go into a nonprofit trust for medical research.

"I always worked toward owning the controlling interest in my companies. I never touched my capital after the initial investment of ten thousand dollars and plowed every penny back into investments. Most important of all, I worked very, very hard.

"One of the reasons I went on until I had this fortune was because I knew once I retired I would never want to pick up the gauntlet again.

"There was one more vital factor—I became deeply involved with a man who became my mentor, advisor, and friend. It was a love affair that could never be resolved."

She didn't want to talk further about Anthony since she suddenly realized that their relationship could be resolved now that his situation had changed drastically. Hearing his voice again had stirred up feelings she though were long past.

"Are you going to tell me about him, Arabella? I want to know everything about you."

Arabella slipped out of Nicholas's arms and said, "I can't—not yet. I'll tell you all of it someday soon but that's all I can say for now."

Nicholas pulled her back and embraced her in his strong arms; she knew he understood.

Chapter Thirteen

It was the third afternoon out of Cherbourg, with three more days before docking in New York on the Hudson River. Life on the maiden voyage of the *Tatanya Annanovna* resembled a perpetual party. Everything seemed to flourish in the party atmosphere, especially longstanding marriages that had been drifting apart because of time, work, money, age or the availability of beautiful single women.

The Mike Mackays were one such couple. This big Texan who began the voyage under duress surprised even himself when he realized what a good time he was having. What surprised him even more was how much he still loved Marcia. His admiration and desire for women, his sexual attraction to any number of beauties on board, and his obsessive need to work and have power were suddenly tempered, put into perspective. He began to recognize the games that men play. That realization made it easy to make love again with Marcia, to appreciate what they had together and enjoy it.

Extraordinary romances were born, some explanations found, some new questions asked. Cotille Jefferson, who had been running for a lifetime, finally felt enough peace to find out why. Voyages such as this were a fantasy time where the outside world disappeared and the inner self emerged. Much better and far more pleasurable than a sleep cure, and in most cases having the same effect, six days at sea could change a lifetime.

One wonders how playing deck quoits with two middle-age widows from West Hartford, Connecticut, could enhance the life of a super-secretary like Missy. One might even ask how could they be a diversion. But they were. The women's very averageness was a welcome change from the world of high finance. They gave Missy a taste of middle-class America she was not at all familiar with. Their openness, their simplicity, their ordinary world and harmless pleasure-seeking helped to take the edge off Missy's usual super-efficiency and her speediness. They relaxed her, made her more easygoing. They warmed immediately to her wise-before-her-time character, solid and reliable, combined with her aggressive nature. She also presented an unbeatable combination in the eyes of Pete Peters, the first-class purser.

Before he met Missy, Pete had a penchant for older women, not just middle-age women, but really older. He found in them a kindness and acceptance of their position as transient lovers that he never found in younger women looking for romance on the high seas and a ring on their finger at the end of the voyage. The older women removed his anxiety of being trapped, offered him the warmth a professional traveler craves, and guaranteed him sexual success.

But Missy was different—free, easy, independent, in love with her work and filled with a *joie de vivre* that thrilled him. She seemed to be very like him. Missy enjoyed her flirtation with Pete, and he was falling in love.

Since Cherbourg, Xu's contributions to the sporting activities on board ship were respected and admired by his fellow passengers. Socially, too, he was in demand. By the third day out Xu was having a full and happy vacation.

Isador Katz was lying in a deck chair next to Arabella. He watched and listened to Xu enthusiastically tell his employer the joys of golf and how much progress Mr. Katz had made in the morning's Tai Chi sessions. Isador thought how wonderful this voyage was turning out to be. Where else could you meet a servant as interesting as Xu, or a beautiful woman in a silver jumpsuit who had the world on a string and asks you to teach her golf? Her attentions to him were like the kiss of life.

Pete Peters and Booker St. John, the senior medical officer on board, stood together on the bridge of the S.S. *Tatanya Annanovna* waiting for Captain Hamilton. Pete always found the bridge awesome: the vast glass windows with their enormous windshield wipers sweeping six feet across, the sensitive Decca Navigators, the latest computers, Marconi forecasters, the radar systems, the intricate equipment set into the pilot's console, the control consoles, and the bearing repeaters. Pete Peters was in love with the sea and the great ships who traveled her. For him, the *Tatanya Annanovna* was like a dream come true.

There was an ease on the bridge that comes with quiet, sure efficiency. It always made Pete feel he should whisper. There was, as well, an alertness, a constant watching, waiting for a signal coming from the safety-control room or a sign of danger from the machines recording the outside world and the elements for hundreds of miles around the ship's position. The bridge gave off an atmosphere of stability, safety on a grand scale. At the same time, there was a feeling of imminent action at the least sign of danger.

In the center of the safety control room down below was a desk that bore an illuminated master plan of the ship. At the turn of a handle any particular area could be shown, all safety precautions available displayed. This desk carried direct communication links with the bridge and the engine control room. Pete's office also used two computers, but these performed much more mundane tasks such as the prediction of fresh water requirements and the control of foodstuff storage and supply.

The purser stood there, arms folded, with Dr. St. John, waiting for Captain Hamilton. He so enjoyed the efficiency and magnificence of the coordination and control on the bridge.

Captain Hamilton ran a tight ship. There wasn't an officer on board who didn't respect him for it. He was a man with complete control and authority over his ship. He made periodic checks to see all was in order from the engine room to the dining room. He demanded that every man who worked on the *Annanovna* be happy and satisfied in his job, that every passenger was more than content, that his ship be maintained to perfection.

The two men were waiting now for one of the captain's walkabouts, which he did with two or three different members of his staff through different parts of the ship twice a day. He approached his waiting officers, saying "Sorry to have kept you waiting, gentlemen. Let's start our little walkabout today down in third class and work our way up. Shall we?"

The men were alone in the elevator as it started down into the depths of the ship.

Captain Hamilton said, "Gentlemen, I've got an interesting idea for you to mull over with me. The weather is changing, the temperature is dropping fast, and the updated forecast is very cold and very clear. What do you think of giving the maiden voyagers of the S.S. *Tatanya Annanovna* an extra treat?"

Pete looked at the doctor, who looked back at him just as blankly. Neither had a clue as to what the captain was proposing.

"There are a series of magnificent icebergs we can easily sail through, no fog and no danger of cloud coming our way. All reports are that they are sensational looking, and since they're unusually far south, our detour will be only a matter of a few hours each way. We could reach them sometime between eleven and one tomorrow. What do you think? Shall we do it?"

Pete's enthusiasm burst forth. "My God, yes, what a wonderful idea! I've always wanted to see some bergs up close."

Dr. St. John laughed at Pete's childlike response. "The passengers may also like it, Captain. I think it's a grand idea."

Pete laughed at himself as well. Captain Hamilton smiled because he liked when his staff responded so energetically, and the three proceeded to the third-class observation deck. The captain greeted some of his guests, including an elderly French couple from Toulouse, a German girl, a pair of newlyweds to whom he promised to send a bottle of champagne, a family of four from Colorado whose precocious little boy was filled with questions about the ship. The captain offered him a special tour of the vessel, including the engine room. He also made a friend for life.

The three men moved on. The captain looked through the glass doors leading out onto the open deck and saw Cotille Jefferson, wrapped in a great black cashmere cape with a luscious long-haired fox collar pulled up around her handsome dark-chocolate face. She was looking out over the cold, dark waves. She had a black-and-white silk scarf tied around her hair, not under her chin but at the nape of her neck, so as not to mar the perfect face or hide the magnificent jaw line.

Captain Hamilton was struck by her beauty. "I saw that woman yesterday," he said. "She's the model with the photographer who asked for special permission to use my bridge as a background for her. There was something—a quiet desperation about her that upset me. I hope she's happier with us today."

He put his hand to his hat in order to hold it in place while he pushed the door open into the cold wind. The two men followed.

"Good afternoon, madam. I am Captain Hamilton."

She turned away from the sea and faced him. She looked over his shoulder past him to Booker St. John. Not taking her eyes off Booker, she put her black kid gloved hand out and said, "Good afternoon, Captain Hamilton."

"It's getting very cold out here, Mrs., er, er..."

"Jefferson. Cotille Jefferson," she put in.

"Ah yes, Miss Jefferson." Immediately picking up her preoccupation with Dr. St. John, he turned and said, "I should like to introduce you to Dr. St. John and Mr. Peters, our first-class purser."

The three acknowledged the introduction. The captain then asked, "Are you enjoying your voyage?"

"Oh," she said, "honestly, I don't think I was until this

morning when suddenly it all changed for me. I'm liking it more now," still with her eyes on the doctor.

"Miss Jefferson, I'm giving a dinner party for Nicholas Frayne tonight. Perhaps you haven't heard, but he has announced his candidacy for the governorship of the state of Rhode Island. It would be a great pleasure to have you join us as my guest."

He saw the woman hesitate and when she began to speak, he stopped her and said, "Please don't decline my invitation." Looking at Booker St. John, he added, "I leave it to you, Doctor, to escort the lady this evening."

Turning back to a now-smiling woman, he said, "Ah, that's better! I'm pleased you will come. Now then, Miss Jefferson, come along. You must be quite cold. I know I am. Mr. Peters, please see that this lady is given a nice cup of hot bouillon."

Back in the enclosed deck, the captain kissed her hand and felt a sensual animal magnetism about the woman. He was delighted with his little act of playing Cupid. Captain Hamilton was not an insensitive man—he recognized an interest on Booker's part as well.

The men started toward the stairs on their way to second class. Peter lagged a little behind to give orders to a deck steward.

The doctor said to the captain, "That was a very nice gesture, sir."

"Are you saying thank you, Booker?"

"Yes, I think I am, Captain."

The two men, who had become close friends over the last few years on board various ships, looked at each other and smiled warmly.

"Well, just be careful, Booker."

Chapter Fourteen

Arabella Crawford was wearing a white linen jumpsuit. Her long gold and silver hair hung loose and curled around her face and down over her shoulders. She stood with her knees slightly bent, her weight on the heels of her flat shoes, a golf club in her hands.

Isador stood behind her, his arms around her arms, his fingers over hers, manipulating her hands into the proper way to hold a golf club. They gripped the club together and he directed her swing slowly up in an arc, high over her head, and slowly they swung down again. They practiced the action again and again.

They were now moving as one. She felt his body tight up against her back and for a split second she was confused —Anthony flooded her senses. No, no. That was years ago.

They practiced the swing over and over again in silence. She leaned back into him and moved with the motion of his body. It was involuntary. Everything about Isador drew her to him. A warmth, a kind of loving, a cautious, quiet masculinity enveloped her. This conservative, New England, middle-class man in late middle age was giving off the same magic and chemistry that had drawn her into Anthony's life. There was a powerful manliness about him. She felt it crying out to her. Brief images of Anthony flashed before her and she was unable to wipe them from her mind.

Again they swung together; the club went up in the air and again they came down together, their bodies touching. She knew she should move away, but she felt a sense of power over this man whom she was toying with.

It had been the same with Anthony. She found out she

could drive a man to sexual extremes and awaken him as he had never been before. She had done just that with Anthony, and it had been thrilling. Yet she had somehow been enslaved by it for years. Had she mistaken lust for love? No, she thought, I made no mistake. And I won't make a mistake with this man either. I'd like to be his friend and count him among mine. It's really the warmth of Nicholas's arms that I crave. She broke their embrace and turned around, still close to him, and handed him the club.

"Come and have tea in my suite, Isador."

After Isador closed Arabella's stateroom door, he followed her into the center of the room. When she turned to face him, he broke the tense silence. "I'm a staid, conservative, happily married man and I like being those things. I even take a pride in being just that."

"Yes, I'm sure you are and you do. That's one of the things I find so attractive about you, Isador. That's why I invited you to tea and why I hope we will always be friends. I also sense you are a passionate man, and I'm flattered to think you may have thought of me that way."

Isador picked up her hand and stroked it. "Your words help. They make me feel a little less foolish for having had thoughts I haven't had in years."

"You may not believe this, Isador, but you remind me so much of the great love of my life. It's quite incredible because you are so completely different and yet you have a similar chemistry."

"I'd like to know all about him. And about you, Arabella. You know, I've been married over thirty years. I have a terrific life with Libby. Yet I've never wanted any woman as I want you. Do you believe me?"

"Yes, I believe you. Will you settle for having me as a friend, Isador? A fond friend?"

"Can *you* settle for having a friend who is a little in love with you, Arabella?" Isador Katz was embarrassed and enthralled all at the same time.

"Yes, I could do that. I'd be very flattered and very pleased to have you as a friend, Isador."

He looked at her solemnly, with puppy-dog eyes, and said, "Then we'll have to be careful friends and never speak about it again."

Arabella rang for tea. While they waited for it to arrive, they sat together on the sofa and talked about golf and Tai Chi, Paris and Connecticut, antiques and mines. Occasionally Isador would pick up her hand and squeeze it, she would smile, and he felt he was with her. They were an unlikely match having a splendid time together.

The tea arrived, Indian, with cucumber sandwiches on brown bread sliced as thin as a dime and a fresh Madeira cake. Henry, the steward, served them and left. They had their tea in silence. Arabella was fighting a steady flow of *déjà vu* and losing; it swamped her. Many years ago another older, just as unlikely man had come into her life. Isador understood her silence and was satisfied just to be there with her.

Eventually he took the cup and saucer from her hand and put the pretty Lenox china down on the table. He helped her to her feet. Suddenly the silence felt awkward. Isador cleared his throat, drawing Arabella's attention to him. She smiled and he said, "Your man, Xu?"

"Yes," said Arabella.

"Getting to know him these past few days has been a real privilege. I value him as a friend. He is something special, your Xu."

"Yes, he is, Isador, very special indeed."

"Is it rude to ask who he is? Where does he come from? He's such a silent, introverted person. As curious as I am to know more about him, I simply cannot bring myself to question him. That he is well educated there is no doubt. I've guessed that he is a Zen Buddhist, and it's evident that he is a natural athlete. He's quite extraordinary in so many ways. He says so little, yet holds one in conversation. He appears simple, and is far from simple, infinitely more knowledgeable and intelligent than most people one meets."

Arabella listened pensively. She poured Isador and herself another cup of tea and said, "You're rather extraordinary

yourself, Isador. I hope you know that. There aren't many
people who would understand or even begin to fathom just
how special Xu is. He has a remarkable story, which I'll
tell you in confidence and only because I think he wouldn't
mind your knowing."

She proceeded to tell him the incredible story of Xu's
life and how the trust was established between them.

"There is a great bond between us," she said, "and we
both know that we will always be together. He travels everywhere with me. I am his employer, the only woman in his
life, his best friend, and his Western family."

"What a remarkable story," Isador said. "Remarkable,
savage, and yet beautiful because he is the least bitter person
for all that he has been through."

"Ah, yes. Well, you see, he works at a life beyond life
and death, love and hate. You are right, Isador, he *is* an
extraordinary man. I'm really happy that you and Xu have
become friends. We all need friends."

"I must go now," he said. Putting his arms around her,
he held her close and gave her a gentle kiss on each cheek.
Slowly, and with great emotion, he released her from his
arms and left.

After he had gone, she closed the door and leaned against
it. She smiled a mysterious smile and said, "I really wanted
you, you know."

Arabella poured herself another cup of tea and added hot
water to it with a slice of lemon. She picked her cup and
saucer up and walked over to the porthole overlooking the
bows of the ship. She tried to think of the very nice and
charming Isador Katz, her new friend and admirer, and
hoped she had let him down gracefully with her sincerely
meant words. But her thoughts kept getting muddled with
Anthony Quartermaine. She sensed him so strongly in the
room; he was still so much a part of her life.

She could not understand why Isador Katz had triggered
such profound feelings and desires for Anthony, feelings
that had been dormant for so long. She shrugged it off,

rationalizing that it was the combination of Isador and Anthony's unexpected phone calls that was digging up old, worn-out emotions.

She watched the ship plow through the waves, gazed at the vast ocean all around her, the setting sun, and the clear sky. She felt the wind rocking the ship and putting a froth on top of the heavy waves. She tried to forget both Isador and Anthony, but the past would not go away—it was forcing its way into her life. As she drifted off into thoughts and memories, she heard the telephone ringing in the distance. Arabella continued daydreaming as she moved inside and lazily picked up the receiver.

She finally said, "Hello?"

"Hello," he replied. "I didn't wake you, did I?"

"No, you didn't wake me."

"Are you alone?"

"Yes, I'm alone, Anthony."

"Alone, but not for long, is that it?"

"Yes, that's it," she answered, feeling very vulnerable, but safe from their love affair because he was on the other side of the ocean.

"Ah," said Anthony. "You sound very sexy. I recognize that touch of lust in your voice. Is he a good lover?"

"Yes," she replied, "a *very* good lover."

"I think you are deriving some sort of pleasure in telling me that, but be careful, my darling Arabella, make no mistake. He is not important in your life. Once you step off that ship, he'll step out of your life. I don't mind if you are just making do. I know very well how sexy you are."

There was that old seductive teasing in his voice. In spite of herself Arabella was reacting to it.

"I wish I were there with you now," continued Anthony. "I'd like to be there playing with your skin, caressing you, petting you, touching you. Laying you open, licking you, kissing you, sucking you, making you ready to receive me. Remember how you loved being open, moist, ready for me whenever I wanted you? We have one of the greatest, most marvelous things going in this world, you and I."

"Why are you doing this, Anthony?" asked Arabella, unable to hide the passionate tremor in her voice.

"You know very well why I'm doing it. Because I love you when you are excited. It makes me excited to think about it, about us, making love. Are you in bed?"

"No," she replied. Despite intellect, she was beginning to be aroused. Her body was tense, ready to be caressed.

"Where are you?"

"Sitting in the drawing room, in a big comfortable chair."

"Dressed?"

"Yes." She exposed her breasts, touched them tenderly, pinched the erect nipples. She watched herself in the mirror across the room.

"But underneath? No panties?"

"No, no panties," she answered, feeling like an echo.

"The thought of you makes me hard. I'm lying in bed, holding myself, thinking that you are here with me. Remember the exciting, wonderful things we've done together? They were some of the happiest days and nights of my life."

"And mine," she found herself saying helplessly.

"Ah, I'm aching to be inside you. Arabella?"

"Yes," she answered huskily.

"Raise your legs up and open them as wide as you can. Put one on either arm of the chair. Oh, my glorious Arabella, do this for me so I can imagine you exposed, pink and luscious, ready to be licked. Do that for me right now," he said urgently.

There was a moment's silence, then he asked, "Have you?"

"No," she lied, "I haven't." She didn't want him to know the control he still had over her, yet she couldn't help but feel aroused by this disembodied voice. She could see herself reflected in the gilt Queen Anne mirror. Unnerved by the sexual tension created by Anthony's taunting and teasing over the telephone, she tucked a cushion under her bottom with trembling hands.

He said, "Don't lie to me. I can sense you've done as

I've asked. That old electricity between us is still there even over a telephone line. I know every nuance of your body. I can tell you are wet now."

Arabella touched herself. Her legs spread far apart, she was indeed moist. She thought about being entered. She imagined a cock, but she saw no face.

"Touch yourself, Arabella. I can feel you sliding onto me. Can you feel me?"

She didn't answer. Didn't want to succumb to him, but she continued to pleasure herself.

"I wish I had you here right now. Remember Bangkok and that beautiful madam I introduced you to, the one who taught the most famous women in the world how to make themselves tight and derive infinite pleasure from their own contractions. Have you any idea how exciting it is for me to have been the instrument of granting such exquisite pleasure?"

Arabella could barely speak between the memories of that night and the knowledge that he too was masturbating on the other end of the telephone.

His voice went on, deep and husky. "It seems almost yesterday that I held you in my arms in the dark on the verandah of that marvelous old hut on one of those lovely Thai canals. The moon was so bright it lit up the old compound and the couples making love. Tell me you remember."

She whispered into the telephone, "Yes, yes, Anthony," knowing full well that he too remembered and was charged with passion almost to the point of no return.

"I held you in my arms and you were so beautiful in your nakedness. I reveled in your beauty and the way you gave yourself up completely to lust. Do you remember watching the naked girl being taken by twelve handsome men, each in a different way, without one second's rest? I think you would have liked to be that girl!

"Ah, how wet you must be by now!" Anthony's voice cracked.

Part of Arabella wanted to slam the phone down, but she

was so mesmerized by Anthony's voice, so turned on to her body and its sensations she couldn't even speak. She didn't want him to know how he had completely seduced her.

"Arabella, I loved keeping you wet all the time. I love it even more now. I have my cock in my hand and my heart is pounding with desire to be with you, in you. I want to be there licking you, sucking up every drop of you. I want to hold you in my arms and move in and out, in and out until you cry out for me to come."

"Stop, stop!" cried Arabella. "Why are you doing this to me?"

"Because I'm not there. To remind you that no matter how much ocean is between us, I can reach you. I want you to come all over me, that's what I want you to do. Do it now, Arabella, while I come."

Arabella was nearly panicking with passion. He had always been able to get her in this state. They both knew it. It had always been wonderful and right in the past but now, now she had met Nicholas, and she somehow felt embarrassed by her depravity with Anthony.

"I've loved you, Anthony, loved you completely, given everything to you. But I think I have figured out what I really need—a man who will make love to me with his cock *and* his heart, the only thing you ever held back from me."

As she said that, Arabella sat up in her chair. She would make love with Nicholas later. She didn't need Anthony to turn her on anymore. It was suddenly very clear.

After she hung up, she put her hand between her legs and touched her wetness. She came almost instantly.

It was there again, that terrible feeling, one she had never felt before she met Nicholas Frayne—the feeling that for all those years she might have fooled herself into believing what she and Anthony Quartermaine had for each other was love. A love that could not be because of circumstances beyond their control. Perhaps it was no wonder there had been no possibility of building a life with Anthony. The basics had all been wrong. It was not just that he had a wife, that he was close to the Queen of England and could not bear the scandal of divorce; nor was it that he was a devout Catholic with four children. It tormented her now to think that she may have been kidding herself about this love affair with Anthony. Was it possible that he had found a damaged girl, damaged by an inner loneliness, and he had used that to get her, just as later he had used his conservatism, his inhibitions, to build up a sexual relationship with her and label it "impossible love" to keep her?

Anthony Quartermaine, the man she loved, had been her "godfather" because he had recognized the ailing girl and had in many ways healed her with his loving presence. But he had also been the lover who had introduced her to sexual madness, eroticism, lust. Arabella had been completely seduced by him, as he had been initially by her.

Only now did she realize that when he had stepped aside for her to assume a glorious role in the world alone, she had really been alone, *all* alone. Her fantasy was that it had been a genuine sacrfice for him to give her up, as it was for her to be given up. How clever he had been to hold her all these years. He had pushed her out into the world but never let her go. He held her by sexual lust and hung the label of secret love on them.

It occurred to her that until she had signed those documents in Paris and freed herself from the past eighteen years, not one of the men in her life had ever really had a chance because Anthony had never let her go. Then she had freed herself.

Freedom, real freedom. That's what she had now and the first man to appear is Nicholas Frayne, and he has a chance. Or does he?

She remained paralyzed in the chair, not able to escape the memories Anthony evoked in her.

Arabella remembered her thirty-fifth birthday. She was in London at that time and Anthony was very much a part of her life. She recalled being on a ship with Anthony—a

ship with wings. She and Anthony spent three wonderful
days and nights aboard a flying boat, and she could recall
every detail of that glorious adventure.

It was the last Friday in May. It should have been a sunny
day, a day when the crocuses and daffodils were pushing
up through the new bright green grass, reaching for the sun
and swaying in the soft spring breeze. But instead it was
pouring buckets, the sky was pale gray, and all the flowers
were bent from the pelting of the rain.

Arabella, dressed in a white silk shirt and a black-and-
white checked raw silk jacket under a white belted raincoat,
adjusted her perky black hat in the Art Deco mirror in the
back of the limousine. It was Anthony's favorite car—his
vintage Silver Ghost Rolls-Royce. In front were his driver
and Xu. The interior of the car was paneled in gray suede
and the seats were upholstered in dark-gray leather, sump-
tuously padded and as comfortable as an old armchair. The
dashboard and the partition between driver and passenger
were of finely carved ebony, as was the bar discreetly encased in the middle seat armrest. The car was carefully
restored to its original splendor, and Anthony's only conces-
sions to modern equipment were the tinted glass windows
to ensure privacy and the stereo sound system that filled the
air with music, displacing the abrasive traffic noises of the
London streets.

They were driving along the Birdcage Walk, and Arabella could just make out Westminster Abbey and the Houses
of Parliament blurred by the sheets of rain pouring down
the car windows.

She checked her watch against Big Ben as they rode past
the famous clock tower. They both read one minute to
twelve. The Silver Ghost swung around the front of the
Houses of Parliament, so majestic and dramatic on the edge
of the River Thames. The car eased along through the pud-
dles of rain water, passing awesome Westminster Abbey,
and continued toward the House of Lords.

What bad luck, she thought. My thirty-fifth birthday and
it had to fall on a Friday. The worst day for Anthony and

I to be together. By Friday noon he was usually on his way to Heversham Park, if not there already. She sighed, thinking how eager she was to return to Paris. These past few months working in London again only made her acutely aware of how impossible their relationship was and how conflicted she felt. She thought about how sweet he had been the night before, and embarrassed, pretending he had forgotten her birthday. Anthony assured Arabella he would make it up to her. Then there had been more embarrassing apologies, for all he could offer her on her birthday was a brief lunch in the restaurant at the House of Lords before he took off for the country and his weekend with his family and important guests.

Arabella had been quite surprised, however, when he had suggested they meet in such a very public place for all to see. Not at all like Anthony, she mused.

The Silver Ghost pulled up to the entrance and came to a halt. She watched Xu step out into the rain opening a large black silk umbrella. The chauffeur jumped out into the deluge and opened the door for her.

Anthony, the Earl of Heversham, greeted them in a formal, almost aloof manner, as they walked into the House of Lords. As Arabella began untying her raincoat belt, Anthony stopped her, saying "No, don't do that. The dining room is damp and cold. You might be chilly. Do keep it on."

Arabella thought, This is going from bad to worse. He's so obviously nervous about my being here. Feeling suddenly uneasy herself, she said in a rather impersonal tone, "Anthony, it was kind of you to suggest that Xu and I come by for a tour of the House of Lords."

"I was happy to arrange this. Follow me and I'll take you down and introduce you to a page who will give you a tour of both the House of Lords and the House of Commons."

He gave Arabella a brief, twinkling smile and said, "Come along. We haven't much time."

As he hurried them through some of the dark and elegant

rooms, she caught a fleeting glimpse of the famous and wonderful Henry VIII room, with its magnificent oil portraits. She was swept past the House of Lords dining room, but even at a glance she could see it was not at all the drab, chilly room Anthony suggested it was. It was, in fact, one of the most exclusive dining rooms in the world, reeking of the privileged, of aristocracy.

She was feeling embarrassed and somewhat humiliated as he rushed her through the magnificent rooms facing the Thames and then down a long corridor. They seemed to be heading toward a less used, more remote part of the building. The atmosphere was declining rapidly as well.

Arabella could barely keep up with Anthony. She lagged behind feeling more the tourist than the mistress of one of the most powerful men of the land. The rooms they passed now were deserted, the corridors empty. Many members had obviously already left for the weekend. They went down a flight of stairs that were positively dingy and then through a pair of dull-gray metal swinging doors. Finally they reached a large wooden door bolted at the top and bottom. Arabella felt the dampness and the cold as she watched Anthony reach up and shoot one bolt back, then bend down and do the other one. He pulled the door open and the gray light poured in and filled the corridor. For the first time that day he smiled at her.

"And this," he said, "is Parliament Pier, and that," he continued, raising his arms in a gesture of offering, "is your flying chariot, madam. Happy Birthday, my love."

The cool, reserved facade was dropped as he took Arabella in his arms, kissed her, and began to laugh.

"She's called the *Belvedeer Clipper*, one of the last of the great flying boats. I bought her, saved her from disappearing into oblivion, restored her, and had her fitted with new engines and a new interior. As a birthday present for you, I've planned a wonderful trip for us, my dear. We will have three days together, and the *Belvedeer Clipper* will be our magic carpet."

Arabella was speechless with surprise. She looked through

the open door and through sheets of pouring rain to the magnificent great white flying ship moored at the historical stone pier where Henry VIII and Sir Thomas More might have docked. The door of the plane opened and two men jumped down on to the pier. Xu stepped around the couple out into the rain, opened the umbrella, and raised it for them to step under. The first thing Arabella said was, "You got me this time. I had no idea whatsoever." Then she looked at Xu, smiled, and said, "You knew?"

"Yes, I did, Miss Crawford."

"Well, of course he did, darling. He helped me. I couldn't have done it without him. Now no more questions."

A loud crack split the air, cut through the sound of the pouring rain; puffs of white smoke briefly escaped as the engines began to roar. The three hurried through the rain and Anthony and Arabella boarded the plane. From his breast pocket Xu took a pigskin case, handed it to Anthony, and whispered, "Miss Crawford's passport, sir."

Anthony thanked Xu and turned back to Arabella, who had missed the exchange. They both waved good-bye to him as the crew jumped aboard, having released the plane from its mooring.

The *Belvedeer Clipper* taxied out onto the Thames. Like her current owner, the flying boat was a part of English history. She had been in service on the Lisbon–London flight during World War II. Adventure and romance were very much a part of her past. Many a soul who had boarded her with the Nazis close on their heels had been carried to freedom during the worst time the world had ever known. She was big and bulky, with a cabin that seemed to hang beneath the wings. On the outside she had been restored exactly as she once was, and the interiors had been redesigned to satisfy Anthony Quartermaine's needs while retaining a certain period charm. He saved her so she could take him on adventures up the great rivers of the world, to explore mountain lakes, and to travel in ultimate privacy.

They were standing in the main cabin, a luxurious but simple room with high-backed wing chairs covered in brown silk velvet that were screwed down to the richly carpeted floor. It was all walnut paneling and subdued colors. A pair of tables was also bolted to the floor.

. Anthony took her by the hand, rushed her forward to the cockpit, and introduced her briefly to the pilot and his navigator, then helped her back to a chair. They strapped themselves in. The *Belvedeer Clipper* began picking up speed as they passed under the Westminster Bridge up the Thames. Arabella looked through the window, the rain pouring down and beating against it. The spray from the river displaced huge amounts of water, nearly obliterating the view. A good distance upriver the airship turned and charged downstream again at full speed, passing once more under Westminster Bridge. Just as they passed the Parliament building, the clipper ship climbed up off the water into the air. Arabella looked back at the House of Lords and saw the faithful Xu standing in the downpour, a waterfall of rain from the umbrella dancing all around him. She waved and he waved back.

When they were finally airborne, the storm cleared, their ascent completed, Anthony unbuckled her seat belt and helped her from her chair. They walked back into the main cabin together.

"Happy?" he asked. "I really got you this time, didn't I?"

She nodded.

"Did you really think I would offer you nothing more for your birthday than a sandwich at the House of Lords?"

She nodded again.

He touched the tip of her nose with his forefinger and looked into her eyes. He said, "When next you're in London, I'll take you to lunch in the dining room of the House of Lords. The food is exquisite, the room magnificent and warm, the company usually fascinating. I always lunch there when I'm in the House. I would deem it a privilege to take you there for a fine meal, but even that is not good enough for your birthday."

Then their eyes met and he took her in his arms and

kissed her, softly at first, then deeper, then passionately, never releasing her lips from his. Anthony put his hands on her shoulders, then down her arms until he held her hands in his. He stepped back, still holding her hands, and said, "Come on. Let me show you our room." And he led her toward the back of the ship.

It was a simple room, not overly large, just adequate to accommodate a dresser, a chair, a dressing table and a real bed rather than an airplane-style berth. It was not a glamorous room, but efficient and pretty in its simplicity. Off to the side was a lovely bathroom. The most surprising thing about these rooms for Arabella was that Anthony had organized them so that all her clothing, accessories, and toiletries were there and laid out for her.

"Good Lord, how did you ever manage it?" asked Arabella.

"Simple. I had Missy and Xu buy duplicates of everything you brought with you from Paris. Even the flowers are the same ones I sent to you at your hotel this morning."

Anthony opened a bottle that had been chilling in a cooler on the dresser. He poured two glasses of the champagne. As they clicked their glasses he said, "Happy Birthday," and they drank.

He slipped her jacket off her shoulders, unbuttoned her blouse, and removed her bra. He touched her breasts, placed his face between them, and began to kiss them, moving his head from side to side. He caressed them, fed her nipples into his mouth, and sucked long and hard on them. Slowly, reluctantly, his kisses tapered off, leaving her trembling. She dressed as he filled their glasses again, and they drank. Anthony ran his fingers through her long, luscious hair and pulled her face up to his, touching his lips to hers. He put his arm around her shoulder and said, "Come on. Let's go up to my chart room. I want to show it to you—the hub of the *Belvedeer*, where I plan my adventurous journeys."

They entered the room just as they were passing over the white cliffs of Dover. As if by magic the gray light disappeared and the sun broke through. The English Channel sparkled like a vast sheet of sequins.

Just as she saw the white cliffs of Dover receding under the bright sunlight, Anthony put his arm around her and said, with a wry smile, "You know, I made a terrible mistake a long time ago. I should never have encouraged you to make a life of your own, away from me. I should have kept you like a prisoner, locked up only for me when I wanted you. I should have kept you as a sexual slave, to be toyed with, played with, as I saw fit. I have complete control over you and our few days together, and I like that feeling. It excites me. I can do whatever I like with you and you can't possibly get away."

"Oh, you think not?" she said laughingly.

"I know not," he said. "I have your passport." Removing it from his breast pocket, he waved it at her.

"I have you now, Arabella Crawford. Complete control over you and your movements, for three days. I am going to give you the gift of three lovely, adventurous days and divine nights, beautiful sights, delectable food, and lots of lovemaking." And he did.

There is a romantic aura about Rome. Poets, painters, lovers for centuries from all over the world have run away to live and love and even die there. Glorious, sunny Rome. A worthy city to be busy in, but blissful to do nothing whatsoever in. A city for the poets and lovers of the world to be idle and play in. Glorious, beautiful, romantic Rome, where the beautiful, well-dressed women strut rather than walk and the dark, sexy men swagger. Gorgeous Rome, with her cafés, flower stalls, and moments of history frozen in stone. Divine Rome and her vanity, a constant, delightful charade. Rome and the Romans who can give a performance that is polished and faultless, so much so that you believe that they are what they pretend to be: elegant, disdainful, superior.

The *Belvedeer Clipper* flew low over St. Peter's Square, always imposing, full of grandeur. Arabella and Anthony sat in soft chairs absorbing their bird's-eye view of the exquisite piazzas and little churches, the old areas of Monti and the Ghetto. They were dazzled by the majestic ruins of the Fora.

Anthony turned away from the window, looked at Arabella, and said, "I love Rome. I always have. And I know how much you adore it too. That's why we are stopping here for lunch." He checked his watch. "Two twenty. Right on time."

They flew over the Colosseum, then down the center of the Tiber River that wends its way through the heart of the city like some exotic, watery serpent.

The *Belvedeer Clipper* touched down on the Tiber and cruised upriver, docking against a small crumbling pier where there waited a customs officer, several policemen, and a representative from the mayor's office. Once they were moored, the *Clipper*'s door opened and the couple stepped out on to the pier and into the sunshine and warmth of Rome.

They were in an older section of the city with narrow, crooked, cobbled streets and tilting buildings of soft warm colors of ochre, faded persimmon, worn pale yellow, soft pink.

Anthony greeted the officials, cleared passport control, and left the remainder of the details to the pilot. While he was tending to those things, a small crowd had gathered to see who was going to emerge from this odd-looking plane. Once convinced no movie star was on board, the people began dispersing back into the little streets and shops.

Anthony recognized the owner of the Hosteria del Orso, who was there to meet him. The three shook hands and walked the short distance through the picturesque streets to the famous restaurant. They entered the ground floor to the sounds of romantic Italian music being played by a small group of elderly musicians. In the bar they drank Negronis, a Roman speciality of orange juice, gin, and campari, and petted and touched each other like young lovers. A beautiful young girl appeared with a cluster of perfect white gardenias.

"*Scussi, permisso,*" said the girl, and pinned the gardenias in Arabella's hair. "*Bellissimo! Buono, buono. Bellissimo.*"

"She is right, you know. You are very *bellissimo* indeed."

They were taken to a table upstairs by the *maître d'*. There, in the utterly romantic and enchanting atmosphere of the elegant restaurant, they dined on exquisite food. First they had white asparagus in a superb hollandaise sauce that was as light as air, served with an exceptional bottle of white wine from the deep cellars of Frascati, which date from ancient Rome. Then came *gnocchi verdi* in a cream sauce, followed by *osso bucco* served with spinach sautéed in garlic and oil, accompanied by a full-bodied red wine. Finally they were served a pyramid of *profiterole*, airy puff pastries filled with rich, homemade vanilla ice cream covered in dark-chocolate sauce and topped with heavy whipped cream.

They sipped espresso laced with sambucca under the hot Italian sun on the balcony of the Hosteria del Orso and looked over the rooftops of Rome. They talked about the beauty of St. Peter's, the imposing Bernini's colonnade, the magnificence of the Sistine Chapel. Anthony spoke about the two great English poets, Keats and Shelley, whose remains lay under the broken columns and marble fragments covered by acanthus leaves, honeysuckle, wild flowers, and red camellias growing in abundance under shading pines, laurels, and myrtles in the English Cemetery of Rome, where the famous expatriates of the world are buried.

Arabella felt the romance of Rome, the romance of poetry and the romantic side of Anthony to the depths of her soul, and was seduced by them yet again.

They regretted there was not time to go to the Villa Borghese and see the Canova masterpiece of Paolina, Napoleon's favorite sister, reclining in marble. Nor was there time to visit the Museo Romano. They decided to go to the incomparable Piazza Navona, where they rode in an open

carriage pulled by a pair of horses. They stopped at the
Piazza d'Espagna and walked to the top of the stairs hand
in hand, then down again, buying all the flowers they could
carry from the old vendor with his stall set under a pair of
umbrellas in the middle of the steps.

They rode in the flower-filled carriage back to the *Belvedeer* and were arranging flowers in all the cabins as the
plane slipped from her mooring and traversed the Tiber
slowly, through the city. They went into Anthony's room
last, where they placed the remaining flowers in a vase.

"What a wonderful birthday lunch," said Arabella, and
she put her arms around Anthony's neck. "Thank you, darling."

He kissed her neck and then her throat. "That was just
the beginning, Arabella. Just the beginning." And he led
her toward the bed.

It was dusk when they flew away from Rome and just
barely light when they circled the lake and the pilot rang
through to Anthony and woke the couple.

"Come," he said. "Come to the window. We're making
our next birthday stop. Come quickly and you'll see something wonderful."

Arabella went to him. He pulled her forward in front of
him. She stood there naked in the darkness of the cabin,
looking through the window, and saw, far below, the faint
outline of a large lake.

He pressed his own naked body against hers and kissed
her back while looking over her shoulder. After the *Belvedeer* completed its third circle over the lake, he slipped
his arms around her waist and held her breasts in his hands.
She felt his full erection against her bottom.

"Watch now," he said.

A light flared bright in the darkness on the edge of the
lakefront, then another, and another, and on they went ringing the lake, each of the flames about fifty yards apart.

He caressed her bottom, bent her over slightly, and whi-
pered huskily as he spread her open, "They look like the

candles around a great birthday cake, don't they?" Then he eased deep inside her with a rampant throbbing cock.

Arabella let out a sigh of surprise and ecstasy as she felt him fill her completely.

"You feel wonderful inside me like this. And what a birthday cake. It has to be the birthday cake to end all birthday cakes, Anthony. But surely this is not all arranged for me?"

"No, darling, not for you. But it's a lovely idea, isn't it?"

And, with his hands firmly clamped on her hips, he began to move slowly in and out of her. In and out, bending her body down forward, he kissed her back as he made love to her in the dark room flying over the fire-lit lake.

"God, it's sexy taking you this way from the back, bent over, watching the lake light up. Oh," he said, increasing the intensity and speed of his thrusts. "I like taking you like this, standing up in the sky."

"Oh, yes, I like it too," she answered breathlessly. As the *Belvedeer* began to descend, a small light flashed in the cabin announcing their imminent landing. Anthony gripped her more firmly, his passion broke loose, and he moved in her fast and hard, shooting into her as the plane skimmed only inches above the water. He continued to move in and out of her, and Arabella came just as the *Belvedeer Clipper* eased down into the waters of Lago Bolsena.

Anthony picked up her beige silk kimono and helped her on with it. Then he walked across the room to the dresser, took out a pair of dungarees, and slipped into them. He pulled on a navy-blue cashmere sweater, reached his hand out to Arabella, and said, "Let's go have drinks in the main cabin."

"Anthony, that's a lovely idea and this is all so exciting, but where exactly are we, and where are we going?"

"We are now on Lago Bolsena, about a hundred and fifty miles north of Rome. Our host is the Count of Bolsena. We are going to a ball in his castle tonight. The torches have been lit to receive all seaplanes landing on the lake this evening. The ball is in honor of the restoration of the family castle. The count is the patriarch of a very old Italian family, but one which, like many others, lost everything but its name over the years. Roberto has worked very hard to regain the family's fortune, restore their position as successful landowners. He has carved a place for himself in Bolsena and has even served a term as mayor of the town. All Italian society will turn out for this ball. It should be a very lively party, filled with the beautiful people gowned and bejeweled to dazzle. You'll love it."

"I am sure I will, but I do wish you had told me that this afternoon. Oh, Anthony, you should have told me while we were in Rome so I could have picked up something very special." Here she was on her thirty-fifth birthday, pouting like a child.

"Poor Cinderella," he said, going to her and kissing her tenderly on the lips. "My poor Cinderella."

He walked across the cabin to a desk, opened the drawer and quickly removed something. "Think quickly," he called out and threw a key across the room to Arabella who caught it.

"It's a key to the cabin next to yours. Pretend that it's a silver wand and I am your fairy godfather. If you use that key, you will find a gown for the ball, a birthday present from me."

Arabella jumped out of the chair and into his arms. "I've never known you like this! This is the most romantic, exquisitely detailed, loving birthday imaginable. You've thought of everything, taken so much care to make me happy. It's lovely, absolutely lovely to be cared for by you like this."

Anthony became very serious for a moment, stroked her hair, touched her cheek with the back of his hand, and said, "I know I am a selfish man, Arabella. I don't give you nearly the care and attention or the love you deserve and want. But I do the best I can."

Arabella went to the ball dressed by Valentino. The gown was grand and elegant, made of Dupioni silk in a rich ivory

color. It was strapless and cut daringly, meant to excite.
The soft silk hung precariously low over her breasts, just
covering the swell at the sides before it disappeared into the
waistband on the hip, leaving a completely bare back. The
skirt appeared to be made of endless yards luscious silk. It
hung to the middle of the ankle in the front and gradually
flowed into a three-foot train at the back. Her evening coat
was of the same silk in black, with a collar of white ostrich
feathers. It had long, snug-fitting sleeves and was cut to
cover the very full skirt of the gown.

She wore the rubies he had given her for their first an-
niversary together—smuggled on board thanks to Xu. She
looked as splendid as any one of the many great beauties
at the ball.

Arabella did feel like Cinderella from the moment they
left the *Belvedeer Clipper* and walked onto the jetty. They
were swept away by a chauffeur in one of the count's vintage
cars, an open Bugatti. The night was very black and warm,
with just a few stars in the sky. The scent of wildflowers
filled the air. They drove through narrow tree-lined roads
where the only noise was the night sounds of the woods.

In the center of the town the road they were on merged
with the main road and they were joined by a stream of cars
moving slowly toward the castle. They inched up to the
roadblock where the police guards waited. Every passenger
in every car was made to display an invitation, which was
then checked against a guest list. Once cleared, three young
boys from the town dressed as medieval pages ran in front
and at the sides of the car holding high flaming torches.
They ran as an escort through the darkened streets lined by
townspeople clapping and waving all the way to the foot of
the castle's entrance. There the passengers left the car and
were led by another young boy, also carrying a torch, up
the steep castle stairs to the balcony, where they were greeted
by the count.

It was a splendid sight. The entire town was lit only by
torchlight and candle. Anthony introduced Arabella to the
count and they proceeded into the castle.

The party was glamorous and fun. Never before had Arabella ever seen a more beautiful group of people under one roof. Dinner for four hundred was served at round tables of ten, glittering with silver and crystal, white linen, wild-flowers, and candlelight. The tables trailed all through the wide corridors and main rooms of the castle so lavishly restored to its old splendor. They drank wine and dined on suckling pig dressed with apples in their mouths and wild-flowers behind their ears. Just watching the beautiful people was a feast in itself.

Arabella had expected to find the most beautiful women at this ball, but what a collection of men! Oh, the men! Most of them were elegant and dark, olive-skinned, and terribly handsome, dressed in smart, well-cut tuxedos, soft black silk bow ties, jeweled studs, and white silk dress shirts. They were the cufflinked brigade out to conquer the women at the ball with charm, a silver tongue, and whispers of love. They were outrageously flirtatious, extravagant with compliments, the image of Latin lovers at their best. That was what the men were like at the Bolsena Ball.

It was one of the most happy and dazzling parties she had ever been to. There was laughter, there was kindness, there was a surprising warmth among the guests. It was just one of those rare, perfect parties.

There was dancing in the great hall to two orchestras that played continuously. Arabella and Anthony twirled around the restored ballroom hung with garlands of laurel and wild-flowers and lost each other to other beautiful partners and found each other again at dawn. At last they thanked their host, returned to the *Belvedeer Clipper*, and, in each other's arms, slept the Saturday away.

Arabella was awakened by a combination of sensations. A sensuous rocking and bobbing up and down, as if she were lying in the bottom of a rowboat. There was the sound of muffled voices somewhere outside. She felt a sexiness brought on by a pair of lips and a roving tongue. She opened her eyes, wriggled her pelvis round and round, stretched and opened her eyes to her lover, who gathered her in his arms and said, "Good morning."

Anthony kissed her on the cheek and briefly on the lips. He said, "Hello there."

"Hello there yourself," she answered.

"Did you sleep well?" he asked.

"Yes, very well. But I kept feeling as if we were taking off and landing, sometimes as if we were out at sea, cruising on a boat."

They lay there silent in each other's arms for a while, and then she said, "There must be a storm coming. The lake feels different and rough." Then she noticed the bands of sunlight coming through the windows and crossing the bed. She looked out of the window and said, "Just look at what a glorious day it is out there. You know, I'm famished."

"Me too. It's half-past two in the afternoon. Come on, we'll be late for breakfast."

Arabella got out of bed, went over to the window, and gasped. The *Belvedeer Clipper* was bobbing up and down on the waves half a mile off an exquisite white sand beach. She ran to the other side of the cabin and looked through those portholes. There she saw more white beach, a crumbling, weatherbeaten wooden dock reaching out into the water, and a tiny crumbling village with no more than ten or twelve houses. On the other side of the village, sparkling under the hot sun, was a magnificent ancient temple of some kind and the ruins of a once magnificent amphitheater.

Arabella flushed with excitement and wonder. "I *didn't* dream it. We flew away. Where are we? It's magnificent! Unbelievable and magnificent. Fantastic! Let's go and see."

"Stop," said Anthony, laughing. "One thing at a time. Put on a comfortable dress and put a swimsuit on under it as we might want to swim."

While dressing, she caught a glance of some men—dark, rugged, rough-looking peasant types. It had to be Greece or Turkey—maybe even Syria. It had to be someplace magnificent and remote. She felt the airship turn and taxi toward the dock.

They had breakfast at a rickety table with wobbly chairs set on the beach at the end of the village a few feet from the water. They were served fresh fruit, warm bread, grilled fish, sweet butter and honey, hard-boiled eggs, homemade yogurt, and tiny cups of Turkish coffee by a young Turkish man who ran back and forth from the village restaurant.

Anthony explained that they were in Side, once a great seaport, on the Mediterránean coast of Turkey, close to Syria. The village was very small, only a few houses, bleached by the sun and sea salt, the villagers hesitant but friendly. There were no signs of twentieth-century culture or artifacts. Camels and donkeys were used for transportation. Well-worn kilim rugs and crude pottery could be seen through open doorways. Men and women alike wore layers of loose-fitting, flowing robes. Shopping and commerce were done in open stalls. There were no paved streets, electricity, or cars, and no tourists. It was divine there, sitting under the hot sun. Arabella could hardly believe this was all happening to her.

After breakfast they walked arm in arm along the water's edge through the ancient port and visited the tiny museum, which housed several ancient bas reliefs in white marble. Then they visited the amphitheater, a remnant of the Greek culture that had once ruled this part of the world. The quality of the architecture, the carvings, was remarkable. There was a strong aroma from the spring flowers that grew between the marble seats. Arabella and Anthony sat high up and looked down into the amphitheater and out over the Mediterranean.

"Stay here," he said, and rushed down the twenty rows to the center of the amphitheater floor. Then, in a whisper, he sang "Happy Birthday." The acoustics were so perfect she heard every word from where she sat high above him.

They walked from there back through the village to the deserted beach. It was a very long, narrow beach beyond which the land rose slowly and was covered thick with wild bushes, some flowering. Though it was almost sunset, it was still warm so they dropped their clothes on the sand, held hands, and ran out into the shallows to swim in the sea. They swam together, played in the water like children. They floated on their backs drinking in the view of the glorious coastline. Arabella threw her arms around Anthony's neck and kissed him.

"You are an amazing man. I'm so happy. I thank you so much," she said, kissing him deeply.

He floated on his back and she saw that he had an erection. She released it from his trunks and, slipping through the water between his legs, she licked the salt water from his cock and fed him to herself, sucking him deeply. It was an act of affection, not passion, and they both knew it and enjoyed it. She tucked him away once again and lay next to him on her back in the shallow water, her arm around his shoulder, and they floated together.

It was getting late and cool, and they were about to swim to shore when they saw four white horses break through the thick foliage onto the beach, led by a great white stallion—a magnificent beast with a long white silky mane. They ran across the sand and leaped into the water with a great force of animal energy. Arabella and Anthony watched the magnificent horses running back and forth into the crashing waves. They swam away from shore in a single stream, following their leader, and then abruptly, as the tide came in, they reversed direction and headed back toward the shallow beach.

It was a magnificent sight never to be forgotten. Arabella and Anthony, not wanting to frighten the horses off, stopped and waited until they ran out of the sea and up the beach. Two of the horses continued to run, disappearing once again into the bush from whence they came. Silhouetted by the setting sun, the white stallion mounted the remaining mare. They coupled with a surge of animal instinct and rhythm and for a brief moment remained locked together, standing as sculpture against the evening sky. Suddenly the stallion leaped back and the two horses turned in unison and ran back into the trees.

There was something about that scene that was so special and so sensual that they could hardly speak about it. It was a special moment of beauty in a special moment of time.

They went back to the *Belvedeer Clipper*. They departed quickly and flew over Lake Damsa Baragi. As they soared over Cappadocia, Arabella viewed the magnificent, exotic landscape—more like a moonscape than the middle of Turkey. It was hard to believe that nature and time had formed the weird and wonderful landscape. Miles and miles of hills and valleys extended along dry and arid land. From the air they looked like tiny Henry Moore sculptures.

In the twilight the Goreme Valley looked like a city of soft forms, a city made not by architects but nature. She recalled it was once occupied by Byzantine monks, fleeing from oppression. They made churches and chapels, hermits' caves and monasteries by digging steps up the cone-shaped cliffs—creating their caves high above where they could feel safe, and closer to God. For the love of God, they decorated them with murals sensitive and primitively beautiful enough to make one weep. They lived and prayed, roasted in the summer and froze in the winter, in this wind-swept landscape. The vivid history and passage of time and space seemed surrealistic to Arabella as she continued to stare in silence through the porthole windows of the aircraft and saw the moon rise high over the Goreme Valley. It was full and white and reflected the conical churches and Byzantine chapels. The moon turned the valley to silver, creating shimmering stark images on the landscape.

Anthony told Arabella old Turkish fables that he learned from an archeologist friend in London. They sat close and talked softly through the dark hours in the air, guided by the stars. They watched the sun come up and turn the sky red, then pink that Sunday morning. Finally they flew over sea and land again and headed home.

Chapter Fifteen

Arabella was jolted from her reverie by the sound of the telephone ringing. It went on ringing as she made her way through to the bedroom.

"Hello?"

"Hi," he said. "You must have been in a deep sleep."

"No, not really," she said, very pleased to hear Nicholas's voice. She went on. "I'm so happy you called. Have I told you I love your voice?"

He laughed and suddenly she saw his handsome face, the open, clean-cut smile.

"No," he said. "But that's a beginning. Did you sleep?"

"No."

"You must be exhausted! We had no sleep last night and when I left you I thought for sure you'd catch a nap at least."

"Well, I was going to but then I decided to go for a walk to get some fresh air. I had a golf lesson too, with that nice Mr. Katz. We came back here, had tea, and since then I've lost track of time. I'll take a nap now."

"Darling, how? It's seven. I called to ask you what time to pick you up. I must be at the captain's party on time. He's made a point of holding the dinner in my honor."

"Oh, Nicholas, I'm sorry."

"Darling, there's nothing to be sorry about. It's just that I'll have to ask someone to escort you other than myself. You do understand?"

"Of course. Don't worry, Nicholas. I'll be there before you all sit down to dinner. Nine, isn't it?"

"Yes, nine. I'll send Marvin down for you."

"No, there's no need to do that."

"I've invited Xu and Missy—or rather, the captain has at my request. Would you prefer me to send Xu?"

"Yes, fine. Send Xu. I'll be ready by eight forty-five. If I make it before that I'll just arrive. I know my way. I'll be with you as soon as I can."

"Okay. See you then."

She put the phone down and went to the dressing room, put on the lights, and looked in the mirror. She wanted to look ravishingly beautiful. She wanted to give Nicholas her best. Arabella was excited. It suddenly came to her how remarkable it was that she and Nicholas found each other at this time. Just as she was turning her life around, so was he, trying to work out a new life to satisfy a hidden dream. And perhaps they each were destined to be a part of the other's life.

The captain's dinner for Nicholas Frayne was in the Trocadero, the largest of the first-class dining rooms. It was Arabella's favorite—not only for its Art Deco design and all the Lalique etched glass, not for the orchestra that played in the well, but because it was where she and Nicholas had had their first lunch together.

Arabella hurried toward the Trocadero. It was eight forty. Miracles had been created swiftly and brilliantly thanks to Missy, who delivered the hairdresser, manicurist, florist, and M. Gerard, the jeweler.

Arabella had given Missy a message asking Xu to remain at the reception. She wanted to arrive alone in her own time. She made a supreme effort to be at the party as quickly as possible, because she instinctively felt Nicholas wanted her there to share this, the first of the receptions to honor him in his new political career.

She thought of the man behind the movie star, the real Nicholas Frayne, relating to her, Arabella Crawford. She felt strangely young and slightly immature with excitement at the ease and joy, the old-fashioned simplicity with which he courted her. The handsome, admiring looks he gave her seemed to mean more to her. It was as if she had been released in some way that allowed her to think of him openly—his looks, his hopes and dreams, his lust—with her heart as well as her mind and body. Maybe "openly" was the operative word. That was how he came after her—openly, out front, before everyone, quietly but powerfully.

She knew he had taken her like a tidal wave. Only now could she fully appreciate how very like a *tsunami* he was. She thought of him up on the big movie screen, how his staggeringly handsome presence, his open clean looks, swept over viewers, engulfed, absorbed, then released them, making them feel as if they had been touched by the gods, the sun.

In bed, on screen, with people, at work or play, this man, this tidal wave, was a subtle but powerful force, a winner.

Arabella clearly remembered every detail of the tidal wave. A few years ago she was making a routine visit to a small island in the South Pacific with some very boring businessmen. It was an island rich in bauxite and nothing else. The only nice part of the trip was flying low over tropical islands floating in the vast ocean.

There was nothing there but the bauxite company, a few very unattractive villages, and the inhabitants of the island who all worked in a profit-sharing arrangement with the island's one industry. A scientist was the only other resident. He kept a small seaplane and a helicopter. A one-man institute of oceanography, he was working there not on bauxite, but waves—ocean waves. He had a number of extraordinary detectors set up on the bed of the Pacific Ocean around the islands that did nothing but measure waves. He was an interesting man with an interesting project, so she accepted his invitation to fly with him. He was looking for a specific wave that his detectors reported as different from all the other waves in the ocean. She thought he was mad and wanted to see for herself if indeed he could spot a specific wave from the plane.

Two hours and fifteen minutes out from the bauxite island, he found his wave. He put the plane on automatic pilot, and they followed the length of the wave while he plotted its path. He showed her a small dot on his map, which he said was a deserted island called Alona Noa, and assured her that he could predict that the wave they were following was a tidal wave of vast proportions that would wipe out the island. He was extremely relieved because he knew there was nothing but an old deserted harbor and coconut palms growing down onto white sandy beaches.

The detectors had reported that this particular wave was only half an inch higher than the others. No more than that — just half an inch. Now five hours since that report, the wave was a few inches higher and traveling at a speed of 350 miles per hour.

She ignorantly said, "Surely you're not going to tell me that that long wave, which is just barely higher than the others, is a killer wave, the sort that destroys homes, factories, wipes out islands, sweeps away entire communities in seconds?"

Then he explained that the trouble comes when those long waves just a few inches higher than the others, all moving a few hundred miles per hour, pile up on a coast. It is there, on the shelving floor, that they build up to giants, higher than houses, and cause swift torrents that can drain and refill harbors, causing immense damage.

Flying just barely above the blue ocean waves sparkling in the afternoon sunlight, it all seemed impossible. One could barely see a difference between the waves.

Tim Huggins, the scientist, explained that the killer waves are not caused by tides but by undersea earthquakes that suddenly change the ocean's level. A little shiver is recorded from the first seismic wave of the earthquake through the rock of the ocean floor. What follows, about ninety minutes later, is a slow, regular oscillation of pressure that comes from motion on the sea surface. Over approximately two hours, the sea rises and falls about four times by about half an inch, and your killer wave is born.

She listened to Huggins as they flew twenty-five feet above the ocean, following the length of his quite substantial wave. It was interesting, fascinating, but that was all. She could not believe the wave he had chosen could, in her wildest imaginings, turn into his monster wall of water.

He double-checked his calculations as they flew back to the bauxite island, claiming he could predict within fifteen minutes when that wave was going to hit. She accepted his invitation to fly with him by helicopter the forty miles to Alona Noa to watch the disaster.

When he was reassured by his associates that she was an excellent helicopter pilot, he was delighted. Tim happily delivered the aircraft into her hands so he could concentrate on recording and photographing the event.

His enthusiasm was infectious. Arabella remembered thinking, while taking the helicopter up, how devoted and slightly mad he was. There was no way she could miss seeing his dream come true.

They spotted the wave twenty minutes off the shore of Alona Noa. They flew the length low, almost skimming the top of the wave. She sensed it was longer, much longer, and her feelings began to change. She could see a difference now. It was no higher but it seemed more powerful and was moving very fast toward the fringe of palm trees trailing along the beach.

They flew over the once thriving little harbor and village, then across the island. It must have been about six miles long and three miles across. There was no sign of life. They flew back to the center of the harbor and the white powdery sand beach that stretched for miles on either side. They hovered there, waiting for the wave to form itself and hit.

Tim laid out the plan. He instructed her to stay as close to the front of the wave as she could and fly with it down its length. That meant flying the length of the beach. He said that it was a bonus having a pilot and she was to handle it the best way she thought but not to depend on him; he would be too busy recording data.

Just then the entire coastline of rippling blue waves pulled back from the beach. It simply disappeared farther and farther out to sea. Arabella couldn't believe her eyes. All she could think of at that moment was: It's Krakatoa, that old movie, without the volcano and I'm in it.

She followed the retreating coastal waters out to sea. Slowly the once harmless-looking wave started to rise higher and higher into a massive wall of water. The buildup was extraordinary. It was slow, powerful, its energy dynamic. Soon it was as high as an eight-story building.

She was flying much lower than the top of the wave; she was drawn to it. It was as if she was being sucked into its eyes. The wave was taking her over. She was part of that wave. There was an enormous sexuality about it. She wanted both at once to be taken by it and be it. She wanted it to crash over her, to engulf her. It made her think of the most gigantic orgasm ever. She wanted to have the white froth gently flow over her, followed by a crashing flood that would drown her and then she would come out of it, reborn.

She rode that wave like a surfer, riding the inside of the pipeline—only she was in a helicopter instead of on a surfboard. She had the heartbeat of that wave and flew its length through its tube of water, all the time traveling in with it toward the shore. Then she sensed the moment to get out as it hit. With barely seconds to spare, she pulled out and up, just clearing the coconut palms as they disappeared under the wall of water. She swung around and rode above that tidal wave until the island was gone. Then the much diminished killer wave rolled away cross the Pacific, where it slowly dissolved.

The proper name for a tidal wave in Japanese is *tsunami*; its literal translation is "harbor wave." It was extraordinary and thrilling, from its humble beginnings to its peak, then its strike, and finally its end. It was a profound experience that she never, ever thought she'd have again. But she had. She had it with Nicholas.

She said to herself, Nicholas, when you make love to me, you take me like that tidal wave, and with you I come like that tidal wave. You devastate me with the power of us.

Arabella was rushing toward Nicholas with enthusiasm

and excitement. She wanted to share every moment of his debut, of his first public appearance as a political candidate. Arabella understood him. She was watching the public birth of a future President of the United States. This was his night, and she wanted to support him.

Nicholas was like the tidal wave. He was just that little bit higher, that little bit more special that all the others, the one that slowly grows and becomes all powerful. This was the man she wanted to be with!

Arabella looked magnificent. She knew it, as all women know when they are looking their very best. She felt the way she looked and every head then turned as she walked through the passageways confirmed how glorious she was. She wore a silver and gold brocade jacket of a thousand exquisitely worked butterflies. It was a glittering, magnificently designed St. Laurent, of pure silver thread with accents of gold and occasional tiny Cabuchon rubies set as decorations in some of the butterflies' wings.

The jeweled jacket finished just below her hip, dazzlingly elegant and severe against the soft, cream-colored crêpe de chine strapless dress that offered a tantalizing amount of cleavage while remaining within the limits of propriety. The dress hung straight but softly from the waist to the ankle, with a daring slit to the top of the thigh. She wore her hair pulled back with diamond hairpins, and clasped to the hairline at the nape of her neck were four very tiny, magnificent orchids of cream and lavender.

She walked into the Trocadero dining room behind a party of four who were greeted by the *maître d'* and shown to their table. The room was nearly half full, and many of the diners gave her discreet glances of admiration. Arabella felt their eyes upon her and was ashamed of herself for enjoying so much attention.

She thought, That's what comes from staying in the background too long. Watch out for overreacting, Arabella. Don't let it go to your head! But then she thought, Why? Why can't I enjoy it, revel in the attention? I'm not on a business trip. I never will be again. I'm here to live my life! To be with the man I love! To hell with restraint! And she smiled broadly, laughing on the inside, really, and sailed through the room.

She saw the captain's table—a long, wide, rectangle set with glittering crystal, silver, and magnificent Minton plates, for about fifty people. Down the center were beautiful floral arrangements of full-blown red tulips, irises of cerulean blue, deep purply blue, arranged cleverly among masses of white baby's breath. The arrangements were in silver baskets with handsome wide red, white, and blue ribbons tied around them, trailing down the center of the table. Ten heavy silver candelabras with white candles were ready to be lit.

The *maître d'* returned and Arabella said, "Good evening, Henri."

"Madame Crawford. Ah, madame, may I take the liberty of saying you are looking absolutely splendid this evening?"

"How kind of you to say so, Henri. I'm looking for the captain's party."

"They are on the lower level, having cocktails."

He led her to the head of the curved staircase where he unhooked the pale rose-color velvet rope and Arabella descended. She was a few stairs from the bottom when she stopped to admire the glittering scene from a perfect vantage point. As with every carefully planned detail of this magnificent ship, the lavish two-level room with the majestic staircase was designed to enhance the image of graciousness. Each evening the women dressed in their finest and descended the staircase, alone or escorted, making an entrance. Some made an effort to be dazzling, and the impact was impressive. Others were deliberately casual. The elaborate staircase entrance, reminiscent of the great liners of the past decades, was no longer featured on modern ships except the *Tatanya Annanovna*. Arabella observed that in the center of the small room, in the well where the orchestra usually played, was an enormous ice sculpture, seven feet high and seven feet across, of the American eagle. Lights were playing on the crystal-clear ice. It was amazing. Around the ball of ice on which the eagle perched were bright, healthy, green ferns.

The captain and Nicholas were standing in front of the sculpture receiving the guests. Several people greeted Arabella as they passed her on their way downstairs. A feeling of pride, an extra shot of enthusiasm for life, the world, the power to do good, were all scrambled in her thoughts as she looked out across the room and at Nicholas.

He was giving off the same magnetism that Jack Kennedy had, the intelligence of F.D.R., and the grass-roots honesty of L.B.J. She thought of the many good men with talent and a political understanding of their country and the world. In retrospect they were knights in shining armor. In any case, those days seemed to be the end of a certain kind of strength in America—but one that was waiting just below the surface to rise again, if only the right man were in office to make it happen. Maybe Nicholas Frayne could be that man.

Memories kept surfacing, thoughts of the past that had been stored away as in a memory bank.

She looked at Nicholas with the same sense of sureness she had experienced hundreds of times before about people, deals, future projects and their outcomes, political shifts that would go down in history books. Arabella knew it was possible that Nicholas could be President of the United States someday, and his decision to seek the office of Governor of Rhode Island was a daring step toward that goal.

She was, after all, qualified to judge who would make a good President. Politics were her background, dormant but still in her blood. It occurred to her as she stood viewing the scene below that for eighteen years she had been reading and following the political situation in her country as an interested citizen and storing it away. A woman with as much power as Arabella had in the corporate world was a woman who understood objectively how her own country, the United States, rated in world politics.

Her thoughts were broken by a voice. "Ah'm no cheapskate, Miss Belle," said a smiling Mike Mackay as he walked past her with his wife, Marcia. They stood a few stairs below Arabella as he went on. "Ah said, ah'm no cheapskate, Arabella. Ah'm not offerin' ya a penny for your thoughts, ah'm offerin' ya a thousand dollars!"

She smiled and said, "Hello, Marcia, hello, Mike. Make it ten thousand dollars as a political contribution to Nicholas Frayne, the first political contribution to the next Governor of the State of Rhode Island, and I will tell you."

He looked down at Nicholas and then turned back to Arabella and said, "You're sure not askin' me to back that boy just for that tiny little state? What you are askin' me, gal? What you got to tell big Mike?"

He looked at Nicholas again and turned back to Arabella. "Ah said ya were a gamblin' woman. You all really think your thoughts are worth that kind o' money?"

"Yes, I do. It's the tip of a lifetime, Mike," she replied, prettily, teasingly.

Weston Warfield came down the stairs at that moment, greeted them, and took Marcia's arm. Together they walked down the remaining stairs and into the reception line. Marcia and Mike complemented each other perfectly in style and disposition. Marcia was softspoken and reserved, whereas Mike was gregarious and emotional. Marcia appreciated Mike's wit and outgoing nature. They understood each other's behavior and motives although Marcia was more subtle in her actions than her husband. She knew that Mike wanted a few moments with Arabella and used it to her advantage to join the handsome man who appeared at her side at the appropriate moment.

Mike watched them go, then bent forward and said, softly, "Miss Belle, ah'll go for it. Ten thousand dollars the first contribution to that boy, if y'all tell me what you all was really thinkin' when ah offered to buy your thoughts. Seems to me that's a fair bet."

"Done," she said. "I was thinking, 'Arabella Crawford,

you are looking at the next great President of the United States. Too bad he is a Republican.'"

"Hell, girl, what do you mean, too bad he is a Republican? Ah say, thank God he's a Republican! Thank God again and again, girl, if your prediction comes true." Mike pulled away from her and looked her up and down and said, "Arabella, don't tell me you all is a Democrat? Never, no, you all too smart for that."

She slapped him on the back and mimicked him, "Ah sure am, pardner!" They both laughed. Mike turned away and looked down at Nicholas. He remained silent for a few seconds and then took the stairs to stand next to Arabella.

"Ah'll be God-damned, girl! He sure does have a look about him! He does have a way about him. When we were skeet-shooting this afternoon, ah said to myself, 'Mike, there's somethin' I like about that boy. There's somethin' about that boy that makes me proud to be with him.' Arabella, ya just may well be right. Ya know, I've never had much patience for politicians, but this one may be an exception. Now that you've got my ten thousand dollars, what else do ya want me to put behind that boy?"

"Mike, he's going to need men like you. Men bigger than life, self-made millionaires who believe in him, big corporate men who trust him, oil men who know about energy and where and how to tap it around the world for their country. You stick with him, learn what he has to offer as a world leader, Mike. You have a ten-thousand-dollar investment there."

"You're some number, Miss Belle. Ya really took me, didn't yah? Bought me cheap, hooked me in. Who are ya, ya shrewd, clever devil? *Why* are ya, Arabella Crawford?"

"I'm just a woman called Arabella Crawford. A woman who retired just a few days ago from the world of big business. I sold out for a great deal of money. You are looking at a retired lady, which is what I'm going to be for the rest of my life."

"Ah wouldn't bet on it. I think you are playin' me up, gal. How much did ya sell out for?"

"One hundred million dollars."

With a deadpan look on his face, Mike asked, "Gross or net?"

"Net."

"You daredevil! Ah knew it! You clever gal, ah knew it! Ah knew you were somethin' else."

Then big Mike Mackay roared with laughter. Arabella could not help it, she loved it, and laughed with him.

"You sure are somethin', some lady!"

Their laughter caught Nicholas's attention. He excused himself from the couple he was talking to and went to join them at the foot of the staircase.

Arabella and Mike walked slowly down the last few stairs. Nicholas picked up her hand and kissed it, then he shook Mike's hand and said, "Good evening, Mike."

He turned back to Arabella and their eyes met. For a split second the world disappeared for them and they were alone together. Arabella felt her heart skip a beat. She was thinking, Tidal wave . . . he's just like that tidal wave. He's sweeping over me again.

He picked up her hand in his and murmured, "For a minute there I was completely lost, swept away by you."

Then they smiled at one another, and he said, "I have never seen a woman more beautiful, more elegant. You look like a goddess revisiting earth. I shall never forget you as I see you here now."

Mike Mackay had been pulling out a giant Havana cigar and lighting it. "Those are pretty words," Mike said. "Ah'm sorry ah didn't get 'em out first. Matter of fact ah'm sorry ah didn't shanghai her that first night out."

"You were too late even then, Mike," Arabella said teasingly, as she gave him a peck on the cheek.

Mike held his hands up in a gesture of surrender and said goodnaturedly, "Ah give up, ah give up, ah'm a man who knows when he's beat." Then, looking at Arabella, he added, "Nicholas, ma boy, ah would like to make a contribution to your campaign for the governorship of the smallest state in the Union. Where do I send ma check?"

"That's very generous of you, Mike, but not at all necessary."

"Yes, it is, boy. Ah'm a straight talker so I might just as well tell ya, I want to see you win, watch how ya handle yourself and, if I like what ya have to say, then ah wouldn't be a bad guy to have on your side for the big election. Never mind the details, boy, ah see your Kandy man ovah there. Ah'll find out from him."

Mike shoved a hand out and the two men shook hands. "Good luck, Nicholas Frayne. As for you, Miss Belle, he's right—you are one gorgeous-looking woman." Then he left the two alone.

"Come on," said Nicholas. Still holding her hand, he walked her over to the captain. The three stood below the great ice eagle and were swamped by the invited guests.

Nicholas's announcement and the captain's invitation set the passengers free to pay all the attention and homage they had discreetly held back until now. The three were inundated by well-wishers. Arabella tried to slip away but Nicholas was quick. He unobtrusively grabbed her hand and, holding it tight, was able to keep her at his side.

It was exciting and thrilling for Arabella for the first fifteen minutes but then, suddenly, she had enough. Not enough of Nicholas, supporting him, watching him handle himself with the public. She just had enough of the people, of being the center of attraction, or, to put it more accurately, of standing next to the center of attraction. For someone who had remained in the background for so many years, it was still new to her, this standing in the limelight with a man.

She caught Xu's attention, giving him a look she had used many times before to say "rescue me at once." Xu was subtle in whisking her away from Nicholas's side. Before he realized what had happened, she was on the other side of the room talking to a few guests in a corner.

Eventually the quartet arrived and wandered among the guests, playing the music from the film in which Nicholas won his first Oscar. The waitresses who had been serving silver platters of pâté and smoked salmon canapés disappeared, and at the same time half a dozen waiters walked among the guests retrieving champagne glasses and asking them to join the captain in the dining room for dinner.

Nicholas found Arabella. Going up the stairs, he said, "After dinner we'll leave as soon as we can. I've arranged for a quiet corner table in the Vanya Bar for us where we can talk. Okay?"

"Yes," she replied. "That's very okay."

The glittering party walked to the dining table in pairs. Nicholas, with Arabella on his arm, was following directly behind the captain so it was not difficult for the captain to overhear their plans for escape. He turned to Nicholas and said, "I'm pleased you have made your arrangements to be together, Nicholas, because she's mine for dinner."

Nicholas looked perplexed as the captain handed Millie Merton over to him. Then, taking Arabella by the arm, the captain smiled and said in her ear, "He's not the only man who would like a little of your company, madame."

"Come along," said Millie, leading Nicholas by the arm down the length of the long table to its center, where they were placed. Opposite them were the captain and Arabella.

Arabella looked across the table at Nicholas. He had Millie Merton on one side and the octogenarian Princess Irina Navratalovski on the other. Arabella recognized her as the elegant, elderly woman in the Casino the previous night. He shrugged his shoulders as he and Arabella smiled at each other over the red, white, and blue decorations and soft candlelight, accepting their places with good grace.

The dinner was a great success. Later Nicholas remarked to Arabella how completely surprised he was and entertained by what he thought was just a silly Millie. Princess Irina was enchanting, amusing, and intelligent.

Arabella in turn told him she thought the captain had arranged the seating brilliantly. How during dinner everyone was engrossed in conversation or food and the atmosphere was electric with good cheer. How she was well entertained by Marvin Kandy and how she found Cotille amusing and kind. She also told Nicholas about the warmth and caring that Dr. St. John dispensed to Cotille.

The company, food, and wine were all enhanced by the excitement of the occasion, and several toasts were made during the meal. There were a few after-dinner speeches organized by the captain. The speakers, including Mike Mackay, John Van Renders, and Marvin Kandy, rose to the occasion admirably.

Eventually the captain rose from his chair and helped Arabella from hers. The party broke up. The guests drifted away, arranging the rest of the evening for themselves after thanking the captain.

Arabella waited with Marvin, Cotille, and Dr. St. John for Nicholas to get around the long table and join them. She could not help hearing Cotille say to Marvin, "Marvin, when I appealed to you for help in the early hours of this morning you really delivered. I'm very happy to be here with you and the others." She slipped her arm through Dr. St. John's and added, "Thanks, Marvin."

With that the couple bade them good night and left. Arabella looked at Marvin and said, "That's a grateful friend, Marv."

"Arabella, I love people—all kinds of people, but especially I love ladies. I love to get into ladies, not only sexually, but inside their hearts and their heads. I love the female mind. The way a lady thinks, the way a lady loves, the way a lady is made. I have a neverending love of the female. I love everything about the body of a woman and I know how to make a lady happy. Answer a lady's needs, give ladies what they want, and they bloom like wildflowers in a field."

"And what did you give Cotille?" Arabella asked.

"Friendship, mostly. But I also introduced her to Dr. Booker St. John, a terrific guy."

Arabella was touched. She said, "I can understand why Nicholas is so close to you, why you mean so much to him."

Nicholas arrived just at that moment and smiled at her. As always, since the very first time they set eyes on each other, she felt herself drawn to him. Unconsciously she took a step closer to him. He put his arm around her waist and they looked into each other's face, smiling.

He said, "Hello there."

"Hello."

Someone passed by them at that moment and wished Nicholas luck. He had to release her to shake hands.

Then he said to Marvin, "It was really nice, didn't you think so, Marv?"

"Yes, I sure did. It was a lovely kick-off for you, Nick. So far, so good. All's going as planned, even better than planned. Wait till you read the telexes of support and congratulations! I'm beginning to think you should have run in California! You're a very popular guy there, and the questions of why you didn't run for office there are already coming in."

He then turned to Arabella and said, "Arabella, don't keep him up too late. We have a great deal to get through before we dock. Good night you two." He picked up Arabella's hands and kissed first one, then the other as he said, "Good night, glorious Arabella Crawford. I'm very happy you're with us on this maiden voyage."

"You like him, don't you?" asked Nicholas, as he walked with her from the dining room.

Arabella said, "Yes, I do and I liked your glittering debut as well. The captain did you proud. I felt very privileged to be there with you."

"I'm grateful to the captain. I thought it went off very well. Everyone seemed to be enjoying themselves tremendously. But I wanted you next to me. I must've looked across the table at you a hundred times! I'm so happy you're here, Arabella."

"So am I. I'm beginning to think more than I've realized."

They were interrupted by a state senator from the Midwest and his wife who wished Nicholas well. They had taken only a few more steps when a well-known retired judge approached them, and then the chairman of the board of a Fortune 500 company who offered his congratulations. Nicholas was gracious and charming. Standing next to him, Arabella realized he was sincerely touched by their good wishes and, yes, even a little humble.

They took the stairs down to the deck below and walked toward the Vanya Bar. They passed a door with a neat bronze sign that read "Linen Room." Nicholas pushed the door open and, seeing the room empty, switched on the light. He looked up and down the empty passageway and quickly, before anyone could catch them, pulled Arabella into the room.

He stood with his back against the door. The walls were nothing but shelf upon shelf of bed linen—clean, white, sweet-smelling bed linen, stacks upon stacks of neatly folded white sheets and pillowcases. In the center of the room was a large trestle table.

He gave Arabella his best movie-star look of seduction, all the while grinning madly.

"You're mad!" she said, laughing. "Someone will catch us."

He turned and looked for the lock. There was none. "Never mind," he said, laughing too. "You're right. I'm mad—mad about you. Come here; no one's coming in to look for linen at this hour."

He took her in his arms and suddenly their laughter disappeared. He held her tightly to him and she felt herself giving way. Giving way most tenderly, most lovingly. He whispered in her ear, "I wanted to do this all evening and couldn't wait one more minute."

He released her just enough to enable him to look at her face, stroke her forehead, her cheek. Then he kissed her deeply, passionately. Every inch of Arabella's skin began to tingle. She raised her arms and put them around his neck. The two looked at each other with both passion and affection.

His hands stroked her hair that had been piled up away from her face, then caressed ever so lightly the cascade of white moth orchids that hung full and soft at the nape of her neck.

"I've never seen hair more lovely than yours this evening. Or, for that matter, a woman more lovely than you are."

He put his hands on her shoulders and turned her around so her back was to him, in order that he might have a better look at all of her.

He said, "You're a miracle!" He caressed Arabella's shoulders and her lovely, virtually bare back. He slipped his hands underneath her arms around toward the front and lingered on the firm full swell of her breasts while he kissed her several times over her back and shoulders.

Feeling passion rising in him, Arabella turned her head, trying to look at him. "Nicholas, this is madness."

"Yes, it is madness," he agreed in a husky whisper and removed a huge square-cut diamond earring from her ear, replacing it with his mouth. He kissed and sucked on her earlobe and said, "I can hardly help myself—you're so delectable. I wanted to tell you all day how special you are, how much I think about you. I find you irresistible."

Arabella removed the hand caressing the side of her breasts, turned the palm upward, and put it to her mouth to kiss it. He felt the touch of her tongue on his palm and a shiver of delight went through him. He put his cheek to hers and then slowly released her.

He turned her around and put the diamond back on her earlobe, then put the palms of his hands over the erect nipples he could see through the crêpe de chine dress. Nicholas held her that way for a few seconds, closing his eyes, trying to regain his composure.

Then he dropped his hands to his sides and asked, "Shall we go to my cabin or the Vanya Bar?"

"The bar, I think. We're celebrating, remember? We're celebrating Nicholas Frayne, Rhode Island, and America!"

He picked her jacket up off the table and helped her on with it. Very gently he lifted her hair off the nape of her neck, not wanting to damage the still fresh and succulent flowers.

Arabella straightened the jacket and then picked up the small purse she had laid on the table. She opened it and found her ivory Fabergé powder box. She checked her face in its small mirror, repairing the tiny smudges of lipstick at the corners of her mouth, and then used the powder puff. She closed the lid firmly by the clasp, an emerald cut in the shape of a leaf, and replaced it in her purse.

She then said, "Well, handsome, if you want me to vote for you for President, you had better get us out of this cupboard first! And you had bloody well get us out unseen! We hardly look like a maid and butler!"

He laughed and took her by the hand, opened the door a crack, and looked down the passageway to the left, then to the right. He turned to her and said, "All clear."

Leading her, he was halfway out of the door when he heard people coming around the corner. Quick as a flash he pushed her back in the closet and closed the door. The fear of being caught made them both giddy and excited. They suppressed their giggles and were very quiet while the people passed the linen room.

Nicholas whispered, "I may be mad, but I also think I'm getting stupid! I have you alone in a room filled with sheets and pillowcases and haven't even tried to take advantage of you! And there's even this most exciting table to do dastardly deeds upon!" He raised his eyebrows and twirled an imaginary mustache. They heard the voices disappearing in the distance.

"Oh," Arabella said, accepting the challenge. She placed her handbag on the table and then, looking him mischievously in the eye, she opened his jacket and proceeded to unzip his fly. He stood his ground bravely until she slipped her hand into his underpants, then he said, "Remember, Arabella, there's no lock on this door!"

Arabella was dropping to her knees when he caught her by the elbows and pulled her up. They were both convulsed with laughter.

"Now you've done it!" he said. They both watched as he tried to tuck away a very substantial erection.

"What a wicked woman you are! You know very well how much I like that. I should teach you a lesson and make you carry through even though I know you're afraid of being caught in the act. I'll get you for this, you teaser!"

The affection, mixed with the sexuality, resulted in one very big bear hug. Nicholas put out the light and took Arabella close to him in his arms. After a few silent minutes in the darkened room Nicholas opened the door a crack.

He whispered, "The passageway is clear."

She said, "Are you sure? I think I'd better double-check."

She did, it was, and they left.

Chapter Sixteen

Arabella walked into the Vanya Bar on Nicholas's arm. "It's wonderful! Oh, Nicholas, what a room!" she said, as she looked up two stories to the silver-gilt-carved ceiling and the rock-crystal chandelier.

"I think it's my favorite room on the ship. As a matter of fact, it might be one of my favorite bars in the world," he said.

A magnificent seven-foot-long slab of jasper with chamfered edges five inches thick served as the bar's top, resting on a carved base of the same stone with sections of rock crystal. The opaque, semiprecious stone, a quartz of rich violet—the rarest color of all—was exquisite. It was made even more interesting by the contrast with the very masculine look of the dark-paneled room. It was unmistakably Russian opulence, very Catherine the Great.

Nicholas walked her around the room to admire the paintings of Armenian dancing girls. They sat down in one corner in deep, comfortable, jasper-colored velvet chairs. The rock-crystal table between them had a huge ornate silver champagne cooler on it and two exquisite, cone-shaped crystal glasses, their stems and base of gold encrusted with amethysts and red coral beads.

A waiter arrived at once and opened a bottle of vintage Dom Perignon champagne and filled their glasses, "With the compliments of the gentleman in the corner," he said. When he left Nicholas picked them both up and handed one to Arabella.

"Do you know him?" she asked.

"No, I've never seen him before."

"This is your first bribe, then, as a politician!"

"Arabella, of course not. He sent it over to you, I'm sure. Look at him! He's got puppy love, not politics, written all over his face."

"Well, let's both toast him then." They raised their glasses in the direction of their benefactor, then they touched the rims together and Nicholas said, "To Tolstoy and Nabokov—how they would have loved this room! Ah, if they saw you here as I do, they would make you one of their heroines. Tolstoy would have woven a love story around you and made you even more dazzling than Anna Karenina."

They looked at each other. Then with hands stretched out across the table, they clicked their glasses together again and drank.

Nicholas felt a little embarrassed, as if he had given a deep secret away. He hesitated and after a moment of awkward silence said, "What makes this room are the details. I would love to know the details about the details—how they carved that bar, where the materials came from, how the people lived who did the work and who they did it for. I suppose that's really what my passion for history is all about—details."

"I think I understand, Nicholas. You believe that people and places are extraordinary, that the combination of facts and backgrounds makes each one of us unique and full of promise."

"Yes, that's right. And I think what makes two people work as one happy couple is the right balance of similar and opposite in those details. And timing."

"Timing. A year ago we never would have given each other a chance. I was so involved with my business and you were ensconced in Hollywood. Now we're both at crossroads in our lives. Maybe that's what's making us so open to possibility."

"Possibility and vulnerability. We're both giving up things we're sure we're good at for a chance at something else."

"It won't be easy for you, Nicholas. There will be some terrible burdens."

Nicholas took a long puff on his cigar. He then refilled

their glasses and, picking her hand up, he said, "You're right. You see things so clearly. If it will be difficult for me to change, I think it will be just as difficult for you. My changes are more public, but yours may go even deeper. You are counting heavily on yourself. If you let me, I can help you, teach you. I have a knowledge of many things you want to do in your life. Please let me be part of it, enjoy life with you. I want to see you bloom with discovery. I want to be part of the joy and fun you're going to have in your life now."

Arabella was touched again by the all-American inno-cence, the kindness, the sincerity, and always the beauty—the handsome, masculine, physical beauty of the man. She had to control the desire she had to move over and climb into his lap, to be cuddled by him. Instead she took the hand that was holding hers and kissed it.

She said, "That would be heaven for me! Oh yes, yes, I accept. There's so much I missed, so much you've done that I want to be a part of. I may be a good businesswoman, but I'm virtually ignorant of most of the classics. I don't know how to ski, and I can't remember the last time I took a walk in the woods. I know the work of a few painters, no more than one or two poets, a piece or two of Mozart, Haydn, Bach, Beethoven, Wagner, and touches of modern and other classical composers. But I've never had the time to sit back and enjoy them as I will now."

"And how to cook," he added. "I'm a pretty good chef but will have little time for cooking, so I'll teach you. Oh, Arabella, we're going to have a really fine time together!"

"Nicholas, it will be perfect. While you're sweating over the major issues of the day and learning the ins and outs of federal legislation, I'll be spending endless, frivolous hours at the hairdresser and in the shops, having lunch with girl friends and going to galleries and museums, decorating the most wonderful houses and planting enviable gardens. . . ."

A little tipsy by now, they both started laughing at their enthusiastic scenarios.

"We're beginning to sound like an old movie—you know,

the one with Mickey Rooney and Judy Garland: 'Gee, my dad's got a barn. We could put on a play!'"

Nicholas laughed and said, "The whole world will wonder how I'm able to keep such a great beauty at my side! They'll all gasp with wonder and vote for me simply on the basis that if I'm clever enough to win such a lady, I'm clever enough to be their President."

The second bottle of champagne was being opened and both of them were well on the way to inebriation.

"And what about me? What will the whole world say about me?" asked Arabella. "Who is she? How does she have the luck to have Nicholas Frayne, the Governor of Rhode Island, as a friend? Do you know that she makes a divine mayonnaise and spends most of her time in the hairdresser?"

Suddenly the two became giddy, could hardly stop laughing.

"That sounds ridiculous," said Nicholas.

"It is," said Arabella. "I can't make mayonnaise!" The two of them burst out laughing again.

"Oh, stop, stop!" said Arabella. "I want to be serious. Talk to me. There's so much I really want to know about you. Tell me everything so I can weave the details with the passionate man I already know. How will I be able to help you, support you, if I don't know everything? I want to, you know, just as much as you want to be part of my life and help me."

"Arabella, there are so many things I want to tell you about myself. I want you to know me. Where to begin?

"This sounds ridiculous, egocentric, but I don't mean it that way. I suddenly feel in awe of us. It's as if I, Nicholas Frayne, had climbed out of my skin and am standing a few feet away watching us sitting here. It could be that I'm in a state of wonder, astonishment, bewilderment at having arrived here this night."

He squeezed both her hands in his and continued. "It's been said that a man's choices are conditioned by his past experience. I've always believed it to be true. I also believe that I'm here because I've made the correct choices. It feels to me that it's always been an easy thing to do—to make the right choice. Maybe that is my gift. In this unfair world I seem to have lived a charmed life. It's possible that the one great tragedy of my life is that there is no tragedy. That there never has been, and I have a tiny spot in my brain that reassures me that there never will be."

Nicholas told her how he had married his childhood sweetheart, why he loved her and left her, why she loved him and made him leave her. What a joy his son was to him, how supportive they were to each other, with a mutual respect and admiration, a deep love rarely found in a father-son relationship. He told her of Sylves, his mistress and best friend, the woman he loved but liked much more than he loved. The woman who had satisfied him sexually but who he had no passion for. Sylves and Nicholas—two friends who tried desperately for so long to love each other, who finally gave up and settled for friendship.

"I come from old New England stock who believe that you have to catch every gust of wind to form yourself. I'm from Newport, sailing people, people who believe that death is always with you, an inch away; that one must form oneself, use oneself up before death arrives. The life you live until that moment is strictly of your own making.

"That idea has served me well—from a happy childhood, through my college years and the navy, to being an actor. As a husband and a father sometimes I may have been less thoughtful than I should have, but I think I've matured now, and I have truly remarkable relationships with my ex-wife and son.

"I'm one of those uncomplicated people who has enjoyed their life and work completely."

"I don't think I've ever known anyone beyond six years of age with your optimism," Arabella answered. "It's wonderful. I can't say that has always been the case for me, but I can say that it's going to be. It's extraordinary, the opposite experiences we've had. I've lived so much of my life with tragedy around me. I may never have been fatally wounded, but I've been bruised. Even when the bruises healed, they did leave marks. No, I can't say that I've enjoyed every minute of my life."

"I want you to enjoy it now, with me. Arabella," he went on, taking her hand in his. "I'm sure you know how reporters and fans love to spy on world-famous people. Especially world-famous lovers. It could make you paranoid, very secretive. I would hate to be even partially responsible for that happening to you, or to bring you any kind of discomfort. But I want you to be part of my life."

The world disappeared for Arabella and Nicholas. They sat together, silenced by the thinly veiled declaration that they should become world-famous lovers. Having been previously conditioned to love a man in the shadows of his life, Nicholas's announcement that they should parade their love for each other, out in the open, before the world, pricked Arabella's emotions so deeply that tears appeared in her eyes.

Still silent, Nicholas reached out and picked a tear up from her cheek onto his finger. He waited and then, when he had given her a minute to calm herself, asked in a voice filled with concern and warmth, "Are you all right?"

She nodded, then she spoke. "Until this moment here with you, I've never realized how very alone I've been in the past. The realization combined with too much wine, the excitement of your celebration and your loving me is enough to bring a tear to any girl's eye!"

She smiled at him, a tired but loving smile. The sensitive Nicholas understood. He said, "You must be exhausted. Come on, I'll put you to bed."

They left the bar with his arm around her waist, her head leaning on his shoulder. Nicholas took Arabella's handbag from her as they approached her stateroom door. He found the key and let them in. They walked through the darkened staterooms to the bedroom where he put a small light on and walked her to the bed.

Arabella was physically and emotionally exhausted. She said, "Nicholas, I am so sleepy, but so very, very happy."

She put her arms around his neck and laid her head on his chest. She was limp with tiredness and a sense of relief— somewhere in her soul she felt that she had found the man she hadn't let herself believe existed.

He removed her diamond hairpins and said, "I'm going to undress you and put you to bed. I won't stay because I think you should sleep. I'll come for you in time for lunch. Until then do get a good rest." He kissed her gently on the forehead, the way a parent kisses a sleepy child. Her gold and silver hair tumbled down around her shoulders. He ran his fingers through it. He stood back, still holding her, and took a long look at Arabella. He was filled yet again with admiration and love for the woman before him. He took the diamonds off her ears and helped her off with the sparkling, jeweled jacket and draped it over his arm.

As she sat on the edge of the bed, she said, "Nicholas? Do you think it's possible to love two people at the same time?"

"Yes, my darling. But you can only be *in love* with one. You love in different ways," he answered. "Why do you ask?"

"Emotional house-cleaning," she said slowly, trying not to slur her words. She bent toward him and kissed him. The warmth of her soft lips and the depths of her passion were exquisite to Nicholas.

"Forgive me, Nicholas," she said. "I've had too much wine."

"I know," he said, patting her on the cheek. "Don't worry, you'll soon be asleep."

He bent down and removed her shoes, putting them neatly to one side. The slit of her silk dress had fallen open, showing her long, luscious legs. He ran his hands over them and up under the dress, peeled off her stockings, and kissed her naked thighs. He helped her off with her dress, and she stood naked before him. Gently he folded her in his arms and placed his head on her shoulder. He was surprised to find himself trembling with passion for her. He ran his hand over her lovely back and curvaceous bottom. Then he picked her up in his arms and laid her down on the bed, partly covering her with the pale-peach satin eiderdown.

He went to close the curtains over the porthole. When he returned to her, she said sleepily, as she lifted the eiderdown, "Come, lie down with me. I want to feel you next to me until I fall asleep."

No sooner had he taken his shoes off and was lying beside her than she was drifting off into the first stage of sleep.

He put his lips to hers and kissed her tenderly, lightly, not to wake her. Nicholas was amazed at how completely he had fallen in love with Arabella. Lying on his side and leaning on his elbow, he studied the woman he loved. He looked at her bare breasts, his eyes lingered over her midriff, the soft, supple flesh, lovely smooth skin. His gaze wandered to her luscious mound of golden hair and over the lovely contour of her hips.

Overwhelmed with joy, he lowered his face to kiss her once more. Then with tenderness he slowly pulled the cover over her shoulders, quietly slipped off the bed, and turned out the light.

Walking to his stateroom, Nicholas knew that two lucky people had found the love of a lifetime.

Chapter Seventeen

Awesome, magical and awesome—those were the only words to describe it. The passengers on board the S.S. *Tatanya Annanovna* were spellbound as the ship sailed through the massive floating icebergs: giant, rugged pieces of terrain, nothing but snow and ice. Mountains with peaks and valleys, blindingly white under a bright sun, they loomed up from a dark-blue Atlantic Ocean. It was a freezing cold day with not a drop of wind and a crystal-clear atmosphere—not a cloud in sight. Even the sky looked white from the glare of the sun on the snow-covered icebergs.

A miracle of nature, they were a winter wonderland—so pure and proud, untouched by man. There was a godliness about the experience. It was heavenly—what one could imagine was lying behind the pearly gates. The ship's passengers were speechless, wordless, bowled over but rooted to the rails where they stood, dazed by the mysterious, enigmatic power and beauty of the icebergs. There were not two or three but more like a floating field of twenty-five or thirty, reaching to gigantic heights—mini-Annapurnas, –Mount Everests.

During her slow passage through the open channels among the icebergs, the *Annanovna* was completely surrounded by the snowy peaks for over an hour—mountainous landscapes in a frozen world.

Captain Hamilton had been right. It was an extraordinary treat for the maiden voyage of the S.S. *Tatanya Annanovna* and its passengers. Up on the bridge with his officers and the ship's sophisticated equipment, the captain was able to navigate through the clear channels with complete safety, clearing one or two of the icebergs with as little as ten feet to spare. The icebergs they sailed through surpassed all man-made wonders.

Arabella, swathed in sable against the cold, stood next to Nicholas, who was dressed in his heavy gray herringbone trousers, cashmere sweater and jacket under a brown leather coat and tweed cap. Under her sable coat, Arabella was naked. She failed to advise Nicholas of this fact when he arrived to share this spectacle of nature with her. She had felt a little wicked but highly excited when she made the decision to surprise him.

The couple took this voyage through the icebergs together on Arabella's private deck. The experience was so exhilarating it made Arabella feel high, as if she had been drugged and had landed on another planet. The constant motion as the huge vessel rocked and swayed back and forth, bobbing up and down in rhythm with the waves, excited Arabella. It seemed as though the ship abandoned itself to the force of the waves. She also felt a total sense of abandon.

The ship maneuvered between two particularly large icebergs whose craggy peaks appeared more treacherous because they plunged from such enormous heights straight down into the depths of the ocean.

The sensations of danger, the exhilaration of the ocean and the huge phalliclike icebergs surrounding her created such sensations within her that Arabella could no longer contain her excitement.

Nicholas seemed oblivious and was totally entranced by the magnificent sights before him. She took his hand, guided him to the reclining chair closest to the outside edge of the deck near the water. He was startled by her actions and by the sudden fine, icy spray that swept over them.

"Arabella, what . . ."

He was speechless as Arabella pushed him gently down into the chair. She stood over him, facing him, straddling the chair, and slowly opened her coat. He was transfixed. Her high level of excitement stimulated him. She looked directly into his eyes, cautioning him not to speak, as in one fluid motion she freed his erection, lowered herself onto him, and enclosed them both in her warm, luxurious fur.

They held each other in silence, making no voluntary movements but letting their bodies move in rhythm with the sea. At moments they just held each other and floated as though on a placid lake. Then, unexpectedly, huge chunks of ice crashing into the sea would cause the ship to lurch against the waves with a violent motion.

Time seemed endless and they held each other through orgasms unlike any they ever experienced.

The last channel was hardly straight sailing but the *Annanovna* followed it faithfully, carefully, through its twists and turns. Then, suddenly, as if coming to the end of a maze, it was over. There was nothing but the great wide-open Atlantic as far as the eye could see.

The end of the iceberg voyage was no less dramatic than its beginning. Once the ship left the channel and the icebergs behind, the ocean returned to its old way of rough-and-tumble waves, the wind picked up, even the sounds came back—waves hitting the bow as it cut through the water.

It was enough to make one wonder: Was it a fantasy, this little mysterious voyage among the icebergs? This voyage within a voyage?

Arabella slowly stood and moved away from Nicholas. She took his hands and pulled him up out of the chair. They walked to the starboard side of the deck, leaned over the rail, and watched the icebergs recede. When they were no more than white dots on the horizon, Nicholas put his arm around her and they walked back into Arabella's drawing room. They both had tears mixed with salt water crystallizing in their eyes. Arabella shivered. Her hands were pink with cold. She put them to her mouth and blew on them, hoping the warm air from her body would thaw them out quickly. Then she pulled her coat tight around her body.

Nicholas pulled off his cap and dropped it on a chair, then he quickly shed his brown leather coat that was stiff with cold. He pulled off his fur-lined gloves and went over to Arabella and began rubbing her hands. He removed the coat and quickly wrapped her in the cashmere robe he picked up from the chair. They both remained silent.

Then he kissed the tip of her nose and said, "Christ, Arabella, you're frozen!"

"Well, so are you!" replied Arabella. "Your ears are bright red!"

He put his hands to his ears. "You're right, I can hardly feel them, they're so numb."

Just then Xu appeared from the pantry with a silver tray carrying two hot toddies. Arabella walked to the sofa and sat down. Holding the hot silver cup with both hands, she drank the warming liquid.

"Oh, that's better!" she said. Looking around the room, she focused on the vast array of fresh flowers. She turned to Nicholas and said, "My, but you spoil me! How did you do it? When I woke up this morning and came into this room the last thing I expected was this," she said, waving one arm as if to encompass the whole room.

Nicholas began to laugh. He said, "Divine, isn't it? It's a good thing we dock the day after tomorrow. I've hardly left a flower in the shop!"

Arabella rose from the sofa and went to him where he sat in the big, deep easy chair. She gently folded herself onto his lap and when he had put his arm around her, she snuggled next to him. They remained that way while drinking their hot toddies. They did not speak, simply sat drinking and looking at the room Nicholas had turned into a Garden of Eden.

There were azaleas in every color, dozens of pots of them in varying sizes; tulips and hyacinths; lily of the valley and lilac; iris and jasmine; carnations and honeysuckle and more white long-stemmed roses than Arabella had seen in her life. Baskets and vases, plants in pots of every size had been placed with great thought and care while she had been sleeping.

Warmed by the hot toddy, Arabella said lazily, "What contrast—sailing through a field of icebergs and then walking into a spring garden."

Nicholas replied, with a twinkle in his eye, "I will never forget that part of the voyage. I don't think I've ever understood nature, the power or the beauty of it, but I certainly do now!"

She looked over to him and said, in an impish sort of voice, "Are you going to feed me? I'm famished."

"Sure, I'm going to feed you. Come on," he said, reluctantly getting up from the chair.

"Oh," she said, with a slightly mischievous look in her eyes. "I think I'd better dress for the occasion. Don't wait. You go on and order us a sumptuous lunch. Surprise me. I'll be there as quickly as I can."

He watched her run through the rooms to dress. He shook his head, smiling, and happily went to do as he had been told.

The Gorky Grill was empty. It was a very pleasant room to have lunch in—small, no more than ten tables, all white walls and carpet with comfortable dining chairs covered in yellow velvet and small square tables covered in sparkling white linen. It boasted the only dinner service in the world designed by Miró.

There was one single large crystal chandelier in the middle of the room and recessed pinpoint lights illuminated each painting. The walls were covered in oil paintings, gouaches, watercolors, and drawings—all by Gorky. It was the finest collection in the world. The slashes of vibrant color, emotion, drama of the abstract paintings were exciting and made even richer and more wonderful because they were mounted in heavy, richly carved eighteenth-century frames.

Nicholas apologized to the waiter for being so late and, as usual, the straightforward and strong Nicholas Frayne charm worked wonders. The chef was happy to stay and cook anything for him he liked. He was presented with an enormous menu to choose from.

First he ordered a bottle of the best Roederer Cristal. The waiter was dispatched immediately to put it on ice and bring the cooler to the table. Nicholas and Arabella were to be the only diners in the room that made him think of Italy, sunshine, the Mediterranean, a small cove near Portofino. One day he would take Arabella there.

Nicholas said to the *maître d'*, "Italian—we would love to have Italian food. Yes, a fine, gorgeous Italian meal. Is that possible?"

"But of course, sir" came the answer. "One minute, sir."

The man returned with the chef and together the three selected a menu: mussels steamed in their own broth; pasta—a tagliatelli in a sauce of smoked salmon in cream with fresh tarragon and mint; escalope of veal in a lemon sauce; braised spinach with garlic and oil; for dessert, zabaglione; for wines, the best Italian whites and reds selected by the chef.

Nicholas looked at his watch. Arabella was still not with him. He stood up, put on his glasses, and gave himself a tour around the room looking at the paintings. That was how Arabella found him. She walked up behind him and slipped her arms around his waist.

"Hello," she whispered. "What beautiful paintings! How very, very beautiful."

She stepped to his side and stood with him, admiring a small Gorky, one of the artist's earlier works.

"Who painted them?" she asked.

"Gorky," he said. "Fantastic, aren't they?"

"Oh, yes," she said, "very fantastic. You see how ignorant I am? I've never seen or heard of Gorky."

They walked around the room looking at the artist's work. The headwaiter sent a waiter over to them with two glasses of champagne on a tray. They drank and ambled around the room discussing the artist and his work.

Over a slow, lazy lunch of the most sublime food and wine, they spoke of many things. Places they had been, things they had done, paintings they had seen, houses they had lived in.

Nicholas told her of his beach house in Malibu, his ranch overlooking the Pacific Ocean up in Santa Barbara, the winter lodge he had built on top of a mountain in Idaho, reached only by skis or in the Fraynes' own funicular, the houses he had bought and conserved in eighteenth-century Newport.

When he asked Arabella about the houses she lived in, he was quite shocked to learn they had, for most of her life, been hotels, temporary dwellings, except for the family house on the Potomac.

"But not anymore," she said.

"Hence the real estate portfolios," he said.

"Yes. I'm thrilled I'm about to put down roots, have a real home."

She asked him to tell her about Newport, the Newport he knew as a boy and grew up in; Rhode Island, now the place he wanted to govern.

Over that lovely, lazy Italian lunch, surrounded by Gorky paintings, Nicholas began.

"Well, the Newport, Rhode Island, I come from is not the Newport of the great summer palaces on Belleview Avenue and Ocean Drive, although I've been a guest at one or the other from time to time. The splendors of Belcourt, Ochre Court, Marble House, The Elms, The Breakers, and my favorite, The Moores, are absolutely fantastic. Those old homes, those glorious, late-nineteenth-century forty-room 'cottages' on the water are the nearest thing we have in America to palaces. They're outrageous and decadent, but I adore them.

"My Newport is colonial Newport. All the Fraynes, on both sides of the family, trace themselves back to 1639, when the town was settled. We were sea captains and entrepreneurs mostly, and later city elders and even a mayor. Newport was the most prosperous seaport on the Atlantic Coast and the Fraynes were always a well-respected part of the community.

"They were hard-working folk who prospered and became fairly wealthy. With their money they built sturdy but increasingly elegant homes. They took pride in their homes and gardens and still do today, and within the family everyone refers to the houses by the name of the first member who lived there. I grew up in Captain John's house.

"Wait till you see it, Arabella. You'll love Newport and the wonderful old houses—vestiges of what it once was. It's remarkable how many of the great houses were destroyed during the American Revolution, yet still the city has more buildings of colonial origin than any other city in the United States."

"It sounds just glorious, Nicholas. And to hear you so excited about it is amazing. After all, you've been all over the world, exposed to lots of things, and yet I sense you're really looking forward to living in Newport again."

"Absolutely! I can't wait. Captain John's house isn't vacant. My sister Peggy lives there with her family now, but I've had my eye on a great little place for years. It's the Williams house—complete with pot-belly stove and fireplace in the kitchen, wide floorboards, and a view of the ocean. Peggy is trying to buy it for me now."

"It sounds lovely. It all does. Newport, I mean. All that solidity and continuity must help create a secure childhood. In Washington, everything changed with every election. What do you think of when you look back on growing up in New England?"

"Our trees, the leaves changing color in fall. There's nowhere in the world I've seen a sight like that! And the coast, with its deep harbors and bays, and the mysterious Atlantic Ocean. The beaches and sand dunes, the tall, wispy dune grasses. Lots of lobsters and clambakes on the beach. Sailing and swimming. It's all very innocent-sounding, but it was a wonderful time for me. I didn't even mind going to school."

Arabella laughed and asked, "Is this a campaign speech?"

"Yes, it sure is! I'm trying to win you over, make you give me and my state a voice of confidence. I want you to love Rhode Island. We aren't all history either. We've progressed both in negative and positive ways. Times have changed. There are drug problems, and economic problems, and political differences galore. The WASPs are now fighting not to become the minority among the ethnics. The state is a cross-section of America as it is today, a microcosm of the whole United States.

"Don't look at me that way, Arabella."

"What way?"

"As if I were a salesman for the American Dream. I know I am, but I shouldn't have to sell it to you. I only want you to know what I am and accept it."

"I *do* accept you. I'm even proud of you because you're trying to do right, to do something you believe in. What I don't understand is why you ever left!"

"It wasn't anything I planned. Things just happened to me. And I rode the tide. One day I was a high school football player in love with the girl next door, then I was offered a chance to play for Yale. The summer before my freshmen year I was a lifeguard at the Cape. I started hanging out with some kids who were doing summer stock, and I was bitten by the bug. At Yale I was able to find great teachers who helped me get my first jobs in the theater when I graduated. The next step, going to Hollywood and doing films, just seemed to be a natural progression.

"I've had such a rich life, Arabella. I owe so much to my country, to my family, and to my heritage. I have always maintained a home in Newport, always thought of it as 'home,' and always found time to return at least once each year and do something for the community. I'm drawn back to Newport now. It's the natural place for me to launch my new beginning."

"It sounds wonderful, your Newport, your Rhode Island!"

"You don't know it at all?"

"No, not at all, except for some real estate brochures I've seen. To hear you speak of your youth and the way you were brought up makes me understand why you think you're so lucky. My background was so very different.

"You would love the Crawford house, though. The house I sort of grew up in. My mother still lives there. I think you'll fall in love with her—everyone does. I must take you there one day. Maybe when the roses are in bloom."

"No, I don't want to wait until then. I want to know all about you, see where you were born, what your life was like, how you became the woman you are now."

"It's funny. I've never said this out loud to anyone before, but I think I've always pictured my growing up as happening at very distinct moments, rather than gradually."

Arabella felt herself grow nervous, her palms sweat. She was revealing more to this man than she had intended— more than she ever had shown of herself to anyone at all— yet she felt compelled to do so.

"Tell me, Arabella," Nicholas said, reaching for her hands across the table.

"The first time was when my mother came home from the war and the knowledge of the pain of life came with her. The second moment was when my father died and I understood the finality of death. The third happened over a long period of time." Arabella held Nicholas's hands tightly in hers. She looked into his eyes steadily, as if trying to measure what impact her next words were having on him.

"I had a lover for many years. He was very important to me in many ways. He was much older than I, and married. Our relationship was very complex; we fulfilled a lot of needs in each other, but he never left his wife for me. I used to cry myself to sleep, alone, and wonder why fate had been so cruel to me. What I finally learned, after many years and much pain, was that I had chosen this route after all; that *I* was always in control of my fate but had failed to recognize that. I'm still learning that."

"Arabella, what happened to him? To the two of you?"

"We've seen less and less of each other over the years. He lives in England and we'd meet in London or Paris. I think at some point we were actually addicted to each other— physically and emotionally. It wasn't very healthy, I'm afraid."

"When did you see him last?"

"Seven or eight months ago I saw him in London, but

it felt like a chore, having to look him up. The joy has been gone for a while."

"Have you spoken to him since?"

Arabella took a deep breath and another sip of champagne. "Yes, actually, I spoke to him today. He's been calling me every day since we sailed."

"What! All of a sudden he's calling every day? What's gotten into him?"

"Nicholas, it's so ironic. I used to fantasize about it, and now it's happened and I could care less. It's just too, too late—the moment passed years ago."

"What's too late? What was your fantasy?"

"My fantasy was that his wife would die and he would marry me."

"She's died?"

"Yes. And he wants to marry me." Arabella felt tears well up in her eyes; whether it was from tension or sadness she wasn't quite sure. Nicholas reached across the table and held her shoulders firmly.

"And what do you want?"

"I want to start a new life."

"Then that's what you're going to do. Come on, Arabella, I'll help you if you'll let me. First and foremost, I want to be your friend!"

"Oh, Nicholas." Arabella had tears rolling down her cheeks now, but she was laughing. "That's the fourth one. I mean the next big chunk of growing up was thanks to you!"

Nicholas took out his handkerchief and wiped Arabella's tears away.

"All of a sudden," she went on, "I feel that I understand love. It's graceful, it's honest. Finding you was like finding the other half of my soul."

Nicholas walked around as Arabella stood up. Without a word they hugged each other fiercely. After a long moment they stepped apart and realized they were in a public dining room, but since it was late, their only audience had been their waiter, who stood off in the corner a bit misty-eyed.

Afterward the pair walked into the kitchen with three quarters of a bottle of champagne for the chef to thank him for such a glorious lunch. Arabella could hardly believe it when she heard herself ask the chef for the recipe for smoked salmon and cream sauce.

She turned to Nicholas and said, "Well, that's a first! I usually ask for the financial statement for the last two years when I'm interested in something special," and they both laughed.

They strolled along the enclosed promenade deck and were shocked to see their fellow passengers dressed for dinner. Nicholas looked at his watch and said, "It's after eight! Quite unbelievable! Where has the time gone?"

They then went to Nicholas's cabin, where they found the two secretaries and Marvin Kandy hard at work dealing with the day's telexes and speeches for the forthcoming press conference. It was Arabella, not Nicholas, who suggested that she should leave, saying that she was taking up too much of his time, that these were important hours to be working before they landed and she did not want to be a distraction.

"What will you do?"

"Happily go back to my own cabin and get on with my own affairs. Make some decisions, read some recipes, start working on my new life."

Nicholas offered to see her to her cabin, but she would have none of it.

He saw her to the door and whispered, "Will you leave the door open for me? Can I come and sleep with you?"

"Yes," she replied.

When Arabella arrived back in her stateroom, she stretched out on the sofa and thought about this incredible day and this remarkable man, Nicholas Frayne. She felt surer of him in these few days than she ever had of Anthony. But how would they fit into each other's lives? Pondering all this, she went to the pantry to make herself a cup of tea. She carried it back to her seat and placed the cup and saucer on the coffee table. She then went and brought a wastepaper basket and placed it next to the sofa.

She sat for a few minutes sipping her tea and looking around the magical garden Nicholas had created for her. She etched every flower in her mind so she would remember them always. One by one she picked the real estate portfolios up and examined each before dropping it into the wastepaper basket. All except for one—a house called The Moores— a magnificent late-nineteeth-century home set in a hundred acres of parkland, moorland, and oceanfront, in Newport, Rhode Island.

The telephone rang. It was Missy asking if she and Xu could come to see Arabella about making arrangements for their departure from the ship. Arabella set the time for eleven the next morning.

Missy's phone call had been a reminder that in a little more than twenty-four hours the S.S. *Tatanya Annanovna*'s maiden voyage would be over.

Chapter Eighteen

He walked in, already removing his clothes. Arabella watched him from the sofa where she was lying, reading her book. She swung her feet down onto the carpet and stood up.

He was emanating love, passion, and an urgency to take her, to have her. Arabella walked toward him, thrilled at the thought of giving herself completely to Nicholas. He reached out and took the book from her hand. She trembled. Yet again he had caught her off balance. Yet again their extraordinary affair shifted in some way. They had first made love three days ago. She felt as if it were a lifetime ago.

They had a wonderful time in bed. They worked through all the levels of erotic love. They found continual delight in their flesh and explored each other's bodies with tongues, hands, and his penis. They gave each other total fulfillment, denied each other nothing. Through it all Arabella felt a closeness, love, and caring sweeter than anything she had ever known. During the hours lost in sex there was no slackening of intensity. It was always fresh, always new. They were both enamored of the thought that they were able to excite each other. They were all good things to each other. All good times. What they learned that night was that their erotic passion was increased because whatever one needed, the other one could give. There were no walls, no boundaries. There was no manipulation or control. Both took and both gave.

Somewhere, off in the distance, Arabella heard, "Wake up, my love. It's a beautiful day. Wake up."

She struggled through the last stages of sleep and opened her eyes. She felt a soft, delicate kiss on the back of her neck. Slowly she rolled over and faced Nicholas. Their eyes met, and Arabella thought it was the happiest moment of her life.

She put her arms around his neck and they kissed.

"Good morning, Nicholas."

"I think you might be angry," he said sheepishly.

"Angry?" she asked.

"It's only seven o'clock and I've already rung for breakfast, so we can eat in bed. You'd better slip something on. It should be here in about ten minutes."

"Yes, sir," she said and scampered off the bed. She called from the bathroom, "Nicholas? Seven o'clock, why seven o'clock?"

"Because it's our last day out and there's a mountain of work I've let slide and must do, but I want to spend as much time as I can with you."

"All very good reasons," she said. "I approve of them all."

Arabella returned to the bed wearing a pale-pink satin dressing gown with insets of pale-lemon lace. She looked fresh and beautiful.

He said, "You look so *young*, so very *young* and pretty!"

She slipped into the bed next to him and he put his arm around her. "Like a girl of twenty."

"I feel like a girl of twenty."

After breakfast they dressed and made their usual daily visit to the kennels to see her birds and dogs. Then a long, leisurely twenty lengths of the pool. They parted at half-past ten after agreeing that she would be dressed and ready by seven for their last evening together on board.

He said, "Do you trust me to plan our evening?"

"Yes," she said.

"Then decline any and all invitations."

"Ah," she said, smiling, "surprises!"

"Yes," he replied, "surprises and no guesses!"

Then he was gone.

Missy and Xu arrived at exactly eleven. Their appearance made Arabella's shipboard romance seem even more dream-like, unreal. She realized that neither she nor Nicholas had had one second of anxiety about the end of the voyage. They were behaving as if they were going to be together forever, without a comment or even an indication from either of them that it was so. Arabella's joy was so intense it wiped out all doubts about a parting.

Arabella took Missy and Xu into her dressing room to go through her Louis Vuitton luggage and steamer trunk. Xu took them out and opened them, and soon they littered the entire floor.

Missy sat, pencil and pad in hand, on the chaise sur-rounded by Arabella's luscious evening dresses draped over one end, her exquisite daytime ensembles draped over the other. She watched Arabella and her heart was filled with joy for her boss and friend. In all the years Missy had been with her, she had never seen her like this.

It had been a glorious voyage for Missy, who thought she too might be falling in love. How would one know until the voyage was over? Shipboard romances had a notorious record of failures once the boat had docked. And pursers, especially handsome pursers with university degrees in lit-erature like Pete Peters—how many broken hearts had he delivered down the gangplank? Well, she would know more tomorrow, soon enough.

Arabella swung around from the armoire to face the mir-ror and held up an evening dress. It had a soft, supple, gray suede bodice, a sash of shocking-pink satin, and a long full black taffeta silk skirt that rustled like tissue paper. She draped it against her, pressing it in at the waist.

She stood back a few paces and said, "Well, maybe," turned away from the mirror to face Missy, and said with a smile, "Quite a departure, isn't it, Missy? Indecision— the luxury of indecision—and indecision about what to wear at that! A far cry from the corporate world. Isn't it wonderful?"

Her two faithful servants said in unison, "Yes, it *is* wonderful." The three of them laughed.

Their laughter was interrupted by a knock at the door and the appearance of Arabella's cabin steward, Henry.

"Hello, Henry."

"Hello, madam," he said, presenting her with a radiogram on a silver salver. "This has just come through for you, madam."

Arabella knew instinctively that it was another message from Anthony. She was annoyed by his intrusions. Instead of bringing them together, cementing the love they had felt for each other for so many years, everything he did now seemed to drive them apart and Arabella closer to Nicholas. Or did it?

The envelope on the tray made her feel queasy and a little frightened, but she knew that was nothing more than fear of loss after an attachment of so many years. A shiver went through her spine and then it was gone.

Nicholas's love for her, the admiration and desire he had for her, the overpowering emotional and erotic love they felt for each other, so real and natural, was so earthbound on this dream of a voyage. The message on the silver salver appeared a calculated maneuver to bring her out of a state of intoxication, but since both she and Nicholas were sober in their feelings for each other, and far from drunk on love, it really became an annoyance. And it also made Arabella sad that Anthony could not just be happy for her.

Arabella reached out to take the envelope from the tray, then stopped, her hand in midair. She turned to Missy and said, "Please see to this," then turned back to her armoire, determined to make a final decision on what she would wear that evening.

She heard Henry making arrangements to help Xu with the packing and shipping of the cases to a storeroom where customs would check them on board before they docked, allowing Arabella a quick exit in the morning. Several other

VIP first-class passengers were to get the same treatment. Henry had turned out to be a treasure of a cabin steward for he had even arranged for them all to be cleared through passport control in Arabella's staterooms first thing in the morning—dogs, birds, and all.

Arabella closed her eyes and froze when she felt Missy come up behind her and place a hand gently on her shoulder. She said, "I am afraid this message demands an answer. It's very personal."

Arabella opened her eyes, draped an elegant black-and-white evening dress over her arm, and took the radiogram handed to her.

She read:

You are making a grave mistake. In your desire for a new life you are overlooking what we have always dreamed of—my being free, a life for us together. Being Lady Quartermaine and the mistress of Heversham Park can be a new life for you. In twenty-four hours your fantasy voyage and frivolous shipboard romance will both be over. I accept it as just that and nothing more. I love you. Call or send a radiogram as to whether you will fly to me by the first available seat on Concorde, or shall we marry in New York?

—Anthony.

Missy saw Arabella stiffen, grow pale as she walked to the chaise to sit down. Arabella said in a voice devoid of emotion but filled with resolve, "Missy, please radiogram the following message to his lordship: 'Anthony, I am growing up and liking it. Have no plans to come to London. Please do not come to New York. Perhaps you need a cruise to clear your head. Recommend the *Tatanya Annanovna*. Regards, Arabella.'"

She handed the paper back to Missy and then slowly smiled and said, "Black—black and white, I think. Elegant,

sophisticated black and white is what I will wear this evening. Don't you agree, Missy? Black, white, diamonds, and
pearls."

The two women smiled at each other.

Arabella finally made her selection of clothes for that
evening and the next day, and together she and Missy made
arrangements for their departure from the ship early the next
morning. All the potted flowering trees were to be sent to
her suite at the Carlyle and whatever cut flowers that were
still fresh to the psychiatric wards at Bellevue Hospital. The
cars were to be ready and waiting on the dock, then they
would proceed at once to the Carlyle. Arabella gave strict
instructions that she would not talk to the press—either
about her retirement or her romance.

She had planned a day of pure self-indulgence, and as
soon as all her plans were completed, she proceeded to lunch
at the Pool Room with Marcia Mackay. She wore a divided
skirt of dove-gray suede, a deep-peach silk shirt with a
double row of frills at the neck and cuffs, and over her
shoulders a short jacket with a bodice of golden-brown sable
and dove-gray suede sleeves. Dove-gray ribbed silk stockings covered her beautiful legs, and on her feet she wore
gray-and-white English brogues.

The Pool Room made her forget she was on a ship, forget
it was winter. The olympic-size pool, lit from underneath,
was surrounded by huge palm trees and tables laid with
white linen and lovely china, crystal, and silver. It was like
eating at the most exclusive swim club in the world.

Arabella really liked Marcia, who gave off an air of true
happiness and a zesty good nature. The women agreed to
meet in two months at a luxurious health spa Marcia knew
of called Diamond Lil's in Texas.

After lunch Arabella excused herself and went to the golf
course to meet Isador. Her game had picked up somewhat,
and he was delighted with his student's progress. When they
sat down for tea in the main lobby, Arabella smiled at him,
a slow, tender smile, and said, "Isador, we will see each

other, be friends. Yours is one of the friendships I've made on the *Tatanya Annanovna* that I'll always want to keep and take along with me in my life. Will you be my friend always?"

"Yes, always" was all he replied.

It was midafternoon when the two friends parted, having exchanged addresses and telephone numbers. Both determined that their new friendship would not fade away, they made a tentative arrangement to speak within the week.

There was a definite change in the atmosphere aboard the S.S. *Tatanya Annanovna*. There was an extra air of excitement, a new busy feeling of people shifting gear, preparing themselves for the end of the voyage. In the passageways there was a continuous two-way traffic of cabin stewards and maids bustling to and fro.

Arabella had an appointment to keep. She went to the main staircase of the ship, hurried down two flights, and knocked on the door marked *"Salon du votre plaisir."* The middle-age woman in the white uniform introduced herself as Olga and handed Arabella a white silk dressing gown.

"Please put this on. I will wait for you in the next room." Arabella did as she was told. As she entered the next room, she noticed several things at once: the rough, utilitarian carpet was replaced by thick wool piled rugs; the harsh fluorescent lighting gave way to soft, pinkish-toned indirect glows; a strong scent of tuber roses; and the rich, subdued sound of classical music filled the air.

A tall dark man appeared and extended a silver tray in her direction, saying, "Madame, a vin royale." Arabella took the glass and walked to where Olga was standing. Already she felt transformed, transported. She took another sip of the drink.

"We will begin now, yes?" asked Olga.

"Yes." She put the glass down. Arabella felt herself sink into a soft white leather chair. As Olga began to wash her face with cotton soaked in an herbal cleanser, another woman placed an ottoman under her feet and gently placed them in warm, soapy water. A third woman took Arabella's hand and began removing her nail polish and massaging her fingers. Olga proceeded from the facial to washing Arabella's hair and relaxing her scalp. A fourth woman came in to style her hair and dry it with heat lamps.

It seemed as if the manicure, pedicure, facial, and hair styling were all part of perfectly coordinated effort to prepare Arabella Crawford for the most important night of her life. She felt herself go limp under the busy and assured hands and then all the rejuvenated parts of her came together with a new and vital energy.

She looked at her watch and then slipped her arms through the sleeves of her jacket. She had decided to take a walk around the open deck and enjoy what was left of the light on the endless horizon of the ocean.

As she walked the open decks in the cold, crisp air and felt the salty wind on her face, Arabella licked her lips, wanting to taste the elements. She was loving every minute of her voyage and wanted to remember every detail of the magnificent vessel, from the highly polished mahogany rails to the very last hump of the rivets holding sheet upon sheet of steel together under its overcoat of glossy white paint. She wanted to remember every deck board, every porthole that plowed forward through the cold, rough waves of the ocean.

Arabella held her hand up to her head like a visor and looked at the horizon, wanting always to remember, passionately remember the endless distance of open water they had traveled through these last five days. The nothingness and, at the same time, the everythingness of the ocean. She felt exhilarated, invigorated as she walked and walked the decks, happy to be alone with herself and thoughts of Nicholas. She came upon a section of the deck that protected her from the wind and there she stood, nearly mesmerized by the prow of the *Annanovna* plunging down into the waves and rising up again proud and high with cascades of foaming waves breaking over the lower decks as the ship plowed forward at top speed.

Alone out there in the wind, the water stretching out in front of her, she felt happiness, real happiness, and genuine, deep love and romance more acutely than she had ever known them before. Only five days aboard the S.S. *Tatanya Annanovna*, only five days of knowing Nicholas Frayne and Arabella could barely remember what her life had been like before this voyage.

The years before her embarkation in Cherbourg seemed to be drifting farther and farther away as the ship's engines pumped hard, driving her closer and closer to the States. Whatever lay before Arabella, she knew it would be fresh, clean, beautiful, rich, and lovely. Her thoughts turned to Nicholas—the handsome, intelligent, sexy Nicholas; Nicholas with the smile that put an extra beat in her heart; the sensuous eyes that made love to her and the voluptuous mouth that transported her far above life itself. Involuntarily Arabella wrapped her arms around herself, hugged herself, not because of the cold but because she wanted Nicholas to be there: the need to have him hold her—no, not the need, the *desire* to have him hold her.

It suddenly hit Arabella how very generous he was to her, open and generous; how much of himself he had offered her. She wanted to give him something, something other than herself. Something beautiful, of real and rare beauty: a painting, a small but exquisite painting to remind them always of their first extraordinary voyage, their maiden voyage together.

Arabella glanced at her wristwatch and was relieved that it wasn't too late. She hurried from the open deck through the double doors. There was still time to go and find the purser, Pete Peters, and ask him to take her to the hold where her excess luggage was stored. She had decided to give Nicholas the painting she had bought in Paris the year before. She thought, I'd so much like for him to have it. I don't want him ever to forget this voyage because I never will.

*   *   *

At the same time, Nicholas closed the door of his suite and walked back to the center of the drawing room, looked at his friend Marvin Kandy and said, "Well, that's it then. How about a drink? I suddenly find myself wanting a drink and a good cigar." He went to the console and from a silver tray picked up a cut-glass decanter and poured two bourbons with a big splash of branchwater in each. He reached into the ice bucket with his hand, picked up a fistful of ice cubes, and dropped them into the crystal tumblers. The clink and crack of the cubes as they adjusted to the alcohol sounded refreshing.

Nicholas handed a glass to Marvin, then went to an easy chair on the far side of the room. He put his glass on the table next to the chair, sat down, and bent forward to untie his shoes. He slipped out of them and leaned back. From his breast pocket he took out a cigar case, removed a cigar, and threw the case across to Marvin who caught it in his left hand. Nicholas cut the end off his cigar and turned it slowly over the flame to light it evenly. He pulled his feet up on the seat of the chair and reached for his drink. The first swallow was so welcome it told him he was more anxious than he had realized. He loosened his tie and unbuttoned the top button of his shirt. His thoughts drifted toward Arabella.

It was difficult for him to think of Arabella without wanting her. He could never remember being as in love with anyone as he was with her. To remember her eyes, the feel of her skin, the charm of her laughter, the swell of her breasts, the softness and scent of her filled Nicholas with carnal desire. From that very first sight of her through the binoculars he had wanted her. Now he had her and every time he did, it was as if it were for the first time.

Nicholas looked across the room at his friend Marvin. "Why so silent, Marv?"

"Would you believe I am trying to be discreet?"

Nicholas smiled and said, "It doesn't suit you. What are you thinking?"

"Have you popped the question yet?"

"No, not yet."

"You are going to, I hope?"

"Ah, then you approve of Arabella?"

"It's not a matter of approval, Nick, more a matter of timing. There is no way, old buddy, either one of you will end up any way other than married to each other."

"I'm glad you think so. It's hard to believe but I'm in love with her. I can't imagine my life without her. I never knew how much loneliness there was in my life without the intimacy I share with Arabella."

"Going down that gangplank tomorrow into the darkness of the unknown with the love I feel for her makes it so much easier. Before Arabella, I thought I could be one of the greatest public servants for my country. Now I know I can, because I've experienced the rewards of truly giving oneself away. And I feel her support buoy me.

"You know, Marv, I know now I was never able to live happily with all that guilt-free sex. There was always a sense of loneliness about it—sex that was used as sport."

"And when do you plan on telling all this to the lovely Arabella?"

"Tonight. I've planned a wonderful night for us filled with romance, and sometime during the evening I'll ask her to marry me."

Marvin stood up and started across the room toward his oldest and dearest friend. Nicholas did the same. The two men looked at each other affectionately as they met. Nicholas smiled; it was an emotional smile. Marvin slapped him on the back and said, "The Hollywood in me only wishes that this voyage was just a little bit longer so the captain could marry you and the Nicholas Fraynes could walk down the gangplank together. I'm very happy for you, Nick. She's one hell of a lady!"

The two men hugged each other.

Chapter Nineteen

All the lamps were lit in Arabella's drawing room. The lamplight played tricks on the trees and flowers, adding to their beauty and lusciousness, making the stateroom appear even more like a magic garden. A tape of the rich sound of Charlie Byrd and Stan Getz Brazilian music filled the room, giving it an even more steamy, sexy, "Garden of Eden" quality. The gallery where Arabella now stood overlooked the drawing room. Through the floor-to-ceiling windows she watched the twinkling lights on the decks below her and the blackness beyond, broken only by splashes of bright, shining stars in the sky, disappearing and reappearing as the heavy wind pushed the clouds over them.

The windows appeared as black glass because all the light was inside; so they gave a perfect reflection of Arabella. She caught sight of herself swaying to the music and was filled with a happiness she could barely contain. She stopped dancing and adjusted the five-strand diamond-and-pearl choker. Its center clasp, a natural baroque black pearl the size of a quail's egg surrounded by a row of large, cushion-cut diamonds, was not quite on the center of her long, slim neck. Once adjusted, she arranged the other two strands of perfectly matched eight-millimeter pearls and the strand of diamonds between them. She moved one of the large diamond earrings to a better position on her ear so it would not pinch and admired the magnificent jewels that now hung so perfectly on her bare chest.

How vain, she thought, how very vain to stand and admire oneself in the window! What a reversal in roles from the woman who for years would rather have looked at a portfolio for a corporate takeover!

Arabella smiled, enjoying every minute of this new role, being a hundred times more vain than ever, being in love, wanting to please, to be the most perfect, delicious, delectable, beautiful, sensuous, happy woman for the man she loved.

She looked deep and long into the face that looked back at her in the black glass. Her silver and gold hair, brushed in natural soft waves off her face, hung loosely down around her shoulders. Her makeup, pale and peachy with cheeks highlighted in a pale ginger and soft coral-color lips, gave her eyes an added depth and sparkle. Or, she wondered, is it all just love?

She was proud, truly proud of how she looked for her man and for herself.

She adjusted one of the sleeves of her magnificent Mary McFadden dress, delighted with her choice for the evening, admiring yet again the black and white tiny check silk of the sleeves that hugged her arms with tailored puffs on the shoulders from where the dress plunged straight down square across the breasts revealing a deep cleavage. The bodice was a perfect fit down to the silver kid belt shining in the reflection in the window. The black crêpe skirt falling to the ankle faded into the glass against the black night as if her lower half had disappeared. Only her ankles and feet in their high-heeled silver kidskin shoes reaffirmed there was indeed a whole beautiful body there.

The beat of the Latin music interrupted her moment of self-admiration. She began to swing her hips and, moving her feet, raising her arms up, she swayed with the music, moving provocatively. Arabella watched the movement of her hands, the long, ringless fingers with the nails tipped in rich coral polish. Lovely, seductive hands that would soon be caressing Nicholas. Sensitive hands and fingers that she knew how to use making love to him.

Once his name came into her head she could no longer think of herself but only of him—his face, beautiful body, intelligence, kindness, and warmth. It was then that the doorbell sounded. Her body jumped! she put her hand over her heart and felt the beat.

She called down, "Xu, it's Mr. Frayne. Will you let him in, please?" She stood at the balcony rail looking down when he entered the room.

She heard him say, "Good evening, Xu." Although she said nothing, just stood there looking at him, he sensed immediately where she was and looked up. He smiled at her and said, "Terrific music."

Arabella walked across the balcony to the rhythm of Byrd, Getz, and bossanova, saying "Hello, darling." She looked at him longingly. The long slit down the front of her skirt fell open as she walked and he saw her lovely long, shapely legs flash quickly as she hurried down the half a dozen stairs to him. She held her arms out and he clasped her hands in his, lifted them to his lips, and kissed first one, then the other.

He said, "Darling, you look dazzling, so beautiful." Holding on to her hands, he stepped back a pace and added, "You are always doing it to me."

"Doing what?" she asked.

"Dazzling me. Just when I think I know you, you appear and knock me off kilter again. There you are, much more wonderful than I thought, and always with a new touch of mystery to you." He pulled her quickly into his arms, his need was so great to hold her. He kissed her on the cheek and then passionately on the mouth. Slipping his arm around her shoulder, he moved so that he could hold her close by his side. He looked down into her eyes, lowered his voice, and said huskily, "You look so delicious, I'd like to eat you right here and now. Take a golden spoon and eat you up, spoonful by spoonful, pearls, diamonds, and all."

"Yes, yes," she said, teasingly moving her hands to his swelling crotch. "Now, now!" She began to laugh.

The two walked together through the room. Suddenly he stopped abruptly and said, "I want you, Arabella. I spend a great deal of time wanting you. Have you any idea how much?"

"Oh, I think so, Nicholas. You're almost as crazy about me as I am about you. I stand up there on the balcony looking through the window into the night and all I see is a reflection of myself and all I can think of is that I want to be better than I am, more divine, for you. I want to give myself to you, make love to you so that you can feel a little of how wonderful it is when you make love to me. How can I give you a fraction of the excitement you instill in me? Do you think I'm a woman in love?"

"You had better be," he said as he laughed warmly, "and it had better be with me."

They kissed again and then she said, "Do you want a drink, Nicholas?"

"Don't evade the subject. It is me and only me, isn't it?"

"Need you ask? Now, what do you want to drink?"

"Nothing," he replied, and took her by the hand. Starting toward the door, he turned and looked back over his shoulder at her. He saw complete joy and contentment exuding from her like the heavy scent of perfume.

Their eyes met and he asked, "Hey there, what are you looking at so intensely?"

"Just the handsomest man in the world. I've never seen you in a gray pinstripe suit, complete with waistcoat and such a handsome tie. Quite a dashing man with your navy-blue and white polka dot silk hanky tippling out of your jacket pocket! I think you're wonderful and we're two of the most beautiful people in the world! I'd like to go out there in front of everyone and shout, 'Look at us, look at us!'"

"Who's everyone?"

"All the world," she said.

"Maybe we'll do just that later." He laughed as he pulled her along.

She reached for her evening bag and called back over her shoulder, "Good night, Xu. We'll see you in the morning."

"Good night, Xu," Nicholas called and they were gone.

In the passageway they walked side by side, greeting

some of the stewards they passed. At one point Arabella nearly lost her balance and Nicholas caught her by the elbow.

"Are you all right, Arabella?"

"Yes. The sea seems a bit rough tonight, a little too much pitch and roll for high heels."

"I think our captain has got the engines open full out. When I spoke to him this afternoon he said something about a rendezvous with the pilot boat at six in the morning."

They stepped into one of the elevators and were a little embarrassed by the silence they generated among their fellow passengers. Two decks up Arabella and Nicholas walked to the stern of the ship.

"Is this a mystery tour?" she asked.

"Yes," he said. He slipped his arms through hers. "This is *our* night, our last night on board ship and, in many ways, maybe our first night."

Arabella was very moved yet she noticed a slight nervousness in Nicholas. It was the tension that comes from deep emotion.

"Nicholas," said Arabella, putting her hand on his sleeve, "relax, my love. There are two of us here who feel like that."

They stopped walking and kissed—a long, deep, passionate kiss—and when they drew apart they smiled. Arabella could see in Nicholas's face that he was calm again and very, very happy. They were standing in front of a pair of high walnut doors with a finely carved architrave and lintel of musical instruments tied together with a wooden ribbon. Curly decorative engraved letters announced on the lintel "The Empress Catherine Music Room." To the left of the doors was a simple walnut easel and on it a placard announcing "This room is closed to the public this evening. Thank you."

From his pocket Nicholas drew a key, put it in the lock, and turned it. He kissed the tip of Arabella's nose and pushed the pair of doors open.

The sight took Arabella's breath away. She gasped with pleasure and said, "Oh, how wonderful!"

The room was a jewel that could have been fashioned by Fabergé. It was a small music room, completely paneled and limed an off-white color. There were rich carvings accentuated in a faded teal blue and gold leaf over the doors, windows, and covering the complete shell of the rostrum. The heavier carved cellos, violins, flutes, and guitars were tied together by garlands of leaves and flowers held in the mouths of deer, antelope, leopards, wolves, rabbits, and pheasants, lending an undeniable charm to the room.

The floor of rich inlaid woods in triangles and squares within larger rectangles of ebony looked as if it had been glazed with honey.

Four rock-crystal chandeliers designed to look like hanging baskets of flowers were softly lit by dozens of white candles. There was a pair of extremely fine period satinwood pianos inlaid with pearwood and walnut flowers, elongated in shape and nestling into each other with their outside curves. Next to them, four gilt chairs faced each music stand.

Two French windows—not portholes but long glass panes—stretched from the wainscotting to the ceiling where they arched and became six feet of skylight. A round dining table of substantial size was set in one of the windows in such a way that, once seated, Arabella and Nicholas could face the room and dine under the stars. The table glittered, set magnificently with Sèvres and antique Venetian crystal. In the center a baroque silver candelabrum, with many branches, held white candles, all lit and casting a romantic light on the dozens of white moth orchids—the same species as Arabella had worn in her hair a few nights before. They were intertwined over the base of the candelabrum and its arms. Silver dishes sparkled and filled the rest of the table.

Several torchères holding handsome silver candelabra strategically illuminated the room. One of them stood next to a magnificent medieval wooden unicorn resting on its haunches. The proud animal was the size of a full-grown antelope; its horn of pure ivory was inlaid in faded gold leaf. The mythical beast lay surrounded by half a dozen lovely luscious green ferns. It was enchanting.

Nicholas and Arabella went to look at the lovely animal. And there was more to be seen in the room—a pair of silver-leafed wooden dogs the size of Russian wolfhounds, Louis XIV period, sat under another torchère. There was a magnificent marble birdbath filled with water and overflowing with flowers, a life-size bronze crane inlaid in fine pencil-thin gold designs, drinking from it. Smaller birds of bronze stood on the bath's edge, one with its wings set as if fluttering in the water.

It was utterly romantic and magical. As they walked from one group to the other, the soft sounds of a harpsichord drew them to a corner of the room they had yet to discover. There, behind an ivory carved and pierced screen, they found the instrument and a musician playing one of Scarlatti's most charming and exotic seventeenth-century sonatas.

Nicholas had created this for Arabella—the most romantic, exquisite evening any man could make for the woman he loved. He slowly drew her away from the harpsichord. "Come, let's have a glass of champagne."

Arabella was so overwhelmed she could not speak. As the music swelled and filled the room, so did her heart. A waiter seemed to appear from nowhere with a wine cooler. He greeted the couple, then opened the Dom Perignon with deft fingers before serving them and then disappearing through a door in the paneling.

"Wonderful, just wonderful—that's what you want to say, isn't it?" asked Nicholas.

"Oh, more, so much more, but I'm too overwhelmed. How, how could you possibly have got all this together for us?"

"Later, I'll tell you everything later. But now let's just wander through the room, listen, and look. It's yours, you know, the unicorn—a gift of love from me."

They kissed and walked back to the unicorn, the irresistible unicorn. Arabella ran her hands over the long, smooth horn and then went down on her knees to look straight into the beast's magical face. Nicholas sat down on the other side of its head. There they sat and drank, completely enveloped by the moment.

Hidden from the musician, Nicholas moved over next to Arabella, took her empty glass from her hand, and then laid her across his lap as he held her in his arms. They kissed, and he caressed her lovely bare throat, surrounded only by the precious jewels. He lowered one of the puffed sleeves off her shoulder and kissed it, then lowered the other. The bodice of her dress thus loosened, he lifted her breasts free.

Arabella watched his handsome face intently. She recognized love turning to passion as he held her naked breasts cupped in his hand. He was tender and sweet with his caresses. Arabella's senses began to swim. The beauty of the room, her man, the enchanting animal and rarefied sound of the music, the taste of his kisses nibbling at her mouth aroused in her incredible sensations. She felt a flush rising in her cheeks and a wetness and warmth between her legs. They were silent lovers, holding back so as not to embarrass the harpsichordist or themselves.

The room, the music, the ship disappeared. Only the sensations of love and passion remained. Not until Nicholas had tenderly touched her cheek with the back of his hand and eased her off his lap into a sitting position did she realize that the music had stopped and Nicholas had covered her breasts and replaced the puffed sleeves on her shoulders.

He helped her up. They stood next to the unicorn looking down at the beast with admiration for its romantic beauty.

"I hardly know where I am," said Arabella. "All this—" She waved her hand, encompassing the room, then kissed him as he held her in his arms.

"All this," she repeated, "and heaven too. I never dreamed I could have so much."

They were walking toward the dinner table, his arm through hers, when she said, "There is nothing that can surpass this evening and our being together."

"Yes, there is. Being together always. Joining our lives,

our dreams, our hopes forever. How about being partners in love, passion, and life for eternity? How about marrying me?"

They had stopped and now looked into each other's eyes. As if by magic the sound of the harpsichord swelled again from behind the ivory screen and filled the Empress Catherine Music Room.

"Say yes . . . just say yes," he begged, as he raised her hand to his lips and kissed it.

Arabella wanted to say yes. Her heart, body, and soul yearned to say yes. Only her mind, full of the stored-up years of loving Anthony, held her back. Thoughts rushed through her head. After years of hoping, at last he offered her marriage, a life together—all she had dreamed of and yearned for for so very long. Now she looked into Nicholas's face and was mesmerized by the love, excitement, and emotion in it. Those were the very same things she had imagined she'd seen in Anthony's face time and time again. Yes! she realized; she had *imagined* those things! She had never really seen them, except perhaps during their lovemaking, their passionate and sometimes depraved sexual odysseys. Then she saw Nicholas lower his eyes and she felt him slip a ring onto her finger. Never releasing her gaze from him, nor herself from the tension of the moment, she felt a tidal wave of emotion sweep over them both.

Nicholas raised his eyes again and looked into hers. In that look Arabella saw a flicker of fear and anxiety, vulnerability, a stab of intense pain and desperation over her silence. In a voice cracked with emotion, he repeated the same words. "Yes—just say yes."

Arabella's heart was filled with a wave of love so profound it snapped her out of her own shocked silence. She put her arms around his neck and whispered, "Yes, yes," then louder, "Yes," and even louder, "Oh, yes, yes."

Arabella was aware that here was a love stronger, more emotional and powerful than anything she had ever felt for another human being. She was painfully aware that in all her years with Anthony never once had he opened himself, surrendered himself completely to her as Nicholas did now.

It was with a deep sense of sadness that Arabella now understood she had loved, given everything totally, surrendered herself completely, happily answered all Anthony demanded from her. She had done it with a naturalness that comes with love and the desire to please.

She knew now, with her "yes" to Nicholas still on her lips, that she had given too much to Anthony and he had given too little. It was a shock because she had never measured how much love to give, but she knew now that Anthony did and was mean with it.

Nicholas closed his eyes, took a deep breath and let it out slowly. Then he smiled at Arabella. He held her up off the floor, against him, and she kissed him passionately on the lips, then his cheeks, his chin, and then once again on his lips. All the while she murmured, "Yes, yes, yes. Oh, yes." When she stopped he put her down and they smiled at each other.

"I can't believe it," he said.

"You had better believe it," she said, laughing. "I'll not let you go now!"

"I don't know what happened but for a minute there I thought I'd lost you, that you were thinking of . . ." Nicholas broke off in midsentence and went on. "Never mind that minute.

"When?" he asked. "When? Shall we try and get Captain Hamilton to marry us tonight here on board ship? I think captains can still do that, can't they? No," he answered himself, "not on board. Let's have our closest family and friends around us. What do you think?"

Not giving Arabella a chance to answer, Nicholas carried on. "Just tell me when and we'll plan our wedding together. Arabella, you've made me so happy. I'm the happiest man on earth. We'll have a wonderful life together. I promise you that."

"I know we will, my darling. Nicholas, let's decide all that tomorrow—the when and the where. Right now I'm floating on a cloud of love and trying to adjust to the reality that this is no dream, no shipboard romance that will be over tomorrow when the ship docks, but a love that now has the commitment of continuity to it.

"You are not the happiest man in the world. *We* are the two happiest people on earth. I love you with all my heart, Nicholas Frayne."

With her hand held up in front of her, the two of them admired the square-cut diamond ring Nicholas had slipped on her finger.

They walked to the torchère lighting the two wooden silver-leafed Russian wolfhounds in the middle of the music room and held the gem up to the candlelight. The blue-white diamond sparkled, sent off flashes of light, and flecks of rainbows danced on the sculptured animals.

"It was made for you! It fits perfectly. I knew when I saw the stone nothing else would do."

"Nicholas, I simply adore it! It has such fire. It's so alive! I love it!"

He kissed her on the cheek, then lifted her right hand, saying "That's only the frosting, darling. Here's the cake."

He slipped a magnificent ivory wedding band inlaid with square-cut diamonds all around it on the third finger of her right hand.

They kissed. Arabella said, "Thank the Lord for the ship's shopping mall, and M. Gerard's boutique, your good taste and generosity, and, most of all, your love for me."

"Wear it now, Arabella. I'd love you to wear it always," Nicholas said before they kissed again.

"Oh, Nicholas, I will. It's so elegant, unusual, and beautiful. But this is a ring I'll always wear for what it means, not for its beauty alone."

"I'll borrow it for five minutes just before our wedding ceremony and then slip it on again before the eyes of the world and God and all that," he said, kissing her again.

"Where did the unicorn come from? How did you manage it in the middle of the ocean?" Arabella asked.

"It was easy and I was lucky. I bought it in Paris from

an extraordinary collector of decorative arts from the Middle
Ages and the reigns of the kings of France. I went to look
at it with a friend. I was as shocked as everyone else when
I walked away having purchased it!

"It was in the storeroom on board. I planned all this and
had the case opened this morning after I left you."

The eloquence of the harpsichord silenced them. Suddenly it took over and filled the room with the bravura
passages, ornamentation, romantic rhythms, and fine dynamic shadings of Joaquin Rodrigo's *Concierto de Aran-
juez*. While the piece had been specially arranged for the
harpsichord, it still sounded like the guitar and orchestra it
had been written for. It fired the imagination, and they could
have been in a secluded courtyard somewhere in Seville,
surely not on the ocean waves. Only the sensuous rocking
sensation of the *Tatanya Annanovna* was a reminder of
where they really were.

Nicholas had created a secret fantasy world where a magic
carpet flew them from one happy sublime place to another
by pricking the senses.

The room, like the music, was bursting with life, an
extension of them and what they felt for each other. They
gravitated silently toward the harpsichord, sat on the floor
of the rostrum, and listened. As the last note was played
and the room was silent, neither of them moved. An essence
of Rodrigo vibrated around the room. Arabella slipped off
the rostrum and walked to the pierced ivory screen and the
young harpsichordist sitting there silent.

Nicholas pressed a service bell underneath the dining
table and almost immediately a waiter appeared through the
hidden door in the boiserie. Nicholas asked him to pour
three glasses of champagne. He watched the young musician
rise and kiss Arabella's hand before joining them. The three
drank a toast to Rodrigo for his genius. Then, rather self-
consciously, the young man made his exit through a small
door in the boiserie.

Nicholas put an arm around Arabella and said, "I give
you honest and fair warning right now. It's not always going

to be like this. I'm usually a simple man who likes to sail his boat, hunt with his son on our mountain in Idaho. This new, romantic Nicholas Frayne who can only think of ways to make you happy is as new to me as he is to you."

"Okay." She laughed. "I'm warned."

"And you're still willing to take me on?"

"Sure, you bet I am!"

"God, I adore you! Come on," he said. "I've arranged for delicious things to feed you, give us strength, make us sexy. Are you hungry?"

"All this and food too?" she teased.

"I believe we are ready for dinner, George."

"Thank you, sir," said the waiter. He then disappeared behind the boiserie, reappearing with an assistant and a serving table. They removed domed silver covers from serving plates and lit burners under chafing dishes. George opened a chilled bottle of vintage Roederer Cristal while the second waiter piled their plates high with chilled oysters on the half shell; big, fat, delectable Belons, so sexy to taste and feel in the mouth. The waiters retreated behind the paneling and waited to be called to serve the next course.

Arabella sank her teeth into the succulent oyster lolling on her tongue. As she swallowed the taste of sex filled her thoughts as the slippery crustacean slid down her throat. Her eyes met Nicholas's; something in his look combined with the eating of the oysters made her feel sexy and warm all over.

She picked up the empty shell, sucked the juice from it, and then said smiling, "They're so sexy to eat they're almost indecent!"

"So are you," he said.

"Don't look at me that way, Nicholas. It's as indecent as the oysters!"

"How can I help it? You're provocative, sucking on those shells."

He reached out and slowly moved his hands over her throat and bare chest. "You're so beautiful. Everything else in the world seems bland next to you."

He leaned over sideways, pulled her chair a few inches closer to his, and ran his tongue down between the cleavage of her breasts. He kissed her passionately on the lips; their mouths opened and their tongues met.

Nicholas took her hand in his and buzzed for the waiters. Two of the waiters removed the shell-laden plates while the other walked around the table to one of the chafing dishes and stirred the steamy bubbling soup with a silver ladle.

Arabella watched as he ladled the thick liquid into two Sèvres soup cups. He served them to the lovers and then placed a small silver jug of thick white double cream between them and was gone. Nicholas leaned toward Arabella, kissed her on the tip of her nose, then slowly poured some cream over the thick turtle and green pea soup.

"Oh, it smells divine!" said Arabella.

Nicholas reached over and took Arabella's left hand in his, then they picked up their round soup spoons. The cream had spread like a thin film over the epicurean delight. Arabella broke the surface of the cream and filled her spoon with the thick green soup. The cool, velvety rich cream and hot pungent taste of turtle and pea combined with the smooth texture of the soup was mouthwatering and devastatingly sensual. Nicholas knew quite well how erotic the food they were dining on was. He had, after all, planned the menu.

After the fourth spoonful he squeezed Arabella's hand and felt a tightening in his crotch. Swallowing the ambrosia only served to remind him of how wonderful it was to make love with the woman at his side. He licked the empty silver spoon and placed it in the saucer under the soup cup. He undressed Arabella with his eyes.

The harpsichordist had returned, and he was now playing a Telemann piece reminiscent of springtime, of nymphs and satyrs in a wood or dashing through fields of wildflowers. Arabella stood up and bent down to kiss Nicholas, who took the opportunity to put his arm around her waist and press his face to her breasts. "Let me touch you," he said in a husky voice. He saw desire in her face, heard her sigh and felt her change her stance, her legs move wider apart. He slid his hand through the long slit of her dress up between her legs and was delighted to feel the luscious thick pubic hair unhindered. He pulled her tight to him and his fingers played up and down the length of her. He was thrilled by the heat and silky smooth wetness he found there.

"Oh, how I wanted to feel you! You cannot possibly know how exciting and divine it is for me to sit here fondling you like this."

Arabella couldn't answer him. She let out a soft moan. She was torn between wanting to ease his cock out of his pants and move on to it and thinking they should stop. There was, after all, someone else in the room, albeit behind the screen.

She whispered in his ear, "Send the waiters and musician away so you can take me now, here, now...."

She could feel his erection throbbing against her.

"No," he said. "Let's wait. The evening has just begun. You're making a dirty old man of me. Let's wait at least until dessert!"

Arabella stepped back and adjusted her dress. Her face and chest were flushed and her eyes sparkled. Nicholas rang for the next course and George duly prepared it: lobster stuffed with wild mushrooms and covered in a succulent shrimp sauce, served hot from one of the chafing dishes. The waiter covered the little burners with their silver caps, putting out the flames, thanked the couple, and asked them to ring should they want anything. He then retreated behind the door.

Nicholas said, "I chose our dinner from the sea for this evening. Sexy food from the sea. Proteins and minerals to give us strength to match our passion is an added bonus for food so delicious, don't you think?"

"I have to say one thing, Nicholas. You certainly have planned a perfect evening. Tell me, are there any rules about our night?" Arabella asked.

"Well, let me think," said Nicholas. "Yes, there should always be some rules. How about anything and everything our hearts desire as long as our bodies can stand it?"

"Ah," she said teasingly, with a raised eyebrow, "this is going to be some night!"

"You're damned right!" he agreed. "The first night of our new life together."

Over the lobster they tried to talk about the future, what they would do, where they would go, the people and things they would share together, where they would live. But it became difficult, trying to be practical. The sexual tension and overwhelming desire to explore each other physically and emotionally overpowered everything else. They lapsed into such romantic, sweet, and profound silences. At one point Arabella picked up her dinner plate, placed it next to his, and shared the large wing chair with him, sitting half on his lap. With her plate in her hand, resting against Nicholas's chest, Arabella finished her dinner.

It was between the lobster and the dessert—luscious peeled oranges from Seville caramelized with lemon and raspberry—that Arabella began to assert her feelings for Nicholas. Lying snugly in his arms, half on his thigh, half on the chair, she unclasped the buckle of his belt and slowly drew down the zipper of his fly.

"The waiters won't just suddenly appear, will they?" she whispered in his ear.

"No," he replied, "not unless I ring for them."

"And the harpsichordist?"

Nicholas laughed. "We're safe unless the music stops."

Arabella thrilled to the touch of him. Released, his semi-erect penis and heavy, luscious rounded testicles lying against the gray pinstripe of his suit made her sigh with admiration.

"Oh, Nicholas, you're so handsome, so alive! You have such perfect genitals—the sort Greek gods were supposed to have, that Rodin would have sculptured in bronze and labeled *Man*. I love your cock, Nicholas."

Her words were enough to bring him fully erect. He sighed and said, "I don't believe I've ever had a woman who felt that way about me, let alone enjoyed me as you do."

Arabella fondled him tenderly, with a delicacy that made Nicholas tingle all over. The full, throbbing erection cried out to be made love to. Arabella stroked him lovingly, first with one hand, then the other, again and again as she lay in his arms.

He closed his eyes in a state of rapturous ecstasy. She whispered in his ear, "Nicholas, keep your eyes closed. Don't look at me, just enjoy me. There are things I haven't said to you yet that I want to say now. I've wanted to all evening. If you look at me, I'll lose myself in you and your love for me and I won't be able to express myself."

With eyes still closed, Nicholas turned his head and found her lips with his. Their lips parted and they kissed; their tongues explored the moist warmth of their mouths and fired a stronger, more passionate fondling of him. Slowly their kiss melted away. Nicholas, eyes still closed, raised his hand. Fingers trembling with emotion, he traced his lips, pressed them lightly as if not to let the kiss go.

Arabella lay in his arms and toyed lovingly with his cock as she said, "Nicholas, I love you. I love you more than any man I've ever known. I've never felt as completely alive, as full of love as I do now when I'm with you. I've never felt the oneness with any other human being that I do when we're together, nor have I ever felt the strength of my very own self until now. You know, the strength of the self without all the ego.

"I know how much you want me and it's important that you understand I want you just as much. Our love is in balance. Sometimes, when you touch me, even look at me from across a room, I want to turn myself inside out for you, become totally exposed. There are times when we're making love that I feel as if my flesh has been seared, branded by you.

"These are things a woman dreams she would like to feel with a man; never daring to hope she might, she buries even the dream deep in her subconscious. You've taken me to the heights of exquisite pleasure and I will never take that or you for granted."

She raised herself a little from the chair and kissed Nicholas, tears of emotion in her eyes. He put his arms around her and pulled her on top of him; with eyes still closed, he kissed her. Then he opened his eyes and said, "I will never, ever forget one word you have just said to me. I love you with all my heart now and forever." He bent forward and buried his face in her breasts, then he kissed her and they were quiet together, allowing the peace and love between them to flourish and his cock to relax.

Nicholas looked at his watch. "It's half-past ten. How about another glass of champagne and our dessert?"

Arabella returned to her chair as the waiters arrived and cleared the table. They were served the dessert and then the waiters left, rolling the service table away between them.

The oranges were sublime, yet another taste to tantalize the tongue. The erotic passion between them had subsided. Nicholas had adjusted himself, straightened his tie and shirt, was relaxed, content, and happy.

"You don't think I'm going to wake up and find this is all a dream, do you?"

Nicholas, all smiles, bent forward and pinched her as hard as he could on the arm.

"Ouch!" she exclaimed.

He said, "That should tell you!" Then he kissed away the pain teasingly. "I did it as hard as I could so you wouldn't forget the pain. It will serve as a reminder that you need never ask yourself that question again. Maybe you had better pinch *me*!"

She did and hard. He pulled back and said, "Now neither one of us need ever ask that question again."

"I want the whole world to know we are a couple," she said.

"I know, Arabella. So do I. Let's go and shout it out."

"No, don't get carried away, darling! If we do, we'll be sorry. This is our moment, our night, and I want us to have it as much as possible to ourselves. Let's shout it out quietly, like, tell anyone who gives us the least chance to spill the news!"

They both laughed and Nicholas said, "Okay. But if any celebrations are offered, we decline—except for brief ones."

That innocent childishness of wanting to tell all and yet keep it a secret added still another dimension to their happiness.

Nicholas went on. "Right. Let's try our subtle approach in the Vanya Bar. We might find Marv there. He knew I was going to ask you and made me promise to call when you said yes."

"Marvin, M. Gerard . . . who else knew you were going to ask?"

"Well, all the porters who helped get the room together, the chef, the waiters, the musician, the captain—he helped arrange for us to have the room to ourselves."

"Good grief! What if I had said no?"

"It doesn't bear thinking about!"

"You mean, they're all waiting to hear if I've said yes or not?"

"I suppose so."

"Xu?" she asked. "And Missy?"

"Yes," Nicholas paused. "I needed their help on the ring size. Xu seemed pleased, or as pleased as Xu would show, and wished me well. Missy looked apprehensive, worried. I told her not to feel she was betraying you by keeping my secret and if she was thinking about your suitor, Quartermaine, she was not to worry: the best man would win out and we would all know who that was by morning."

Anthony's name on Nicholas's lips shocked Arabella, and while she wondered just how much he knew, she was too happy to pursue it.

"You are amazing," Arabella said, with a good deal of respect and admiration for the sureness the man had of their love for each other. She put her arms around his neck and kissed him. He pulled her tight to him and fondled her breasts through the silk, then kissed her again and ran his hands over her bottom.

"Oh," she said, in a sexy, husky voice, "you're wonderful! I want to make love to you right now."

He said, "Keep that thought," kissing her on the tip of her nose. "One drink in the Vanya Bar, tell a few people, and then you can take me to bed and have your way with me!"

Chapter Twenty

There were about thirty people in the Vanya Bar, most of whom the engaged couple knew and liked. Mike Mackay was settling his bar bill and tipping overlavishly in the process. He was the first to greet them.

"Ah'm sure glad ah bumped into you two. There're no last farewells for us tomarra mornin'. Ah'm hookin' a ride back with the pilot boat. Marcia's furious 'cause ah won't wait for all the hoohah of this floatin' hotel's first dockin' in the States. Tell ya the truth, ah had a great time but I sure can't wait to get into a little oil tradin'!"

"Did this here rogue pop the question, Miss Belle?"

"How did you know he was going to?"

"Not hard to guess, gal! If he's goin' to be Governor he can't be stupid, and if he's aimin' where we know he's aimin', he sure as hell can't be stupid! An' that's what he would've been had he not grabbed you 'fore this ship anchored.

"By her face and that hunk of ice danglin' off her finger, ah take it she said yes, Nick?"

"Yes, she did," answered a happy Nicholas.

"Ah said she was a damn clevah girl."

Mike Mackay picked up Arabella's hand to kiss it and let out a low soft whistle, saying "He's done yah proud, girl!"

The big gregarious teddy-bear Texan called for snifters of the best Napoleon brandy, and the three moved to a table. Arabella and Nicholas sat next to each other on a seat, Nicholas with his arm around Arabella.

"Here's lookin' at you. You be happy, ya hear?" toasted Mike.

"You're a fascinatin' couple and you're gonna make an awful lot of people miserable. Ah sure as hell am glad ah'm not runnin' against you for governor. That poor sucker hasn't a chance. Nick, when you run for President, if your programs and policies are as good as your intentions and your appearance, there's no man alive who's gonna have a chance against ya! Here's to you both!"

The three clicked glasses and drank.

Marcia and Weston Warfield were the first to approach the table. The two men stood up, and Marcia knew immediately from Arabella's face what had happened. The two women kissed and Marcia hugged Nicholas. Suddenly it seemed to be a party. Warfield called for champagne, and Marcia invited Arabella to join her for lunch at the Plaza before her return to Texas. Captain Hamilton arrived then with Millie Merton on his arm and toasted the engaged couple. Missy, looking very pretty, arrived holding hands with Pete, who seemed very taken with her. Nicholas asked them to join their table.

The group drank and drifted across two tables, more champagne arrived, and laughter rocked them all. Pete Peters excused himself. Arabella followed, wandering from the table after whispering in Nicholas's ear, "I'd like to go and see those people at Xu's table. I'll be right back."

"Why don't I get a bottle of champagne and join you?"

"Oh, lovely, Nicholas. I'd really like that. I want to talk to a new friend, Isador Katz. I know you'll like him. Also Xu must hear our news from us."

Arabella walked across the room to Isador's table. Xu, who was a guest of the Katzes that evening, stood up and drew a chair over for her. Libby Katz, Mrs. Tillman, and Mrs. Davis were delighted to have her join them, and shortly after that Nicholas arrived with a waiter carrying two bottles of Dom Perignon.

The couple announced their news. The West Hartford ladies were enchanted and thrilled at a shipboard romance with a happy ending. Xu looked so pleased that Nicholas could see just how devoted he was to Arabella. Isador was sincerely happy for them both.

Nicholas excused himself when he saw Marvin, Cotille, and Booker St. John come into the bar and went to greet them. By the time Pete returned everyone was table-hopping, drinking champagne, and enjoying being part of the great love story.

Several waiters were shifting tables toward the walls and one corner near the piano was cleared. The next thing the Vanya Bar's guests knew Miss Margaret MacNab and her Edinburgh All Girls Orchestra fluttered through the door like a flock of black ostriches flapping their feathery wings. They were an assortment of women, tall and short, fat and thin, with hair piled high or fluffed out in varying shades of gray and white, except for the band leader, Miss MacNab, whose hair was rinsed a watery navy blue.

They had several other features in common besides being musicians—all wore black chiffon evening dresses to the ankle and pointed black satin shoes with a medium-height heel. All wore corsages of deep-red roses and lots of spider-web green fern held together with a silver ribbon. They sprouted out of the ladies' shoulders, except for the violinist—hers looked as if it replaced a bosom—and the bass player's looked as if it had erupted from her waist.

Their average age was sixty-six. They were all elegantly frumpy, and each carried in her right hand a musical instrument. They flounced, fluttered, and chattered, trying to arrange themselves decoratively. The corner they were allotted appeared to be spilling over with black chiffon.

Nicholas whispered to Arabella, biting his lip as he spoke to prevent himself from laughing, "Don't you dare get the giggles. I've a feeling this has been done for our benefit."

"It's not going to be easy! Wherever did he find them?"

Missy and Pete joined them just then and, overhearing Arabella's question, the purser answered, "Down in second class in the tea dance room. Come along, I must introduce you."

They approached the ladies and Pete managed to make

himself heard after several seconds. Miss MacNab swung around in a cloud of black chiffon and dangerously long ropes of yellowish pearls, a pair of pince nez clamped on the bridge of her nose, the black silk cord dangling down in a loop.

She said, in a thick Scottish brogue, heavily trilling her r's, "Aye, a happy event. My congratulations, my dears," before they had even been introduced. She then swung around and used her ivory baton loudly and sharply on top of a table close by. All went quiet in the room.

Then came the opening bars of the Rodgers and Hart song, "My Funny Valentine." Nicholas and Arabella discovered something else about each other. They both loved the sentimental ballads from the big band days of the forties. Simultaneously they said, "They're playing our song!" They attempted to be serious as they gazed into each other's eyes and sang the familiar words. The others at the table joined them in song, and then everyone burst into applause and joined in toasting the happy couple.

Miss Margaret MacNab and her Edinburgh All Girls Orchestra followed with "Just in Time," the perky Styne, Compton, and Green tune. Then they hit on the Fred Astaire and Ginger Rogers music, "Isn't This a Lovely Day," "Cheek to Cheek," and so on.

Arabella and Nicholas danced. Xu and Libby Katz danced and the Mackays took the floor. It was the best band Arabella had ever danced to. The orchestrations of "You Can't Take That Away from Me" and "The Way You Look Tonight" were pure Hollywood. By the time the orchestra played "Night and Day," Arabella and Nicholas were lost in each other yet again.

Arabella whispered in his ear, "You're a wonderful dancer. Nicholas, ask me again, the way you had planned it."

The music stopped at that moment and the dancers stopped. Then the music began again. It swung into a slow, sensual rendition of "Body and Soul." Nicholas took Arabella back in his arms and they moved with the music. He whispered in her ear, "Arabella Crawford, I fell in love with you from afar and every minute I am with you and know you I love you more. Make my life complete and marry me."

"Yes," she whispered. "Yes, just like this song, with my body and soul."

They stopped, forgetting where they were, and kissed passionately, their bodies melting into each other.

Arabella whispered, "Take me. Oh, I want you so much to take me."

"Soon," he whispered, "soon."

They kissed again and the party applauded them loudly, taking the two of them out of themselves. Arabella felt weak-kneed with desire but managed to walk tall and beautiful, hand in hand with Nicholas to the bar. They decided it was time to make their exit so went to thank Pete, then Miss MacNab.

Finally the couple discreetly slipped out of the Vanya Bar.

They were in the passageway to Arabella's suite. It was deserted, empty and quiet except for the muffled churning from way below in the engine room. Arabella gave Nicholas the key to her suite. He put the key in the lock, opened the door, and gave Arabella a decidedly lustful look. He picked her up in his arms and, holding on to her tightly, kissed her eagerly as he walked into the room and kicked the door shut.

Arabella could feel his heart pounding as he devoured her with his warm, urgent kisses. She swung her legs up and wrapped them around his waist. He lifted her skirt free up around her middle and fondled her naked bottom as he walked with her through the darkened rooms.

Arabella's bedroom was lit by a beam from the moon. It shone across the waves through the porthole. They were transported into the sensuous, romantic atmosphere generated by a secluded cabin on a ship on the high seas.

They collapsed together onto the bed into the soft peach satin eiderdown. He tousled her hair, pulled the earrings gently from her ears and placed them on the night table next to the bed. Pushing her long silky hair away, he sucked on her earlobe, nibbled and bit her.

"You're wicked and wonderful, wanton and wonderful!" Nicholas said. Still clinging together, they rolled over until she lay on top of him. She sat up and straddled him. With her knees pressing into the bed she asked, "And what about you?" as she loosened his tie and began unbuttoning his shirt, pulling it out from the top of his trousers.

"Tell me that's not lust and desire I see in your eyes." She slipped her hand under his shirt and caressed him. It was like an electric shock for Nicholas. He pulled himself up into a sitting position against the pillows, still pinned down by her, and pulled at his tie until the knot came undone. He tore off his jacket and threw it and the tie across the room.

They were looking into each other's eyes and souls as he unbuttoned the cuffs of his shirt and stripped that off. She leaned forward and with splayed fingers ran through the thick, curly golden hair on his muscular chest.

As he ran his fingers lightly across her back she felt a wave of sexual electricity charging between them. The anticipation was thrilling. With a feathery touch he stroked her exposed thigh with the palm of his hand. Their caresses and kisses were soft and tender, masking the passion that was building in each of them.

Nicholas placed his watch on the table and switched on the lamp. Arabella slowly slid her evening dress from her shoulders, all the while looking directly in Nicholas's eyes. She slipped the sleeves down off her arms, pushed the top down around her waist, and ran her hands over her luscious breasts, caressing them and lifting them in the palms of her hands, flicking her thumbs across her nipples.

Nicholas watched and even the silence between them reeked of passion. Arabella bent forward and Nicholas kissed her nipples, first gently, then stronger. Then he sucked them, watched them grow erect. He took them between his teeth and nipped at them, then licked, then nipped them again. He lay back and watched her arch her back and move her hips erotically back and forth along his bulging trousers.

"You're playing with a raging fire, Arabella."

"Mmmm," she moaned, still moving on him. "I don't want to put the fire out too quickly," she said and swung around with her back to him, bent forward between his legs and began to untie and remove his shoes and socks. She looked over her shoulder at him and said in a playful tone, "Do you want me to get the present Marvin gave me before?"

She pulled off one shoe and twirled it up above her head, then dropped it on the floor. She took off his socks slowly, sexily. He couldn't believe the ways she knew of arousing him. "Yes, but not just yet."

Nicholas caressed her voluptuous behind, the curve of her hips, and pulled her back roughly into a sitting position on top of him. He sat up and bit her through her hair on the back of her neck. She said, "Ouch!" and raised her hand to cover the bite.

"Okay. Why don't you go and get the present." He gave her a gentle push forward, a smack on her bottom, and she scampered off the bed. As she walked out of the room, she looked back over her shoulder and said with a smile, "I never knew love could be so much fun."

When Arabella returned, Nicholas was standing in the middle of the room admiring the ocean under the moonlight as it rushed past the porthole. He was an extremely handsome man with a civilized animal quality that Arabella couldn't help but respond to.

She watched him eating her alive with his eyes as she walked toward him, naked now but for black high-heeled shoes, black stockings worn high up on her thighs and held in place by a pair of black-and-white frilly garters.

She also wore the diamond bracelet and a diamond and ruby necklace, with matching huge Cabuchon Burmese ruby earrings encircled with a double row of diamonds. On her hands she wore only her engagement and wedding rings. She had perfumed her body under her breasts, between her legs, and along the side of her neck. She had made herself as sexy and seductive as possible, hoping to trigger every sexual fantasy he had into a reality to be practiced on her.

He said nothing but the lust in his eyes spoke. She watched him unbuckle his belt and slide it out slowly through the loops on his trousers.

As if reading his mind she said, "Oh, yes, I want to give myself to you as if I were every woman in the world. I want you to take me like you would all of them."

"Yes," he said. "Let's be generous with our flesh and our spirit as men and women should be who want each other as much as we do.

"Arabella, I don't know how you understand me so completely. I also want our flesh to speak, to cry out and have nothing to do with propriety, ownership, jealousy. I want to penetrate you, tame you, and I want to be tamed by you. I want my flesh to speak to you freely."

The belt still held in one hand, he opened his zipper with his other.

Arabella, standing provocatively, watched him, aware that every word she uttered, every movement she made with her body seduced him.

Now he was naked. She saw his cock in full erection and his wonderful, large, heavy balls. She looked up from his cock and smiled.

He led her to the foot of the bed and sat her down on the edge. Then, gently putting his hands on her shoulders, he pushed her down flat. Spreading her legs wide apart, he stood between them.

Arabella trembled at the sight of him looming up over her, not knowing what he had planned, what his fantasies might be. He leaned over her and reached for two pillows, which he tucked under her shoulders, saying "Watch us, my love, my wife-to-be."

He said it calmly, with a controlled passion, then he stood silently between her legs examining every inch of her with his eyes. Slowly he went down on his knees and pulled her gently toward him until she was partially off the bed, her knees spread wide apart, her feet planted on the carpet.

He ran his hands seductively over her luscious long legs encased in the black stockings and played for a few seconds with the ruffles of the black-and-white garters. She watched with mounting excitement as Nicholas admired her.

She watched him take the palm of his hand with fingers spread and run it up over her mound, catching the silky flaxen hair. She shivered with anticipation as he squeezed his fingers closed and pulled her pubic hair. He massaged her like this for a while, then with both hands he spread her open as wide as he could and bent his mouth to her.

Nicholas licked slowly with the most delectable long strokes. He sucked and licked, first one side, then the other. He inserted his tongue as deep as he could into the tender opening of soft, sweet flesh. It was exquisite and delicious. It was like being eaten alive. Her hips began gyrating on his willing tongue, and as her movements quickened he knew she was about to come. As he placed two fingers inside her she shuddered with release.

He stood up a moment later and looked at her lovingly. She was spent, legs still wide apart, her face pink with the flush of orgasm. She was beautiful in her nakedness with the magnificent jewels and whorish black stockings. A picture of elegant depravity.

He said, as he pulled her legs up around his waist and stepped closer to her, "I love the taste of you. It drives me mad with passion, makes me want to absorb your flesh into mine."

She said nothing, her eyes riveted to his rampant cock, blood pumping through the veins that stood out on the throbbing thick penis. It looked as if it had a life of its own. She watched as he lifted her closer toward him and with one quick, hard thrust he drove into her. He was so strong, more wild and tough than she had imagined he could be. It was thrilling to be taken this way. He pulled her higher up off the bed into a position where he supported her as he moved in and out of her again and again with total abandon and lust. It was divine. It was powerful. It was joyful. She grabbed him with her vaginal muscles and squeezed as hard as she could on him.

"No!" he called out. "Don't do that. I'll come too quickly. Just relax and let me do it all. Lie there and enjoy this."

Arabella did as she was told. It was marvelous. He was so proficient and obviously reveling in her. It was glorious.

Nicholas was, as always, extremely imaginative between her legs. He was amazing, let every fantasy fly. He reached over to the nighttable and grabbed something. Before Arabella could see what it was, Nicholas was improvising with a kidskin dildo so that she felt as if two cocks were moving in and out of her at the same time. It was an incredible feeling. He saw how much she enjoyed it and that gave him the courage to be wilder.

Arabella submitted to him joyfully. His erotic arts gave her infinite sexual pleasure. Because they were performed with premeditated love and affection, they were an exercise in passion without hate or violence and carried out with care. It was sex with the desire to please, which resulted in yet another kind of love, yet another bond of affection.

The animal had taken over, broken free. Nicholas lifted Arabella to the carpet, on her hands and knees, and mounted her from behind. He rammed into her until they came together in an orgasm that seemed to go on forever. They were spent, worn out. They lay in each other's arms, crumpled and limp on the floor next to the bed. Placing a pillow under her head, Nicholas covered them up with the satin eiderdown.

Arabella recovered quite quickly, but was still amazed at their debauchery, which was enhanced by Marvin's unique gift to them—a treasure chest of sex aids and toys. They had not spoken one personal word to each other as Arabella and Nicholas, but as a man and a woman they had had a dialogue to last a lifetime.

Nicholas kissed Arabella tenderly, with love and affection. He reached between her legs and felt their wetness. He said, "You are divine. You give it all too, you know. For the first time in my life I've been able to really let go.

For the first time in my life I've experienced sexual love that is honest and open."

"It's perfect, isn't it?" asked Arabella.

"It's ideal love, darling. It was and is always wonderful for us because I can deny you nothing. We can deny ourselves nothing."

Nicholas stroked Arabella's hair tenderly, kissed her on the cheek, and slowly drew the eiderdown away from their bodies.

He said, "I lost myself and found myself at the same time. I'll love you all my life for letting me lose myself in you."

Arabella kissed his cheek and caressed him, snuggling up as close as she could to him.

"I feel incredible. You were exquisite, wonderful, everything I've ever wanted in a man, a partner, a husband, a friend."

They kissed a few times, then he said, "It's time I undressed you and put you to bed."

He removed the jewels from her ears and around her neck, her bracelets from her wrist. He reached up and put them on the table. Then he spread her legs apart and slowly slid the garters off her thighs, removed her black high-heeled shoes from her feet, and slowly rolled down the black silk stockings.

"I'd like to take you to bed now, naked except for our betrothal rings, and make love to you not as a woman but as Arabella *the* woman, *my* woman."

"Yes, I'd like that too."

He stood up, straddled her breasts, and offered to help her up with outstretched hands. Arabella did not take them. He knew by the look on her face what she wanted. He lowered himself over her mouth and she swallowed all of his soft, flaccid penis. It grew hard and filled her mouth quickly. Slowly, lovingly, she kissed him and licked him with her tongue. As she disgorged him, they both smiled. He helped her up and they went to bed.

They made a gentle kind of love all night and through

the early hours of the morning, sleeping intermittently. When they were not making sexual love, they remained locked in each other's arms and made love verbally and emotionally. They made plans for their private future and talked of dreams for their public life.

It was a night of sexual delights, but different from any night they had spent together because it was emotionally controlled by their commitment to marry.

Nicholas's mind woke first with a sense of joy and happiness that Arabella was going to be his wife. His body next woke with a full morning erection, ready, waiting and wanting Arabella. He opened his eyes to see if she was awake. She was not there.

The door to the bathroom was open and he could hear her singing softly, "You must remember this, a kiss is just a kiss, a sigh is just a sigh. The fundamental things apply . . ."

The sun was streaming through the portholes and the waves sparkled silver from its rays. It looked cold, choppy, but exciting. There was so much out there waiting for him, waiting for them. He wondered about the time, eager to dock and begin his new life with Arabella.

He sat up and looked through the bathroom door. She was busy putting on her makeup and doing her hair. He smiled to himself then called out, "You're singing off key, my love."

"Good morning to you too!" Arabella said, laughing.

"Good morning. What's that at the foot of the bed?"

"Ah," she replied. "It's a present from me. In all the excitement of our engagement I forgot to give it to you last night."

Nicholas reached out for his glasses and put them on. The large, rectangular package wrapped in silver paper could only be a painting. The writing on it in bright coral lipstick simply said, "I love you, Arabella."

"Sorry about the lipstick, but it was all I could find impressive enough to write with at this hour. I bought the painting a year ago to hang over my bed in my new home. I took it out of the hold yesterday wanting to give you something so you would remember the loveliest voyage I have ever had." She paused before continuing. "That was before you offered me the voyage of a lifetime. I hope you like it," she called out.

He began tearing the silver paper from his gift, then stopped for a second. Realizing what was before him, he looked up at her and said, in an almost somber tone of voice, "I want you to know that no woman has ever done this—given me such an extravagant gift. I'm overwhelmed."

"*You're* overwhelmed! What about me!" she said, holding up her hands and looking at her rings. She twisted her hands around for him to look.

Nicholas leaned the painting back against the post again and went over to her. Arabella spread her arms out wide and Nicholas walked in up against her. They kissed.

He said, "Thank you, my love." They kissed again.

Then they both went to tear away the silver paper. They made sure the picture was set level and steady on the bed before they went around and sat in the middle of the bed next to each other. They looked at the Henri Rousseau in silence. It was one of his jungle scenes with a silver moon high up in a black sky. A naked maiden lay on her side in the foreground in a small clearning near a babbling brook, white orchids in her hair.

Nicholas was utterly speechless. He was absorbed into the painting, which was entitled "Maiden with Orchids in Her Hair."

For what seemed like a long time, they sat on the bed silently, enjoying the genius of the painting. Arabella was captured once again by the sensuous, luscious garden, the power of the moon, the naïveté and sweet innocence of the naked girl. There was a whole world, a universe in the painting set before them.

It was the presence of Nicholas, naked except for his glasses, sitting back on his haunches, that finally drew her

away from the masterpiece. She watched him, completely
engrossed in the world of Rousseau. An overwhelming tide
of emotion began to swell within her. Eighteen years of an
exciting full life flashed before her, yet she felt as if she
were drowning. She was suddenly shattered by the aware-
ness that she, like the maiden in the painting, had been
alone in the jungle until now.

Oh, Anthony! she thought. Eighteen years. Eighteen years
of loving you. Eighteen years of substitutes, diversions,
loneliness I would accept as such because you could not or
would not give me what Nicholas has given me in five days.
Oh, Anthony, Anthony! What a loss!

Nicholas turned to Arabella. He reached out and wiped
the tears from her cheeks. Neither of them spoke as he took
off his glasses and put them on the table. He removed the
robe Arabella was wearing. Gently and tenderly he lay her
down on the bed, himself over her, as he kissed the tears
from her eyes. He felt enormous pity for the sadness she
suffered, but from this day on he would kiss her sadness
away forever. Together they made the sweetest love either
of them had ever known.

He pulled her into his arms and covered them with the
eiderdown.

"No one has ever been so generous with their love for
me," she said.

"Nor me," he said, and they snuggled tightly in each
other's arms.

Three long, melancholy blasts from the ship's horn startled them awake.

"What's that?" Arabella asked.

"That, dear heart, is telling us that the pilot boat has
arrived and the customs men are boarding. We should be
getting dressed."

The phone rang just then—it was Missy announcing that
it was eight o'clock, three hours until the ship would dock.
She and Xu were in the kennels arranging to bring the birds

and dogs to Arabella's cabin where the customs men would clear the entire Crawford party at nine o'clock.

Arabella turned to Nicholas after she hung up.

"Okay, Mr. Frayne. Are you ready for the real world?"

"You bet, Mrs. Frayne!" He leaned over for one more kiss. "I'll go back to my cabin, shave and dress. After we clear customs we'll go to the private gangway the captain has arranged for us and then on to the press conference.

"I think the best plan is that we meet in the dining room at nine thirty. What do you think? Does that give you enough time for the things you want to do?"

"Sounds fine," answered Arabella, just as the phone rang again.

It was Marvin, who was waiting for Nicholas in his cabin to go over last-minute details of their exit from the ship and the reception waiting for them on the dock.

While the two men were talking, Arabella suddenly remembered Marvin's engagement gift to them. She looked at the Japanese lacquered box with its magnificent panels of erotica sitting on top of the chest of drawers. The doors were open and the three drawers were pulled out a few inches.

She thought, I must check the box and make sure the toys are all put away. That's definitely not something I'd want reporters to find!

She slipped out of bed and put on a white cashmere galabeah heavily trimmed in pale olive-green silk braiding and checked each of the silk-lined drawers to make sure that everything was in its proper place. Something was missing.

Nicholas hung up the telephone and looked at her. "Well, you have to admit that it's a marvelous, exciting present! Objects of great beauty and certainly a great sacrifice as Marv bought them for himself from the late King Farouk's collection of erotica."

"I think it's amazing and quite extraordinary, but I must say when I spoke to him just now I didn't quite have the nerve to thank him for it," Arabella replied.

"I guessed so. I did it for us both."

Nicholas went to Arabella and kissed her on the side of the neck. He stopped for a minute and looked over her shoulder. He saw something in the bottom drawer they had not used. He reached around her and pulled out a beautiful pair of lavender jade balls, exquisitely carved as a pair of lovers. One ball depicted the couple having oral sex and the other showed the couple entwined, making love with the woman on top. There was a shiny new silk cord four inches long separating the two balls, and a six-inch cord with a loop on the end hung from one of the balls.

Arabella held out her palm and Nicholas dropped them into it, saying "My God, they're so beautifully carved! A great work of art and very, very sexy."

"Will you put them in me now?" asked Arabella.

Nicholas gave her a lustful look and said, "Not now. These are magnificent, probably made for a lady of the court or an empress, and most worthy of being kissed by your luscious vagina. I could place them inside you and you could wear them all day, have delicious little orgasms as they tease and roll around inside you. But I think not. If we get started now with all that, you might have a problem getting through the day!"

"Pity," said Arabella. "I could have pretended they were your balls, fantasized that I had a part of you inside me, feeling me, giving me orgasms while we stood among the crowd." She rolled the balls around in her hand, let them click together, and put them back in their place in the erotic treasure chest. She closed the cabinet door and locked it with its original bronze slide lock. Nicholas nipped her on the side of the neck and then licked the sweet flesh.

"Enough," he said. "Put it with your jewel case and you can carry it with us always. They are, after all, your new interior jewelry!"

"For a New England Puritan, you're awfully sexy and cheeky!" she said, just as the phone started ringing again.

Arabella picked up the receiver and put it to her ear. Nicholas was getting dressed in front of one of the long mirrors. He could see Arabella reflected in it as she talked on the telephone. Feeling no need to wear a tie as he had to undress again in a few minutes to shave and change, he rolled it up, put it in his pocket, and adjusted his open collar.

Suddenly he saw Arabella go deathly pale. Concerned, he turned around and went to her. He stood behind her and put his hand on her shoulder to reassure her. He could feel the tension all through her body. He heard her say, "Yes, Anthony."

Then he understood.

She went on. "What an impossible suggestion, Anthony! Have breakfast with you? I'm not even in New York yet and you're in London."

Nicholas, sensitive to the situation, bent down and kissed Arabella on the top of her head and made motions in the mirror that he was going into the drawing room.

Arabella continued with her conversation. "That's unbelievable, Anthony. How can you possibly be on board?" There was a long pause while Arabella listened to Anthony Quartermaine's explanation.

Then she spoke. "Please don't do that, Anthony. I'm not dressed and the cabin is soon going to be full of people, dogs, and birds. The customs men will be here soon."

She listened and then said, "I certainly am not afraid to see you."

There was another pause and then she went on. "Well, of course I don't sound enthusiastic about your dramatic arrival. So much has happened to me since I left France, not the least of which is your delayed announcement of Fiona's death. You want to both bribe me and marry me, but I mustn't ask any questions that might embarrass you!"

She listened to him again and then answered, "I don't know what I expect, Anthony. Silence on both our parts for a very long time, I suppose."

He spoke at length and then Arabella conceded, saying "All right, I'll see you. But give me twenty minutes to finish dressing."

Arabella hung up the telephone and let out a great sigh of relief. She put her hands over her face. She could hardly believe it. Nicholas and the five days on board the S.S. *Tatanya Annanovna*, her future, all disappeared from her mind. After all these years Anthony was coming after her, ready to give her what she had always wanted from him: a commitment to an open life together. Now, when it was probably too late to have the children they might have had, be the family they might have been. Now, when someone else had swept her away from him he offered her all.

Arabella lowered her hands away from her face and looked long and hard at herself in the mirror. She shook her head and the lovely gold and silver hair with its well-cut shoulder-length bob fell beautifully into place around her face. She had to keep moving, get through the next few hours with self-possession. This was *her* life. The time was now. No more maybes.

She put the finishing touches to her makeup, then looked critically at herself again in the mirror. She knew that her face was more beautiful, youthful looking, fresh, and alive than it had been for a very long time. She stood up and took off her galabeah. She slipped into a brown silk chemise trimmed in ecru lace, then sat down on the chaise and drew over her long, shapely legs a pair of nylon stockings over which she pulled on a pair of Maude Frisson chocolate-brown suede boots with high heels.

There was a tap on the dressing-room door. Arabella stood up in front of the mirror, a gray suede skirt in her hand, and called out, "Come in."

Nicholas walked toward her with a reassuring smile. He saw her bite the inside of her lower lip nervously.

He said, "What an outfit! God, you look sexy in those boots! Come on, I'll help you into your skirt."

He took the full gray suede Armani skirt and held it open by its waistband for her to step into.

Arabella could not bring herself to say anything. Looking at them both in the mirror, she stepped into the skirt and adjusted it so that it sat correctly, then she zipped it up. Nicholas walked behind her and kissed her naked shoulder.

He said, "The blouse, darling."

He saw an edge of anguish in her face reflected in the mirror and he squeezed her reassuringly on her shoulder. Nicholas then turned and picked up the gray suede top with its bat-wing sleeves and a band of chocolate brown around the hem. He unzipped the back and held it up over her head.

He said, "Put your arms up, Arabella."

She was amazed to realize how comforting it was to hear his voice, calm and reassuring. She came to life and moved as Nicholas put the top on and zipped it up.

"You're going to knock them dead going down that gangplank. I know just what the gossip columns will say: 'Arabella Crawford, the reclusive business tycoon, the woman who walked away from the corporate world with millions and, as rumor has it, the future Mrs. Nicholas Frayne, was one of the passengers disembarking from the maiden voyage of that most extraordinary of ships, the S.S. *Tatanya Annanovna*. She is a magnificent, mysterious beauty who dresses casually with an elegance and chic we have not seen for a very long time . . .' and so on."

Arabella and Nicholas did not once take their eyes off each other in the mirror while he gave his little review. They both knew that Nicholas was waiting for her to say something.

Arabella raised her hands and adjusted the blouse so that it fell a few inches over the waistband of the skirt. The magnificent engagement ring Nicholas had presented her with the night before sparkled in the mirror. It managed to flash her back to the reality of Nicholas. She turned around to face him. He took her hand in his and pressed it.

He smiled at her and said, "I have to go now. I'll meet you in the dining room just as we planned."

He squeezed her hand again and started to leave. Arabella held onto his hand so he turned and looked at her.

She spoke for the first time since he had entered the room. "Nicholas."

"Yes?"

"That was Anthony Quartermaine on the telephone."

"I gathered as much."

"Nicholas, he's here, on board the *Annanovna*. He took the Concorde from London to New York yesterday and managed to get a lift on the pilot boat this morning. He's here on our ship!"

"What does he want, Arabella?"

"Me."

"I take it you haven't told him about us?"

"No, not all about us."

"Listen, my love," said Nicholas. "I understand that you have to see him. I understand much more. Anthony Quartermaine has been the great love of your life, an influence on you for many years. I understood that when you first said there was an unfulfilled love affair that helped drive you on to your phenomenal success. I selfishly held back from asking about him because I didn't want another man between us. Not even one from the past. But we don't always get what we want. He is here, in the flesh. Now I have to face his existence. You have a very big decision to make now, though I thought you'd made it last night."

Arabella began to speak, but Nicholas stopped her by placing his index finger lightly over her lips.

"Shhh," he said, "don't say anthing now. I'll meet you in the dining room at half-past nine, just as we've planned. Hey, don't look so worried. There's a big, wonderful life out there waiting for us one way or another."

He gathered up both her hands in his and then turned them over, kissing first one palm and then the other. He hugged her tightly, then smiled at Arabella and walked away.

She felt her heart racing, the adrenaline pumping and the excitement that comes with emotion and change, decisions and going forward.

Arabella then draped half a dozen necklaces of various lengths around her neck. They were all ancient gold necklaces—Egyptian, Phoenician, Roman, Mayan. The gold against the gray suede enhanced the richness of the metal, the elegance of the shapes, the antiquity and drama of the beads.

Missy and Xu came in with the caged birds and the dogs, who dashed to the dressing table and Arabella. They barked and yelped, jumped and twirled around her until she had petted and played, given all her attention to each one of them.

"They must be so happy to be out of those kennels," she said to Missy and Xu. The dogs busied themselves sniffing around the dressing room while Missy and Xu congratulated Arabella yet again on her engagement to Nicholas.

Arabella was touched by her two faithful helpers' sincere wishes. She gave them a smile of appreciation and said, "Missy, Xu, I have something to tell you. Lord Quartermaine is on board. He came on the pilot boat this morning with the customs officials. He knows nothing of my engagement."

"Oh, my goodness, what are you going to do?" Missy asked.

"I'm going to see him, but I'd like you to stay here in the stateroom while he is with me."

"We'll be here," she said.

"Of course," seconded Xu.

"Don't look so worried, Missy. I'll work it out. It'll be all right, you'll see."

They all continued packing up as Arabella tried to sort out her feelings.

Understanding where her head and heart were vis à vis the two men was not easy. She knew full well that she was in love with Nicholas, that beautiful man who gave her everything without her asking. She knew she wanted to go out into the world with him as her lover, husband, and best friend. Yet there lingered a residue of that total commitment she had made to loving Anthony all those years ago. But Arabella was beginning to see it more clearly as an addiction to loving Anthony, rather than loving the man himself. He was the love affair of a lifetime; Nicholas was the love of a lifetime. But instinctive understanding did not quell the fire of emotion she felt for the two men.

Anthony's appearance on board could change everything she thought her future was going to be.

Arabella turned to Xu and said, "Please bring my sable coat and hat to the dining room at half-past ten. I'll need them to be out on the open deck watching the ship dock."

The doorbell to the suite rang sharply at that moment and Henry let in Lord Quartermaine, the Earl of Heversham. The dogs sprang to life and started for the drawing room. Outwardly Arabella appeared to be very much in control, but she felt fragile and anxious about the overpowering emotional effect Anthony had always had on her.

She said, "Xu, please get the dogs under control."

The handsome Chinese man said but one word, *"Leyon,"* in an authoritative but kind whisper. The animals rushed at once to him and sat perfectly still at his feet.

Arabella went to meet Anthony.

Chapter Twenty-one

Anthony was standing with his back to the drawing room, looking out of the porthole.

Arabella was not sufficiently braced for the impact of his presence nor the effect it had on her. She felt her mouth go dry, her heart pound and tension shoot through her spinal cord at such a speed she felt a stiffness in her neck. She was short of breath and wanted to scream at the same time. Instead she bit the inside of her lower lip, closed her eyes for a second, and took a deep breath. That brought back a measure of control and before it disappeared again, she spoke.

"Hello."

He turned quickly and started toward her, saying "What an extraordinary place for us to meet! Hello, Arabella." He extended his arms as if to greet her with a hug. She managed to bypass them, and as she walked farther into the room, she was startled to see how much he had changed. In her mind's eye she had been picturing the Anthony she had first known in Alexandria. But this man was different, not simply older with a few more gray hairs, but there was something tense and desperate about him. Where was the authoritative, aristocratic manner he used to have? He was certainly still handsome, but she sensed a new air of pomposity and suspected that he was trying to hide the fact that he knew he was not, for the first time, in absolute control of her.

"You look so beautiful, so very, very beautiful," he said.

Arabella heard the signs of intense emotion in his voice and saw in his eyes what could have been held-back tears. She went to the porthole and looked out toward New York. It was snowing; great sheets of heavy white snowflakes swirled past and dissolved from the salt air as they landed on the deck.

"How extraordinary," she said. "It was snowing when I left Paris and now, three thousand miles and six days later, it's snowing on my arrival in New York."

He said, "I can't believe you're here."

She turned from the window and they looked at each other. For a fleeting moment the years seemed to melt away, and for a split second they were together as if they had never been parted.

Anthony asked, "May I sit down?"

"Yes, of course, Anthony, please do sit down. Can I get you something, a cup of tea, a glass of champagne?"

"No, nothing. Just come and sit near me and let me look at you. You seem very much changed to me. Changed and, if possible, more exciting."

Arabella sat down in the easy chair opposite him. She said, "Two years is a long time, Anthony. Two long years it has taken you to ring my doorbell."

Anthony said, "Arabella, please, come sit near me. Two years *is* a very long time, long enough. Don't be silly. I can hardly see you across the room through all these flowers."

"How are your children? They must be very grown up now."

"Yes, very grown up except, of course, for the last one, Chisholm."

"Oh, yes," she said, "Chisholm would be eight years old now," the gorge rising in Arabella as she spoke. To herself she said, Oh, yes, Chisholm. The reality of the big lie that Anthony and Fiona no longer slept together, that their marriage was no more than a social and marital arrangement on paper only.

Arabella tried to contain her anger as she asked, "And Heversham Park? Glorious Heversham Park?"

"Thriving, beautiful."

"And Fiona? Or do I take it that I'm not to ask anything about Fiona and her demise?"

"I never said that. It's quite natural you would want to

know about her death. Fiona died after being thrown by her
horse during a hunt. She was riding with the Belvoir. It
was icy, the horse slipped, but Fiona, a brilliant horsewoman,
took the jump, in this case a fatal miscalculation. The horse's
leg broke and Fiona suffered a fractured skull. She died on
the way to the hospital."

The coldness with which he catalogued his wife's death
gave Arabella the impetus to press on.

"Why are you here, Anthony?"

"I want you to come away with me, Arabella. I want to
take you home. Home, Arabella, back to England. I want
to marry you."

Every word she had longed to hear for so many years
hit her like so many darts piercing her skin. Arabella was
bleeding.

Henry came in at that moment with a tray.

"Just leave it please, Henry. I'll serve, thank you." Arabella reached for the jug of peach juice, praying that Anthony would not see her hand trembling.

"No, please allow me. I still remember how you like
them." He prepared the drink for her, filling the Baccarat
crystal champagne glass half with peach juice and half with
champagne. He handed it to her.

Arabella took the drink gratefully, much relieved to
quench the dryness of her mouth. She looked at him and
recognized the lust and desire he still had for her.

"They were long and lonely, those years without you,
Anthony. Your friendship, at least, would have eased the
pain of our situation. I needed friendship, a closeness between us, but you offered me none.

"Now I'm allowed to come out of exile because your
wife has had the good grace to die an accidental death,
setting you free with your honor intact, having been a good
and faithful husband to the end."

Arabella picked up her glass and drank.

Anthony chose to disregard her words. He said, "I want
what we have had all these years. What we *still* have. That's
why I'm here."

"Why now? It's three months since your wife died. Why now and not three months ago? Didn't you think enough of our friendship to let me know Fiona was dead?"

"Three months ago you were an executive whirling around the world making money. When I heard of the business coup that jolted the international stock markets, I knew you were behind it. I was delighted for you, *am* delighted for you now. I thought if I came to you then and asked you to marry me, you would have been terribly torn. I knew that if you had pulled out of business, as you always said you would if we could have been together, that was the worst possible moment for you to do it—just as you were riding highest. And I couldn't bear the thought of you turning me down. Now that you've retired, it seemed quite natural to assume we would marry."

Arabella was speechless. Anxiety flooded over her. Anger mixed and mingled with memories of the utter devotion she had given their love. He had been her first priority and she his last. He was setting her up again in the same way, except this time he proposed marriage. What could she say? Her tongue was tied with heavy cords of emotion.

Arabella rose and Anthony followed, taking her hand in his, ignoring the engagement ring, just as he had ignored the existence of Nicholas Frayne.

"Look, Arabella. This meeting is a shock for both of us, but I'm very uncomfortable here. Let's go upstairs, my dear. We'll have breakfast and we can make plans for our future, where we are going, what we are going to do—"

He was interrupted by a knock on the stateroom door. The dogs started to bark. This gave Arabella the opportunity to call for Xu.

From that moment the drawing room filled rapidly with people. The Immigration Officer and customs official appeared, ready to check passports, luggage, dogs, birds, and people.

"Anthony, I need some time to finish a few things here. You go on ahead. I'll meet you in the reception area of the dining room as quickly as I can."

She walked him to the door and politely but firmly saw him out. She introduced Missy to the officials and then hurried to the privacy of her bedroom.

She closed the door and went immediately to the telephone to call Nicholas.

He answered and Arabella said, "Oh, Nicholas, I'm so relieved I caught you. Are you through with the customs officials?"

"Yes, I have been for about fifteen minutes. Are they with you now?"

"Yes, they are, Nicholas. I'm on my way to the dining room."

"I'll see you in five minutes then, Arabella."

"Nicholas," she said apprehensively, "I've seen Anthony briefly. He wants to have breakfast with me."

"Oh." There was a moment of hesitation, then he went on. "That's no problem, Arabella. They can set another place for him at our table."

A vulnerable, nervous Arabella suddenly felt sad at the mere sound of Nicholas's voice. Then he hung up.

She could not believe this was happening: breakfast with both Anthony and Nicholas. Arabella picked up her large, dark-brown Hermès alligator handbag and slipped it on her shoulder. She checked herself in the mirror and looked around the suite for the last time, then thanked the officials for their kindness. After giving last-minute instructions to Missy, she left.

Arabella found Anthony standing alone among some of the other passengers. He still had a debonair look that made him attractive. He certainly appeared happier than he had been in her cabin.

She went up to him, saying "Sorry to have kept you waiting, Anthony."

"Well, I daresay I have kept you waiting a great deal longer! But that's all over now. Come along, I'll buy you a super English breakfast."

"Anthony," she said, releasing herself from his arm, "I've asked a friend of mine to join us for breakfast."

Anthony looked at Arabella, raised an eyebrow, and said, "Was that necessary? We have plans to make."

"I told you I have a friend named Nicholas Frayne."

"Your movie star. I would have preferred this breakfast reunion to have been just the two of us. But if you find it necessary for us to meet, I suppose I can handle it."

At that moment, Nicholas arrived and Arabella introduced them.

Her heart froze, her emotions were numb. The men exchanged a few pleasantries with each other, but she couldn't hear them. She felt as if she were swimming under water and everything was moving in slow motion. She floated with them into the dining room, thinking how bizarre it was that her past and her future should meet like this. People in the restaurant kept intruding on the three to say farewell to Arabella and Nicholas, and she nodded and smiled appropriately. Yes, she thought, Anthony is my past and Nicholas is my future. I'm sure of that. Very sure.

Sitting between the two men at breakfast, Arabella was highly anxious though outwardly she was in complete control of herself and her position. She listened to the two men talking to each other about Concorde, the S.S. *Tatanya Annanovna*, the dining room, the menu, the weather. She watched them as if they were performers on a stage doing a play just for her. They were fencing, using their conversation as swords. They were like two duelists—one man would win, the other be left wounded. Just as for duelists, the reason for the combat, Arabella, was far less important than the challenge between the two men.

As an escape, to try to calm herself, Arabella watched the snowstorm swirling around the ship. She was drifting between long-time love, Anthony, who still had some power to rekindle the old flame, and a new love, Nicholas, who had flared up quickly in her life and burned brightly.

Not many women are made to watch a duel between their lovers, and Arabella was not enjoying it one bit. She was engrossed in her own thoughts, but her ears perked up when she heard Anthony say, "The cinema. What an extraordinary way to live, playing in the cinema! It must be very amusing always using someone else's character to live behind."

Arabella recognized the smooth, elegant English put-down and looked at Nicholas, who gave Anthony his most devastating, handsome, open smile. He looked across the table at Arabella with slow sexy eyes and then turned his attention back to Anthony.

"Oh, yes, Lord Quartermaine, you have no idea what a luxury it is. It allows one to work out the inner feelings of the character one is playing. Why, I've even played an English lord in one of my films. It gave me the chance to shoot grouse."

Arabella had to keep from laughing at this jab of Nicholas's. He continued speaking while Arabella drifted again. Anthony's world was one she didn't belong in. She wanted to go home, to America, after all these years away. Aristocracy held no special mystique for her anymore. The honesty, warmth, and laughter she had had with Nicholas was something to be treasured, nurtured. Anthony had meant well, or at least in his mind he had, in concealing Fiona's death, but it was so symbolic of the way his mind worked— and now it seemed unnatural and manipulative to Arabella. She was beginning to feel sad for Anthony, for he had never, and probably would never, have a relationship like the one she had with Nicholas—totally open and spontaneous.

Dishes rattled around her, bringing Arabella out of her reverie once more. Suddenly she realized that she was ravenous. The coffee smelled wonderful and the Eggs Benedict looked divine. She began eating with great gusto when Nicholas said, "Arabella, those eggs must be stone cold."

She looked at his plate, then at Anthony's. Clearly they had finished eating some time ago while she had been day-dreaming. She looked at him, and as she began eating said, with a big grin, "When you find a good egg, you've got to hang on to it. No matter what!"

Nicholas smiled back and understood he had won.

The three were then interrupted by the arrival of Xu, who brought Arabella's coat and hat. He drew an empty chair from the next table and placed her things on it.

"Will there be anything else, Miss Crawford?" he asked.

"No, nothing. Thank you, Xu. I'll meet you all on the boat deck."

Then they were interrupted by Missy who excused herself, went to Arabella, opened a red Moroccan leather looseleaf notebook, and asked, "What would you like me to do about these two things, Miss Crawford?"

Arabella read, Would you like me to disappear with Xu and the animals or does the plan remain the same?

Arabella took the felt-tip pen from Missy's hand and wrote, We all leave the ship together.

Then she read, Have you any last-minute instructions?

Arabella looked up at Missy, smiled, and wrote, No, nothing for the moment, and handed the book back to her.

Now, feeling quite in charge of herself and her emotions, Arabella felt she should guide this meeting to some kind of graceful end. Abruptly she stood up and, picking up her coat and hat, swinging her handbag over her shoulder, she said, "Gentlemen, there is a lady I'd like you to meet. Follow me."

Obligingly, Anthony and Nicholas followed Arabella up to the observation deck. There the three joined the other passengers in the glass-enclosed room that offered a full view of New York harbor.

"It looks like one of those tourist souvenirs of New York City—you know, the little glass globe filled with water and white bits with a minute golden Statue of Liberty. You shake the globe and *voilà*! The Statue of Liberty in a snow storm, just like this," said Nicholas, with his arm outstretched presenting the scene to them.

Arabella laughed. "It's true, good God, it's true! Oh, it's wonderful!"

The three walked to the stern on the port side of the ship and stood silently until the statue was swallowed up in a whirlwind of snow. Several people stopped to speak to them.

Arabella recognized the look of annoyance she knew so well on Anthony's face. He was out of his element and felt uncomfortable. Many people milled around Nicholas, wishing him luck.

"Let's do get out of this, Arabella, and find some privacy," said Anthony.

Nicholas disengaged himself from the crowd as quickly and graciously as he could. "Arabella," he said, "I have a few things to attend to. I'll meet you on the boat deck very shortly. I'll say good-bye, Lord Quartermaine, in case we should miss each other."

The two men shook hands, and Arabella mustered her strength for the conversation she must have with Anthony.

Anthony linked his arm through hers as Nicholas went off in the opposite direction. They rounded a corner in the deserted stairwell and Arabella started up the stairs. Anthony blocked her way by putting his arm against the wall in front of her. She stopped and looked at him. He pulled her quickly to him and held her tightly with one arm. He grabbed her face roughly by the chin, tilting it up to him. He must have known, she thought, that she had made up her mind, yet now he was desperate.

He kissed her passionately, saying "Don't be foolish. Remember Alexandria, all our years of passion? We can have it all now!"

She had been afraid that Anthony Quartermaine could still, after so many years, practice his power of animal lust on her. But now in his arms Arabella felt nothing, only, possibly, a slight sadness at his touch.

She ducked under his arm as soon as she felt his grip relax and continued up the stairs. He walked up behind her and put his arm around her waist. "Forget all this, this ridiculous drama. Let me take you back to England."

She quickened her step up the stairs, leaving him behind. He followed and she heard his familiar laugh. She stopped for a moment on the landing and closed her eyes. Then she realized it was a joy to hear his laugh. She loved and adored it, and had longed for and missed hearing it very much.

She might no longer hunger for him as a lover, but he would always be part of her life.

Then, very seriously, he said, "I must have been mad, mad not to have chained you to me years ago."

"No," she said, swinging around to face him on the landing, "no, you weren't mad, just married."

Then she pushed the door open. He was laughing now as they stepped out onto the glass-enclosed section of the boat deck.

"I'm glad you still have some wit about us," he said.

"And memories, Anthony, wonderful memories." She reached out and held both his hands in hers. "I hope you'll always remember it, Anthony, as I will."

He squeezed her hands and nodded. Tears had welled up in his eyes. "Yes, Arabella. I will always remember and cherish what we had."

One of the two sailors in attendance interrupted them. "Is this gentleman with you, Miss Crawford?"

She looked at the young sailor and smiled warmly at Anthony, answering, "For the moment at least."

"Thank you, ma'am. We have to check that no people other than yourself or Mr. Frayne's party are allowed out here."

Suddenly there was an enormous explosion. The snow turned pink and then another whizzing sound and a bang as red rockets shot up across the gray sky. A cacophony of horns, bells, sirens, fog horns rang out. The ship was bathed in a rainbow of light from the fireworks display of a flotilla of twenty tugboats surrounding the *Tatanya Annanovna* on her way up the Hudson River to her berth.

It was extraordinary, wild, and exciting. The display was remarkable for its timing as it surrounded the ship with a constant flow of purples, oranges, yellows and reds, silver and gold, all diffused by the heavy snowfall. The ship sailed through it like a great wonderful goddess of the sea, announcing her arrival with great blasts of her horn.

Arabella was thrilled by the display and by the great relief and joy she felt. Xu, Missy, and Henry arrived with the birds, dogs, and hand luggage. It was a mad, noisy group, and Arabella loved every minute of it. Finally she gave up trying to hold back and clapped her hands in delight. They no sooner had the four dogs under control with Xu handling them on leads when Nicholas and Marvin Kandy arrived, followed by the two secretaries.

Then a waiter appeared with a large silver tray holding crystal glasses filled with champagne and passed them around. Even Anthony had to give way to good humor.

Through the snow they saw the Anglo-French line's terminal building draped in red, white, and blue bunting. The ship began to swing around, to make its maneuvers to dock. Several sailors appeared to remove the glass walls, open up the section at the rails where the gangway would be pulled in from the top floor of the terminal. Arabella felt a gust of wind begin to lift her hat off. Nicholas caught it, smiled, and handed it back to her. She put it on and adjusted it securely. It was a gray felt Adolpho, magnificently shaped with a wide brim and chocolate-brown satin band around the crown.

Nicholas gave her nose a quick kiss and told her she was beautiful. She looked up at him, pulled up his collar against the snow, and said she loved him. They both had forgotten that Anthony Quartermaine was there.

The snowflakes were now whirling in at the three as they leaned on the polished rail. They watched a young sailor swing open a section of rail, getting ready to receive the gangway. They heard the clanking sound and felt the vibration of the anchor as it dropped.

The great fat hemp cables were already lassoed around the moorings and the ship was doing its last-minute sidling up to the dock.

Arabella could see them now, hundreds of people waiting in the terminal. Its wide doors swung open so the crowd could see the ship and its passengers. She was standing between Nicholas and Anthony. Nicholas turned to her and said, "Look, Arabella, that's my son there, that boy waving."

"Oh, he's very handsome, Nicholas!" Nicholas waved back at his son.

"And my parents are next to him!"

Arabella saw a handsome, white-haired couple.

"Oh, look," said Arabella. "Look at your family!" They were all waving enthusiastically at Nicholas. He waved back.

Arabella saw her Rolls-Royce with Oskar beside it, in a special cordoned-off area in front of the media people. She saw him go around the car and open the door. She was surprised, overwhelmed, and delighted to see her mother step out and then Robert, her brother.

"I never expected this," said Arabella. "What a surprise! Nicholas, look over there. It's my mother and brother."

Arabella turned to Missy and said, pretending to be stern, "Did you know about this?"

"Sorry," said Missy, laughing, "but I was sworn to secrecy."

By now streamers were being thrown onto the ship from all over the open viewing areas in the building. Hundreds of people waved to the *Tatanya Annanovna*'s passengers. Thousands of brightly colored streamers were tying the ship up to the terminal.

Covered gangways, great tubes, now connected the building to the ship, and the passengers were already disembarking. An open gangway was being shifted from the building to the ship for them, and when Arabella heard it bang on the deck itself and saw the sailors make it secure, everything fell into place for her.

An officer from the ship walked across the open gangway to the building, testing that it was safe. He waved them to come across.

Nicholas looked at Arabella. Marvin interrupted their gaze, saying "Arabella, I think we'd better have Nicholas go first and begin the conference. Then you can come down without being besieged." He turned abruptly away from Arabella to Nicholas and said, "This is it, Nick. Good luck, Governor." Then he went off down the gangway.

Nicholas looked at Arabella. He ducked under the brim of her hat, kissing her on the cheek. "I love you and always will."

Then, before she could react, he was off. She watched Nicholas disappearing away from her.

Anthony stepped up to Arabella and said, "You're going to marry him, aren't you?"

Arabella looked at him, studied his face, the face she had thought about so many nights when she was alone.

"Yes, Anthony, I am. Anthony, I love, you possess. I don't want to be possessed. I wanted to be loved. You've waited too long, left it too late."

"Yes," he said very softly. "I know that now. Good-bye, Arabella. Good luck to you both." The Earl of Heversham turned without another word and walked away.

She had taken only two steps when she saw Nicholas running back up the gangway toward her. Her heart leaped.

He said, "I don't want to do it. I don't want to walk into a new world without you."

She smiled and said, "Thank goodness for that! I don't want to start a new life without you either."

He took her by the arm and together they walked down the gangway.

"Don't be nervous. When we get to the microphone, I'll introduce you to the press."

"As the future Mrs. Frayne, I hope. Oh, and by the way, you can also tell them that the bride is not willing to wait more than three days for the wedding."

They were three quarters of the way down the gangplank treading carefully in the swirling snow, the bustle and noise all around them, dogs leaping and prancing around Arabella's feet, Xu a few yards behind her with Missy.

Nicholas stopped her and said, "Do you mean it, *really* mean it?"

"Yes, yes, I really mean it," she replied.

He took her in his arms. She pulled the pin from her hat, took it off her head, and, with a strong toss, she flung it up into the wind. Photographers and TV cameramen broke through the barriers trying to get the picture. They raced up the gangway.

Arabella's eyes followed her hat as it took flight and disappeared. She said, laughing as she looked into Nicholas's eyes, "Well, you change your life, you change your hat. That's two in less than a week. Where do we go from here?"

"Home," he said, laughing.

About the Author

Roberta Latow is an American and a world traveler, who is currently living in England. Her previous novel is THREE RIVERS.